A WALK TO REVENGE

SAM THOMPSON

Sam Thompson Books

2

A WALK TO REVENGE

CHAPTER ONE

JUNE 1977, MANCHESTER, ENGLAND.

The car eased through the automatic gears as it proceeded into the drizzly Manchester night. No different from the hundreds of times the driver had done this before; a night on the town, a few more drinks than normal, the mood throughout was free and easy. It began at seven in the evening with a few drinks shared with four friends, which increased to eight by ten-thirty. It seemed the usual crowd had the same idea on that warm, sultry night, until the yellow, closing sun gave way to the first dark clouds, and then the rain. The city centre was quietening down as the midnight news on the radio was followed by the dulcet tones of Bryan Ferry singing the Dobie Gray classic, 'The In Crowd'. It all seemed to match the mood of the night.

A taxi ride of only a few miles seemed pointless compared to the disruption of returning on public transport in the morning, only to drive back home in the Saturday hustle and bustle of the shopping fraternity.

As the car floated around the corner of Portland Street into Peter Street, an unwelcome vision appeared in the rearview mirror. The police patrol car was looking for any disruption in the city streets.

In a moment of panic, the police car woke up the street with flashing blue lights and unfriendly sirens.

Here we go, the driver thought. However, as quickly as the thought came into his mind, the orange and white car flashed past the BMW, racing towards a more pressing problem elsewhere. It must be my lucky night. The feeling of invincibility cast, the driver relaxed into the seat and the radio button slid to the off position.

Within a minute, a body hit the car with a dull, sickening thud, followed by a head hitting the windscreen! The pedestrian was instantly recognised. Paul Jennings! They knew each other, they sometimes drank together, always chatted and shared a laugh when they met. This was different. Paul Jennings had been struck by the car and, as if in slow motion, Jennings rolled up the bonnet and onto the windscreen. Their eyes met and, in what must have been a split second but felt like five

4

minutes, they instantly recognised each other, before the strength of bone outmatched the strength of glass and the crack in the windscreen appeared like a sheet of ice forming on a freezing pond.

The body lay, contorted, on the wet kerb, nobody was around, the rain must have kept people off the streets. What decision must be made? Was he dead?

The car drove out of the city with a bruised bonnet, a cracked windscreen, a driver high on alcohol, whilst a stiff, motionless body lay strewn in the street.

The morning began in the same way as any for Paul Jennings, although this day was different in that the sun was up, which was a rarity throughout this summer. A hot day with showers was forecast later, bringing back some normality. His plans for the day were to go to the factory where he worked as an engineer. He honed the skills required to bore crankshafts and camshafts in diesel engines in a factory that produced engines for the bus and shipping industries. He did well to get into such a highly skilled area of work. That was to be followed by a night out with his friend, Billy Jones. Billy worked in the Royal Ordinance Factory about half a mile away as a draughtsman. The ROF did work for the Government of the day, usually ammunitions and sometimes very confidential work, which, meant employees were required to sign the official secrets act.

Paul was popular with his workmates, always a joker, and always willing to help where he could. His passion was football, and Manchester United in particular, which would often set off some heated discussions with Billy, who supported arch-rivals Manchester City. Arguments would often centre around who were the better team, both past, and present – Paul arguing the Best, Law, and Charlton teams, and Billy debating the merits of Bell, Summerbee, and Lee. Like the painting of the Severn Bridge, it would always be an ongoing task for each to convince the other.

The bell rang at four-thirty to indicate the end of another working week. Paul and Billy shared the journey home in Paul's car, it was his turn to drive in the alternating car share they had in place. The traffic, as usual, was busy and the three-mile drive from Eccles to Worsley took forty minutes, the same as it usually did on a Friday night, as the cars snaked up Worsley Road. The hot, sultry day made Paul feel sticky throughout; he wore his overalls off at the top, with the arms tied around his waist. This, in turn, had attracted a layer of dust on the old, Slazenger t-shirt he wore. The sweat made him wipe his forehead throughout the day, resulting in a blackened face that made him look like he'd just exited a coal mine rather than a factory. He felt tired, but he knew the energy would return after a bath, an evening meal, and a change of clothes.

Paul and Billy arranged to go into the city for an eagerly awaited drinks evening. They had not been out together since Paul and Susan's wedding day three months earlier. Paul and Susan were together about a year before she broke the news that she was expecting their child. This hastened the inevitable wedding, which took place when Susan was only four months pregnant and just showing a small sign of the infant that was working away at the importance of growing.

Paul was a good-looking man without standing out in a crowd. His blonde hair was beginning to recede and, up until the news of the baby, it was his biggest problem in life. Bill, on the other hand, with his six-foot frame and muscular build, helped by the regular gym work, was always the centre of attention and everybody loved him. He was one of those rare people who attracted both men and women. Men, because they wanted to be near him in case any trouble started with drunken gangs looking for top-dog status for the night, and women because of his chiselled good looks encompassing his mix of English and Italian bloodlines.

By ten in the evening, they met up with a few friends and the pints turned quickly to Jack Daniels and coke to ease the pressure on the already bursting stomachs swilled with pints of Boddington's and Holts' bitter, the local Manchester ales.

As usual, Billy was popular with the girls he was showing a particular interest in a bubbly blonde doing a bad rendition of Candi Staton's 'Young Hearts Run Free' on the pub karaoke. However, the short skirt and big smile seemed to make up for that.

"I think I'm going on to a club with young Candi," joked Billy after another pint or two.

"No problem," replied Paul. "I should be getting home. I promised Sue I wouldn't be too late," He looked at his watch. "Catch up on Monday. Keep me posted about the date with Candi, sharing her one and only life," he added, making a quip about a line in the song.

They laughed and shook hands. Paul left the bar and walked out into the city night. A swift look at his watch told Paul it was just approaching midnight. A jog to Piccadilly Gardens and the all-night bus was within his grasp. He turned his fast walk into a steady jog, which soon turned back to a fast walk as the consumption groaned against his brain and made him feel sick. He strode at the fastest pace he could muster, if not entirely straight, onto Peter Street and headed towards the town hall.

Although he had not drank excessively, he was not used to drinking these days, as he and Sue tended to stay in more and watch TV on what was a tight budget. Added to the fact that he felt drained after a day's work in the heat, the alcohol seemed to be attacking his system easier and quicker than normal. He felt a little vague and the feeling of numbness in the head was a feeling he knew from a hundred nights out before. Overall, his senses were working, he knew where he needed to be, and what time his bus was due.

The road was clear as he began to cross. Suddenly, heading from the direction of Oxford Road was a black BMW. He became transfixed on the car. It was hurtling towards him at around forty miles per hour. He froze. Normal life slowed down. He tried to turn back to the safety of the kerb, but he slipped slightly, probably due to a mixture of drink and a wet road surface. His left leg went down when the car hit him. He saw the driver as he rolled over the bonnet of the car. He recognised the face in the split second, a clear reflection of life passing, as it always does before life ends. Then… darkness.

CHAPTER TWO

JUNE 1977, VERONA ITALY

Nate and Claire Hughes reached the final two days of a two-week vacation, and the real reason for their visit had finally arrived. The year had accelerated at the pace of a space shuttle increasing with the speed of passing time.

Verona is famous for its Roman amphitheater, and Nate and Claire's excitement finally reached a climax with the arrival of two tickets to see the opera Aïda. The arena is located in the city's largest piazza, the Piazza Bra. Completed around 30 AD, it is the third-largest amphitheater in Italy after Rome's Colosseum and the arena at Capua. That night, around 25,000 spectators were filling its 44 tiers of marble seats. Nate took in the flavour like a child trying its first chocolate bar. Nate and Claire were attending the open-air opera on this warm, summer night. The reason was to celebrate their first wedding anniversary.

Nate read that, nowadays, at least four productions took place each year between June and August. It was one of these evenings that had driven Nate to make this day as romantic as he could. He booked a performance of the opera in the amphitheater. Not that they loved opera, or, had ever seen opera before; but it was a chance to do something different and in a unique way to remember this important date.

After booking tickets in January as a surprise for Claire, he placed the tickets on her pillow in the four-star Malcesine hotel that they'd booked for the first thirteen nights of their stay. She was so excited, and the fact that she would be sharing it with Nate made it all the more special for her. It wasn't his six-foot-two masculine frame that she liked, although that was the initial attraction. When they first met at University six years earlier, as 19-year-old students at Iowa University, she loved his easy-going ways and his love for the outdoors. He would take her camping in the mountains, where they would gaze at the stars with no refracting city lights. It was one of the most beautiful sights she had seen.

Iowa was the place they loved and settled to share their lives. She loved his gentle way and how the physical side of him made her feel protected.

She saw him work his way up from the student of six years ago to grow quickly as an up and coming expert on art, with a specialism in nineteenth-century Canadian artists. It brought him a very comfortable income, which they both enjoyed to the full. The first painting he bought was a Frederick Henry Brigden of the gorgeous Canadian Don Valley, a pilgrimage Nate promised to do, but was yet to achieve.

They spent a leisurely day working their way from the spectacular town of Malcesine on the shores of Lake Garda, travelling the 54 miles south to Verona. The day began with breakfast at 7 am, their bags already having been loaded into the hired Fiat the evening before, allowing them to set off on their journey at 8.30 am prompt.

Their second stop, at Sirmione, was even more impressive. They visited the Scaliger Castle, which was an impressive thirteenth-century castle, a rare example of medieval port fortification that was used by the Scaliger fleet. The castle stood tall and proud in a strategic position at the entrance to the peninsula. It was surrounded by a moat and could only be entered by two drawbridges. Claire stood, transfixed, looking over the wall and watching fish glide in the clear lake water formed the moat. The castle was established mainly as a protection against enemies, but also against the locals. The main room housed a small museum, which Nate and Claire looked around. They saw local finds from the Roman era and a few medieval artifacts. Nate was in his element.

"This has to be the most romantic country in the world," he said.

"It is like going back in time," Claire cooed as they entered the small church of Sant'Anna Della Rocca, which stood next to the castle.

They ate the best ice cream either of them had tasted in their lives followed the tour of buildings. Nate made fun of Claire's choice of banana and chocolate before the Fiat was fired up, and directed down the road to Verona via the A4 and finally onto the autostrada to link the final leg to the romantic city.

They arrived in Verona later that afternoon and ate a late lunch of a shared pizza, followed by a very quick registering in the Giulietta e Romeo Hotel. Nate booked this specific hotel because of its proximity to the amphitheater, as they were expecting to be leaving the Opera in the early hours of their last night in Italy.

Their final visit for the day culminated in a visit to Juliet's House, where they stood in the courtyard below the famous statue.

Nate turned to Claire. "The power of storytelling should never be underestimated," he whispered.

Every year, hundreds of thousands trek to Verona to see the balcony where Juliet stood while Romeo declared his love. None of the tourists milling around the house cared if the story was true or not, or the fact that Romeo and Juliet were figments of Shakespeare's imagination. This was the most powerful love story ever written in Western culture and everybody wants to live a little part of its dream – though, not its tragic ending.

Inside the house, there was a small museum and, in the courtyard, a bronze sculpture of Juliet.

"People rub her right breast for luck," Nate told Claire. However, the ultimate romantic gestures were the many love notes stuck on the walls and doors in the entrance to the courtyard.

"Wherefore art thou, Romeo?" Nate and Claire passed on this tradition.

They spent the evening in the hotel restaurant where they enjoyed a glorious meal. Which was accompanied by easy chatter and excited anticipation between the couple. They chose an expensive bottle of red wine, from Valpolicella, a district in the Bardolino winemaking region, the wine complimented Claire's baked manicotti with meat sauce and Nate's seared loin lamb chops with red wine sauce, equally. Claire, in particular, was feeling excited, as the butterflies in her stomach rose, while her hands kept changing from warm to cold and began shaking.

Finally, the moment arrived and they took their seats in Verona's amphitheater. They sat on the steps with a cushion to save the expected battering their backsides would take from the aged stone.

Nate booked tickets for Aïda, the opera in four acts by Giuseppe Verdi to an Italian libretto by Antonio Ghislanzoni, based on a scenario often attributed to French Egyptologist Auguste Mariette. Nate knew very little about opera but knew the atmosphere in the arena would make it a once in a lifetime experience.

By the time the first scene finished, a hall in the King's palace, Nate and Claire were transfixed, like rabbits looking into the headlights of an oncoming truck.

By the end of the opera, they witnessed Aïda dying in Radamès' arms. With the final chorus being sung in the romantic Italian language, a whole range of emotions had been met, from laughter to emotional intensity, and finally, tears and sobs as the opera unfolded.

Claire turned to Nate. She was sobbing uncontrollably and put her head into his chest. "Thank you for the most wonderful wedding anniversary a girl could ever have," she said. Nate put his arm around her.

"I could not have imagined a better day to celebrate our anniversary, Nate," Claire said as they walked back, arm in arm, to the hotel.

"I am so pleased," replied Nate. "This has been the most complete day for us to share."

They fell onto the bed at the hotel in each other's arms. The relaxation felt following a perfect day led to gentle and tender lovemaking, before finally succumbing to sleep, the finale to perfection.

CHAPTER THREE

JULY

Father Waring listened to Helen, admitting how she was wavering from the Catholic faith that she had followed all her life. Brought up a practising Catholic, Helen went to mass every Sunday and confession on Saturday evenings every month. She was, brought up to believe that the Lord worked in different ways. She believed he did everything for a reason; however, this leap of faith was being put to the test now.

"There seems no way any good can come from this," she told the considerate, calm, and easy-going priest.

"Sometimes, the reason doesn't show itself until a later day," replied the priest. He continued to quote Isaiah 51:11. "Those who have been ransomed by the LORD will return. They will enter Jerusalem singing, crowned with everlasting joy. Sorrow and mourning will disappear, and they will be filled with joy and gladness."

If this was correct, why was Helen Jennings standing in St Mary's cemetery watching the coffin of her son, Paul, being slowly lowered into the hard Manchester ground, with the sun beating down like a day in the Bahamas? Helen felt numb in disbelief that this could happen. She was unaware of the heat being radiated by the burning sun. There were no hysterics on her part; just a sombre, straight-laced face staring out and beyond any vision brought up by the horizon.

She stood in an embrace with Sue, Paul's bereaved wife, who was sobbing uncontrollably. She was not showing the same ice-cold persona of Helen, and the exertion of crying in the hot weather made her perspire quite heavily from the forehead. Helen was dabbing Sue with the white cotton handkerchiefs they purchased when they went together to buy black suits for the day. Helen bought a tight-fitting two-piece suit comprising a pencil skirt and a box jacket, with plain black high-heeled shoes and a man-style white shirt open at the neck, with the collar placed neatly over the lapels of the jacket. Sue chose something more modern in style – her jacket flared in at the waist with a six-inch vent cut into the back, along with a short skirt that sat about five inches above the knee, with a three-inch pair of black patent high-heeled shoes. Sue also wore a white, loose-fitting blouse because of the ever-increasing baby inside her. Both women dressed to suit their age and were perfect for the occasion.

Sue sobbed relentlessly and tried to speak in broken words between the gulps for air.

"Why did he leave us? Why did he go out that night? Why? Why? WHY?"

Helen pulled her in tighter and responded, "I don't know, darling, I don't know. But we will be strong and get through this."

Sue heard the news of the death by a knock on the door from a faceless policeman. There is a coldness being told that your husband had died by someone you did not know. It felt like they had privileged information about your family that you didn't.

"It isn't true!" she'd told the police officer. "It can't be true. He is in Manchester with his friend Billy," Her hands flew up to cover her face.

"They looked after each other," she continued. "Why are you telling me this?"

Gradually it dawned on her that it was, indeed, true. The realisation settled on her heart like a branding iron, causing the burning pain. Then the tears. She collapsed in the police officer's arms.

"Maybe I should come in the house with you," he said. "I can make you a drink."

At the same time, WPC Jean Solway was parking outside a terraced house in Sadler Street, Eccles. A faceless woman, behind the door of Number 7, was about to receive the worst news of her life. Jean took a moment to settle; she noted the nicely kept patch of grass, which was too small to be classed as a lawn. There was a brick wall, three feet high, and a simple path of paving stones leading up to the dark blue front door.

Helen was not as dramatic in receiving the news as Sue. She just sat quietly sobbing into a handkerchief. She was much more pragmatic in her questions.

"Did he suffer? Is he scarred? When can I see him? God, why Paul?"

Now, at the funeral, it was finally dawning on Helen. The life she had shared with her son, whom she treasured and shared so many deep memories and scars from a life living in a working-class estate in Greater Manchester, was at an end. She'd never had the opportunity to hug him and say goodbye.

Helen stood by the grave, her mind elsewhere. Within days, she met the detective charged with the responsibility of finding her son's killer.

Jonty Ball was a tough-looking man in his late thirties to early forties, with cauliflower ears from years of semi-professional boxing. He stood six foot six inches and weighed in at nineteen stone. He loved nothing more than getting involved in a fight with Manchester's finest. He was the top dog and everyone knew it.

He asked the routine questions. "Where was going?" "Why was he going?" "What was he doing there?" Stupid questions that were not relevant. The lads had been going for a pint on a Friday night in the City. He was determined to find an end to this, despite Helen's response.

"Hang on a minute here," Helen said. "My son is the victim, not the aggressor. Please treat this case as such,"

"I know," Jonty said. "I will do all I can to find the person responsible and give you closure."

Helen still had the body of a young woman that belied her age of 38. She was still an attractive woman, although the long, blonde locks of yesteryear now replaced by yellow hair from a bottle in an attempt to disguise the grey.

Paul's friend, Billy, put his arm around her. "Helen, I am sorry. If only I had…"

Helen interrupted. "Billy, it's not your fault. You can't legislate for a bastard driving a car, then running away like a coward. Take me for a stiff drink, will you? We have had a time we will never forget and we never asked for."

Billy was close to Helen, through his friendship with Paul. Her husband, Frank, finally left the home after years of drinking too much beer and gambling his weekly wages away on cards in the pub and horses in the weekend sessions. It was like Christmas the day he left. He was there today, drunk and slobbering about. Helen felt sympathy, but never empathy for him. He was an old man without a future, where his best friend was a whiskey and coke. He was at home, except for feeding and sleeping. He eventually left after a session in Wales with his mates and decided to move there and start a new life, to get away from all the 'evil' people he lived with.

Helen was determined Paul would never take after his father. She did a sterling job bringing him up straight and honest, and in Billy, he had a kindred spirit with the same values. Helen always felt that Paul and Billy would have a lifelong friendship supporting each other long after she had passed. The only problem was, it did not work out as planned.

By 11 pm, all but one person had left the Jennings' home that evening. All the condolences had been said and relations not seen for years were saying "We must meet up again." False promises, that everyone knew would not happen, until the next funeral or wedding.

There was only Billy left now with Helen.

She looked at him. "Billy, where do I go now? I don't know if I can find the strength to go on without Paul."

"Helen," replied Billy, "You are one of the strongest women I know, you will find a way through."

They hugged and cried on each other's shoulders. After a minute, Helen pulled herself away and wiped her eyes.

"Thank you, Billy, you were a good friend," she said. "It's all raw right now. Go home, I need some sleep. My eyes are as red as a United shirt."

Billy smiled and responded. "Your eyes will never look as bad as a United shirt."

They both laughed. As Billy walked out into the starlit night, he looked up at the sky. He walked down the garden path, but then stopped and turned back to look at Helen. "I wonder which one he is?" he said as he jerked his head towards the stars. With that, Helen closed the door with a smile and a tear in her eye.

Sleep was hard to find that night for Billy. But eventually, the eyelids turned to lead weights falling to cover his eyes, and sleep was finally sought that would last the ten hours.

***

It was early December. Paul had been dead five months and some normality was returning. A typical Manchester morning, dull and mild that usually tipped over from a damp, mild November. This particular day was no different. The dark hours turned to daylight hours around 8.30 am. Helen was already on the road, caught in the bumper to bumper traffic jam on the motorway towards Hope Hospital to officially meet her new grandson, Thomas Paul Jennings.

When she arrived at the maternity ward, Christine and Steve Collins, Sue's mother and father, were already there. Christine stood up and greeted Helen with a beaming smile and a bear hug.

"Oh Helen, how are you?"

15

"I am very good, Chris. How is the new addition?" Helen acknowledged Steve with a "Hi, Steve". His joy was bursting out like a March daffodil upon seeing the first ray of light.

"They are wonderful, just wonderful," said Christine. "The labour was eighteen hours and Sue was tired, but they are both just wonderful."

In true Steve style, he said to Christine, "If I had a pound for every time I heard the word wonderful in the last twenty-four hours, I would be a millionaire."

"Oh, shut up," Chris retorted. "And I am sure it's being happy that keeps you going." She turned to Helen and rolled her eyes, but kept her head level, not allowing Steve to see the gesture. "Men!" she said, they both laughed.

"Come on," said Helen, "let's go and meet Thomas Paul."

They left Steve with a cup of coffee from a hospital vending machine as he sat his 19-stone flabby body on a chair and a half in the waiting room, the buttons on his XXL blue shirt bursting open, revealing a stomach trained on full English breakfasts, pizza, and takeaway burgers all washed down with an average of ten pints of beer a day. He always blamed the recession; after being made redundant, he struggled to find employment. Both he and Christine knew that, deep down, he was lazy – the total opposite of Christine, who worked long hours as a care worker visiting the elderly and vulnerable. The work was rewarding but the pay was low.

Christine linked arms with Helen as they walked down the corridor, both giggling like a pair of school-girls and so happy to share this cherished moment.

The years that followed would be tough for Sue and young Tommy. With no main income coming in from Paul, they had to claim benefits, which helped with a council house, some child support, and income support. Sue was a hard-working girl that would always be on the lookout for a job.

CHAPTER FOUR

BOONE COUNTY, IOWA

The ambulance was travelling down Highway 30, ready to turn onto Story Street, where it would travel the short journey to Boone County Hospital. The passenger was a lady in labour and about to give birth to her first child.

"Nate, I am scared," she said.

"Don't be," replied Nate. "This baby will be the perfect addition to our family."

Claire Hughes squeezed her husband's hand and grimaced as another contraction weaved its way into her body, advising she was getting nearer to being a mother than ever before.

The labour lasted 24 hours. A tall man with flowers in his hands cruised through the Boone corridors like a train set to its tracks, its destination confirmed by the pre-laid rails giving no doubt as to its arrival point. Nate entered the private room that he shared with his wife after the birth of their son some six hours earlier. He had been home, showered, and shaved while Claire caught up a little on some well-earned sleep.

Jake Hughes was born into a family with moderate wealth and unbound love, with a comfortable future lined up. However, the first six hours of his life was not a time to consider such things, when sleeping was much more fun.

As Nate sat looking at his son and wife in the bed next to the seat he occupied, his mind drifted to a place many years ago. He remembered what he'd learned in school about Boone County Hospital, the hospital he was born in, and visited as a child with various broken limbs from scrapes and tumbles. His mind cast back to an old teacher, long since passed away, speaking at the head of the class.

He knew that Samuel Moore, a prominent Boone financer, had purchased the land that Boone County Hospital now occupied to build a new home. Instead, however, he decided to donate the land to build a hospital after learning from Dr Deering, a railroad physician, that a

17

railroad worker died and could have been saved if there had been a hospital available in Boone County. After building the hospital, Mr. Moore named it the Eleanor Moore Hospital, after his mother. Mr. Moore then invited Boone County residents to furnish rooms in the hospital. The response was generous, a tradition within Boone. Nate thought *the railroad worker was a martyr for all, including Jake Richard Hughes, my son.*

"Mrs. Hughes and Junior need some rest, Mr. Hughes," came the sound of a cheery female voice, bringing him back to the present.

Nate looked up to see an attractive thirty-something blonde nurse smiling at him. "They have had a long day, as all of you have."

"Of course," said Nate as he gave Claire and Jake a kiss each on the cheek, wishing them a good night. He left the hospital on a wave of euphoria as he made his way to the parking lot.

His drive home took thirty minutes, but it felt more like two. He thought about Italy, the place Jake was conceived. He thought of Aïda. He thought of the green lake and the warm temperatures and sailing on Lake Garda and wishing it would never end. *Life is perfect, just perfect!* he thought.

CHAPTER FIVE

Five years had passed since the death of Paul Jennings. Billy Jones's life was moving forward. He had been hit by the decline in the Manchester factories, where all the skilled engineers and craftsmen in the surrounding areas of the city were plunged into the recession of Margaret Thatcher's reign, in a world that was changing Britain into a country of 'shop keepers,' With the vision of the service sector being the future. Manchester had a way of reinventing itself time after time. The eighties were not going to cause the city to decay and give way to the bullish thoughts flying out of Westminster like a barrage of locusts visiting a summer cornfield.

It was a Friday in June. Billy and his wife of six months were getting ready to enjoy a holiday in Cumbria, a holiday away from the city smoke. They needed the fresh air that only Cumbria could bring, and the scenery around Keswick was not only amongst the best in England but the best in the world. They were travelling up that night and the car was loaded. He and Maggie were looking forward to the break. They did not have a honeymoon, except for a few weekend breaks together in Blackpool; but this was different, as it was their first time in a hotel. Thanks to Billy's newfound income, they booked a five-star hotel outside Keswick in a hamlet he'd read about, called Rosthwaite.

As they travelled north on the M6 motorway, the terraced houses soon changed to fields, which changed to views of the distant lakes and mountains around the city of Lancaster. This then changed to full countryside, lakes, and a fading blue sky that was rapidly turning pink, like the inside of a marshmallow with all the fluffy white clouds wrapped around it. Finally Keswick, then Rosthwaite in all its glory.

"It's five years since Paul died," Maggie told Billy. "I love you, and what happened to Paul was fate." She was trying to ease his guilt.

"You were the last person we spoke about, remember?" Billy added.

"Yes, you cheeky pair of buggers. Candi Staton."

They both laughed as the final suitcase was unloaded from the hired Vauxhall Cavalier. Not a Porsche, but it was brand new thanks to the national bank, Bill's new employer.

Maggie yearned for the Lake District. She had holidays there with her parents many times as a child, although it was a first for Billy. He bought some walking boots, as he knew he was going to be, introduced to walking up and down the fells after listening to Maggie's stories from past times. It was not a prospect Billy was looking forward to, but anything for an easy life.

***

"What would you like for breakfast, Jake, darling?" Claire asked her son.

"I would like some candy please, Mommy."

"Well, you can have cereal and juice," Claire said with a smile. "I have told you, no candy in the morning."

"Ok, Mommy."

Claire looked at her four-year-old son. *Where on earth has the time gone?* she thought to herself.

Nate was doing well at work, but working too many hours for Claire's liking. However, it brought in the money, and she liked the lifestyle that a large income gave them, such as the large, detached home with five bedrooms – far too big for the three of them, but luxury living had its place in the Hughes' household, and Jake wanted for nothing. She looked at the little blonde boy with loving eyes that only a mother can give her son.

"Did you have a lovely sleep?" she asked.

"Yes, Mommy."

"And did you have any nice dreams?"

"Well, I don't know if it was nice…" Jake replied. "I dreamt of old buildings in black fog, with men running around."

"What were they running after?" Claire enquired, drinking her coffee.

"I don't know, Mommy, it seemed silly. I also dreamt of playing with friends on pavements with dirty streets and fog that was black."

Claire didn't ask any more questions. She locked onto the words, knowing she would return to the subject again. She changed the subject and began telling Jake about Milan, as it was around five years ago that she was there with Nate. She was convinced Jake was, conceived on that wonderful anniversary evening following the performance of Aïda in Verona.

It was Saturday. Maggie had arranged an early morning walk to convince Billy of the beauty of the Cumbrian Lake District to ensure he settled in the area. They had a full English breakfast in the hotel dining room overlooking Derwent Water. Maggie was in full flow, pointing out various mountains, with the largest in sight being Skiddaw, at around 3,400 feet.

"What is your first impression, Billy boy?" she teasingly asked, smiling like the proverbial Cheshire cat.

"It's stunning," Billy answered. He felt the sun and could smell the air. It was fresh and clean. A faint smell of eucalyptus faded in and out of his senses

"I have a walk planned for the day."

True to her word, they left the hotel at 11 am. They crossed the road and over a bridge about half a mile from the hotel and into a village called Grange in Borrowdale. It was stunning. A quick left turn and they were below the mountains and walking along the flowing Derwent River. Both were taking in the views and sounds; the sound of birds singing cutting the otherwise silent land. They stood still.

"Listen?" said Maggie in a hushed voice. Nothing. Then, the sweet song of a blackbird broke the silence; it was a sound heard in the city, where the traffic was the conductor, with the cars, trains, and overhead planes the orchestra. Here, the blackbird was singing a solo performance and it was beautiful. Both Maggie and Billy were feeling relaxed in each other's company.

Billy looked at the woman he loved. Maggie was a serious girl, who had been out of character the night she sang on the karaoke. It was a drunken night celebrating a friend's twenty-first birthday. The alcohol gave her the courage to pick the microphone up and sing the title song to their romance, 'Young Hearts Run Free'. In reality, Maggie was 'Margaret' only in front of her well-to-do parents, Maggie's father being a partner in a large solicitors' practice. In all, they were comfortable in their middle-class Cheshire lifestyle.

Her parents liked Billy from first meeting him – although, at first, his energy and strength of character made them wonder if he was the type of 'gent' they had in mind for their coveted daughter. However, after a raging argument between Maggie and her father, he saw the light when her backdrop for the plaintiff was that "Billy was a genuine and honest man. And anyway, at what point does love come into your plans for me, Father?"

After that heated discussion, a few days saw Edward Le Conte understand the logic of his daughter as only a good defence lawyer would.

Maggie joined the law firm after a few well-chosen words in the right ears from Edward, and she quickly worked her way up to managing a conveyancing team.

Cat Bells was as popular as ever with people walking along the top, like ants foraging for anything they could pick up on their travels. That wasn't Billy and Maggie's target today. The walk took them along the scars of man, where quarrying preceded with the German miners who'd come a hundred years earlier using their undoubted skills, which were generations advanced from the British. The area mined for mainly copper and lead and, although now well disguised, there were still signs of the past. Skill and desire to maintain the landscape made it a beautiful part of the world.

As they continued walking, until, with no warning, the view opened up and to the right was the small pinnacle of Castle Crag. They turned to their right and began climbing the steep hill. The mini fell was under 1000 feet and Billy's strong frame found it easy to stride up. As they were neared the top, the previously green land turned to grey slate steps, which took them up to their final ascent to the summit. There, they reached a cairn constructed with the names of the men who fell in the Great War.

Maggie looked at Billy and smiled. "Father told me that, when you do your first walk around here, you either love it for life or hate it. What is your view, lover boy?" she teased.

"I hate it."

"That face is not a face of hatred." she smiled back.

Billy laughed. "I love it."

They gazed at the range around them. Skiddaw in the distance looked like a mother bird protecting her chicks, which were the smaller mountains. Maggie and Billy turned 180 degrees, both in awe at the range headed by Glaramara

"I have never seen anything like this before," Billy said. It was the same everywhere he turned. It was as if they were the cog of the wheel, and the spindles of the wheel were the mountains, in every direction they looked. "I am a subscriber to this fantastic way of life. I am a lover."

Maggie smiled. "Leave room for me."

They enjoyed a week that got better by the day. They walked all around the area, covering fells like High Spy, Maiden Moore, and a walk to Watendleth, which was the most beautiful place. They picnicked at the tarn before heading back into Rosthwaite, where Billy promised he would buy a house when they retired.

The week was over too quickly. They begrudgingly packed and turned the engine over to make the drive back to Manchester,

"At least when I go back to work it's a job I enjoy and not the factory," Billy said.

Then they were off along the banks of Derwent Water before re-joining the M6 and the long haul back. The journey was quiet for the reason that utopia had been met for one week only, and it was now over – for now, at least.

CHAPTER SIX

Jake was growing up fast. He was now ten years old and a bright lad for his age. He showed an interest in sports, although only as a ten-year-old would. The childlike, robotic movements were there when kicking a ball or running, however, a flash of talent would show when he was playing junior league baseball. Despite his enjoyment of the sport, nothing excited him more than a walk around the creeks and rivers. He felt at one with the beauty that nature had blessed on the Earth. This was his perfect family day out with Nate and Claire, today was no different. It was a warm Saturday morning, the temperature already hitting 25 degrees and it was only 7.30 am. They were spending the day at Ledges state park, a 15-mile drive from Boone.

Jake loved the fact that wildlife and plant communities were interwoven with the human history of Ledges. Humans have appreciated this unique area for thousands of years. Archaeological evidence found within the park dates to around 4,000 years. At the time of European settlement, the Ledges area had been inhabited by American Indians such as the Sauk, Fox, and Sioux. Native American mounds in the vicinity contain artifacts acting as silent reminders of the area's past inhabitants.

The beauty of the canyons and bluffs of Ledges made Jake feel alive and it was a joy to see for both Nate and Claire. Ledges were proposed as a state park as early as 1914. The first park custodian, Carl Fritz Henning, was, appointed in 1921. In 1924, the Ledges officially became one of Iowa's first state parks. Park facilities, constructed of native timber and fieldstone by the Civilian Conservation Corps (CCC) in the 1930s, are still standing today. These examples of fine craftsmanship include an arch stone bridge, a shelter in the oak woods, stone trail steps, and the stone shelter in lower ledges.

Jake was exploring the park, while Claire and Nate were trailing him by fifty yards. Claire turned to Nate and looked him in the eyes.

"I am a little worried about Jake and some of the dreams he is having," she said.

Nate looked at her. "What do you mean?" he replied.

"He keeps having this recurring dream," Claire continued. "He has the same dream about three times a week."

"Does it seem to affect him?" asked Nate.

"No, not really," was his wife's reply.

Nate looked at her. Claire was glowing in her walking boots and shorts, that came just under the cheeks of her bottom, with a bright pink sleeveless t-shirt. The outfit seemed so appropriate for the day, but he was still aware of the shape and sexiness she oozed. He would never lose his desire and love for her.

"What should I do?" Claire said, shunting Nate out of his moment of desire for her.

"I would keep an eye on it and see if it continues," said Nate. "Just keep asking him and keep me up to speed."

Jake turned around and called out to them. "Are we having some soda? My throat is as dry as a dead raccoon's ass,"

"Jake! What have I told you about that language?" Claire shrilled.

"C'mon, Tiger, I'll share one with you," said Nate with a badly disguised smile on his face.

CHAPTER SEVEN

Billy and Maggie were having another weekend break doing what was now their favourite past-time. It was 25 years since that first magical adventure for Billy, when Maggie suggested they go to Cumbria, walking the fells. Having now completed over one hundred of the Alfred Wainwright 214 fells described in the seven-volume *Pictorial Guide to the Lakeland Fells*, Billy knew they were now more than halfway through the walks.

Wainwright will always be famous for his guides to the fells, which he compiled between 1952 and 1966. These handwritten and hand-drawn works of art have given inspiration to all true fell walkers. Billy had accumulated all seven of the books and had given himself the target to complete all the climbs. However, Billy's main ambition, possibly in retirement, was to walk Wainwright's famous 192-mile coast-to-coast walk. In 1973, following many months of research, Wainwright compiled his book of the walk he devised from St Bees on the Cumbrian coast to Robin Hood's Bay on the Yorkshire coast. This was entitled *A Coast to Coast Walk* and, in the intervening years, it has become the most popular walk in the UK and is ranked the second most popular walk in the world after Milford Track in New Zealand. It has the tradition of dipping one's toe in the water at the start and replicating this tradition at the end.

The day started with the fourth climb up Skiddaw, a favourite because the views at the top were simply breathtaking. The south of Skiddaw is the flat vale of Keswick and Derwent Water, across which there are clear unobstructed views of the Skiddaw range. To the west is the head of the Newlands Valley and Bassenthwaite Lake, which cut Skiddaw off from the North Western Fells. North of the Skiddaw range there are low, rolling hills and, to the east, is the upland basin of Skiddaw forest, separating the formidable Blencathra, with the most dramatic 'Sharp Edge' on its north-eastern flank, which invariably takes several lives per year.

Today, though, was the first time the full mountain was to be covered. All previous climbs started at the car park, which was 2000 feet below the summit. Billy always felt this was cheating and, today, all of the 3,054 feet of the mountain was going to be met, including the summit of Skiddaw Little Man.

To summit the mountain, sustenance was needed, so the day began with a hearty breakfast in the nice and expensive hotel. This was now affordable to Billy following years of increasing income, making Maggie and him very comfortable financially.

The walk started at the beautiful town of Keswick, and some flat walking for around a mile took them over the road that leads to the foot of the mountain. No matter how fit Billy and Maggie were, the zigzag path of between 1000 and 2000 feet was always a challenge as it felt almost vertical.

The day was warm the sun was setting on the Cumbrian hills. The rabbits were playing hide and seek with the lambs as they gamboled in the fields. The sheep shared the fields with the countryside of Rosthwaite, probably the most beautiful square mile in England's green and watered pastures.

The walk went without incident, just a thoroughly relaxing and enjoyable walk enjoyed by both Billy and Maggie.

The clock chimed 9.30 pm in the lobby of the hotel, where most evening diners were either finishing or had finished their meal, guests were taking the last of the evening sun as it lowered in the sky like a big orange ball.

Billy turned to Maggie and smiled. Somebody had put 'Young Hearts Run Free' on the jukebox. The song was always a favourite following Maggie's rendition of it on the karaoke, they insisted on it being played during their wedding ceremony, but they compromised with Maggie's father, who disallowed it. If Billy had his way, they would have played it; however, the most beautiful girl in the world had kept all parties happy.

Billy looked around to see who put the song on the jukebox. There were, three couples in the room, one couple looked like they were here for the gorgeous scenery and not walkers. Billy guessed they were in their eighties, but they looked happy and were enjoying a glass of wine after what was a very select and well-prepared evening meal.

The second couple were too young, somewhere in their early to mid-twenties, and probably only came across the song now and again on the radio. The third couple were around Billy's age.

He turned to Maggie. "Do you fancy a five-pound bet it was that young couple who put the track on the jukebox?"

"Yes, I would, Billy," Maggie replied with a giggle. "A big bet, because I saw the young lad put it on while you were powdering your nose."

Billy made conversation with the young couple. "I would have thought you were too young to know this song?"

"I am." was the reply from the younger man. "But it is a favourite song of mine."

"What a coincidence," said Billy. "It is a song close to our hearts, too." Billy did not mention Maggie's rendition of the song on that fateful evening when Paul's life ended in such a brutal way.

"That's not a local accent," continued Billy. "Where are you from and how come you're around here?"

"I am from Iowa," said the younger guy, "and I'm doing the Wainwright coast to coast walk with my wife, Emily."

Billy smiled and replied. "Anybody who does the Wainwright coast to coast walk has to be a good guy in my book, I plan to do it myself one day. My name is Billy and this is my wife, Maggie."

The couple approached them and they all shook hands. "Pleased to meet you," said the young man. "This is Em, and my name is Jake."

CHAPTER EIGHT

Jake first met Emily at university, where they both studied law. They had always got on well and shared the common interest of coming from Boone. Although they never knew each other in Iowa, they knew a lot of the same people and wondered how their paths never crossed and had to wait until moving to the local university before meeting. Although, with the 211 campus buildings, that was a slim chance, too.

The University of Illinois at Urbana-Champaign was founded in 1867 as a state-supported, land-grant institution with a threefold mission of teaching, research, and public service. The University has earned a reputation as an institution of international stature. Recognised for the high quality of its academic programmes and the outstanding facilities and resources it makes available to students and faculty. Scholars and educators rank it as being among a select group of the world's greatest universities.

Located in the adjoining cities of Champaign and Urbana, approximately 140 miles south of Chicago, the University and its surrounding communities offer a cultural and recreational environment ideally suited to the work of a major research institution, with professional programmes through the Colleges of Law. National surveys consistently rank the University of Illinois at Urbana-Champaign among the top ten institutions in many fields of study, with several colleges and departments ranked among the top five.

Jake and Emily, or Em as he called her, hit it off straight away and quickly became close in the group of around eight friends that hung around together. She had the typical American looks that Jake liked – long, jet black hair and shining blue eyes, with a smile that could light the whole of New York City.

They had so much in common and were always comfortable in each other's company. Both sporty and athletic, she introduced Jake to horse riding. Her father held a few Arab racehorses, which he raced around the American circuits. She taught him about bloodlines and discussed how all Arab racehorses came from only a few horses, one of which was the most famous, named Eclipse.

29

Em told him that Eclipse was foaled during the great solar eclipse in 1764. His exact place of birth is unknown. She told him of Eclipse's breeder, H.R.H. William, the Duke of Cumberland in Windsor Park in Berkshire. This is where his sire, Marske, stood at stud, having been swapped for an Arabian by Marske's breeder, John Hutton. Eclipse's dam, Spiletta, was purchased by the Duke from her breeder, Sir Robert Eden. And that is how the racehorse we know today was born.

Jake quickly learned how to ride and many a long day in the saddle shared. In return, Jake's love for walking and climbing was, shared with Em. They would often toss a coin to see which was to be the day's pursuit.

This quickly changed through the years from friendship to love to marriage, like a performance car going through the gears to achieve maximum feel. They were now celebrating their second wedding anniversary – not in Italy, which would have been the choice of Jake's parents, but in England, for what is classed as the world's second-best walk, Wainwright's coast to coast, beginning in the stunning county of Cumbria and ending in the equally beautiful town of Robin Hood's Bay on the East Yorkshire coast.

Day one of the fifteen-day target saw the couple walk from St Bees to Ennerdale Bridge. They started by dipping their boots in the water and collecting a pebble. Taking the steep path up South Head, the walk had begun. That was yesterday. Now, at the end of day two, they had pre-booked a hotel in Rosthwaite. They mastered Loft Beck, climbing out of the valley and followed the faint track to the right of the beck. At the top, they turned right to follow the stony and rugged track beneath Grey Knotts. They then covered the old Tramway, a well-laid path, steep in places, that takes you down to the slate mine at Honister and eventually reaching their destination.

"Only thirteen days to go," Em stated as they returned to the small and comfortable hotel, where they again bumped into Billy and Maggie.

"Where have you been today?" Billy asked. The adventures of both couples covered verbally as stories and their love of the walks were swapped.

"Is this your first visit to England?" asked Maggie.

Everybody seemed to be getting along well. However, Jake felt uneasy, even though he didn't know why at first. He never showed his feelings to the people he was sharing the time with; even Em couldn't sense it, and nobody knew Jake better than her.

Jake and Billy discussed each other's likes and dislikes, and Jake picked up on Billy's passion for football, Manchester City in particular. They were chatting away quite easily, and Billy began describing a goal by an old Manchester City player, Denis Law, who was a hero at Manchester United before signing for City. Billy laughed as he told the story of how Law scored a backheel goal against Manchester United in 1974 at United's Old Trafford ground. Manchester United needed to win to avoid being relegated to the second tier of the English football league.

Jake went cold, not that he cared about football, Manchester City, United, or Denis Law. He suddenly caught a vision, so clear in his mind's eye that it could have been on a cinema screen in ultra-high definition. He saw the sun shining on a blistering hot day; he saw a team in sky blue shirts attacking a red team's goal. He saw a footballer in a blue shirt miskick a ball, and a blonde player in another blue shirt anticipate, with electric instincts, the path of the ball heading towards him; he positioned his body and back-heeled it past the goalkeeper and into the net. Jake saw that the goal scorer was not celebrating, despite scoring a goal against their biggest rivals.

He had a vision of thousands of spectators running onto the field from the other end of the pitch. There must have been ten thousand, maybe more, all wearing tartan scarves wrapped around their wrists. Jake realised his view was from the pitch. He looked down and realised he was running on the pitch, a tartan scarf wrapped around his wrist; he wore a tight t-shirt over baggy jeans and a pair of Dr. Marten boots. This vision was very real. He was suddenly brought back into the present when he heard Billy speaking.

"...And Denis didn't celebrate the goal because he had played for United, but I can tell you, I did!" A big smile, spreading from ear to ear, erupted on Billy's face as he continued. "All the United fans ran on the pitch trying to get the game abandoned so they could get the game replayed. No chance, they were going down. A great day in City's history."

Jake felt faint. He tried to concentrate on what Billy was saying. Em looked at him anxiously.

"Jake, are you feeling ok? You've turned white!" She felt his forehead, checking to see if he had a temperature.

"No, I feel a bit sick," said Jake. "It must be the events of the day. I need to go to bed, I think. I will be fine in the morning."

31

"It's been great meeting you," said Billy. "I have enjoyed our chat. Enjoy the rest of your walk."

"Thanks," said Jake. "It's eleven-thirty already, and we have to be up early in the morning. Let's get some sleep," He nodded to Em.

When they got to their room, what Jake did next astounded Em. Instead of making a zombie-like move towards the bed to generate some much-needed sleep, Jake went to his rucksack and brought out the laptop they brought with them to allow them to email back home.

Jake fired up the machine and instantly began to google Manchester United v Manchester City. Pages of hyperlinks came up, but nothing that he was looking for. Then he searched for Denis Law scoring against Manchester United. This had a link to a YouTube clip. He pressed the link and the vision he saw replicated, to the smallest degree, his vision of Denis Law back heeling the ball into the net. A sunny day and then thousands of people running onto the pitch with tartan scarves wrapped around their necks and wrists. He couldn't help but smile at the silly clothes they wore – some wore boots, some wore platform shoes, and they all fashioned long feathered haircuts. This was England in the mid-seventies.

"Jake, what is wrong?" asked Em. "You've been acting strangely for the last hour and a half. It's now one in the morning and you are still wide awake."

"Can I sleep on it?" replied Jake. He seemed hyper. "I promise I will tell you in the morning. I'm not sure what is happening."

Jake finally got to sleep at around 3 am. Before then, his mind would not disengage from the world of awareness. When he did finally fall asleep, he began to dream of things he'd dreamt of as a boy – not the dreams of being a fireman or a superhero, but a young lad on what he called 'bogeys' in his mind, which was a plank of wood with four wheels from a long-discarded pram he'd grown out of as a child. He dreamt of running through cobbled streets with terraced back-to-back houses. He dreamt of sliding on icy pavements on bitterly cold days. He dreamt of making dens with wood and string. He dreamt of a large park with boats. He dreamt of a canal with orange water. He dreamt of a childhood Manchester with his friend… Billy!

***

It was eight-thirty in the morning and breakfast was only half-eaten.

"Jake, when are you going to talk?" said Em impatiently. "What on earth is going on, darling?"

32

"Let's get a coffee and talk in the lounge area," replied Jake.

The lounge was almost empty, except for an aging couple who sat reading the morning papers. Most of the guests either hadn't evacuated their beds or were eating breakfast. They ordered some coffee and sat down.

"Em, can we cancel the rest of the walk?" Jake asked. "I'd like to use our fortnight doing something I think I need to do."

"If it is that important, then yes, we can," replied Em, surprised by Jake's request. "But tell me what is on your mind?"

By eleven o clock and three more cups of coffee later, they both sat there in the lounge in silence.

"Jake, do you realise how stupid that sounds?"

"Yes!" replied Jake. "But I know I'm right."

"Well," said Em, "I love you, but I can't believe what you have just told me. It sounds impossible, but I will stick with you on this. Let us see what happens."

By 2 pm, they had packed their things and checked out of the hotel, being careful to avoid Billy and Maggie. They made a phone call to Hertz to rent a car and were soon making their way down the M6 to Manchester.

CHAPTER NINE

They stopped at Killington services between Junctions 36 and 37, on the south side of the M6. They had been driving for about an hour and were halfway to their destination. Whilst they sat drinking a warm coffee, Jake googled hotels in the Manchester area and found a Travelodge. He quickly booked a two-night stay for him and Em, then relaxed and let the tiredness have its way before they eventually left and continued their journey.

They took their time travelling down to Manchester and arrived at the hotel later that afternoon. They checked in, went to their room, showered, and collapsed for a well-deserved catch-up sleep.

It wasn't until around eight in the evening that they awoke. They decided to see the city centre and go for a meal. They took half an hour to get dressed then went on the hunt for a nice restaurant. As they walked along Deansgate, Jake froze.

"Em, I know every street around here."

"Jake, that's impossible," Em replied.

"Well, if I was to say Dale Street and I took you there, what would you say? Or Manchester town hall, or a statue of Abe Lincoln on a street named Brazennose Street?"

"Jake, you are beginning to freak me out now," A shudder went down Em's spine. *What if?* she thought. She knew he had never been to Manchester before.

"Ok," she said, "I will make a deal with you. If you take me to a statue of Abe Lincoln on Brazennose Street, I am with you. If not, we go back to Keswick and continue our coast to coast walk. Deal?"

Jake fell silent for a moment. "Deal." was the final word to come out of his mouth.

He frowned and felt suddenly anxious. What had he just done? A city he had never seen, the word 'Brazennose' he had never heard before, and a US president with a statue in England. *This must be a fragment of my imagination somewhere,* he thought to himself. He shook his head. *This is silly.*

They continued to walk along Deansgate on the left-hand side, with Market Street and the Manchester Cathedral behind them. They saw the most glorious building across the road, about fifty yards away.

"That is the John Ryland's Library!" said Jake instinctively.

Em laughed out loud. "That's not a library, it is too grand. You are losing it, partner."

As they approached the building, a sign outside read, 'John Ryland's Library.' They stopped and just stared at each other. Any shivers they had before now magnified to volcanic eruptions.

They walked further very slowly, holding each other's hands. *If we do see the statue, this will all be true,* Em thought. They inched towards a street with a sign on it. They could not read it from a distance, but it was obvious the name of the street would not be Brazennose as the letters were too few. As they got closer, the words became focused. It read 'Queen Street'.

"I knew it was impossible to have such a wild guess. You win," said Jake. "Let's go for a meal and then sleep. It's all too wacky to be true."

They turned in silence, the John Ryland building still in sight, Em nudged Jake. They looked on in silence. There, as plain as the nose on her face, was a sign. Em read it out aloud to Jake. "Brazennose Street!" The sign was there, sitting proudly on the side of a wall as if to say, "Walk up to me if you dare."

Em was now linking Jake's arm very tightly. He tried to relieve the tension by saying, "You don't hold on this tight when you're on the back of my Harley doing ninety," They both stood still and looked up the street to a magnificent building at the top.

"That is the town hall," said Jake. But there was no statue to be seen, let alone Abe Lincoln. "Let's walk up and see what we can see," he continued. They began walking up the street and still no sign of Abe.

"Perhaps he was assassinated," Jake joked. Just then, the street cut away into Queen Street, the road they had mistakenly gone down, and there, standing eight feet tall and proud, Abe Lincoln.

They crept up to it and, before they read the inscription, Jake turned to Em. "I know why it's there."

Em looked at him and pulled a face. "Go on then, tell me."

Jake took a deep breath. "Manchester in the industrial revolution was the capital of the world and the northwest of England was particularly rich in cotton mills and factories. Cities like Liverpool, Bristol, and London set up a plan they called 'the magic triangle'. They sailed from their harbours to Africa, kidnapped Africans, and used them to do the hard labour jobs on the ships, then, when they reached their destination, the deep south of America, they traded the slaves for cotton and brought the cotton back for manufacturing. This was supporting the slave market whilst increasing their profits, as they did not have to pay for the cotton and in a way helping the confederates."

As he continued, Em was listening with her mouth wide open and her eyes equally as wide.

"However," Jake added, "Manchester refused to do business with any links to slavery and that's why the statue is there, with a thank you from Abe to the Manchester People."

They looked at each other for what must have been the hundredth time in disbelief.

"I don't know where that came from," Jake said, finally.

"Jake Hughes, I love you and I believe every word you have told me," said Em. "But I am also hungry. Let's eat, we have a busy day tomorrow." It was almost 10.00 pm and the Manchester sun was just about to retire beneath the horizon for the evening.

"Pizza?" Jake asked.

"Pizza is fine with me."

CHAPTER TEN

The next morning saw a cloudy day and the overnight rain had dampened the streets.

"I quite like this Manchester place," said Em. "We must explore more."

"I will show you the sights," Jake told her. "But we have to be on our metal today as it is a busy one."

After breakfast, Jake fired up the hired Seat Ibiza from the car park opposite the hotel. He drove out without the aid of a sat nav. Em stared in awe as he was proving, by the minute, that the story he'd told her was, although unbelievable, possible. Very possible.

Jake drove from the city centre for about six miles to Sadler Street and eased the car to a stop outside number seven. They sat there for fifteen minutes, staring out of the windscreen, in silence.

"I am trembling," Jake said at last. "Let's get this thing over with."

They both edged out of the car, glanced at each other, and walked up the short garden path to the door. Jake waited fifteen seconds to gain his composure then rang the bell. Within a minute the latch was being drawn back with the tell-tale sign that only an opening door can share. The woman stood at the doorway was in her late sixties to the early seventies. She had a trim figure and was well dressed in a cream blouse and a pair of faded blue denim jeans, finished off with a pair of ankle boots. Even though her hair was dyed chestnut brown, it was an expensive colour that was done professionally. The tell-tale signs of her age were the fine wrinkles on her face, a face that looked like it had seen hard times; but the wrinkles around the eyes suggested that this lady had seen fun times, too.

"Are you Mrs. Jennings?" Jake asked.

"Yes," the woman replied.

"Mrs. Helen Jennings?"

"Yes!"

"Could we speak to you in private?"

"Not really," the woman replied. "When Americans come here, they are usually Jehovah's Witnesses or something."

37

"I am not a Jehovah's Witness, or a salesman or anything," said Jake. "I just want to chat."

Helen looked at Jake and thought how handsome he looked. He had a very good physique that was emphasised by the navy blue tight-fitting Fred Perry t-shirt and a pair of cream chinos with brown, well-polished, Oxford shoes. Em was equally as smart, in a black and white polka dot ankle-length skirt and a white shirt with black braiding on the top pocket and black buttons.

"No, not today, thank you," Helen responded.

As the door closed in Jake and Em's faces, Em shouted out spontaneously.

"It's about Paul," There was no response. "Paul, your son Paul!" The second comment was as loud as she could muster.

The door reopened. Helen looked at them blankly. "You had better come in then."

Jake and Em glanced at each other and followed Helen into the hallway, then into the lounge. Em quickly felt comfortable in the room with its high, pristine white ceilings and pastel green walls. There was a log burner set in what would have once been an old fireplace, with the original stone surrounding it in the hearth. They were invited to sit on an antique green leather couch, which was deep and wide.

"Well, what do you want to talk to me about?" Helen asked. "Please make this quick as I have to be out in ten minutes."

Silence echoed around the room for thirty seconds until a grimace fell on Helen's face. "Tell me now!"

Jake cleared his throat. "As you can tell, I am from America, Iowa." His mid-west accent drew out Iowa. He continued. "My name is Jake Hughes and this is my wife, Em… I mean Emily. I have never been to Manchester before, but I know my way around it like I have been living here all my life."

"That's right." Em interrupted. "I couldn't believe it."

Helen intervened. "I am pleased for you. Is that what you came to tell me?"

"No." responded Jake. "I have come to tell you I know who killed Paul," The room fell silent. The room felt heavy. The room felt thick and airless.

Helen stared. "So, you, an American who has never been to Manchester, claim to know how my son died, when the best of the British Police couldn't find out. Please, LEAVE!"

38

"Give me fifteen minutes," Jake pleaded. "I need to tell you a story you will not believe. I am not even sure Em and I do, but please hear me out."

Helen looked at him for a moment. *What is this nutcase going on about?* She wondered. Then a second thought. *Oh well, there is nothing to lose.*

"You have ten minutes, then you need to leave."

"Thank you," said Em.

Jake cleared his throat. "I am finding this so difficult to say, as you have lost a son and I don't want to rekindle any sad memories. You will either take my opening line with an open mind or you will think I need psychiatric help."

"What is your opening line?" Helen enquired.

"I am Paul reincarnated."

Helen stared at Jake. "I will take the psychiatric choice. Get out now!"

"But…"

"Out! Now!" Helen's face was red with thunder as she stormed to the door.

Jake began to panic. "You loved Northern soul and went to a club in Manchester called the twisted wheel," he said quickly. "My favourite food was egg as a kid. I fell and bent my front teeth aged about five. I had ten stitches in my calf when I was seven."

Helen looked at him. "Are you stalking me? Have you been doing research just to upset me?"

"You once cooked a fish in butter sauce in boiling water and burst the bag because it said pop bag in boiling water. You told me to never mention it to anybody." Jake was grabbing at straws now.

Helen put her hand up to her mouth. "How do you know that?"

"I don't know," said Jake. "I didn't even know I did until thirty seconds ago."

"You are weird," Helen said. "You can't know all this."

"I remember my father's registration on a Hillman car. BVB 378J, You smoked Park Drive cigarettes and liked strawberry ice lollies, and I don't know where any of this is coming from!" Jake was shouting now. He was raged like a man possessed. Em had never seen him like this before.

"Ok." said Helen "You have all the facts. Let me ask you some questions. How much did you give me for your weekly keep?"

"Fifteen pounds." was the reply.

"What was the name of your toy teddy bear?"

"Scruff. It was passed down from my cousin Jane."

"What date did you die?"

"I don't know."

"Well, if you don't know the basics of when you died, how can you be reincarnated?" Helen countered. "What is your date of birth?"

"The fifteenth of March 1985," Jake replied, but with less certainty.

"You have hit some personal points and I don't know how you came across them," said Helen. "But how can I believe you are my son reincarnated? How?" She waved her hands in confusion. "I have to go now, so please leave!"

"I am truly sorry if I have upset you," Jake replied. "If you want to talk again, here is my phone number."

Jake scribbled his number down on a nice card he'd bought specially for the occasion, working on the theory that there was more chance of Helen throwing away a tatty piece of paper.

"I promise I won't disturb you again. We will be leaving Manchester the day after tomorrow."

CHAPTER ELEVEN

The following day, Jake continued to show Em the sights of Manchester as a way of passing the time but deep down hoping that Helen would call. Em could not believe how well Jake knew the geography of the city. He took her to the site where he believed he worked; although it was no longer a factory, he felt he remembered the basic buildings. He took her to Old Trafford football ground, which looked different from his memory, but the old footage he saw on YouTube was his proof of how it once looked. He saw the plaque dedicated to the Manchester United players who perished in the Munich air disaster on 6th February 1958.

"They are the flowers of Manchester," he told Em.

All the things they saw only convinced Jake more he was Paul Jennings reincarnated. They went to the John Ryland's Library and could not believe the beauty of the building; they found it even more impressive when they toured inside. They took a final look at Abe standing there majestically, with people passing by with no knowledge of why he was there. They were snaking up or down the street, scurrying to their offices or the shops. Jake and Em stopped and stared in awe at the statue that had turned this impossible story into a possibility.

For their final stop, Jake took Em to Peter Street.

"This is where Paul was killed," Jake said quietly.

Em shook and cried. She sobbed as if, Jake himself who had died. The last twenty-four hours had been a journey both would never forget; twenty-four hours that had shaken their belief in reincarnation. Here was where the journey ended. Em knew Jake was a man of his word and he would not contact Helen. A promise was a promise.

The evening was upon them and it was getting late. Jake and Em decided to call it a day and went back to their hotel.

"Let's not dwell on it," Jake said when they were in their room. "We can add a couple of days to the holiday and finish the coast to coast walk. I owe you that for the support you have given me over the last couple of days."

Em stood on her tiptoes and give him a peck on the cheek. "Deal," she said, though feeling a little disappointed that the adventure had reached the end of the line.

The next morning, they woke with an early breakfast at seven, loaded the car, and set off at nine. The plan was to be back at Rosthwaite before lunch and pick up the broken coast to coast walk.

The traffic was heavy leaving the city centre and it put the two of them about forty-five minutes behind schedule.

"Well, that's the end of the story, morning glory," said Em as they finally hit the M61 going west towards Preston. They were sitting quietly, thinking what might have been, then they both jumped. Jake's phone was ringing. Em answered as there was no hands-free in the car.

"Wow! Gosh! Really!" Em said into the phone. "Why didn't we think of that? Ok, we are on our way now!"

"Who was that?" Jake asked.

"It was Helen!" said Em excitedly. "She said that she'd been thinking about your date of birth."

"And?" Jake asked.

"She said that Paul died on June fifteen, 1984."

"And?" Jake asked again.

"Well, you were born exactly nine months after Paul died. The period your mom was carrying you."

Jake looked at Em. It was all fitting into place again.

"She wants to see us now." Em's voice raised to an excited shrill.

"Sadler Street, here we come," Jake replied with equal enthusiasm.

***

The door opened at 7 Sadler Street. Jake had dreamt of this property as a child and he understood now that his mother was concerned about his childhood dreams. He now realised that all the dreams were Manchester-based – football, factories, childhood memories… They were dreams that he had no right to own. They belonged to somebody else. They belonged to Paul Jennings.

The street was different from how it had been all those years ago. The few trees lining the neighbouring streets had grown. Helen's front door had changed from a dark blue in Jake's mind's eye to deep green, shimmering in the Manchester summer sun.

Helen could not be described as appearing happy as the door swung open, but Jake and Em picked up on the fact that she was much friendlier than the last time they met. This time, they were offered a cup of tea, which they both happily accepted.

Helen got straight to the point. "Look," she said. "I still don't believe all this stuff. It sounds ridiculous."

Jake and Em sat watching her, not daring to take their eyes off her.

"But the truth is," she continued, "I can't get out of my head some of the details you mentioned the other day."

Helen gazed distractedly at the recently vacuumed carpet, cream with a bold red and green floral design emblazoned on it, and she laughed to herself. Jake and Em did not join in, afraid of breaking the moment.

"The pop in the bag thing with the fish… I thought I had to pop it, as in burst, then realised it meant pop as in place."

Helen shook her head without breaking the smile that was lighting up her face. Jake and Em began smiling with her until they all laughed. It eased the situation.

"And knowing Scruff, and everything else…" she added.

Em and Jake remained quiet, waiting for Helen to continue.

"As I said," she continued, "I don't believe you deep down, but ten percent of me – no, two percent – says what if? It's an avenue I must look at. I need closure, but I don't want you to be pulling some kind of trick or scam. Please spare me that."

Jake looked her in the eye. "I am only just beginning to realise what is happening. I would have been none the wiser had we not decided to do the coast to coast walk."

Helen did not know what the coast to coast walk was, she let the comment pass. "We need to get some ground rules set here," she said with a tone of authority. "There are lots of people involved. Paul had a wife, and now has a son he never met."

Jake looked at Em and back to Helen. "Agreed," he said. "We will not mention it to anybody until it is safe to do so. In return, we expect the same from you, especially regarding Billy and Maggie Jones."

Helen's eyes darted quicker than a lightning bolt. "Billy? What has Billy got to do with all this?"

"As I said," Jake continued. "We were on a coast to coast walk in the Lake District. It would have taken us two weeks to complete. On the second day, we stayed in the same hotel as Billy and Maggie. We met them and shared an evening having a few drinks. God, that man can drink."

Helen smiled briefly then straightened her face again.

"It was during that conversation I started seeing things that I dreamt about when I was younger," said Jake. "He told me about a Denis Law goal – the vision was so clear, I knew I had been at that game."

Helen lifted her head. "Paul was a United fanatic. That match is famous in this city. Paul was at the game."

"Did he wear a tartan scarf around his wrist?" Jake asked. "It didn't make any sense to me. Tartan is Scottish, isn't it?"

Helen smiled. "Yes, it was a fad with the united fans of the time. I think because there were a lot of Scots in the team and they were managed by Tommy Docherty, who was also Scottish."

They took a moment to drink their tea, which was by now going cold. Helen broke the silence.

"So, if we keep this between the three of us, nobody else will get dragged into unhappy memories of the past. I don't want to dig up old memories for my family and friends." Jake and Em both nodded in agreement.

Helen looked at Jake. "The last time you were here, you said you knew who killed Paul?" She was much calmer and Jake was impressed with her self-control, probably a result of the wisdom of growing older.

"Well," said Jake, "the truth is, I have an idea, but so much needs to be proven before I cast any names forward. What if I'm wrong? Let's take it day by day, shall we?" Helen nodded in agreement.

"After all," continued Jake, "how do you prove reincarnation, let alone a murder that happened over twenty years ago? We need to understand fully what is happening to me."

Helen agreed again and, in her way, knowing enough of the topic had been covered for the day, she changed the subject. "Tell me about this coast to coast walk you were on, will you?"

After some idle chit chat about the weather, the coast to coast walk, Helen's nice décor, and the fantastic homemade fruit cake that accompanied the well-needed mug of tea, Jake and Em said their goodbyes. Jake asked Helen if she fancied a meal with both him and Em in a couple of days to reflect.

"That would be nice," said Helen.

"I will give you a call tomorrow and arrange something," was Jake's response.

CHAPTER TWELVE

Jake, as promised, rang Helen. "I have booked a table at the Midland Hotel for six tomorrow evening if that's okay, Helen? I thought we could eat early and have a chat after over a drink."

"Wow," said Helen. "You are pushing the boat out a bit at the Midland."

"Then pick you up at quarter past five?"

"I'll be ready and waiting," Helen replied, "See you then."

Helen sat back and reflected. *What a whirlwind the last four days have been.* She thought to herself. She had gone from slamming the door on 'the nutter' at her door who said he was Paul reincarnated, to agreeing to a meal at one of Manchester's prime hotels. She thought about '*That introduction to fire*' to thinking '*Actually, they are a nice couple – crazy, but nice.*' She thought about Paul and his hard-working ethics. She thought about Sue and young Tommy, the son Paul never met. Tommy was now aged 21 with a family of his own, living in a council house with his wife, Ann. They met through the local pub scene both struggling for money. Tommy had a job in a local supermarket doing odd jobs, stacking shelves, helping customers, working on the checkout, helping unload lorries with their loads of food and drink to keep the hungry community watered and fed.

The work was long hours, and sometimes involved heavy lifting and working weekends, which was becoming more common in an increasingly management-controlled noughties Britain. It was typical of a company that wanted its pound's worth of flesh from everybody. However, the effort put in by Tommy did not match the rewards in the guise as cash.

"I struggle on this pay, Granma."

Helen felt saddened as she thought back to the last time she saw Tommy a week ago. The comment was a regular statement from him; she wanted to help, but she met her monthly bills and outgoings with little spare cash for luxuries. She did help as much as she could, though; she would buy extra food to help Tommy and Ann. Now, though, she was going for a meal at the Midland, something she had never done before in her life.

She thought of Sue, Paul's wife, who struggled on benefits for years after Paul died. They had no life assurance, the mortgage was not fully covered. However, Paul's pension fund did pay twice his annual salary and provided a small pension for Sue, but £24,000 cash sum and £5,000 a year pension would ensure jam and bread, not caviar and champagne.

Sue led a hard life. She met another man, Jim Partridge, and remarried. Unfortunately, Jim's best friend floated at the bottom of a beer glass, and no attention paid to Sue or Tommy. He worked and kept the money coming in, but it was more what was left after the beer, cigarettes, and betting, it was not his first choice to give to his wife and stepson. He never gelled with Tommy, and Tommy sensed this. Although he would get birthday and Christmas presents, there was no love from Jim. The relationship lasted about five years before Sue left him. It was an acrimonious divorce with an unfair settlement, which saw Jim receiving forty percent of the value of Paul and Sue's equity in their first home together. This annoyed Helen as she knew Jim was good for nothing and the money he gained would go to lining the pockets of bookmakers, landlords, and brewery owners.

Sue had been alone for fifteen years now. Helen loved Sue like her own daughter. She'd held jobs as a cleaner, barmaid, and waitress in a café just to make ends meet before finally getting regular work in a local GP practice as a receptionist six years ago. She was at her happiest now since Paul's death, but humans are resistant and a near-poverty-line existence becomes the norm, something Sue had learned to live with.

Helen then thought of Jonty Ball, the detective who tried so hard to find the person responsible for the hit and run on Paul. She liked Jonty a lot. They'd had a brief affair whilst he was working on the case; they enjoyed evenings out for meals or shows. She had a special evening with Jonty at Manchester's Palace Theatre watching an all-star cast in the stage show of *Westside Story*. Jonty was surprisingly in love with the theatre, given he was brought up in a one-parent family. His social life as a youth was boxing clubs and fights, before breaking free when he joined the police force. He owed a lot to the force; it saved him and kept him on the straight and narrow. Helen remembered he mentioned at least six times that night at the Palace Theatre how the show was never, meant for film, that it was perfect on stage. "It is based on Romeo and Juliet, you know," he had said. Helen made a little noise as she cackled. She was not in her home now, she was at the Palace Theatre with Jonty some twenty-plus years ago, enjoying the show and wishing it would never end.

The romance petered out after Paul's case closed – not because of the case, but it was hard dating a police officer. Long hours that were never routine; like a light switch he was unable to switch on and off, he would get calls in the night about felonies, arson, murders, and suchlike. Jonty would need to respond, despite sometimes having eyes as red as the London buses. They kept in touch by phone and Jonty had a few nice holidays after he retired from the force seven years ago; he liked cruising in particular. He threatened to go to Broadway for a week and take in a few shows, that was still a dream as of yet.

During all this reminiscing, Helen showered and climbed into bed, feeling nostalgic about nice times in the past, angry about sad times in the past, and surprisingly excited about seeing Jake and Em the following evening.

She thought about a crazy man who had knocked on her door four days ago. *What if…?* She closed her eyes, sleep soon followed, as sure as the evening moon follows the afternoon sun in the sky.

CHAPTER THIRTEEN

At 5.15 pm prompt, the doorbell rang to inform her that Jake and Em had arrived to take her for an evening meal at the Midland Hotel. Helen had been unsure what to wear but finally decided on keeping it simple with a black A-line dress that fitted at the waist and with a hemline that hit the middle of her knee, a high neckline with no sleeves. She wore black, high-heeled leather shoes with an ankle strap, her favourite Bueche Girod white gold watch, and a solid silver necklace, which sat on top of the dress, highlighting the silver on the black effect that matched the narrow black belt with a silver buckle, silver buckles on her shoes and the silver clasp on her black leather handbag. She loved the simple two-tone effect of black and silver.

Helen was ready and waiting. She opened the door to Jake, as Em waited in the car. She smiled warmly.

"Hiya," she said to Jake. "How are you?"

"I am fine, thank you, Helen," Jake answered. "I hope you are hungry because I know I am."

Helen liked the Mid-West American drawl. As she approached the car, Em got out and moved to the back seat of the two-door Seat Ibiza.

"How are you, Helen?" said Em.

"I am good, thank you, Emily."

"Please, everybody calls me Em, except my Mom on a Sunday, when it's Emily." They all smiled. Jake looked at his wife in the rearview mirror and winked. She went coy and smiled. She liked it.

The drive to the Midland Hotel took around twenty minutes. Jake allowed for a little rush-hour traffic, but the majority was the rank and file driving in the opposite direction, and not all going to the Midland. Jake was listening to the Eagles on the car CD player. Helen said how she used to love the Eagles in the seventies, they were so different and wrote some fantastic songs. She began to sing along gently to Don Henley.

"So you know the words to Hotel California?" Jake asked. "Don Henley has competition?" All three laughed.

49

Helen, unfortunately, was tone-deaf. "I would come second in a one-entry singing competition."

Jake parked in the nearby multi-story car park and they strolled round in the summer evening sun, which was high but dancing and hiding between the tall buildings of the city centre.

"I have to say," said Em, "some of these buildings are spectacular. We went around the John Ryland's Library a few days ago and I loved it."

"There are two or three fantastic libraries in Manchester," replied Helen. "There is one over there." She pointed to the domed roof of the Central Library building in St Peter's Square. "The domed roof there is spectacular. The Chetham's School of Music is worth a look as well."

With that, they had arrived at the doors of the hotel. The building was fully tiled on the outside, in what looked like marble, and it wasn't a small building. There was a commissionaire to greet them at the door, which led to a lobby and to the main entrance to the hotel. Jake looked at the statue on the right. It had a plaque which read:

Presented The Honourable Charles Stewart Rolls
Met
Frederick Henry Royce
In this Hotel on 4th May 1904 a meeting which led to the formation of ROLLS-ROYCE

"Would y'all take a look at that!" Jake said in the American drawl that Helen liked so much. "We are in pretty good company here, ladies." Jake was more impressed than his two dinner partners.

They went to the door that led them to Mr. Cooper's restaurant, where they were met by the head waiter.

"We have a reservation for three in the name of Hughes?" Jake told the waiter. The waiter nodded politely they were duly led to their table.

They were each handed menus and they spent some time deliberating over their choices. Helen felt slightly daunted by the exotic menu. *I best get this right,* she thought to herself. *It will be the only time I get this chance.*

The menu looked fantastic. Jake and Helen both ordered Earl Grey smoked salmon, while Em ordered heritage carrot and goat's cheese salad with hazelnut dukkah and spiced currant jam. *Wow!* thought Helen. *This is new to me.*

For the main course, Helen chose seared sea trout, as did Em.

"As we had to cut short our walk in Cumbria," said Jake, "I've decided to have the Cumbrian beef sirloin, medium rare."

50

The food was fantastic, as was the bottle of house red that they chose to accompany it.

"You must have a good job, Jake, to afford all this?" Helen enquired.

"I am a partner in an accountancy firm, which is doing quite well," he replied.

"Quite well financially," said Em. "But I would still swap that for more family time together."

Helen smiled. "The balance is always more difficult than time versus pay." Helen turned to Em. "What about you, Em? What do you do?"

"I work in my father's law firm," replied Em. "I am still learning to be an attorney, but hope to get there in the next two years. It is a slow go."

Helen was impressed. "It's lovely to see two people doing so well." She felt she was getting to know this couple more and more, and the more she knew the more she liked.

The meal over, they had meandered out of the restaurant and into the lounge. They all decided to order some coffee, as they knew they needed to chat some more about why they were there, namely Paul's death.

"What is the next step, Helen? Where would you like to go?" Jake asked.

"I don't have an answer to that, Jake. Have you thought any more about it?"

Jake looked thoughtful. "We are all in a bit of a flux about things, do we believe it? Or don't we believe it?" He paused. "Am I Paul? Or am I not Paul?"

He took a deep breath. Helen's stare glued to his face, a face that was in control, a face that showed little emotion, a face that was pleading to be listened to.

Jake continued. "I have been searching on the internet and have found a medically qualified brain specialist who has set up as a hypnotist specialising in regression. He says he can't believe some of the results, and that he believes in reincarnation."

"He would say that, wouldn't he." Retorted Helen.

"Yes, he would," Jake replied. "However, I would like as much clarity as possible. Am I Paul, or am I just going mad?"

He looked directly at Helen. "Have you mentioned this to anybody, Helen?"

"No." Helen answered in her soft, Northern lilt, that had Em transfixed.

51

CHAPTER FOURTEEN

The office in London was plush and luxurious. White leather sofas welcomed them as they entered the reception area, which boasted a large, curved reception desk. Two receptionists, who stood behind the desk, looked like they employed a personal makeup artist to keep them looking as perfect as possible, to keep them in line with the plush surrounds. The huge chandelier dropping from the ceiling glistened as the thirty-plus lamps splattered and spangled off the pear-shaped crystals that draped down. It seemed to say, "Ignore me if you dare."

The head receptionist wore a made-to-measure smile by the time they reached the desk. She wore a Chanel-style navy jacket and knee-length skirt fitted tight to a size ten body, while the pure white blouse was in full competition with the sofas.

"Good morning." said the receptionist, whose name badge gave her identity away as Nicola.

"Good morning, Nicola," Jake replied. "We are here to see Dr. Jameson. My name is Jake Hughes."

"Take a seat," replied Nicola. "Mr. Jameson will be along to see you shortly."

The other receptionist, in the meantime, delivered a pot of coffee, a pot of tea, and three bottles of Evian water on the smoked glass coffee table directly in front of the sofas. *This is customer service at its very best.* thought Jake. *Note to self: run my reception like this when I return.*

Helen poured three coffees into the pristine white china coffee cups, making sure not to spill any on the equally pristine saucers. The pinchers used for transporting the sugar from the sugar bowl to its destination in the coffee cup were silver and hallmarked London, with the characteristic Lion facing right to left with a raised paw. The same stamp was evidenced on the sugar bowl it accompanied.

How much is this costing? Helen thought.

Dr. Jameson came out from an adjacent door. He was wearing a long, white coat. He was around six feet tall, of medium build, aged mid-fifties. He kept fit with an exercise regime. He wore deep brown, expensive-looking Oxford brogues, with a surgically sculptured crease running the length of the pure wool trousers, which were brown with a black fleck in them. He also wore a canary-yellow shirt and matching tie, which Em felt let the look down. His half-rimmed glasses were surrounded by a mass of thick, curly, salt and pepper hair, cut to collar length.

Quite tasty. thought Helen.

Helen and Em were invited to sit behind a single mirrored glass window which allowed them to see into the room, they could not be seen from inside the room.

"Does this make you feel like Cagney and Lacy?" Helen said to Em, smiling.

"When they bring the line out, vote number three. It's always number three." Em responded. They both laughed and sat, anticipating what they were about to see.

It was not an identity parade, but Dr. Jameson and Jake. In the room was a large, oak desk with two comfortable-looking oak chairs with green leather insets secured with studs, both for the seat and back. Dr. Jameson sat in a chair behind the desk, Jake sat in the other at a right angle to the desk. A matching leather piece cut into the desk, which matched the two chairs. The whole set looked very expensive.

There was also an expensive-looking cream carpet, file cabinets, and a coffee table with four deep-olive green Chesterfield chairs around it. There was a glass shelf under the coffee table, a few magazines were neatly placed. A large, beech-framed clock on the wall sat in a cabinet that allowed you to see the pendulum swing through a glass door on the front. This clock was loud; its 'tick-tock' was like a detonator ready to explode, in between words it was the only sound in the room. Edwardian bay windows stretched from the top of the ceiling to a window ledge three feet from the floor; the bay was eight feet wide and consisted of four long panes of glass allowing the light to flood in, controlled by pure white wooden window shutters. This room was built for concentration.

Helen and Em stared through the glass-like children looking at the first snowfall of winter. Like children, they were mesmerised. Dr. Jameson broke the steady sound of the rhythmic tick.

"The first thing I need you to do, Jake, is relax. Listen to only two things, my voice and the tick of the clock. Let your mind take you where it wants to go…"

A long minute passed in silence, except for the tick-tock! Tick-tock! of the loud clock.

Then Jameson asked, "What is your favourite pastime, Jake?"

"Riding in the Ledges State Park near Boone County, with Emily, my wife."

Tick! Tick! Tick!

"Think of a hot summer's day, both you and Emily riding your favourite horses' in the Ledges State Park."

Tick! Tick! Tick!

"Can you see and feel it?"

"Yes."

"What year is it?"

"It's in 1996. We are riding Scarlet and Misty. Em is riding Misty, he is a handful. She is a better horsewoman than I am."

Helen looked at Em and gave a nod and smirk. "Ooh, get you."

They turned back to the window as if they were watching their first-ever film in widescreen at the movies.

"Let me take you back to 1976," said Dr. Jameson. "Were you alive in 1976?"

"Yes," Jake answered

Helen and Em looked at each other. They knew he was born in 1985.

Jake continued. "It's really hot, the hottest summer known in England."

"How old are you in 1976, Jake?"

The response came short and quick. "Who is Jake? My name is Paul, Paul Jennings!"

Helen shrieked and recoiled in her chair. She put her hand over her mouth, her eyes wide. "It's Paul's voice. He has Paul's voice!"

Dr. Jameson continued. "What are you doing, Paul?"

"I am eighteen. It's a warm night. I have been in the factory all day, they gave us salt in drinks to keep us going. They still want their work done, even though it's so hot. It's hard to earn a good bonus."

"Where are you, Paul?" asked Dr. Jameson.

"I am sat outside the Broadwater Arms drinking a pint of Boddingtons bitter. The Bridgewater Canal is opposite. The water is usually orange, but it's all stagnant with the drought."

"Who are you with, Paul?" Dr. Jameson asked. Now speaking in a low, calm, soothing voice.

"I am with Billy Jones, my mucker."

Behind the window, Em looked at Helen. "What in God's name is a mucker?"

"It's another way of saying friend," Helen replied without taking her eyes off Jake.

Jake continued. "We are chatting to another man who wants us to deliver some parcels for him at the weekend. He is going to pay us three hundred and fifty pounds each to drive to Liverpool and back. That's more than a month's wage in half a day!"

Helen was mortified. "Is this true?" she said, more to herself.

"What is in each of the parcels, Paul?"

"I don't know. Something is wrong here, but why is Billy so keen?" Jake began to get agitated. Dr. Jameson decided to slow it down again.

"Tell me, Paul, did you deliver the parcel?"

"Yes. Billy talked me into it. He said it was easy money and we could pick and choose when we did it. Just pick it up when we needed money."

Tick! Tick! Tick!

"He lied!" Jake said suddenly. "We were tied in. They were gangsters. We were gun-running and we couldn't get out of it. If we tried, they would kill us. They were nasty blokes."

Em looked at Helen.

"Men," said Helen, before Em could ask what blokes were.

"Where were the guns going, Paul?"

"I don't know. I think Angola. Civil wars were going on," Jake replied. "We couldn't ask, they would kill us otherwise. We would drive the guns to Liverpool and they would be smuggled out, down the Mersey."

Jake then turned his hands into tight fists, his eyes widened and his forehead creased. "Don't let them near me, they will kill me!"

Helen, shocked by what she heard, began sobbing. Em was doing the best she could to console her.

Dr. Jameson could see that Jake was getting over-agitated, so he brought him out of the regression.

"Thanks for the information, Paul," he said gently. "Slowly think about being in London. It is the present day. You are now Jake Hughes. You have moved through the life zones. Take your time and return to Jake."

Jake slowly came round. He appeared exhausted as if he had endured two marathons in one session.

"Stay where you are, Jake. You need a drink." Dr. Jameson pressed a button. "Miss Fenton, will you bring a large mug of coffee in here straight away with a triple shot, please? And ask Mrs. Hughes and Mrs. Jennings what they would like to drink and eat?"

"Yes, Dr. Jameson."

The drinks took five minutes to arrive, by which time Jake, Em, Helen, and Dr. Jameson were sitting around the coffee table in the Chesterfield seats.

"What have we just seen?" Helen demanded.

Jake spoke. "I don't remember a thing. Em, Helen, why are you so upset?"

Dr. Jameson took control. "Mr. Hughes, we regressed you successfully into a previous life. The life appeared dark and manipulated by others, not a happy existence, and…"

"Paul was happy with his life. I have just seen and heard lies about my son!" Helen interrupted.

Dr. Jameson continued. "What I saw is something I have never seen or heard before." His voice was still low, strong, and assuring.

All was quiet, apart from the steady, relentless rhythm of the clock, like an African rainstorm heralding the wet season.

"What age was Paul when he died?" asked Dr. Jameson.

Helen answered. "What has that got to do with anything? He was killed in an accident aged twenty-five."

"Mrs. Jennings," Dr. Jameson said, peering at her over his glasses, "you have just experienced a conversation that was both disturbing and threatening. Bearing in mind what you have just heard, would you consider changing the verdict of the accident to murder?"

"The police looked at this for two years and they said it was an accident," replied Helen, her voice louder than intended. "I had a personal friend on the case and he said it was an accident." She felt she needed to defend Paul.

Jameson again continued. "I do not know if this was an accident or murder." The room went silent; even the clock went unnoticed in the heavy atmosphere. "In my experience, the British police are the best in the world at solving crimes." All three faces stared at Jameson. "To be honest, a simple hit and run in a city centre should not…" Dr. Jameson paused. "Let me change that… *would* not stop a city constabulary from finding a hit and run within forty-eight hours. You only have to watch the news these days. The perpetrators are caught within days."

"What are you saying?" Jake asked.

"All I am saying is that I find it very difficult to believe that a simple hit and run could avoid detection from a major UK police force unless there was very good intelligence in covering it up." The faces were looking back at Jameson as he continued. "I think you should consider it, that's all. Look, I will make you an offer. To show how strongly I believe this, and to prove I don't want any further payment, I will regress Jake free of charge from now on, if I can help any further. That's how confident I am."

Jake, Em, and Helen were shaken to their roots. None of them expected any of this.

"I know the face," said Jake suddenly. "I just don't know the name, or who it is. But I *do* know him from somewhere."

"Him?" said Em, who was equally as shocked.

"Yes, him," Jake answered.

"Well, if it is a 'him', that's a step forward. We know it's a bloke." She turned to Helen and smiled.

"What's a bloke?" asked Jake.

CHAPTER FIFTEEN

Back at their London hotel, Jake, Em, and Helen were very quiet. Jake was the first to break the silence.

"What happened today?"

"It was really scary, Jake," said Em excitedly, the shock now having worn off. "It began with an easy chat about Scarlett and Misty, then before we knew it you were talking about being in Manchester in a heatwave."

Helen interrupted. "It was 1976, the hottest summer on record in the UK. Paul did work in the factory and went for a pint in the Broadwater Arms regularly."

"Before we knew it," continued Em, "you were agitated and explaining how Billy was talking you into gun-running to Liverpool for the Angolan Civil War."

"What!" Jake replied. "I don't know anything about the Angolan Civil War, but surely guns were not being shipped from the UK?"

Helen intervened. "Exactly. It can't be right."

"Hang on a minute, Helen," Em blurted out. "You can't agree on all the things you do know about, but disagree on the things you don't."

Helen turned red and looked at Em. "Listen, lady, if you think I am going to sit here and agree that my son was a gun runner for someone who was funding murders in a civil war on the other side of the world… I can't accept that!"

Em sat upright. "Well, something happened in there!" Her voice had risen to a half shout.

Helen was getting uptight. She could feel her jaw aching. "You think my son was a gun runner? What does that make him?"

Jake intervened. "Hang on, girls, let's not fight about this. Let's have an open mind." He paused for a few moments. "What were the factual points?"

"Well," said Helen, calming herself down. "The summer was hot. Paul did go to the Broadwater pub. There is orange water across the road, and it is the Bridgewater Canal."

"And you spoke in a Manchester accent as if it was Paul's voice." Em added.

"What?" Jake responded. "Is this true, Helen?" Helen nodded.

"And you called Billy your best mucker," Em said.

"What's a mucker?" asked Jake. Helen and Em looked at each other and giggled like a pair of schoolgirls.

"Friend," they replied in unison. The two women stared at each other and instantly burst into laughter again.

"Okay," said Jake, "I was speaking in my best Manchester accent, we need to keep an open mind about all of this. What is the next stage? Can we get help from anybody?"

"Well…" said Helen. "There may be one person."

"Who?" Jake asked.

"The man who ran the inquiry at the time, Jonty Ball."

Jake frowned. "We can't ask the police to look at this. They would laugh at us."

"Jonty is now retired and…" Helen began to blush a little. "We were quite good friends for a while."

"How good friends?" Jake replied, like a professional tennis player returning a serve.

Helen's blush deepened. "Do I have to spell it out for you?"

Jake and Em looked at each and smiled.

"Oh, I see," Jake replied.

"You little vixen, Helen," said Em.

Whatever brought Em and Helen together, they were certainly beginning to feel comfortable in each other's company.

They made their way back to Manchester. Jake and Em's two-week vacation was now rapidly coming to an end, with only three days left before they were due to return to the States.

The first thing Jake did when he got back to his hotel room was to set his laptop up and link it to the internet via the telephone line with an Ethernet cable, which was a slow process. He googled the Angolan war, searched a few hyperlinks, and settled on one that seemed to give a brief overview. It read:

"The Angolan Civil War was a major civil conflict in Angola, beginning in 1975 and continuing, with some interludes. The war began immediately after Angola became independent from Portugal in November 1975. The civil war was essentially a power struggle between

59

two former liberation movements, the People's Movement for the Liberation of Angola (MPLA) and the National Union for the Total Independence of Angola (UNITA). At the same time, the war served as a surrogate battlefield for the Cold War, and large-scale direct and indirect international involvement by opposing powers such as the Soviet Union, Cuba, South Africa, and the United States was a major feature of the conflict.

The Angolan Civil War was notable due to the combination of Angola's violent internal dynamics and massive foreign intervention. The war became a Cold War struggle, as both the Soviet Union and the United States, along with their respective allies, provided significant military assistance to parties in the conflict. Moreover, the Angolan conflict became closely intertwined with the Second Congo War in the neighbouring Democratic Republic of the Congo, as well as with the South African Border War."

Jake turned to Em. "I need to contact the office and let them know I won't be returning as planned. I need to see this thing through, as stupid as it sounds. You get back and keep things going in the States. I will get back as soon as I can."

Em looked at him. "You gotta be joking? There is no way I'm going back without you."

"But we are both putting our jobs at risk," Jake said as an urge of responsibility flowed over him. "We can't afford to lose two salaries,"

"Father will understand," said Em.

"Understand what? That I'm staying in England because Jake is reincarnated from a man named Paul? That we are staying in England because we want to look at some possible gun-running for the Angolan Civil War during the seventies and eighties? Will he buy that?"

"No," said Em, "but he will buy what I tell him, I just haven't thought what it is yet." She looked at Jake before adding, "What are you going to say, Mr. Gun Runner from a past life?"

Jake hung his head. "I don't know."

The following day, Jake rang the Senior Partner in the accountancy firm.

"What are you saying, Jake? Do you want to stay in England? You don't know how long for and I am just going to have to accept it?"

"I know it sounds a bit crazy, but I have met this person who is related to me and she needs some support. I feel obliged to do it."

Ron Rodgers was a hardnosed, hard-hitting executive, who had been Jake's direct line since his promotion eighteen months ago. He never liked Jake, one night during a company Christmas party, he'd tried to pick a fight with Jake outside when nobody was around, meaning there would be no evidence that he had hurt Jake in a fistfight. He would have no problem beating 'laid back' Jake. Ron, after all, regularly did weights and had a six-pack that he showed at any opportunity. He could easily bench press two hundred pounds. Jake would be spending Christmas 1997 in hospital, right? Wrong. As he made a swing for Jake, Jake dropped his left shoulder allowing the swing to go over his head. As Ron lost a little balance, Jake scythed his leg across Ron's calf, causing Ron to topple. A person with normal strength would have fallen to the ground, but Ron's strength allowed him to keep on his feet. Within a split second, a roundhouse kick caught Ron on the jaw, the crunch of bone deafening. Then, in the same move, a punch came directly down the line and made contact with Ron's nose, which spread over his face like a balloon full of water.

Ron was unsteady and hurt. One, final kick to the ribs and a final knee-up to the already disjointed nose while he was bending from the last hit saw Ron collapse like a bag of coal. Nobody told Ron that the new member of his team had accrued a black belt in karate over years of hard, physical training. This did nothing to endear Jake to Ron.

Jake never told anyone about the fight except Em. To explain his injuries, Ron told everybody he fell off his motorbike after a blowout. He could not face the truth.

"I'll tell you what, Jake," said Ron. "I will give you two weeks further vacation, unpaid, then you can look for another job. Do you understand that?"

Jake hung up. There was no point in talking when nobody is listening.

"That went well, then?" Em said as Jake repeated the conversation to her. "Mine went a little better. Daddy says I can stay with you until you get better." She was looking very sheepish.

"Better?" retorted Jake.

"Yes, I said you had an accident while horse riding. I said you have broken your leg and it's a bad break."

Jake looked at his wife with anger in his deep sea-blue eyes. "Why did you say that?"

61

"Because I wanted to make sure my job was safe whilst I still get paid. I said you fell off the horse because you're riding skills are not as good as mine."

Em couldn't help giggling. Jake didn't know what she meant, as she hadn't told him that part of the regression where he admitted she was better at horsemanship than him.

For good and bad, they both managed to extend their stay in England.

"I think we need to find a house to rent. I am fed up with hotels," said Jake. "We will start looking tomorrow."

"Well, my wages will help," said Em with a beaming smile. Jake just gave a grimace, then a grin.

CHAPTER SIXTEEN

Jake, Em, and Helen were sitting in Helen's lounge when they heard the doorbell ring.

"He's here," Helen said as she rose out of the chair and made her way to the door. Jake and Em heard a deep, gruff voice.

"Hello, darling, how have you been? Long time no see. You are looking good."

"I feel good thanks, Jonty," Helen replied. "How was your journey?"

"Good, thanks Luv. Bit of congestion on the motorway, but okay."

As they walked through to the lounge, Em noticed a little flush on Helen's face. It was the type of thing another woman would notice, but a man would miss by the proverbial mile. This made Em smile inside, she hoped Helen would not pick up on it.

"This is Jake and Em," said Helen. "I told you about them earlier."

The nod from Jonty to Jake was returned. No words were exchanged.

"Hello," Jonty cordially said to Em, to which a silent nod was given.

Em started to feel increasingly uncomfortable in Jonty's presence and she knew why. He wouldn't buy into anything that was about to take place, and, he wasn't even aware of the reincarnation point yet, which he was bound to find absurd.

Jonty sat in a corner armchair. It was covered in a green and cream fabric, which picked out the bold green flowers on the cream carpet. It looked like it had arrived only days ago from a Laura Ashley shop. Jonty's police skills were so honed that he unconsciously used them. He was unconsciously assessing Jake from the forty-five-degree angle the body takes between standing and lowering into the sitting position. He saw a clean-cut young man, wearing fashionable blue and white boating shoes, no socks, a pair of Levi jeans, with a blue and white Henri Lloyd T-shirt, all wrapped around an athletic body that could not be attained without working hard in the gym. Jonty knew Jake and Em were American from the earlier telephone conversation with Helen, although he was yet to hear their voices.

Just as Em was feeling something was required to cut this uncomfortable atmosphere, Helen arrived smiling with a tray laden with four large cups of coffee and a plateful of biscuits.

Jonty opened the conversation. "As you are probably aware, I worked in the police force for thirty years and I know how successful the Greater Manchester force is at solving crimes. I was a little shocked when Helen told me that she knew two Americans who had been in this country for two minutes and could add light to a case I worked on. My first thought was, are they saying I didn't know what I was doing, or that I didn't know my job?"

Jake and Em remained quiet for a few moments. Jonty took this situation as a personal slant on his policing skills.

"Well, Sir," Jake began.

A first impression flashed through Jonty's mind. *Typical American... Sir.*

"That was some opening gambit," continued Jake. Everything was quiet. The tension hung over Jake and Em like an accused murderer listening to a Judge pass sentence. Jake knew he needed to be calm and eloquent at this stage, or else his argument would be lost forever, like the key to the cell if the Judge's next word was "Guilty!"

"I am not questioning anything, sir."

"Call me Jonty."

"I am not questioning anything, Jonty. But what if extra light was shed onto the case that seemed, maybe… very improbable?"

It was now Jonty's turn to let the seconds pass. He looked Jake in the eye. "What can be improbable about a hit and run accident, when the only thing missing was that we could not identify the driver?"

Silence reigned again. How would Jake be able to rearrange Jonty's views on a generation of beliefs? Dr. Jameson's theory on hit and runs sprang to mind, but this was about to be changed by Jake.

"I have seen many times on television news programmes that hit and run drivers are found within a day or so," said Jake. "They are usually normal people driving the wrong car on the wrong road at the wrong time."

Jonty's eyes creased in a way that made Jake believe that anger was not far behind the stare.

"Jonty, how many hit and run cases were you involved in, or were aware of your colleagues being involved in?" Jake asked.

Jonty thought to himself, *Do I answer this or is he trying my patience?* He chose to play along for a while longer.

"Hundreds."

"How many would be solved?" Jake reversed the role on the ex-bobby by asking the questions. He felt in control.

"About ninety-nine percent."

"Then why was this case not solved if the strike rate is so high?" Jake felt he was pushing Jonty now, but he also felt he had no option.

Jonty's eyes were showing signs of anger.

"Are you saying I failed at my job?" he said indignantly. "Am I being told by a Yank that I did not know what I was doing?"

Brilliant, thought Em sarcastically. *Well handled, Jake!*

Jake continued with the Jameson theory. "I am not saying that. What I am saying is, would it be possible that you never caught the driver because it was planned... because it was murder."

Jonty was battling with his inner urges not to stand up and punch this upstart. *Who was he to question my skills?* Experience chose the option to use words instead. "If it was murder, there was no motive. If it was murder, there was no rationale as to why an accident happened for no other reason than a lad who had drunk too much and wandered into the road."

Jake looked at Jonty again, his face full of smugness like a champion chess player who had just maneuvered a checkmate.

"But what if it was a perfect murder?" he said. "A murder that looked so obvious that it was an accident and everybody was taken in?"

Jonty finished his coffee, stared at the mug, and slowly met Jake's eyes. "What proof do you have?"

"Proof? None. Intuition? Lots." The American drool tailed off on the last two words.

"I am an ex-bobby, or cop in your language," retorted Jonty. "I work on proof, not intuition. This conversation has ended until you get me some proof."

Helen intervened. "Jonty, please listen. Paul was my son and I have my doubts, too. I think we may be onto something that only a one in ten million chance has brought us."

Jonty looked at Helen. He had overlooked the raw emotion she must be feeling. He saw this conversation as an unclosed paperwork exercise. Helen saw it as a lost son.

"I am sorry, Helen," said Jonty, impressing Em with this display of compassion, but which could turn in the blink of an eye.

"Jonty," continued Helen, "what I am about to tell you will sound absurd. The second part of why we think it was murder will make you think you are watching Mickey Mouse on speed."

Jonty smiled. "You always had a way with words. Okay, hit me."

Helen looked at Em, then at Jake, before turning her eyes back to Jonty. "Jake believes he is Paul reincarnated. And I believe him."

Jonty laughed aloud. "God, I really could have been watching Mickey Mouse on speed on the Disney channel."

"Jonty!" Helen said in a raised voice. "I have lived for over twenty years without knowing who killed Paul. I have seen Tommy grow up, not having any answers about his dad, except that he was killed in a hit and run."

"Okay," said Jonty, "let's assume Jake here is reincarnated, which I find far-fetched. What motive is there?"

"Gunrunning from Manchester to Liverpool to aid the Angolan Civil War," said Em.

At this point, Helen, Jake, and Em expected the ex-detective to close up shop, shout, and ball, relieve himself from the armchair, and exit sharply. What happened next was most unexpected.

"Britain has never been involved in gun-running to support the Angolan war." The words were more or less what they had expected. However, how Jonty spoke had changed. His voice had calmed and softened.

"Do you know about the gun-running? Did it happen?" asked Helen.

Jonty looked at her and rubbed his chin. "There were rumours, no more. But nothing was ever proven, or even investigated."

Jake sensed the softening in Jonty. "What were these rumours? Why were they dropped?"

"I don't know," replied Jonty. "I was never involved. It was just gossip passing around the bobbies in the station. But it is probably nothing. I never heard of UK support for any side in Angola outside the rumours, nothing in the press, etc." He took a few seconds to think, then continued. "Anyway, the point is, where on earth are you coming from on this reincarnation idea?"

Jake covered the story so far, including John Ryland's Library, Abe Lincoln's statue, and Brazennose Street.

Helen intervened. "Jake knew things that were impossible to know, Jon." It was a name Helen sometimes called Jonty when she was after something. "Things that nobody but a mother and a son would know. He even knew the name of his favourite teddy, Scruff."

Jonty frowned. "I can't believe it. It's just not true. There is no such thing as reincarnation."

Helen sat facing Jonty on a stool. She held his hands, her hands wrapped around the strong, sturdy fingers. She felt the strength in his hands and it made her feel safe.

"Jonty, I know it sounds crazy. I sent them away the first time I met them. But, you know the biggest coincidence can be proved – Jake was born nine months after the death of Paul, virtually to the day."

Em intervened. "We went to a hypnotist in London. When Jake regressed, Helen heard Jake talk in Paul's voice."

Helen looked at Jonty, still holding his hands. "Jonty, please, I know it sounds stupid and nobody is challenging your skills as a detective. Exactly the opposite. You were the person I recommended because I trust you so much."

Jonty looked at Helen for a moment. "Who else knows about all this?"

"The four of us and the hypnotist, who was a brain specialist before he learned about regression and reincarnation."

Jonty pondered some more. "Okay, I will help you, Helen. I don't for one minute believe any of it, and the moment I find something that makes me see through this or makes me look stupid, I am out like a rat up a drainpipe."

Helen hugged Jonty and thanked him.

"Welcome on board," Jake said to Jonty. He got a cold stare for his efforts.

Four hours later and after much discussion, they all departed and went their separate ways. Telephone numbers were exchanged, after a belly full of tea and biscuits, Jonty was left wondering what had happened. *Who are these people?* But then he thought, *It's best to be in this thing in case they are trying some type of scam on Helen.*

CHAPTER SEVENTEEN

Jake and Em spent the next couple of days looking at properties as agreed earlier. Em's wages were enough to cover the rent and they agreed easily on a two-bed semi-detached house in Worsley, near the orange basin that Jake had known about in his dreams all those years ago.

As they looked out of the side window during the viewing, Em whispered. "Jake, look." They both looked at a majestic building opposite the canal with lettering above it. "The Broadwater Arms."

The house was a nice two-up two-down property with a cosy sitting room, with views of the village green on one side and the canal to the rear. There was a modern, white three-piece bathroom and a bright kitchen with all the mod cons. They agreed to move in within the next three days and, whilst the rooms were small, it would be ideal for a month or so.

Em turned to Jake. "We will be okay. I earn two thousand five hundred dollars a month, which is about two thousand sterling. We also have savings of thirty thousand dollars."

Jake loved Em's pragmatism. "We will be okay, Em. Thank you for supporting me on this ride." He leaned over and gave his wife a long kiss. "Neither of us will settle until it's laid to rest, then we can get on with our lives for good."

Em was having a well-earnt shower back at the hotel when Jake's mobile phone rang.

"Hello?" said Jake.

"Jake, it's Jonty. I would like to meet you one-to-one to get my head around all this."

"Evening, Jonty. Okay, when and where?"

"What hotel are you in?"

"It's a Travel Lodge."

"Is there a bar?"

"Yes."

"Meet you in there at nine tonight."

"Okay, see you then."

A voice called out from the shower. "Who was that, honey?"

"It was Jonty," replied Jake. "He wants to meet, just me and him, downstairs at nine."

"Well, you best get ready then. I fancy a night watching TV."

That evening, Jake went down to the bar at five minutes to nine, ensuring he would not be late. However, Jonty was already there with a half-empty pint of bitter.

"Jake. What's your tipple?" Jonty said with enthusiasm. He seemed so different from the meeting at Helen's house.

"I will have half a lager please, Jonty."

Jonty was dressed quite fashionably for a man who must have been somewhere in his mid-sixties. He wore a pair of cream-coloured chinos with a navy short-sleeved t-shirt that showed a slight paunch that age and retirement could sometimes induce. He also wore light brown canvas shoes with no socks. Jake, in contrast, had thrown on a lightly crumpled white cotton shirt and a pair of Levi 501s with a pair of red Adidas training shoes.

The bar was decorated in the Travel Lodge's corporate colours. A few tables were spread around the room and lots of bench-type seats that looked like they belonged more in a train carriage than a hotel bar. Jake and Jonty settled on one furthest away from the bar, allowing as much privacy as the room offered.

"Would you like food?" asked Jonty.

"No thanks, Em, and I have already eaten."

"I will get straight to the point," Jonty continued. "I have problems with what's going on." He paused. Jake's expression never changed. "I have three problems, Jake. Number one, I don't believe in reincarnation and I think it is bull. Two, there has never, ever, been a link between the UK and Angolan gun-running. Three, Helen is hanging onto every last hope here and it will hurt her so much if you are a fake."

Jake's expression was still yet to change. "Then why are you interested and why are we here?"

"Because," said Jonty, "I can keep a closer eye on you by allowing Helen to think I am in."

"Are you going to help us then, Jonty?"

"I will keep to my word," Jonty replied. "I will help up to the point I have exposed you as a fraud."

"And, if I'm not a fraud?"

69

"Then you have nothing to worry about. But if you hurt Helen through this, I will hurt you like you can't imagine."

"So, where do we go from here?" asked Jake.

"I want to know everything you know. I want to know everything. Do you understand?"

Jake maintained his composure. He smiled, took a sip of his lager, winced at the bitterness of it, and replied. "Most of my reincarnation memories are from when I was a child. They were dreams and the occasional flashback when I was awake." He took another sip of the lager. It was cold and had the bitter taste of a gas that only electric-pumped beer can offer. He knew he didn't like the gas this beer delivered.

"By the time I was fifteen, I guess the dreams stopped altogether." Jake felt a strange warmth run through his body as he reflected on those times when he was a child. It soon evaporated when he noticed Jonty was using all the listening skills taught in the force. Jake then explained how he and Em were keen horse riders and walkers. He told Jonty that he was a keen climber and liked all sports. This part was unimportant as far as Jonty was concerned, but Jake went with it.

Jake reached the point about arriving in Britain to do the coast to coast walk and how he met Billy and Maggie in Rosthwaite one evening. He spoke how 'Young Hearts Run Free' was the cause of their introduction and how they shared their love of the song, but not why.

"I remembered why Billy was so familiar to me as the night went on," Jake continued. "I knew him from my dreams. I knew him as my best friend."

Jonty looked at him curiously. "Did you only know about the gun-running and death following the visit to that hypnotist guy, Johnson?"

"Jameson," Jake corrected Jonty. "That's all I know of it."

"Then, I think point one is I meet this Jameson and I look at him putting you into regression. Is that possible?"

"Yes, of course," said Jake. "I think he sees me as an opportunity of some kind. He told me he would provide any further services for free. He probably views me as an interesting project, but we can use him."

Jonty took one final look at Jake. "Okay, let's make that our first port of call and see where we go. You arrange a time and let me know."

"Okay," Jake said, and that was the end of the meeting after an hour of bonding, which resulted in no bonding at all!

70

***

Dr. Jameson's office was as before – clinically clean, yet expensive and gave the impression of wealthy clientele. Nicola, the same receptionist as last time, was there with a welcoming smile.

"Good morning, Mr. Hughes. It's good to see you again. How are you today?"

"I am good, thank you, Nicola."

Nicola was quite attracted to the Mid-West accent, as well as the good looks and well-toned physique of Jake. She gave a broader than normal smile as she made a mental note that Jake was not with Em today. His only companion was a large, imposing fellow with a no-nonsense attitude and a very strong presence.

"Nicola, can you tell Dr. Jameson I have a guest today," said Jake. "Mr. Jonty Ball. He will be joining us."

"I will do that, Mr. Hughes," replied Nicola, holding his gaze for a little longer than was necessary. "Can I arrange a drink for you both?"

"That would be nice, Nicola. Coffee for me, please. Jonty?" Jake looked at Jonty, waiting for his response.

"Tea for me, please," Jonty replied.

Dr. Jameson came through to the reception within minutes. "Jake, good to see you. Mr. Ball, nice to meet you. I hope you both had a pleasant journey down?"

It had been Jonty's decision for him and Jake to visit Dr. Jameson. Em understood but also felt a little put out by not having been invited.

"I have been with you on this trip. I believe in reincarnation," she said, looking down at the cheap-looking reproduction coffee table in the lounge of their newly rented house. "That Jonty does not even believe you."

"I know, Em, but it needs to progress," said Jake. "I don't want to disengage him before he is engaged."

"I know," said Em, "but don't let him take over."

Helen was easier to manage. They never told her they were going.

Dr. Jameson decided to sit and chat on the over-comfortable Chesterfield chairs in the office.

"Mr. Ball, I don't know how much you know about regression?" said Jameson. A few seconds passed and the ticking of the clock returned to Jake's ears, reminding him of the last time he was in this room.

"Not much, Dr. Jameson," said Jonty. "And, to be honest with you, I…"

Jameson sensed what the next negative comment might be. "I know Mr. Ball. Not a lot of people believe or want to believe in reincarnation – which, in turn, means they do not believe in regression."

Jonty admired the authority shown by the doctor. He looked very suave in a navy pin-striped suit with shiny black brogues and a pink shirt. The smell of polished leather wafting up from the Chesterfields did not go unnoticed by Jonty. It wafted style, it wafted class, it wafted money.

Jonty continued. "I don't believe this, but Helen Jennings, who is a close friend, asked for my help. At the very best, I would reluctantly be open-minded."

Jameson looked at him over half-rimmed glasses. "Well, I am happy for you to observe, but I do ask you to be open-minded. Reluctant, if need be, but open-minded."

Jonty smiled to himself as he sat behind the screen. It was a place he became comfortable with during his days in the force. He quickly reflected on a few of the times he had sat behind a window just like this, usually with an innocent victim identifying a suspect who had damaged property or, worse, loved ones.

Jake fell under the influence of hypnosis as easily as he did last time, within five minutes of Dr. Jameson talking.

"Where do you want to take us to today, Jake?" said Dr. Jameson gently.

Jake was sitting in the chair, head back, eyes closed, but looking very relaxed. "I can go back to a sunny day in New York."

"How old are you, Jake?" Jameson enquired.

"I am eight."

"Why are you in New York?"

"My Mom and Pop have brought me for a long weekend break."

"What have you done?"

"We have been to see the Statue of Liberty and been on a boat ride down the Hudson. We have been to the Empire State Building. That's my favourite. Whoa, it's high! I am bored in Times Square, it's a grown-up thing. We are there now. I am bored."

"Where do you want to go after Times Square?" Jameson asked.

"Back to the Empire State Building. It's so great, people are scared because it's so high. I'm not scared, though."

"Do you remember Paul Jennings?" Jameson asked.

"Yes."

Can you go back to a time as Paul?"

"Yes, I can. I am working in a factory."

Jonty sat upright. Jake was now speaking in a Manchester dialect. Dr. Jameson continued. "How old are you, Paul?"

"I am twenty-three."

"What are you doing today, Paul?"

"I am working on a marine diesel engine. I am boring the camshaft."

"Wow, that sounds interesting," said Dr. Jameson. "Tell me what you are doing. Tell me in detail and take your time." Jameson asked for details, hoping in some way to prove to Jonty that regression worked.

"The marine engines are about eight feet long and made of cast iron," said Jake. "They are so heavy they have to do the crankcase in two sections and lock them together when people are fitting them. I am working on the top part today. We call it the upper. I have to core drill the camshaft along the whole of the length of it. It is broken down into nine sections to reduce the weight. I have core drilled the camshaft and I am now single pointing it. I have to get it within a tenth of a thou' using a DTI."

This could have been Chinese to Jonty as he did not understand any of this jargon.

Jake continued. "I have to single point it before sending a floating reamer down the eight-foot length. The floating reamer needs to have oil constantly poured on it because I only have two-tenths of a thou tolerance and a thou' run over the length of it."

As Jake made this statement, a flashing vision of him standing as Paul at the side of a machine sped through his mind's eye. He was in a large building with lots of other engineers working like the Manchester bees often depicted throughout the city. He wore a boiler suit, as did all the men working around him. The spindle on the machine was turning; a dial to his left told him it was revolving at eight hundred revolutions per minute. He held a blue oil can in his right hand; it had a spout of about three inches long and a button at the back, just above the handle, to release and block the oil flow at will. Jake saw Paul drizzling the oil on the tool that was cutting through the metal; it was giving off deep blue localised smoke from the contact point. The oil smoke was drifting upwards and an amount went into Paul's nose, offering a sweet smell somewhere between frankincense and burning leaves on a bonfire. It was

73

a comforting smell that took him back to a time that was happy and free; a time, for now anyway, that was immediate.

Dr. Jameson began speaking again. "Thanks for that, Paul. Do you remember anything about gun running?"

Jake quivered. "Yes, I remember, I think they are coming after me!" Urgency rang from his voice.

"Who is coming after you, Paul?"

Jake felt the fear rise through his body. He could smell the sea, the smell of the Mersey with the salt air flowing up his nostrils. He heard the seagulls squawking; he could see them floating on the wind, wings fully stretched and gliding around the edges of land and river.

"I don't know any names," he said. "I told Billy to tell them not to ask me to run guns to Liverpool anymore." Jake was now shouting. "It's wrong, I have done it once, I don't want to do it anymore. Billy, you need to tell them."

"What is Billy saying?" Jameson asked in a calm, considered voice.

"Billy is saying that he can't do that. These are vicious people and we are in it too deep to just get out."

Jake's hands clasped together in an agitated manner. "I am telling Billy I have only done it once and I don't want to do it again."

He now had real fear in his voice. He appeared on the verge of tears. "Billy is holding me by the arms and shaking me. Billy is strong."

Jake went quiet for a second. The clock was consistent. Tick! Tick! Tick!

"Billy is telling me, 'Paul, we are in it now. Once or a hundred times, we are in it. I thought I was helping you earn extra money?'"

Jake's head dropped onto his chest. He was exhausted. Jameson brought Jake away from Paul and back into the present.

***

Nicola had already put the coffee on the table for the three of them by the time Jonty had joined Dr. Jameson and Jake around the table in the Chesterfields. She placed an extra chocolate digestive on the plate for Jake with a smile that lingered for a second or two.

"What do you remember, Jake?" Dr. Jameson asked.

"I remember being in New York and discussing a holiday I had with my parents when I was young."

"Do you remember anything else?"

74

"No," Jake replied.

Dr. Jameson continued. "If I were to say words like DTI or two-tenths of a thou, would they mean anything to you?"

"No."

"What about a single point or a floating reamer?"

"No, nothing."

"Upper or lower?"

Jake answered that question. "Upper is above, lower is below. Is that what you mean?"

Jonty intervened. "I know a lot of engineers from that time. Give me ten minutes and I will make calls to see if this terminology makes any sense."

Like any well-trained bobby, all this was noted down in his best scribble.

Jonty had at least five or six friends from the Manchester engineering industry saved as contacts on his large mobile phone. He quickly tried calling three but received no answer.

The fourth phone call to Dennis McGrath was more successful. "Hello?"

"Menace, how are you?" said Jonty, the nickname being a reference to Dennis the Menace.

"Jonty, I am good, thanks. I haven't seen you for ages. How's retirement?"

"Great thanks, Dennis. But I will tell you more when we meet up, eventually. It must be what, five years?"

"And some," replied Dennis.

"Listen, Dennis," said Jonty. "Can I pick your brain for a few minutes?"

"Of course, anything I can do to help."

"Just a few bits of technical engineering details I don't understand. Each to his own and all that."

Jonty looked down at the list, searching for relevant points. "What is a DTI, Dennis?"

"A DTI is short for a Dial Test Indicator," replied Dennis. "It is a clock-type shape with a plunger at the bottom. When you run the plunger along or around something, the hand moves on the clock. It's usually used for tight tolerances of about a thou or more."

Thou. There's that word again, thought Jonty. "What is a thou, Dennis?"

75

"God, you are green in this area, Jonty," said Dennis. "A thou is a thousandth of an inch," Dennis gave a brief laugh. "However, we are talking old imperial sizes – everybody uses metric these days."

Jonty felt he had been excused for his ignorance. "So, there are a thousand thous in an inch?"

"You are learning, old man."

"Then, what are two-tenths of a thou?"

"Well," answered Dennis. "If a thou is a thousandth of an inch, a tenth of a thou is one-tenth of a thousandths of an inch, so two tenths would be a fifth of a thousand of an inch, To put that in perspective, the thickness of a hair is about two-thousandths of an inch, so two tenths would be a tenth of a hair thickness."

"Wow," Jonty continued. "Then, if somebody was working to a tolerance of two-tenths of a thou' over, say, eight-foot, that would be skilled work?"

"Very skilled, Jonty."

"So a camshaft would need to be that accurate?"

"Yes, that would sound about right, Jonty."

"One final question," said Jonty. "Is there a tool called a single point or floating reamer?"

"Absolutely. A single point would be as it sounds. One single point tool that juts out of a bar and, when it revolves on a boring machine, it would bore a hole. Usually a precisely bored hole, but it wouldn't take out a lot of metal. Say around ten thousands of an inch max."

"Okay, I am still with you, Dennis," Jonty replied, the phone wedged between his chin and shoulder while beavering away with a rapidly eroding pencil point.

"A floating reamer would take only a very fine shaving off for very small tolerances," continued Dennis.

"Perfect for making camshaft bores?" Jonty questioned.

"I'd say so."

"Dennis, it's been great chatting," said Jonty. "You have helped so much. We must catch up soon. Thanks again, mate."

"You're welcome, Jonty. Take care."

With that, the phone call ended.

Jonty returned to the others. He was turning back and forth all the notes he had taken during his conversation with Dennis.

76

He relayed the conversation back to Dr. Jameson and Jake. "Don't think that you are preaching to the converted," he said. "I am still sceptical, Very sceptical!"

Jake smiled. "Thanks for making the phone call, Jonty."

Jonty and Jake left Dr. Jameson's offices in what was increasingly becoming a dark drizzle over London. They were making their way to Euston Station for the 6 pm train back to Manchester as they were doing the trip in a day. No overnight stays for a copper on a police pension, which just about enabled Jonty to live comfortably, and he was not yet on state pension benefits.

They were about ten minutes from Euston, walking along Endsleigh Street. There was nobody around when they both heard a Northern accent calling out.

"Hughes and Ball, Ain't they a comedy act from the eighties?"

"Nah, mate," came a second voice. "That was Cannon and Ball. They were comedians. Hughes and Ball are clowns."

Jonty and Jake both stopped and looked at each other. Jake curled a lip downwards towards Jonty, while Jonty, in turn, shrugged his shoulders. They turned and saw three men lined up behind them. The smallest man was about 6 foot tall, mid-fifties, and wielding a baseball bat. He was of slender build and looked fit and athletic. He wore white trainers, faded jeans, and a white T-shirt under a denim jacket. His shoulder-length hair was wet with the rain.

The second man was taller by about two inches and had a scar down the right side of his face. He was built of muscle and did not carry a weapon.

This is a guy who can handle himself, thought Jonty. *He doesn't need a weapon.*

The man also wore a pair of boots with good tread. Jonty knew this would reduce the risk of slipping in a fight. The man wore a skin-tight T-shirt so nobody could pull it over his head, and he kept strong eye contact with Jonty, probably sensing that Jonty had considerable fighting experience. The man was probably no older than forty. The third man was about the same height, but dressed in dark Italian-style trousers and a dark grey mac, with what looked like a white shirt under it. He wore a grey checked flat cap offering some protection from the rain.

"We don't want trouble," said the man with the cap. "A gentle warning. Don't touch what you don't know. Play with me and you play with fire. Play with fire and you get burnt."

Jake and Jonty looked at each other, no idea what was happening

77

"Look," said Jake. "I think you have the wrong people. Just let us go on our way and we will forget this."

Flat cap replied in a low, deep, aggressive voice. "We do not have the wrong people, Jake."

"What is all this about?" asked Jonty.

"You know what it's about. Stay clear of digging up long-gone days."

"And if we don't?" enquired Jonty.

"I will ask my two boys to have a quiet word in your shell-like."

"I don't like being threatened," Jonty said.

"No threat," responded the man in the cap. "Think of it as advising."

Jonty whispered to Jake through the side of his mouth. "Can you handle yourself?"

"Try me." was the response, equally as quiet.

"Okay," Jonty said turning back to the cap man. "I look at it this way. I don't know what you are here for, honestly."

Jonty turned to Jake and whispered again. "Last chance?"

"Go for it." was the reply.

"As I was saying," Jonty continued to flat cap, "the way I see it is, if we just walk away from what we don't know, you will haunt us forever. So whatever you are asking, forget it."

Flat cap nodded, his face distorted and scowled. "Boys!"

The other two thugs smiled. They were like two crocodiles ready to pounce on a Zebra at the edge of a lake. They took a step forward. The thug with the baseball bat took a double grip and strode slowly out in front. Before Jonty could blink, Jake flashed past him; he dropped his head and shoulder nearly to the floor, allowing room to do a sidekick that bypassed the bat and landed straight on the man's jaw. The instant crunch told Jonty that it was a break.

Jake then turned so his back was tight against the thug, with the baseball bat under Jake's armpit. Quick as lightning, Jake's elbow landed powerfully in baseball bat's nose. Again, there was a discernible crack, only this time Jonty didn't hear it as he was now facing up to the second man. Both boxing style, toe to toe, both experienced and looking for an opening or a weakness in the other's profile. Jonty was the first to be exposed and he felt a quick, short jab in his ribs. It took his breath for a few seconds, but one thing he had learned in the force was not to let it show. He then felt an uppercut to the chin.

This guy is good and fast, Jonty thought.

In the meantime, Jake was in the process of pushing his assailant's arm against its natural movement until he heard a huge yelp and the bat fell to the ground. In less than a minute, baseball bat man had a broken jaw, nose, and dislocated elbow joint. A final kick to the knee and baseball bat was down. Jake leaned over, picked up the bat, and hurled it as far as he could. He did not want to encourage the man in the cap, although he didn't look interested after watching Jake devour his man.

He looked over and could see that Jonty was not getting the better of his foe. Jonty's face was bloody and he was dragging a leg.

Jake hurled himself off the floor and a flying kick landed in the thug's chest. The man recoiled slightly. Jake instinctively widened his stance to give stability and, in the same movement, he threw a right hook towards the thug's jaw. The thug saw this and put up an arm to block it and counterattacked, delivering a punch straight down the centre of Jake's bodyline and landing on his mouth. Jake felt the warm liquid smelter in his mouth. His lip was cut.

Jake bounced forward on his left foot, delivering a perfect roundhouse kick to Thug's jaw. In his anger, Thug seemed to grow in stature, and he growled at Jake. This man knew how to fight. Jake stood and bobbed up and down, keeping his body alert for any swift movement needed. Jake threw another kick, hitting Thug's solar plexus; the blow was hard, it was low and it was perfectly struck. Thug reeled but did not go down. Jake couldn't believe it; nobody had ever withstood this kind of pressure from him, even at the American Nationals he fought in.

Thug straightened and grinned at Jake. "Is that all you have, son?"

It was designed to drain Jake's confidence. Although it wasn't drained, it was wilting. They squared up to each other.

Flat cap shouted, "Jack, behind you!"

Too late. Jonty had dropped the baseball bat over the thug's head like a woodsman felling a tree. The thug fell to the ground, first to his knees. To help him on his way, Jake gave another roundhouse kick, just as Jonty delivered another baseball bat strike across the back of the neck.

They both turned to the man in the cap. "What is this about?" Jonty screamed.

The man turned and ran away at speed. Jake and Jonty did not have the energy to chase after him. Instead, they both set off quickly for the station and got out of sight of their two opponents. Then, as soon as it was safe to do so, they stopped, bent over, hands on knees, and took deep breaths. Jonty put his arm around Jake, puffing and panting.

"I have three things to say," he puffed. "One, are you sure you can handle yourself?" He laughed, then straightened up. "Two, I don't know who they are, or what it's about, but someone's cage has been rattled." He was still breathing heavily and said, "I'm in."

"You said you had three points?" said Jake.

Jonty's response was quick. "Next time you throw a bloody baseball bat away, don't throw it so far!" They both laughed. Jonty viewed Jake with fresh eyes.

By the time they got to Euston, they had missed their planned train and hung around for the next one. Jake texted Em. *"All Ok here, all went to plan, just overran a bit. Will be home around midnight, don't wait up, love J. Xx"*

The journey home was uneventful. Jake was fine, just a few aches and pains. He was young and strong. Jonty, however, had a swollen face with a sore-looking nose and a limp from a dead leg that the thug had delivered.

It took about one hour and thirty minutes to reach Birmingham. There was engineering work, which kept the train at a slower than average speed.

The two men sat in silence for a while, recovering from the shock of recent events.

Jake finally spoke to Jonty. "What went on there, Jonty?"

"I have been trying to work it out," Jonty replied. "I can only think of four points."

Jake noticed Jonty often spoke in points and numbered them as he spoke.

"Point one, somebody knows what we are looking into, which surprises me as only you, me, Helen, Emily, and Jameson know about it. But somebody must have told someone," Jonty looked at his cardboard cup half-filled with cold coffee. "Point two, we are hitting a nerve somewhere. Point three, whoever sent this warning to us panicked and did not have the nerve to sit tight a while longer. That means we are dealing with dangerous people, they must have something very important to hide."

Jonty took a sip of coffee and thought for a moment. "Point four, we have our first lead, a name – Jack. The flat cap man called out Jack before I hit him with the bat."

This made sense to Jake. He was impressed by the fact that, in all the action and confusion, Jonty had the foresight to recall the flat cap man calling out to someone called Jack. He was warming to Jonty and his Northern ways.

They chatted for the remainder of the journey like old friends. They shared battle scars, which brings men together. It earns respect.

"I make the next step," said Jonty. "I will call a few favours in from some ex-colleagues."

CHAPTER EIGHTEEN

Dave Rowlands had been in the Greater Manchester police force for twenty-eight years. He planned to do his thirty years, then retire. He lost some health after suffering a heart attack around three years ago; it was touch and go for a while, but he eventually came through and, whilst he could not resume the life of a police constable on the busy streets of Manchester, he was offered a desk job, helping in administration tasks across the force. His input, though not invaluable, was helpful. He was put to pasture to see out his final days; he knew it and so did his superiors, but he was good at keeping out of harm's way and keeping his nose clean.

In his heyday, Dave would parade the city centre with Jonty. Both were young, fit, and strong. They, and the hooligans that would fall out of the clubs and pubs, drunk and fiery, shared the same goal. They all wanted a good fight, except that Dave and Jonty would always get away with being seen as upholding the law, even though they would have started their fair share of scuffles. However, you could do that in the police force during the seventies. As the years passed, Dave and Jonty, like all men, calmed down, the fights became less important and the real aim of the law came to the fore.

Both were good officers and, even though Jonty took advantage of the chance of becoming a detective, they remained friends throughout. They even used to holiday together with their respective wives, visiting places in the UK, with Whitby being a favourite. They also shared a few holidays abroad in Spain and Portugal, but these tapered out as, first Jonty, and then Dave, were divorced by their wives. The reasons for both were similar – they were in love with the job more than their spouses.

Dave's heart attack initially came as a shock. However, when considering smoking, too much drinking, fast food, and stress from the job, he would always have been in a high-risk category. Like all heart attack victims who survive, the first thing is to thank God you got through it, then make lifestyle changes. He dropped some body fat, reducing his weight from eighteen stones to fourteen and a half. However, old habits die hard and he crept back up to sixteen stones.

"Jonty, how are you?"

"I am good thanks, Dave," Jonty said on the other end of the telephone.

"Great to hear from you. What can I do you for?" asked Dave jokingly.

"I need a favour, but I can't speak about it on the phone."

Dave was intrigued. He knew the favour wasn't to borrow a cup of sugar. "Okay, let's meet. I am off on Friday, so why don't you come round to my place? We can speak privately there."

"Great, Dave," said Jonty. "Is ten in the morning okay?"

"Ten it is."

Jonty ended the conversation by saying, "Make sure you have good coffee in."

Dave was waiting as the doorbell rang on his terraced door. He lived in Kent Street in Salford following his divorce from Karen. He shifted downmarket as his pension fund was taken into account under the pension splitting rules of divorce. He had to either give a large share of his police pension value away either as a lump sum or retirement income for Karen or sacrifice his share of the equity in the semi-detached house they shared in Sale. He took advice from various sources, including Jonty, and decided on the latter. He gave Karen £120,000 from the equity value and protected his police pension – a decision which, in two years, would prove to be the right choice. All he had to do was see out the last two years.

They shook hands on the doorstep.

"Come in and tell me what I can look forward to when I retire?" Dave asked.

Jonty laughed. "Arthritis, peeing twice a night, and glasses that need thicker lenses by the year."

"I can't wait," Dave joked. "You asked for coffee. I've got some fantastic instant in."

"I can't wait." Jonty reciprocated sarcastically.

Dave gave Jonty his coffee. It had bits floating on the top and was in a grimy cup that looked like it hadn't seen a decent wash in five years.

"We shared some fantastic times, Jonty?"

"The best Dave. Where did all the years go? If only we could do it all again."

Dave lowered his overweight frame into a threadbare armchair, whilst motioning Jonty onto an equally threadbare sofa. Dave had let himself go after the divorce; he surrendered to the daily fight that life presents.

The house mirrored this; it smelt of dust and grease. The carpets were black with wear and age; a line ran down the centre where the red and green pattern was no longer seen clearly, with a tar-like texture to it. There was a small television in the corner with a grey, plastic surround that was black in places with the grime. Dave was dressed in old black tracksuit bottoms, which even looked baggy on his sixteen stone frame. He was wearing a light blue shirt, which Jonty was convinced was an old constabulary shirt. Jonty could not believe what he was seeing in Dave and his surroundings.

"They are old, but they match," said Dave in response to the look on Jonty's face. "Well, Jonty, how can I help you?"

Jonty was quiet for a few moments. "Dave, it's a real long shot... Do you remember, in the seventies, when there were rumours about gun-running for the civil war in Angola?"

"God, Jonty, that's a long time ago."

"I know, but I need to know what you can remember about it. You were closer than I was to it."

Dave considered Jonty's question. "If I remember correctly, it was just rumours that nobody could qualify. The thing I remember most was Quinn getting us all in and raking us over the coals because there was no substance in it, and the GMP were not going to invest any time or money in it. That sort of ended it there."

"I didn't realise it had got to the ears of Superintendent Quinn," Jonty said as he grimaced from his first sip of the coffee. "Is he still there?"

"Yes," said Dave. "He has probably missed the boat now, that's why you never hear about him these days."

Jonty sighed briefly. "Look, Dave, what I am asking you to do is have a look to see if there is any truth in it."

"Why the interest now, Jonty?"

"I don't know," replied Jonty. "It's just that a few things have cropped up recently, and I wouldn't mind using my spare time keeping the grey matter going, you know."

Dave looked him in the eye. "Jonty, I have known you longer than most. I know you better than most, and I know you do not just want to keep the grey matter turning over."

Jonty sighed again. "Okay, Dave. Find some information for me and I will let you know what I think. How's that?"

Dave smiled. "Okay, Jonty, I will see what I can find out, but it may take a few days or more."

"Thanks, Dave, much appreciated."

CHAPTER NINETEEN

Jake, Jonty, Em, and Helen sat in Helen's lounge to catch up on events. The mood was sombre.

"I think somebody has told somebody what we have been discussing." Jonty was stern in his delivery.

"I know it's not Jake," said Em, "and I can't tell you why I just know."

Em looked at Jake. "Jake, I don't know anybody in this country. It can't be me."

"It must look like I was the one," said Helen. "But I assure you, I haven't told anybody, honest Jonty. Not even Sue or Tommy, as we all agreed."

Jonty looked at Jake. "Do you want to tell them, or shall I?"

"You." was the reply.

"Okay," said Jonty. "Jake and I were attacked by some thugs in London."

It was hard to try and cover the brawl up as both Jonty and Jake were carrying several large bruises from the encounter.

Em looked at Jake. "Attacked? What do you mean, attacked?" as she searched his sorrowful bruised

and battered face with her hard glare.

Jake looked at Em. "I didn't want to worry you, but we were threatened and a fight started. We don't know what it was about, or why it happened, but they knew who we were." Jake kept the details to a minimum.

"I didn't even know you were going to London." Helen blurted. "What is going on, Jonty? We entered this together, and all of a sudden it's like it's being taken over by the Interpol. You are not in the force anymore. This is my son's death we are dealing with."

She put her head in her lap and cried, the tears flowing like a river bursting its banks. Em sat next to her on the sofa and put an arm around her.

"Look what you two have done," said Em angrily. "You think you can dictate the destination of all this? You are trying to be so macho about it all."

Em was now shouting and her hands were trembling. She could feel her wedding ring tighten as the blood rage swelled all parts of her body, her face turning a deep red.

"Jake," she continued, "Helen and I are in this, or I am going home. And whatever else you have to do you will have to do alone." Helen was still sobbing uncontrollably. "Come on, Helen, it will be okay," Em said, turning her attention to Helen.

Jake and Jonty were looking like guilty schoolboys, both staring at the floor as if it was going to offer them a solution.

"Are we in or not?" shouted Helen, staring at Jake in a way that made him feel uncomfortable. Helen felt a warm, sick feeling surging from her stomach as she spoke. "You are not Jesus and St Peter. We either sort this together, or I want it ending right here and now."

"Well?" demanded Em, also staring at Jake and Jonty.

"Look…" continued Jonty.

"Don't look me, Jonty." Em exploded. Her head felt like it was about to erupt off her shoulders, the rage building like a lava stream bubbling in the volcano before it was released out of the top.

"Well?" she shouted again. Helen looked up, her eyes were red from the tears. Her face looked like it had aged five years in the last two minutes, every sinew stretching from her neck to her eyes.

"Okay, okay!" Jonty finally said. "We apologise. We were just trying to speed things along a bit."

"Em," Jake added, "I told you we were going to London. I didn't mention the attack because I didn't want to worry you."

Em stared at him. "Jake, don't you see we are getting ourselves into something we never envisaged. This could be dangerous, and what I don't know could put us in more danger. Stop acting like an idiot!"

Jonty took over. "Okay, we did wrong. Helen, Emily, I apologise. We will keep you up to speed with things. But, equally, you need to allow me to lead this because things are going on here where only my experience can be most effective."

"Nobody is challenging your skills, Jonty," said Helen. "I want to use every ounce of your skills." All went silent.

"Now, tell us everything we need to know," Em said in a calmer voice. A strong smell of burning came across the room, followed by a vapour of light grey smoke.

"Look what you have done now. You've made the cake burn." Helen shouted as she ran into the kitchen. The others laughed, easing the tension between the four of them.

Jonty and Jake continued to explain the happenings in London. Jonty also told them about his meeting with Dave and that Dave was "as we speak, working on the rumours of the gun-running in the seventies".

Em hugged Jake. "I don't mean to go on, you mean so much to me. But don't leave me out, okay?"

Jake put his arm around her and pulled her in. "I'm sorry, I just didn't know what to do."

She thumped Jonty in the chest playfully. "And you need to look after him,"

Jonty smiled. "From what I have seen, he can look after himself."

***

The spare bedroom at Em and Jake's rented property was now turning into a mock-up incident room. Jonty attained an old piece of large chipboard that he secured against the wall with a screw in each corner. It was very empty looking. Paul's name and a photo were at the top of the board with a piece of red tape leading from his picture to the name of Billy. They knew there was a connection, but we're not sure yet apart from the fact that they may have done some gun-running, which was largely based on an ultra-thin base of evidence that Jake, while reincarnated, recalled in the sessions with Jameson. This worried Jonty. There was a piece of paper with the name 'Jack' written on it pinned in the top right-hand corner, with no place to sit and a question mark next to the name. It wasn't much, but it was organised, and Jonty was in his comfort zone.

"If we can answer these six questions we will be a long way to solving the conundrum," he said rhetorically.

Points and questions again, Jake thought, but it didn't waiver his interest.

"Who?" continued Jonty. "We don't know that yet. But from Jake's regression, we do believe it's a male. How? Murdered by a hit and run? Where We know Manchester is where Paul was murdered."

Jake looked at Em. This was the first time they'd heard Jonty use the word murder.

"What was the reason?" continued Jonty. "We need a motive and we don't have that. When? When was the murder? We know it was 15th June 1977. Why? Why? Oh, why?"

The others looked at each other, not saying anything.

"Time to chat with Billy," Jonty continued quietly, looking deep in thought.

***

Billy received the voicemail from Jonty whilst at work, returning his call at lunchtime.

"Jonty, old friend. How are you doing? Great to hear from you." Billy sounded false.

"I am good thanks, Billy. Just giving you a call to see if I can meet you and chat a few things through. Actually, To pick your brain, if I can?"

Jonty picked up a slight nervousness in Billy's voice. "Yes, of course, you can, Jonty. Always good to see you. Why don't you pop round to my house, say, tomorrow night? It will be quiet as Maggie is going out with some work colleagues."

"Perfect." was Jonty's response. They exchanged details about time and directions and the phone call ended.

Jonty kept his promise, meeting with Helen, Em, and Jake at Jake and Em's house that evening.

"Why don't we make a night of it?" said Em. "I will cook a meal," They all agreed on 8 pm.

Earlier that day, Em told Jake they, may be in trouble with their parents at home. "My mom 'bumped' into your pop back home and got talking. My mom asked how your leg was after the break?"

Jake looked at Em in amazement as she continued. "They want a three-way skype, a new toy my pop has to see what's going on."

Jake looked aghast. "I love you, but you will get me hung."

"Sorry," responded Em weakly. "I have made a lasagne for Helen and Jonty, with garlic bread and tiramisu for afters, so no picking," she said, trying to change the subject.

"Okay," was the despondent response. Jake wanted the call to his parents as much as he wanted a tooth extracted without anaesthesia.

Six o'clock came around too quickly and they prepared for the pre-arranged three-way Skype call. The call was attended by everybody, this included Claire and Nate, who Jake could see were sitting in the sunroom overlooking the hills in the background, with the primrose draped curtains falling between Nate and Claire's view. Claire was dressed for what looked like a hot day outside with a 50s-style knee-length skirt, a pink blouse and a pink cardigan draped over her shoulders. She looked cool and relaxed in the flower-printed wicker chair that matched Nate's, who wore a pair of grey slacks and an open neck sky blue shirt tucked into his waistband, two drinks placed on the table. *Probably an Italian red*, thought Jake knowing his parents so well.

A minute or so later, Christopher and Rachael Connaught, Em's parents, joined the call. One thing Em had always been taught was not to tell lies or you will always get caught out. A sudden vision appeared to her; she remembered being a child and her father telling her this after she had told a tall tale about how she'd tried to convince her father that the candy bar in the fridge had been eaten by Doodle, the family highland terrier. Looking at the laptop screen, she could see that her mom and pop were in the study with the mahogany bookcases lining the whole wall behind them. Christopher was sitting behind his equally stunning mahogany desk, with Rachael sitting at the edge.

Em's hands were feeling sweaty. She could see her father was not in a light mood. He looked rather stuffy compared to Nate; he wore a red and white pinstriped shirt with a red tie pulled fully to the neck, with a very expensive tie pin and a Rolex on his wrist. Rachael was dressed in an expensive-looking brown mohair suit with a white blouse, pressed and fitted under the jacket. Her dyed chestnut brown hair made her look fifteen years younger than her forty-five years.

Mom has had Botox again, thought Em, knowing presentation and looks were very important to Rachael. This was the opposite of Christopher, who, though always smart, always appeared to keep his grey hair unkempt and collar length, more what you would expect from a university tutor than a top-end high-earning attorney.

Nate started the conversation. He still looked fit and strong as he approached middle age; his hair had started to recede slightly, but the steel grey and black hair made him look a little like Richard Gere. Claire liked this look in her husband a lot.

"Jake!"

Em was now shaking and hugging Jake so tight that he felt he had no freedom to move. She was sweating and breathing deeply. She just wished they could get this over and done with.

"Can you tell me what's been going on, son?" said Nate.

Jake sat composed. *Where will this go?* he wondered.

"It's my fault." Em blurted out.

"What do you mean?" asked Christopher. Em thought again about being told to 'never tell lies'.

"We have to stay, Daddy," she began, "because Jake has been reincarnated and we think we know who killed him in a previous life. And when Jake rang Ron, his boss, he was told he wouldn't get paid and I knew we needed some money, so I lied hoping you would pay me. I am sorry. I know I should have told the truth and I am just sorry, that's all…" Em raced through the speech. She tried to get as many words out as she could and hoped everybody was just going to understand. However, this was not the case.

Jake then took over. "We were doing the coast to coast walk, as you are all aware. I bumped into somebody who I knew from a previous life."

"Was it Billy?" interrupted Claire.

"Yes!" was Jake's shocked reply. "How do you know?"

Claire continued. "When you were a small child, you used to tell me about the dreams you had about Manchester. They were very vivid and Billy's best friend was Paul. You used to tell me what you did and it was very real to both of us."

"How do you know you are reincarnated, Jake?" Rachael butted in.

"I saw an expert in London who put me through regression," explained Jake. "Whilst I am not one hundred percent sure, it seems more likely than not. That's why Em lied because it sounds so farfetched that we thought none of you would believe us."

"We are your parents," said Nate. "We will stick by you in thick and thin, plausible or non-plausible."

"You mentioned a murder?" Christopher stated, his attorney side now taking over. "How do you know this person in a previous life was murdered?"

"We are not sure yet, Mr. Connaught." Jake always called Christopher Mr. Connaught. "We're working with a retired detective from the UK police force to help us with it all."

"Do you need any help with this so-called case?" asked Christopher.

"Thanks, Mr. Connaught, but not at the moment," said Jake. "Could I call you if needed?"

"Err, well, yes."

"Of course he will help you," stated Rachael with authority.

"And if you need anything, Jake, you must let us all know, okay?" Claire added.

"You do not need to lie to any of us for any reason," said Nate. "You are our children and you are important to us."

Em was still shaking and her hands were sweaty. She was still expecting the final bombshell, but there wasn't one. She wondered if her father would have been more aggressive had Jake's parents not been in the call.

Christopher then spoke. "If you want me to keep paying you a wage, young lady…"

Here we go, thought Em, waiting for the bomb ready to explode. But it never came.

"I propose we discuss this twice a week on Fridays and Wednesdays, at six o'clock UK time." It was an opportunity for him to use his new technology, and everybody knew it.

"Of course, Daddy," Em replied in disbelief, amazed at how lightly they were getting away with this.

"Yes, Mr. Connaught," was Jake's contribution.

"That's okay with us, too," said Nate.

And that was that. Everything was above board and out in the open. Em felt as though the whole weight of Tower Bridge had been lifted off her.

"Thank you for understanding, Daddy, Mom, Mr. and Mrs. Hughes," she said. Nate smiled. He loved the innocence of the girl whom he and Claire loved as the perfect daughter-in-law and wife for Jake.

"Do not think we understand, though, Emily." was Christopher's response, convincing Em that this conversation would have gone far worse without the presence of Nate and Claire.

"One down, one to go," said Em after the call ended. She looked at Jake. "I best check the lasagne. Helen and Jonty will be here soon."

Jake just had time for a quick shower, as Em had taken residence in the bathroom before the call with their parents, panicking and getting ready. She had, however, done a great job, coming down the stairs in a pair of tight-fitting white jeans that looked sprayed on to her sporty legs, accompanied by a cream cotton round-necked top.

She is looking much more relaxed now, thought Jake.

She went straight to the kitchen and started preparing the meal. "Where are the pasta sheets? Where is the béchamel sauce?"

Jake smiled. *Well, maybe still stressed, just a notch down,* "I'm going up for a shower, Em."

"Okay, Hun. Have you seen the onions? Oh, it's okay, I have them."

Go now, Jake told himself.

Helen and Jonty arrived with five minutes to spare. They looked very comfortable in each other's company. Jonty wore a cream, open neck shirt and grey slacks with a pair of blue yachting shoes with white laces. His outfit complemented Helen's cream sleeveless shift dress and brown shoes with a hint of cream around the top of the shoes. She'd decided to go with bare legs as the weather was warm and she had legs she could still flaunt, albeit only in high-heeled shoes these days.

As they crossed the threshold, Jake couldn't help but notice a warm drift of alcohol surrounding both of their guests. Em was now calm and calculated, with absolutely no sign of the stressed person from earlier. The table was set with a white tablecloth, on which were set four placemats each depicting four different photographs of Manchester buildings, namely the Town Hall, the library on St Peter's Square, St Ann's church, and finally, Em's favourite building, the John Ryland's library.

"Do sit down." urged Em. "I have some prosecco in the fridge, as I know it's your favourite. Jake, dear, will you pour some wine?"

They settled in the dining chairs, the aroma of the lasagne wafting from the oven. The windows were open, letting in the warm air from outside; the birds were singing in the trees, and a steady purr of traffic could be heard from Worsley Road fifty yards away. Em played a CD of Sinatra, knowing it was a choice both Jonty and her father would make. She particularly liked the one about him singing about his life, 'When I Was Seventeen'.

The lasagne was excellent. Helen commented, "Em, that was top restaurant standard. You must give me the recipe."

Em felt a warm glow of pride. She liked the compliment. She liked to be liked.

Once the lasagne, tiramisu, and two bottles of wine had been demolished, Jonty sat feeling full and heavy from the meal. "That was a fantastic meal, Em. You will make somebody a good wife one day." he smiled, patting his stomach.

"Careful, old man." Jake smiled back.

However, they all knew why they were there, and Jonty began the proceedings. "I have arranged to see Billy tomorrow. We need to plan a way of bringing up the topic of Paul and the gun running."

CHAPTER TWENTY

"Where are you meeting him?" enquired Helen.

"At his home," said Jonty. "I have the address. Do you know exactly where it is?"

Helen looked at Jonty in surprise. "You *are* the honoured one," she said. "I don't know anybody who has been there. He keeps his address a secret. I have never been invited, but I believe it's a lovely house in Knutsford, Cheshire. It's worth about a million pounds from all accounts. Support from Maggie's daddy, I think."

"Wow, I can't wait to see it then," Jonty said. He went quiet for a moment, knowing the others wanted to know if he had a plan. He played it like a good comedian planting his punchline, except this was no joke. After ten minutes of discussing and refining Jonty's thought process, an agreement was made and Jonty had a blueprint to deliver to Billy.

The next day, Jonty set off early. He arrived in the Knutsford area about an hour early, so he decided to find the property first. He stopped the ageing Honda CRV and looked for 'Woodcote House', the name of the property, on his sat-nav once again. The system selected the road, but could not identify the property. He slowly drove down the privately-owned road named 'The Forestry'. It did not take much imagination to know where the road gained its name; It was surrounded by trees on either side of the road. There were ash, beech, birch, oak, and elm, they all looked to have been around for a few hundred years. Their leaves were fluttering in the warm, late July evening sunshine.

Jonty proceeded down the road. Although he couldn't see many houses, he could see large gates of different styles and structures; the driveways were so long that they weaved into the mask of the trees, camouflaging the properties from the outside world. Jonty drove for fifty yards to the bottom of the road and, at the head of it, sitting at a right-angle to the road, was a pair of imposing double gates with a limestone tablet stone to the side, about two foot square, with the words 'WOODCOTE HOUSE' emblazoned in gold lettering. Again, there was no house to be seen, but an obvious winding driveway that led up to it.

Right, I have the best part of an hour to play with, thought Jonty. *I will find a coffee and a car wash. I better have the car looking its best in this place.*

Jonty returned after fifty minutes. He guided the navy CRV into 'The Forestry' and slowly crept along the well-tarmacked road to 'Woodcote House'. There was an intercom button on the side of the wall. Jonty pulled down the electric window and pressed the buzzer once. Within a couple of seconds, a voice could be heard from the silver box on the wall.

"Jonty! Glad you found us. Come on in."

He recognised the voice as that of Billy. He may have moved out of Manchester, but Manchester had not moved out of him. The ten-foot-high gates swung inwards in unison, quietly and perfectly timed. Jonty noticed what must have been a very high-quality close circuit TV system; the camera rotated on its arm and followed the car onto the premises. He saw another camera, about twenty feet further along the drive, which was lined by pine trees set about a yard outside the neatly paved approach.

The road meandered for around thirty yards, the trees accompanying him all the way. When he reached the end, a circular garden came into view. It had a diameter of about twenty yards with a stone drive running around its circumference, allowing cars to exit by driving around it in a clockwise direction The lawn was so manicured it could have easily passed for an international bowling green, or putting green at the Augusta golf course, the finest in the USA. A thirty-foot high copper beech tree sat majestically, bragging its leaves and taunting the warm breeze, glistening in its copper tones for the world to see. It was the finest tree Jonty had ever seen.

Set behind the tree was a long white building, the type usually seen in American films or the American TV show *Dallas*, certainly not in the UK. It was two storeys high and there must have been a dozen windows, symmetrically placed, on both floors of the building. A doorway was perfectly balanced in the middle of the property. Jonty was drawn to a large arch-shaped window above the door; although it was tinted, Jonty could make out a wide staircase behind it.

As he pulled up outside the front door, Billy was already making his way down the eight steps to meet him.

"Jonty, my boy," said Billy, smiling broadly. "How the hell are you?"

Jonty had not seen Billy for about five years. Whilst the beginnings of middle age had started to show with grey specks of hair around the temples, and the slight loosening of skin around the chin and jawbone, Billy looked extremely fit. He retained the dark olive skin that only ancestors from a warm European climate could share. He still possessed strong arms, a slim waist, and muscular thighs that could be seen through his cream chinos, which fought against the ever-expanding and contracting thigh muscles as he moved. He wore a tight-fitting, V-neck navy T-shirt that, again, showed off his enviable European colour and a chest that looked as solid as a blacksmith's anvil. Jonty felt insignificant compared to such a physique.

"Do come in," added Billy.

Billy invited Jonty up the steps to the majestic navy-coloured front door. Jonty passed through into a large entrance hall with cream and rust-coloured floor tiling. The hallway was large and hexagon-shaped, with five doors running off it. In the middle was a staircase that was around ten feet wide. Jonty saw the smoked-glass arched window he'd noticed from the outside. Two spindled handrails made of marble went up the full length of the stairs. There was a hint of the rust fleck matching the tiles in the hallway and the steps going up the stairway. Jonty was out of his comfort zone and he knew it.

Don't get phased by this, Jonty, he told himself. *This is Billy, Paul's closest friend, and a close friend of Helen's. You have met Billy many times... DO NOT GET PHASED!*

Billy turned to Jonty. "You must be thirsty. Would you like tea, coffee? Something a little stronger?"

"Coffee, white with one, will be fine thanks, Bill." Jonty consciously used the word Bill rather than Billy to try and put himself on an equal footing. Who was he kidding?

"Coffee it is." Billy walked up to a door and opened it, again inviting Jonty to walk past him and enter the room.

"Make yourself comfortable," he said. "I will make a brew."

There it is again. Brew, a Manchester phrase. He is just a Manchester lad at heart, thought Jonty.

As Jonty entered the room, the first things he saw were four large, wide windows. Two were to the front of the room, which overlooked the manicured lawn, but from an angle that hid the stone driveway. It showed, however, the copper beech tree standing there, in all its glory, as proud as a guard protecting Buckingham Palace. There was a window on each sidewall. One overlooked a large lake with a blue and white rowing boat sitting alongside a mooring pier. The boat looked in need of some paint, the oars placed either side of it. The other window took in the forest of tall trees he'd seen driving up the road. There was a wood-shaven path leading up through the trees, and he could see two red squirrels racing around the treetops. *I have never seen red squirrels before. They are so rare.*

Jonty looked around the room. The house was contemporary. He had always thought that people with money either went contemporary or period; he preferred period, but there was no mistaking that this property was bursting its banks with class and expense. He sat down on one of the two grey, modern leather four-seater sofas which were facing each other, with a smoked-glass coffee table running the length between them. There was nothing on the table and its nakedness added to the class of the room. He looked to his left and eyed a modern white bookcase that stretched wall to wall, floor to ceiling. He estimated there were probably two thousand books in total, with a sliding ladder at one end that could be used to reach the books on the higher shelves. To his right was an inglenook fireplace made of grey marble with a log burning stove that was about four feet wide. There were seats in the inglenook to keep you warm in the winter.

Cut flowers sat in large, light grey vases, sending out the fresh blossom smell of summer flowers. There was a vase in each corner and all sat on matching grey marble and oak jardinières. Just as Jonty was looking through the window, still mesmerised by the red squirrels bouncing around the trees, Billy entered with a tray and what looked like a solid silver pot of freshly brewed coffee.

"So, how are you? You are looking well," said Billy.

"I am good thanks, Billy," replied Jonty. "Life appears to be treating you good," He gestured with his head to show that he meant the house.

"Yes, well, the luck came in falling in love with a girl who has a wealthy father," Billy said. They both smiled.

"Do you still get to see City play?" enquired Jonty.

"Not so much these days. You know what it's like?" said Billy. They both nodded.

"What about you, Jonty? What are you up to?"

"I've retired now," said Jonty. "I just spend days easing myself around, you know."

"Lucky you. I can't wait to retire."

"Well, when you get there, you want to start all over again, trust me," said Jonty, like the wise old owl.

97

The coffee was the best Jonty had tasted in years, and it tasted all the better for drinking it out of a white bone china cup. The quality pot held the heat like Jonty only knew from a plastic thermos flask.

"Well, Jonty," mused Billy. "I know you came here for a reason. Let's talk about what's on your mind." An assertiveness that Jonty had never known from Billy came through.

"Well, Billy, it's probably something of nothing," countered Jonty. "I know you and Helen are close. She sees you as a son after..."

"Paul," Billy finished Jonty's sentence.

"Yes, Paul," added Jonty.

"I think about him every day," said Billy. "We were such close friends. I will do anything to help Helen, you know that. What can I do?"

"Well..." Jonty let the silence hang. He was back in detective mode. "Somebody, and I am not sure who..." Again, he let the sentence hang. "Someone has told Helen that you and Paul may have been involved in something illegal while you were in Liverpool around the mid-seventies."

Billy didn't reply.

"Do you know what she means?" said Jonty.

"No!" was the emphatic reply.

"Try and think," Jonty pushed. He was now drawing on all his skills as a detective to read the body language rather than reading into the answers to his questions.

"Honestly, Jonty, I can't think what this person means," said Billy. "I don't know if Paul was involved in anything untoward, but I wasn't. Friends don't always tell each other everything."

"I know," said Jonty. "But please, just try and think?"

Billy again took a second to answer. "Jonty, I wouldn't need to think so hard if I was doing anything illegal, would I?"

Jonty looked at Billy square in the eye. "You know, Billy, that is exactly what I said to Helen. I think somebody is just stirring up trouble about something that never happened."

He quickly stood up and shook Billy by the hand. "Lovely place you have here. Thanks for the information, or no information." Jonty smiled. "Helen will be really glad to hear that nothing was going on. She will trust your word, I know."

Billy put his arm around Jonty's shoulder and they walked out of the room and back towards the grand hallway, where Jonty had stood forty-five minutes previously.

Jonty turned to Billy. "What do you do for a job these days, Billy?"

"I am a regional manager at the national bank," replied Billy. "I have worked my way up from being a trainee."

"They must pay well?" Jonty commented.

"As I said, the advantage of marrying into wealth," Billy said.

They had reached the main entrance by this time and Jonty was walking down the steps to reunite himself with his trusty steed, the CRV. He turned and took one final look at his surroundings. The sun was setting pink over the west side of Cheshire, a dozen or so rabbits had made an entrance and were playing on the lawn without a care in the world, and the copper beech was turning a pink copper in acknowledgement of the setting sun. Jonty turned to Billy and waved.

"Great to see you again, Jonty," said Billy.

"You, too," said Jonty. "Not so long next time, eh?" He got into his car and started up the engine. He then began the forty-five-minute journey back home, with real people, Manchester people.

CHAPTER TWENTY-ONE

Jonty promised feedback for Helen, Em, and Jake the day after. They agreed to meet at the Midland Hotel for coffee, but no food, as it was too expensive. This was Helen's idea, as she had enjoyed the atmosphere and the time she'd spent having the meal with Jake and Em.

The warm and sunny climes of the previous day had changed to a cool, drizzly day. Jake and Em were the first to arrive, with Jake giving a wink and a slight nod of the head as he walked past the statue commemorating Rolls Royce. The weather did not concern Jake and Em, as the weather in Boone was not too dissimilar to Manchester. It rained more in July and August than at any other time of the year.

"Are you missing home, Em?" Jake asked.

"Some," Em replied. "We have been here two months almost and we don't seem to be moving too far forward."

"These things pick up pace as they go, I guess," said Jake, trying to give some assurance.

They ate lunch at home before making their way to the city hotel for the 2 pm meeting. The rain dampened the dust on the pavements, the smell vaporising through their nostrils from the car park to the foyer.

As they entered the hotel, the lobby was busy with people checking in and out; it was much busier than usual. There were several tables set aside in the far corner with businessmen and women dressed in smart suits; they looked like they were at a conference. The timing couldn't have been better for, within five minutes of Jake and Em's arrival, the suits disappeared into a room for the afternoon session and the hotel seemed to go from the hustle and bustle of a hurricane to the tranquil moment of the eye of the storm. This allowed Jake and Em to find a comfortable sofa and two very comfy-looking cream draylon chairs, all set around a coffee table that had been vacated by the seminar 'mob'.

Within a minute, a waitress asked what they would like and Em explained they were waiting for some people to join them. Helen and Jonty came in precisely at 2 pm. They stood for a moment, surveying the room and looking for Jake and Em. Jake saw them looking, stood up and waived them over, simultaneously making eye contact with the waitress to confirm that they were now ready to order.

"Parking is a nightmare," Jonty said.

"It does seem busy today," Jake acknowledged. He immediately turned to the reason why they were there. "Jonty, we need to know about yesterday's meeting with Billy. Nothing more has been on our mind."

"Mine too," Helen said excitedly. "He wouldn't tell me anything in the car on the way over, he just said we would all talk it over as agreed."

Jonty sat there as the master about to teach his three pupils a lesson on being a cop.

"The first thing I have to say," he began, "is that alarm bells are going off in my head. If you heard them in the street you would think a nuclear bomb was heading straight for us."

Em moved forward in her seat like a little child listening to the teacher read out a story to the class. However, this was not going to be a fairy tale.

"I drove to Billy's house," began Jonty. "Helen, you said you thought it was worth a million. I would say five – at the least – and another half-million on fixtures and fittings."

Helen's face was a picture as her jaw dropped slightly, but enough to let out a little gasp. "But his father-in-law is wealthy," she said in Billy's defence.

"Not so wealthy that he can spend five million on a daughter and son-in-law," Jonty answered energetically. "However, I thought the same. I rang Dave Rowlands at the station. He is looking at the rumours regarding the gun-running for me. I kept the discussion to the gun-running at first and asked how he was progressing with it. He said it was slow going, but he was finding bits out. I then asked him if he knew Edward Le Conte." Jonty paused. "That's Billy's father-in-law." The others looked at each other. "I then asked if he would look up Henry Le Conte's address. I knew he could get it easily, as all solicitors and other professionals that deal with the courts are on a central computer for security reasons."

The three faces looking at Jonty were now like hungry chicks waiting to be fed.

"Within thirty seconds, he gave me the address and postcode." Jonty smiled. "With, of course, the condition that I didn't hear it from him." Everyone smiled

"Anyway, I then went on one of the famous internet property sites, you know the one you look at when you are looking for a house to buy." A trio of nodding heads came back at him. "I looked first at the

101

postcode of properties sold in the last five years in the neighbourhood where Billy lives, and the average was four and a half million pounds. Now, given that Billy's is the best property in that area, it must be a little above that, and that is how I guessed at the five million ballpark figure I stated earlier."

"Wow!" was the only thing Em could think of saying.

Jonty continued. "I then looked at Le Conte's postcode and it's in a lovely leafy Cheshire area. I would want one of his houses if I could afford it."

"How much?" Jake demanded.

"One point seven million!" said Jonty. They all gasped.

"What's your thought process, Jonty?" Helen asked.

"Well," continued the ex-detective, squeezing every pip of enjoyment out of this. "I know everybody would want to support their own children financially. But I don't know anybody who would want to support them to almost three times their living standard." All went quiet again.

"How on earth does Billy pay for what must be an exceedingly high standard of living on area manager's wages?" he asked.

They agreed.

"And there's more," said Jonty "Let me ask you all a question individually. Whilst I do so, I want the other two to watch the body language of the person answering."

They all looked startled but willing. Jonty continued and asked them all a question. "Jake, can you remember the colour of your first school tie?"

Jake thought for a moment. "Blue, with a yellow stripe running at an angle left to right."

Jonty turned to Helen. "Helen, can you remember the colour of your front door when you were a child?"

Again a pause. "Yes, green and white."

"Em, can you remember the colour of the seats in any of your father's cars?"

A third pause. "I can. It was a lovely red leather with white piping. I can smell the old leather now as I speak."

"Thanks," said Jonty. "Now, what did you notice about each other's body language?"

There was silence as the others thought about Jonty's question.

"Did you notice where the eyes went?" Jonty pushed as he was met with more silence. "Okay, I guess you didn't know what you were looking for."

They all felt a sense of uneasiness at having failed. "All three of you, when asked to remember, looked down and left."

"Yes." jumped in Em.

"That is the part of the brain working that asks for a recall. When asked a question, over ninety percent of people will cast their eyes down and to the left. It's a subconscious reaction."

They all looked at Jonty, waiting for the punchline. "I asked Billy if he remembered being involved in any illegal activity with Paul in Liverpool."

All was quiet except for the distant sound of piped music playing Edward Elgar over the hotel speakers. "He answered no, as I expected. But the interesting thing is, instead of looking down and to the left, as you all did, he looked up and right."

Jake intervened. "What is the significance of that, Jonty?"

"Well," replied Jonty, "when people look upwards to the right, that part of the brain is telling them to search for something that is not true. They defend, they lie," He went quiet as if inviting questions. None came. "It's not a perfect science and, like reincarnation, it would not hold up in a court of law, but it gives us enough gut evidence that we should delve a little deeper!"

They sat and ordered a refill of coffees. After a few minutes, Jake asked, "What tools do we have available to us at this point to move forward?"

Jonty was the first to respond. "We have Jameson, who we can ask to delve deeper with Paul."

Em looked at Jake. "Would you want to do that?"

"Yes," was Jake's emphatic reply. "I know it won't stand as evidence, but it might give us some strong clues on where we should be looking."

"Agreed," said Jonty. "We will use Jameson again at some point." He scribbled in his notebook.

"We have Dave working in the background," Helen said, and again Jonty scribbled.

"We have a good idea that Billy is living beyond his means," Em said.

"And that he is hiding something," Jonty added. "I will bet a pound to a penny he is hiding something, but what? And how deep does it go? And who is the man in the trilby and his two thugs? Where do they fit in?" He looked at the other three. "We have some pieces of the jigsaw, we now have to fit them."

CHAPTER TWENTY-TWO

LIVERPOOL 1908

At the beginning of the twentieth century, the influx of Italians into America began to increase. New York was the second-largest Italian city after Naples. In one-quarter of New York, more than half a million people were Italian. The new immigrants, bewildered by the new land and its strange language, lived closely together in the 'Little Italy' neighbourhoods of New York, Chicago, New Orleans, and other cities. They were rendered uneducated by the lack of schooling in American language and culture.

Whilst New York was the highest immigrant area for Italians fleeing their homeland, other parts of the world also took on the masses leaving their beautiful 'Old Country'. According to the UK 1911 census, there were over 50,000 Germans and 20,000 Italians living in England and Wales.

In 1908, one of these families was the Sartori family. Roberto Sartori was the head of his family in a run-down district of Palermo. He was the leader of the highly unorganised group called the blackhand's. People paid the black hands, who were extortionists, with the knowledge that the Sicilian law had no understanding or power to help them, and that the threats made in black hand letters were usually carried out if payment was not made. This threat usually meant severe beatings or, worse, death for repeat offenders. This was an early form of the protection racket.

The name 'black hand' was taken from a secret Spanish society of anarchists, that later spread to other countries, particularly the Balkans, to assassinate monarchs and other chiefs of state.

The black hands were the predecessor group that led to the more infamous mafia. Many Mafiosi entered the countries around the world on false papers, which the Italian authorities were only too happy to provide. The Mafiosi had good reasons to travel, as the law and restrictions against ex-convicts in Italy were crippling. After leaving an Italian prison, the convict would be placed on special surveillance, meaning strict night curfew, no employment without permission from the police, regular reports to the local police station, a ban on carrying weapons, and a ban on frequenting all drinking places. Once they arrived in England, they found an already established Irish underworld. The Irish had left their country to escape the potato famine. The Italians did not penetrate these groups at first, instead of keeping within their communities.

The trail left by the black hands draws a picture of an unorganised body with no central leadership or hierarchical structure. Their extortion letters were written in a mixture of dialects. Certainly, by people originating from different regions of Italy, and the blackhand's symbols varied greatly in design. Some depicted an open hand, others a closed fist, while others showed a hand with a knife.

Whilst Roberto knew most Italians were running to America, he chose England. He sailed into Liverpool silently with his wife, Maria, and sons Roberto Jr, aged eight, and Giovanni, aged five. A new life awaited them.

Within a year, Roberto reverted to what he knew best – extortion. He managed a small team of Italian immigrants and took a cut of any income they provided. This kept basic food on the family table until Roberto died at the age of forty-five in 1918. Both his sons followed him into the extortion racket when Roberto Junior hatched a bright idea in 1921. He read that, in 1920, the prohibition of alcohol in America led to a huge opening for ex-countrymen to bootleg liquor, mainly from Canada. The brothers became, extremely structured, working as teams across America. Each family headed up by a leader known as the godfather; this was *Cosa Nostra*, or the mafia, and the beginning of the largest organised crime system the world had ever known. Roberto wanted a slice of the action; but more than that, he wanted to learn how to manage and be taught, thus enabling him to run a similar operation in England, under the radar. He came back into contact with Bennito Rossi when he telegrammed to advise that his father had died from tuberculosis three years previously.

Bennito (Benni) and Roberto Senior had been friends ever since they were children in the late nineteenth century when there was no money in poverty-stricken Sicily. They grew up together and, rather than work the vineyards or land for a pittance, they decided to take their future income in their own hands. They earned a living by running a very basic form of protection racket, although the proceeds were never enough to allow a comfortable living, it was always a day to day hand to mouth activity.

Roberto Junior accepted an invitation from Benni and travelled to New York on the liner *Mauretania*. With a capacity of 2,300 passengers, it was able to cross the Atlantic in four and a half days, a record which was held for thirty years when the liner *Queen Mary* reduced the crossing time by half a day (four days). Roberto arranged to meet Benni at Ellis Island in an attempt to strike an agreement on the export of alcohol, another source for a New York City that could drink all it could consume and more.

"Roberto, you look well, My, you have grown," said Benni.

Roberto was eight when he and his family left Sicily for Liverpool in 1908. He was now a young 21-year-old man. He wore his best brown tweed suit, which was the only suit he owned, a flat cap, and a pair of boots that came halfway up his calves. His jet-black hair reached down to his collar and he carried the Sartori good looks. He was six foot tall and full of energy with a background of fighting on the streets of Liverpool, earning a life full of petty crime and competing with the Irish. Overall, he made ends meet. He lived with his parents and brother, Giovanni, in a one-bedroom house that was damp and encouraged cockroaches and rats by the dozen. It was no wonder his father contracted and later died from, TB.

Benni, on the other hand, appeared to have found a wealth that Roberto could only dream of. Benni wore a pure white shirt that sat neatly beneath an expensive-looking Milan-made navy pinstripe suit. Roberto noticed the hand stitching on the lapel. Benni looked healthy, with a smart haircut. His hair had turned salt and pepper and, with his Sicilian olive skin, it made him look a picture of health.

"Mr. Rossi, it is so good to see you again," said Roberto. "My mother sends her love."

Benni smiled. "Hey, what's all this Mr. Rossi? You are a handsome young man now, and it's Benni."

Both men smiled. Benni put both his hands on Roberto's arms and stood square facing him. "I was really sorry to hear about your father, we were like brothers. I want to help you and your family for old time's sake, febene"

"Thank you, Mr... erm... Benni."

"Hey, what am I thinking!" said Benni. "You have travelled, you must be hungry. Let's go eat." He looked around him to a man sitting on a wall at the side of the road. "Paulo, get the car, we are going to take our guest to the restaurant Piccolo Italia."

Roberto had not noticed the man due to his concentration on meeting Benni again.

"I need to go through immigration first," Roberto mentioned to Benni, indicating to the immigration signs where he had to have his passport stamped.

"Nonsense!, Come with me," Benni took Roberto by the arm and walked past the queue of people to the immigration guard. "Hey, Charlie! This is my friend, we are okay to go through, no?"

"Go straight through, Mr. Rossi, and have a nice day!"

"Thank you, Charlie," Benni replied.

With that, Roberto was accepted into America. Within a minute they reached the kerbside as Paulo pulled up in a beige Packard Custom Super 8. The Packard V12 was outfitted with bulletproof glass. Benni opened the rear door for Roberto to climb into the car. He had not even got his chest past the door line when he noticed an onboard bar. The smell of leather hit his nose like a bullet out of the fog. By the time Benni had opened the other passenger door, Roberto had settled in the comfiest seat he had ever encountered.

I want a piece of this, he thought.

Benni took him to the restaurant as promised, where he ate the best *spaghetti al Pomodoro* and meatballs. Afterwards, Benni invited him back to his home. Roberto was impressed on his first day in America.

"The next step for you, Roberto, is home. Edita is looking forward to seeing you."

Edita was Benni's wife. She was a childhood friend of Roberto's mother, Maria. As Benni, Edita, Roberto Senior and Maria had grown from children to adults together, Roberto was considered as family. Benni and Edita never had children, although not for the lack of trying; it just never happened for them. The best medical people of the day that money could buy could never give a reason why they were unable to conceive.

Roberto had not even crossed the threshold when he heard somebody calling out, "Roberto, my favourite Roberto."

Edita ran across the best Italian marbled floor, hugging him around the neck. Roberto thought she would never let go.

"I was so sorry to hear about your father, we go back a long way," She looked sombre for a few seconds, then the excitement returned. "Is your mother well? And little Giovanni? I bet he isn't so little these days."

Edita stepped back and looked Roberto up and down, from head to toe. She put a hand on a hip and stood side-on. She wore a light blue dress with red flowers on it, giving the look of summer. "And look at you."

She laughed and clapped her hands in joy. "You are a handsome young man. You are going to break a girl's heart soon." She slapped him on the upper arm as she spoke.

Roberto was then left to freshen up in the room Benni and Edita had set up for him. It was a very large room, with drapes that were twenty feet from the floor to the ceiling in primrose, with matching bedding. It had clean, white walls and a bathroom attached. The bathroom was equally as grand, with a large, white, roll top bath with gold taps and plugs, matching the taps on the large sink set on a marble pedestal in the corner of the room.

They had a huge Italian meal of minestrone soup, followed by the most tender veal imaginable, and a tiramisu that tasted so fresh that, if you closed your eyes, you could believe you were back in old Sicily, washed down with a bottle of the finest wine. Roberto fell into bed around midnight shattered from his first day in the United States of America.

As the weeks passed, Roberto and Benni became inseparable. Roberto saw at first hand the power this man possessed and he saw many people tip their hats at him. They went to the finest restaurants, the best tailors, and did not pay even once. Roberto witnessed organised military-style operations to halt lorries in their tracks, laden with thousands of bottles of liquor. He saw how this way of life had made Benni a rich man, a very rich man, politicians forced plans through for Benni to build properties, hotels, or night clubs after a wedge of money was thrown their way. This was managing a business. This was power. This was a good way to live.

Roberto had been in New York for three months when, one evening, while he was dining at Piccolo Italia with Benni and a few close confidantes, his head turned to see an elegantly dressed woman. She was tall and wore an olive green pair of loose-fitting trousers that were perfectly cut in length, skimming a pair of low-heeled court shoes. A blouse, of a paler green, was tucked into the trousers with a cream belt separating the blouse and trousers. Draped around her perfectly formed shoulders was a cream, finely knitted cardigan. She was talking to a man, who was also smartly dressed in a black suit. He had short, neatly cut hair. The man's back was turned to Roberto, but he could see over his shoulder the perfectly formed face of the woman, her features shrouded by jet-black hair that hung in luxurious waves down past her neck, terminating just above the point where her shoulder blades began.

109

The girl's beauty stopped Roberto in his tracks. She looked over her companion's shoulder and at Roberto. It was the merest of glances and she looked away again within a second. She continued talking to the man. After about a minute, the man ordered what appeared to be two more coffees for the girl and himself, allowing the girl a little break to again look at Roberto. She smiled. Roberto's mouth went dry as he smiled back.

She turned back to her companion and started talking to him again. As he ended his quick conversation with the bartender, the girl gave one final look towards Roberto and smiled again. The couple stood up from the high stools at the bar and walked out. The man was settling the bill and not re-ordering; however, there was enough time for the girl to look over her shoulder and give one last smile towards Roberto as she left the building. Roberto was left with a dry throat and a yearning to see this woman again.

***

Antonia Carlucci was a woman whose family had moved from Attrani in the south of Italy in 1905. Attrani is east of Amalfi, about a five-minute drive away, and one of the most enchanting villages on Italy's Amalfi Coast. Azzo Carlucci earned his living as a fisherman in the village, as had his father and his father before. He'd heard about the opportunity offered in America and so, after two years of discussions and building up hopes that declined with the fear of change, he finally made the decision with his wife, Abrianna, to make the journey to Ellis Island with their two children, Alfeo, their four-year-old son, and Toni, their two-year-old daughter. Azzo settled well in the American way after starting in the fishing industry in the New York state. He quickly transferred his skills from basic fishing in the old country to retailing fish distribution to all the finest hotels and restaurants within a twenty-mile radius of New York.

A few days after Roberto's first sighting of the girl in green, fate took over. He saw her walking past Times Square with a friend; this time, though, it was a girlfriend and not a male. He stopped and smiled. She smiled back.

"Hello," he said. "Long time no see."

She smiled, then turned to her friend. "Janey, I will call you later, to arrange lunch," Janey gave a knowing smile.

"I was thinking of an espresso, would you care to join me?" asked Roberto.

"I prefer an Americano, it takes longer to drink." answered the coy beauty.

"Will your boyfriend wonder where you are?" quizzed Roberto, hitting the awkward question square in the face.

"Boyfriend?" asked the girl. "Ah, you mean Alfi, my brother, He was in the Piccolo Italia for some family business. We have a fish distribution company and Alfi has been trying to get into Piccolo, without much success."

She looked at him. "What do you do?"

"I am in the retail industry," Roberto answered.

"Great, I am Toni. And you are?"

"I am Roberto," was the reply, embarrassed that she had formally done the introduction.

The following weeks saw Roberto and Toni spending every available minute of the day together. They went to ball games and regularly ate at the Piccolo Italia, where Roberto got ribbed from the family guys. He had become immersed in her company, as she was with him. They were inseparable.

CHAPTER TWENTY-THREE

"Jonty?"

"Yes?" replied Jonty to the caller on the telephone.

"Jonty, it's Dave, about the car you said you may want to buy off me. When's the best time to pop round and see it?"

"Is tomorrow okay?"

"Yes, tomorrow is great. Say at ten o'clock?"

"Yes, see you then."

Jonty put the phone down. He stood looking at the phone for a while. Back in the seventies, if a phone call was made and you were worried about the call being tapped or recorded, you used terminology that would be used as a sort of secret code. Jonty and Dave used potential car buying scenarios. Dave knew that Jonty would understand this, and he did. What he didn't know, was why the decoy car discussion had taken place.

The next morning at ten o'clock sharp, Jonty was knocking on Dave Rowlands' door.

"Jonty, come in quickly," Jonty did as he was asked.

"What is going on?" he asked once the door was closed. "Why are you so edgy? What on earth is going on?"

Dave shuffled Jonty through the door of the lounge and drew the curtains. Jonty could see the dust floating in the grubby room. The badly fitting curtains left gaps at the top and sides, where rays of morning sunlight streamed through like an usher's torch in the cinema.

"Dave, settle down and tell me, what on earth is going on."

"Well," responded Dave, "when we spoke the other day about Edward Le Conte, within an hour I was sitting in front of Quinn. He was asking who I'd been talking to and why I had mentioned the name, Le Conte. I said it was about a case an old colleague was involved in and that I'd been talking to Jimmy Shep. Luckily, when I read the case notes, I noticed that Shep was on the list, as Le Conte was presiding over a case that Shep was involved in."

112

Jimmy Shepherd was one of the boys Jonty and Dave would regularly drink with after a shift in the Albert Hall pub, not far from the statue of the Prince Consort in Albert Square in Manchester city centre.

Jonty looked at his mate. "Did he say anything else?"

"No."

"Then he doesn't know anything," said Jonty. "Surely they tracked this track on the central register, and the telephone wasn't tapped. They will know you looked into the system, but they don't know what you looked at. Do you have Shep's number? We need him to be tipped off so he can say he had a chat with you."

Dave smiled smugly. "I'm in front of the game on that one, Jonty. Already done."

"Good," Jonty replied. He rubbed his stubbled chin. *I forgot to shave today,* he thought to himself. *What is going on here? We are touching something that somebody doesn't like, and I don't know what it is.*

"Thanks for looking into it, Dave," he continued. "Did you find anything about the rumours of gun running?"

Dave looked at him. "Jonty, I looked into it all. I searched for illegal Angolan UK relations on the central mainframe search engine. It brought up names that were suspected of being involved in any such relations. I've printed the list." He picked up a sheet of paper from a nearby shelf and gave it to Jonty. There were six names on the list. "Quinn closed the case because there was no further justification, both on grounds of evidence and costs needed to continue with it."

"So, that would have been around the time he called you all in to tell you there was nothing in the rumours?" Jonty asked.

"That's right," said Dave.

Jonty looked down at the list. He did not recognise any of the names. Alongside each name was the name of a city. Jonty assumed this was the place they lived in. He noticed two were from Birmingham, one from London, two from Manchester, and one from Liverpool.

"Did you look on the computer for these names, Dave?"

"Yes, I did," said Dave. "None showed as having a record of any kind. They are all clean."

It doesn't make sense, Jonty thought to himself. *A possible major gun-running outfit, six names, none with a record, which have just randomly appeared. Or so it seems.*

Jonty was relieved to say goodbye to Dave and get out of the house; it was depressing and dirty. He could not believe Dave had lowered his

113

standards so far. Jonty walked the three hundred yards to Grosvenor Road, where Jake was waiting in the hired Seat as agreed. Jonty sat next to Jake and repeated Dave's tale.

"We are definitely on to something. I just wish I knew what it was," Jonty said in a resigned voice, his six foot six, nineteen-stone frame making the Seat tip a little lower on the passenger side.

"Who are the people named?" asked Jake.

Jonty took the sheet of A4 paper out of his back pocket. He was careful to follow the two folds made by Dave to keep it as neat as possible. It wasn't much, but it was all they had.

"George Downs, Stephen Pitt, both of Birmingham. James Morgan, London. John Evans, William Green, both Manchester. Patrick O'Neill, Liverpool."

They sat staring out of the windscreen. The names meant nothing to them. Where could they start? Six names with non-traceable backgrounds was not the lead that they were looking for.

They decided to head back to Jake's house, to update Helen and Em. During the short drive there, Jonty called Helen and gave her an update, asking if she knew any of the names. It was a long shot which, like most long shots, came up short.

"Sorry, Jonty," said Helen. "None of those names mean anything to me."

"We are at a dead-end here, Jake," sighed Jonty. "We need something to break for us to gain momentum."

Both men stared ahead of them as they crossed the Mancunian Way, just as a late July thunderstorm hit the city. The sky turned black and the rain poured as if a bucketful of water had been tipped out of the sky. A flash of lightning was followed instantly by a clap of thunder.

"Not much time between that, was there? We must be right under it," Jonty said, referring to the thunder and lightning. "Just like our clues."

Back at the rented house, Em got the coffee going whilst Jonty and Jake stared silently at the board as if the answer was just going to jump off the chipboard and answer all their prayers. It didn't. Em joined them and sat looking at it, too. After a few minutes, Em broke the silence.

"You know when you talk about long shots, Jonty?" Jonty looked at her. "How long is a long shot?"

Jonty answered. "Well, when a long shot is the only thing you have, it's the hottest trail you have until you can jump off onto a warmer lead."

Jake interjected. "What are you thinking, Em?"

"Well, the names on the list…" The two men listened. "You said that, when you had the scuffle in London, one of the men was named Jack?"

"Yes," said Jonty, looking at the names on the crime board they had set up a few days earlier.

"Well, is Jack not another name for John?"

They looked at each other again. "Well, Em, it is a long shot as you said, but it's the best we have at the minute." Jonty wasted no time in calling Dave Rowlands.

"Dave, when are you next in the office?"

"Tomorrow, Jonty. What's wrong?"

"Can you run me a profile on Jack Evans, from around twenty years ago to the present day?"

"Will do, Jonty." was the closing comment.

***

Jonty was having lunch with an old friend the following day in the Hong Kong Chinese restaurant in Manchester's China Town district. Louise Fleming had been a friend for years. There was a point when Jonty and Louise could have been an item. She was now in her early sixties and looked it. The size twelve figure of twenty years ago had surrendered to many lunches and evening meals socialising with the upper-middle class of Manchester. However, whilst Jonty now no longer found her attractive, he loved challenging the bright brain she always owned. She could talk about what was the best makeup range to the benefits of the atom reactor at CERN and everything in between.

They were just nearing the end of the main course, with Jonty demolishing his vermicelli with sweet and sour pork – not everybody's choice, but Jonty's taste was not like everybody's – when his mobile phone rang to the tune of the confederate anthem, Dixie.

"God!" said Louise in mock disgust, rolling her eyes to the ceiling.

"Excuse me a second, Lou," said Jonty.

"Hello, Dave."

"Jonty, I've fixed the problem with the car and it is ready for a test drive in two hours at my house."

"Great, see you then, Dave."

Jonty just had enough time to finish his meal with Louise and get out of the city to meet up with Dave.

115

He parked the CRV outside the run-down property that let the rest of the street down, and knocked on the door, waiting for Dave to answer, which he readily did. He looked over Jonty's shoulder to double-check that he hadn't been followed.

"I found four people by the name of Jack Evans from Manchester," said Dave. "One had a record for petty crime, burglary, car theft, etc. One was a bit of a hooligan, fighting and drunk and disorderly. One was a drug dealer and user who appeared to spend all his profits on self-use."

Jonty quickly assessed that these did not match the person he was looking for. "And the fourth?"

"The fourth was part of a big player team,' replied Dave. "Theft of high-end cars with the view to exporting them, mainly to America, and a murder trial. None of the accusations stuck," *This could be worth pursuing,* Jonty thought.

Dave continued. "I have a last known address and some notes from the murder trial. I copied them for you!" Dave handed Jonty a buff-coloured manila folder that was an inch thick. "Bedtime reading for you, Jonty."

Jonty laughed. "I best leave *Harry Potter* on the bedside table for a while," They both laughed, although a grunt would describe Dave's reaction better.

"Dave, I owe you a drink."

"Deal!" said Dave. "Out for nowt, you know me," he said in the Lancashire accent.

***

When he got back home, Jonty read the contents of the folder and was particularly interested in the murder trial. The accusation was the murder of a wealthy businessman in the Cheshire area. The trial lasted four weeks and was covered by local TV and press. Jonty paused at a cutting from a press article. It read:

Jack Evans has been acquitted of an assassination-style slaying in a leafy suburb area of Cheshire. He says he is "ready for life to return to normal". However, the victim's sister believed the jury made a huge mistake.

Evans, 33, said that awaiting trial for the killing of 30-year-old Michael Warburton had left him broken.

"I just didn't have any faith in the judicial system after that," said Evans. "I felt like I was being framed and they actually knew the truth, but they didn't care about the truth, it was all about making the paperwork correct. But there is a person, me, in the middle of all this."

Warburton was found near a building in Tiverton near the City of Chester on 6th August 1982. He had been shot four times in the face. Evans, a father of two, said he's ready to move on with his life after Friday's not guilty verdict.

"I'm one of the few people that actually beat the usually rigged odds and I'm grateful," he said. "I'm just grateful to the Lord, grateful that I had an understanding and educated jury that could see through the lies and manipulation of the prosecution."

But Warburton's sister, Julie Needham, told the paper she was "totally shocked!" that the jury "let a murderer go!" "This is not the closure we were looking for," she said. "It's just an unbelievable situation. It's incredibly mind-blowing."

Le Conte, defending Evans, offered his condolences to Warburton's family, but maintained Evans' innocence.

Evans added, "Of course I would want to reconcile with her and let her know, from the bottom of my heart, that I did not commit this heinous crime and harm her dearest brother," he said. "I'm not a murderer. I'm not even a violent person."

During closing statements in Manchester Crown Court, prosecutors played a video of Warburton exiting his nearby apartment in a red hooded Nike sweatshirt before the shooting.

Another video showed a man in the same outfit, from behind, walking past another man and meeting the victim near the murder site moments before shots rang out at around 10 pm. That other man testified at trial that he had walked past Warburton and heard gunshots. He then saw Evans standing over the dead man's body.

Both Warburton's and the victim's fingerprints were found on beer bottles near the scene of the crime.

But the jury did not agree with the police description of events.

The sole eyewitness appeared nervous and shaky in his description of the murder.

"The way he looked, and his body language, did nothing to make the jury believe his story."

Evans' Barrister, Edward Le Conte, said prosecutors had shoehorned their case when another witness testified that the man she saw running away from the murder scene had an afro haircut, which made no sense as Evans had short hair.

"That witness weakened their case," Le Conte said. "That ruined their case dramatically."

The Greater Manchester Police never investigated the murder as a possible robbery, even though the victim's wallet was never found. Police did not recover a murder weapon, whilst CCTV did not capture the actual shooting.

David Hammond, a murder forensic specialist, warned jurors not to acquit Evans just because they thought the investigation was poorly presented. "Do not absolve the defendant because you may think the police were not diligent enough," he said with authority in his closing statement.

117

Relatives of the victim said he had been a builder who worked on upmarket properties around the Cheshire area. He left behind a nine-year-old year daughter and a seven-year-old son.

"Whatever the conflict or how heated it may feel, no one deserves to die like this," his sister told the press.

She said prosecutors told her that Evans was willing to plead guilty prior to the trial to devalue the plea to manslaughter.

"We feel that is not enough. But now there's nothing we can do. We can't even appeal, It's just an injustice," she added. "We just have to get on with our lives as if nothing happened."

Evans' cousin, William Green, denied that Evans would plead guilty in return for manslaughter.

"Jack has nothing to be guilty of," said Green. "Somewhere out there is a murderer who the police have lost because they have concentrated on an innocent man, Jack could have been in jail for his whole life for a crime he did not commit because they relied on a man so dependent on drugs that he was clearly unaware of the reality of the case. And he was their sole witness! Unbelievable."

Jonty travelled over to Jake and Em's and had prepared by printing out another three copies of the transcript so that Helen, Jake, and Em could read at the same time and collect their thoughts whilst they discussed the matter.

"There is also another name we can add to the board," said Jake. "William Green."

"Agreed," said Jonty, who then pulled out the official mugshot that Dave had also attached to the file. There stood a sombre face staring down the camera with no evidence of personality or remorse. John 'Jack' Evans, complete with a scar down the right-hand side of his face. They had found the thug and his name was Jack Evans.

CHAPTER TWENTY-FOUR

NEW YORK, 1927

Roberto was working as a 'foot soldier' in Don Bennito's family under a captain by the name of Joey Costa, whose catchphrase seemed to be "New York is ours to take, As long as we don't cross Charlie 'Lucky' Luciano."

Luciano was a tough New York boss, but good relations were maintained because Benni's and Luciano's fathers had been friends in Sicily. Joey was a short, round guy, about five foot seven inches, and walked like a penguin because his overweight shape made him wobble. He seemed to be built more like a ball than an agile Capitano. However, Roberto soon learned that Joey was not to be messed with. As Roberto got to know him better, and they were comfortable in each other's company, Roberto began to call him 'Popeye' because his huge arms resembled the cartoon sailor. Joey liked this name.

Joey was blessed with thick black Italian curly hair. It was always cut short and neat, but even when it was cut the natural wave in it remained. He always wore a cheesecloth shirt that covered his large belly. He always wore smart cream flannels and a pair of comfy 'Hush Puppy' style shoes. Roberto learned so much from Joey and he had one hundred percent trust in him.

Joey and Roberto's team was in charge of managing four speakeasies around the Bronx and Manhattan areas. They would ensure that they organised the liquor and that the 'joints' were always well-stocked. The most upmarket establishment they ran was in Manhattan, a club called the Palm Spring. The 'Spring' regularly booked top-of-the-bill artists, which included jazz bands and top international singers. The Spring tied in perfectly with the UK operation, with Giovanni sending top-quality Scotch whiskey that would be charged in the establishments for top dollar. The punters could not get enough of it as it made a fantastic option to the lower-quality Canadian imports or, worse, locally made potcheen, which was based on the Irish drink distilled usually from potatoes.

One cool October morning during Roberto's first year, Don Bennito arranged for Joey and Roberto to call into his office to discuss an assignment for which they were to be given sole responsibility. They entered the room, Joey entering first. This was the highest accolade a Mafiosi could gain – to be betrothed to *Cosa Nostra* and the Family. An induction included a knife cut to both the Don and the applicant; as the blood seeped, they would cross the cuts to ensure the blood touched. This was the bonding and initiation, and one would be sworn to the family forever.

The room was large, with a plush red carpet, white walls, and a high ceiling. There was a large window behind the opulent oak desk where Don Bennito sat. Joey walked up to the Don and kissed his hand. A large, twenty-two-carat gold ring sat on a chubby, strong finger. The Don then offered his hand to Roberto, who also kissed it and acknowledged the Don.

They sat down and Don Bennito asked Joey how Roberto was settling in. The answer did not come as a surprise, as he had asked the same question in private days earlier.

"He is settling well, Don Bennito," said Joey. "Roberto is a quick learner!"

The Don looked at Roberto and smiled, then gave a quick nod. Don Bennito was dressed in a smart tailor-made grey silk suit and a grey shirt, with expensive-looking gold cufflinks.

"Joey, Roberto," he began. "We have a problem that needs to be dealt with!."

The receiving ears stayed open, and the mouths stayed closed.

"The Palm Spring is very lucrative, thanks to the efforts of you two, my friends."

Joey nodded in appreciation. Roberto noticed this and followed suit.

"The Socotto family offered me an insulting amount of money," continued Bennito. "They made it clear that it was a take it or leave it offer." All three fell silent for a few moments. "Joey, I need you to make this go away!"

"I understand, Don Bennito." With that, the meeting was concluded.

When they had left the room and were well out of earshot, Roberto looked to Joey.

"Is making it go away what I think it is?" he asked.

"Yes," said Joey, whispering. "If you are not up to it, Roberto, do not worry. I will see it through."

120

Roberto stared at Joey. "Joey, I am in this family because I love the Don. I am on your team because I love you. We will do this together."

Joey put his arm around Roberto. "We are doing nothing until we have had a good, stiff drink in the Spring."

Later that day, Joey put his team to work searching and ferreting around, finding out when and where would be a good time and place to make the hit. They received information after a week from Carlo Mazzola, a family foot soldier who had friends in various families, that Socotto would be in Verdi's, a restaurant, on Thursday for a meal and a meeting with Jimmy Tierney, an Irish leader who readily teamed up with the Socotto family when they needed muscle in number. Tierney also provided cheap potcheen made to Irish recipes for the Socotto bars. They were meeting to put their weight behind something and Joey guessed that it was to take over the Palm Spring.

Thursday came round soon enough and Roberto was feeling on edge. He kept himself occupied all day. He washed his clothes, then washed them again. He went to a barbershop and had his hair cut; he took a Turkish bath; he ate lunch at two separate restaurants, having spaghetti carbonara at Luigi's in the Bronx and a lasagne in Bruno's off Fifty-Third Street. He did anything to keep his mind off the job that he needed to do that night.

Finally, 7 pm arrived and the honk of a horn outside told Roberto that Joey was waiting. Roberto had changed three times, being conscious not to wear clothes that would show sweat stains. He did not want to let anybody know, especially Joey, that he may be nervous. In the end, he had settled for a brown, wide-lapelled pinstripe suit with baggy trousers, a white shirt, and a plain brown tie. He wore brown shoes with a white border and spats. He finished the look with a brown fedora hat flashing a white band sitting comfortably on the brim. He took one last look in the mirror, tilted the hat, and left to meet Joey.

I look calm and collected, he told himself, which was the complete opposite of how he felt. His hands were clammy and churning inside his stomach made him regret the two lunches he'd eaten five hours earlier.

Joey was in the Oldsmobile, waiting. The car was familiar and friendly with its black interior, only distracted by the silver wire around the inside of the steering wheel to be used when the horn was required. The white headlining was discoloured from the constant smoke of cigars that Joey devoured like others chewed sweets.

121

Sitting on the back seat was Molly Rogers, the manageress of the Black Cat Club, one of the Bronx clubs run by Joey and Roberto. Mollie was a good aide to Benni and the Family. She was in her late thirties and had dark brown hair. She wore a tight suit with a fishtail skirt, a style popular at the time, and nylons with a thick line up the back. Drenched in heavy makeup, a cigarette in a four-inch holder completed the look. Next to Molly on the seat sat a violin case. Roberto knew it was a Thompson machine gun – sometimes referred to as a Chicago typewriter. The actual case was not a violin case at all, but remarkably similar in shape, hence the reason why people thought they were violin cases.

"We have discussed a hundred times what we are going to do," said Joey. "Are you okay with everything?"

Roberto nodded in answer to Joey's question.

"Don't worry, kid, the first is the hardest one. It gets easy after that."

Roberto nodded again. He would rather be anywhere in the world than here right now.

They arrived outside Verdi's restaurant at 7.45 pm and parked twenty yards away from the entrance door, tucking in behind other parked cars. Both men shunted down into their seats so that they'd be partly hidden in front of the windscreen. At 7.59 pm prompt, a red and black hand-painted Lincoln drew up outside Verdi's. The paint job was a one-off and not a factory colour. Four men got out of the car; all wore overcoats and fedoras, two were hiding pineapple guns. They began looking around in all directions – over the car, down the side and behind. One of the men nodded and two more men evacuated the car, Socotto and Tierney. Socotto nodded to the men, who returned to the car and drove off.

The first mistake, thought Joey.

Socotto put his arm around Tierney and guided him into the restaurant. Joey and Roberto could see the waiter welcome them and guide them to a table against a wall, midway down the room with a clear view of the door. Joey was ahead of the game. He'd anticipated this.

They let fifteen minutes pass, allowing Socotto and Tierney to settle. At 8.15 pm it was 'party time'. Roberto and Mollie stepped out of the car. Roberto put on a black mohair overcoat, while Mollie put a camel-coloured overcoat over her shoulders.

"Are you okay, Bobby?" It was a name she often affectionately called Roberto.

"Yes," he answered.

Mollie picked up on the dryness in his mouth through his voice. "You will be great."

He really did not want to be there. He thought of Joey's words: *"Socotto will know me a mile away. He won't know you or Mollie."*

It made so much sense to Roberto that this was his job. They arrived at the entrance to the restaurant and entered, laughing and joking to the outside world but trembling inside. Mollie linked arms with Roberto. Both had their collars raised to be less recognisable.

"Good evening, Sir, Madam," The head waiter greeted them with a smile.

"Good evening," Roberto replied. "We have a table booked in the name of Hudson?"

Not very inventive to use the main river that flows through New York! Mollie thought.

They were ushered to a table, where they sat down. They sat six tables away and at a right angle to Socotto's table. Roberto could see the back of Socotto and the side of Tierney. After a further ten minutes, Roberto stood and went to the gents. He was much calmer now. He washed his hands and face and turned to walk back into the restaurant. His trousers were baggy for a reason. His hands were in his pockets, his right hand cradling a .38 pocket pistol – the everyman's gun. Pocket pistols were meant to be carried in one's pocket and used in close-quarter self-defence scenarios. It had just enough stopping power for working up close but would lose its power over a distance. You could buy it in two varieties, the revolver and the auto pistol. The revolver would hold five to six rounds, the auto seven. Roberto chose the revolver.

As he re-entered the room, he had to walk past the table where Socotto and Tierney were sitting. He walked up slowly, smiling at Mollie, who was smiling back. The perfect husband returning to his adoring wife, maybe. All of a sudden, he stopped at Socotto's table a yard away; the gun was out of his pocket and the first bullet hit Tierney in the cheek, the second in his chest. Before Socotto could react, the third bullet was resting in his brain via the middle of the forehead. Another bullet for each of the casualties and Roberto's arm dropped to his side, stiff and straight. He dropped the gun, set his eyes on the door, and walked slowly. Mollie was by his side, having manoeuvred from the table with perfect timing.

The forty-plus diners were panicking and shouting. Roberto heard the shrills of the female screams as one. He was acutely aware of the sound.

123

Everybody panicked and ran to the exit and, just as planned, Roberto and Mollie mingled with them, jogging to the entrance intermingled with the rushing people, using them as a human decoy. They had now reverted back to normal diners.

As Roberto reached the door, Socotto's car screeched to a halt and the four men from before raced out brandishing handguns. They rushed towards the door of the eatery. They shuffled nearer to each other the closer they got to the entrance, all angling for the small door as one. This was perfect, as a small target area was always easier than a widespread one.

Once they were all within ten feet from the door, they were bombarded with a hail of bullets from Joey's Thompson. He'd been waiting in the shadows, just in case. The first man was propelled backward, the second and third just fell on the spot. The fourth man was hit in the leg. Still active, he raised his gun to Joey, but Joey was highly fuelled on adrenalin. He set another volley of a dozen bullets towards the last man until he crumpled like a sack of potatoes.

The exiting diners panicked again. Some froze, some ran left, some ran right, and some turned and went back inside Verdi's. Roberto and Mollie remained calm. Joey smiled and winked. The three of them then jumped into the Oldsmobile and Joey sped off into the night. They heard the sound of sirens aiming for the scene they had created. Roberto's first hit was adrenalin-filled, exciting, and successful. He would never worry about committing murder again!

***

During the first year, Benni regularly sent a small frigate to Liverpool where Giovanni and the Italian family he'd built up in Liverpool stocked a warehouse full of top-grade Scottish and Irish liqueur, which they specialised in. The team travelled far and wide to gain the illicit cargo, from Belfast to Dublin, from Glasgow to London. Giovanni ensured that the small cargo ship sent from New York every other Wednesday to Liverpool returned with not even enough space to load a bottle extra. After a slow start a year ago, where the cargo had been about sixty percent full, the past nine months had been so productive that it allowed Giovanni and his mother, Maria, to move out of the Liverpool docks area and onto the Wirral, on the other side of the Mersey, in a house that they could have only dreamt of a year earlier. It was a modern Edwardian property with running water, a fireplace in every room, and high ceilings with coving around. It boasted lovely views over to the Irish sea. It seemed there was no end to this life of luxury.

In the meantime in New York, Roberto was becoming a major asset to Benni and the Rossi family. He ran the Liverpool job, becoming irreplaceable in many areas of the family business. Don Bennito and Joey were impressed with his handling of the Socotto 'whack'. Another whack about a month later went smoothly – a bent FBI agent, who would not help the family out with vital information after having been on the payroll for five years.

Two years after arriving in America, and with the experience that Roberto gained, it made perfect sense to let him go back to England where the Family could do further joint ventures.

"Roberto," Bennito had said, "We must move with the times. Prohibition has been the goose that laid the golden egg for us, but it will not last forever. England is in turmoil and has just witnessed a general strike. Capitalism is under threat. We must strike while the iron is hot. England must be our next opportunity."

Roberto was delighted to be held in such high esteem by Don Bennito, and felt flattered at being allowed to advance the Family's fortunes. During his time in America, Roberto had married Toni on their anniversary of him seeing her in Piccolo Italia. This was agreed to by her father, mainly because everybody knew not to cross Don Bennito, but deep down he was worried about his daughter's future. Don Bennito, however, was overjoyed that his prodigy had managed to find a beautiful Italian girl to marry. After all, a settled married man was always more stable and less of a risk than a happy-go-lucky singleton.

Toni was still in the early stages of her pregnancy, making this the perfect time to travel to England before she was heavily laden with child – or, indeed, travelling the Atlantic with a young baby. She was excited about the move to England, which would allow Roberto time to grow his 'entertainment' business, something which he did not talk excessively about. The plan was for Roberto to make himself the one and only UK Godfather linked to the Rossi Family, with Bennie taking a skim from the UK activities of fifteen points, or fifteen percent. Whoever heard of the mafia being active in England? It was a perfect guise for both sides of the Atlantic.

And so, Roberto returned to the UK in July 1924 aged 24 and with a pregnant, 21-year-old wife. New York streetwise, a business up and running supplying the ever thirsty New York speakeasies, and a fantastic

125

modern Edwardian house, Roberto was a more than a capable boss. Life was at a good point. Roberto, the new Don of the UK, was going to set up a business exactly as it should be set up, the mafia way. He sat down with his brother, Giovanni, for the first time since leaving for America.

"You have done well, Giovanni. Thank you for your efforts," he said with a warm smile and a nod of the head. "The world awaits. We will sit down many times over the coming weeks and set up the business to mirror the New York operation. We need to think about new areas of the business to develop. Prohibition will not last forever, there is already a movement to lift it across all the states. But we will need to work big if we want to keep this lifestyle."

He looked around the large room they sat in. "We will continue to work with Benni and the Rossi Family. From now on, we are the Sartori Family and I am Don Roberto," *I like the sound of that*, he thought.

"I have been initiated by Don Bennito," he continued. "But, more of that later. First things first. I need to take the family out for a good Italian meal and introduce you all to the most stunning woman Italy has ever produced. My wife, Toni."

CHAPTER TWENTY-FIVE

Jonty sat down in the August evening sun at home enjoying a glass of red wine whilst watching an Agatha Christie film. The setting sun was just beginning to prove that nightfall was slowly edging earlier by the day, a sign that autumn would arrive in the next few weeks. His mobile phone rang, disturbing the tranquility of the evening, he decided to change the ringtone from 'Dixie' to a more acceptable traditional tone. He shuddered at the vision of Louise's face when Dave rang from the Chinese restaurant. He glanced at the screen on his now ageing Nokia cell phone, 'incoming call' notifying him that he did not have the caller in his contacts list, therefore it could be anybody.

"Jonty Ball?" Jonty scowled down at the phone, as he always did just in case it was somebody trying to sell him life insurance or some fantastic 'do not miss this investment opportunity deal.'

"Jonty, it's Shep."

"Shep, how are you? I was only talking about you last week with Dave." The line went silent for a few seconds.

"It's Dave I'm calling about," said Shep. "He passed away earlier today. He had another heart attack, but didn't pull through it this time."

"God, Shep…" said Jonty, shocked. "I don't know what to say. I assume there will be a post-mortem?"

"I don't know, Jonty. It only happened today. Even though the warning signs were there – bad diet, drank too much, no exercise, overweight – it still comes as a shock, doesn't it, mate?"

"It does, Shep." Jonty needed a moment to digest the news. "Can you keep me up to speed with the funeral arrangements? I assume you will be going?"

"Yes, I will," said Shep. "It will be good to catch up again."

The phone went dead. Jonty turned off the film and sat quietly, thinking about the times spent with Dave.

He chose to remember Dave in his prime, a good-looking, tall, dark-haired man with a wicked sense of humour. He smiled as he thought of the childish tricks Dave had got up to in the past. He remembered the time when Dave had stapled Shep's arms at the bottom of his sleeves and tipped in a tubful of maggots; Shep chased him around the building with everybody watching, laughing till it hurt in the stomach. Dave had purchased the maggots from the local fishing shop. Or the time when he'd got Jonty himself; Dave had swapped the soap in the gents for some trick soap that made Jonty's face go black.

Dave told Jonty there was a black mark on his face and asked, "What have you been up to?"

Jonty went to the gents to investigate, but when he got there the mirror had been taken down. Unbeknown to Jonty, it was Dave who had taken it down. He would go to great lengths for a simple two-minute joke. The rest fell in place. Jonty washed his face with the soap in the soap dish and he came back with his face as black as the Ace of Spades. Everybody was in on the joke – except, of course, Jonty. He was received by a barrage of comments like "Has the coalman delivered today?" Shep decided to sing the Al Jolson song, 'Swanee'. Jonty only noticed when he was driving out at lunchtime that the face in the rearview mirror looked peculiar.

Jonty sighed as he recalled the memories. He smiled, raised his glass, and said aloud, "To you, Dave, for all the great times, mate."

The next morning Jonty decided to visit Dave's house to see what he could do to make the house look a little neater for the funeral, that was the least he felt he could do for Dave. He worked his way through the lounge into the small kitchen and then into the back garden. The garden itself wasn't a large area, maybe ten metres square. Like the house, it certainly hadn't been tended, the grass was knee-high. Overgrown roses and a private hedge completed the back boundary. The hedge looked like it hadn't been trimmed for a couple of years or more. The side boundary was nothing more than a dilapidated wooden fencing set in concrete posts. It certainly hadn't seen any creosote or preserver for many a year.

Oh, Dave, lad, where did it all go wrong? Jonty thought, before looking up at the sky. It was a breezy day, with a blue sky broken in many places with cotton wool-shaped clouds racing across as the wind pushed and controlled the flow at will. He had a recharged glass of Scotch in his hand, neat with ice. He became suddenly transfixed at what he saw in front of him. Somebody had been in the garden recently.

He could see that part of the panel fencing had collapsed and that the break was fresh. The wood at the point of the snap was clean. Where the snap in the fence was identified, the knee-length grass was showing obvious signs of having been trod on. There was a line of flatter and lighter-coloured grass showing that a trail had been made. It reminded

Jonty of the trampled crop circles he had seen on TV programmes. It was not to the back of the house, but in the corner of the garden, where a clump of beautiful flowers sat, all in varying colours of red, white, and purple. He was drawn to the purple flowers; they had trumpet-shaped heads and flowed majestically downwards towards the ground. They stood out in the rough-looking garden. From the flowers, the trampled evidence of a path then led to a patio door at the back of the house, on the outside wall of the dining room portion of the kitchen.

***

Later that evening, Jonty met up with Helen, Helen had already turned the house lights on as the day was turning dark and gloomy. She was dressed casually in a pair of tight-fitting Levi's and a trendy postbox red sweatshirt. Jonty liked the look. Jake and Em had both thrown on jeans and trainers, with Jake wearing a dark blue Fred Perry top with light blue piping around the collar and sleeves. Em took the same view as Helen and put on a grey and blue sweatshirt.

Jonty told them of his findings from his visit to Dave's house.

"But, what does that all mean?" Helen asked.

"Well," continued Jonty, "the problem we have is if there will be a post-mortem, or not. The process is as follows." He took a drink of water from the glass that Helen placed on the kitchen table where they sat. "When a death is reported to the office, the report is given to the coroner to decide on the next step. The coroner may be satisfied that the death is due to natural causes and he may choose to take no further action."

Helen smiled at Jonty as he continued. "If, however, the coroner decides it is necessary to investigate further, he will order a post-mortem examination. He tends to do this if the cause of death is unnatural, such as following a fall or assault, or the cause of death is potentially unnatural, or the cause of death is unknown."

Jonty looked around at everyone. "Are you all with it up to now?" They all nodded. "Even if the cause of death is likely to be natural, it is necessary to find out what disease or condition was involved, or if the deceased died in custody or otherwise in the care of the State. You know the sort of thing."

Jonty looked down and his voice lowered. "The problem is, the early signs show that the coroner is tilting towards natural causes due to

129

Dave's history of heart problems. But Shep managed to get enough detail to limp it over the line for a post-mortem because he could be blocking a murder inquiry. All the relevant people agreed to it and a post-mortem is now going to take place."

Jake picked up on Jonty's lack of excitement about the post-mortem. "That's good news, isn't it?" he asked.

"Yes and no," replied Jonty. "It's great news. The only problem is that, if there are no suspicious circumstances found, it will blow our case and all our work dead out of the water."

The others looked at him blankly. Jonty continued. "The coroner has ordered a forensic post-mortem, which is a more detailed examination performed by a specially trained pathologist."

"So, what happens next?" Helen asked.

"When the post-mortem is completed," Jonty explained, "the pathologist will report the causes of death found to the coroner. The coroner will review the information and do one of two things, If the post-mortem shows that the deceased died of natural causes, he will then issue paperwork to allow the death to be registered and take no further action."

"And the second?" Jake asked.

"If the post-mortem shows an unnatural cause of death, or if the cause of death could not be found at this stage, the coroner will open an investigation or an inquest. This is an inquiry which may be followed by a fact-finding court hearing about the circumstances of the death."

They all sat listening to the picture being painted by Jonty.

"How long will it take?" Helen asked.

"When a post-mortem is needed," replied Jonty, "the next step is to order a summary of the deceased's medical history from their GP. This helps the pathologist interpret their findings, and we cannot order a post-mortem without it. We are reliant on the GP surgery providing this promptly. Shep is chasing the GP as we speak." He went straight back on track. "It will take about five to seven working days from when the GP's summary is received. Results from a specialist post-mortem may take a little longer. What is it today? The 1st of September, so we should know by 14th September or the 21st maximum."

They all acknowledged the process needed to take its course.

"There is one more thing I need to tell you," Jonty added. "For me to get nearer to this case, it would be easier if I was back in the force. As Dave has now left a vacancy, Shep has organised for me to meet with

Superintendent Quinn, the day after tomorrow. It's early days, but to be honest all this has made me realise how much I miss the job."

Jonty arrived at 1.45 pm, fifteen minutes early for the 2 pm meeting with Quinn. Ros Drinkwater, Quinn's secretary, knew Jonty well. Ros was a vibrant thirty-something with legs that always had the constabulary heads turning. Her main hobby was skiing, which made her legs the perfection they were. She was quite plain-looking, with blonde shoulder-length hair. She knew her limits, strengths, and weaknesses, which she compensated for by always wearing a short, tight skirt with high heels. Above all, she was a very loving and generous person, which was what Jonty liked about her.

"Jonty, I saw your name in the diary. How are you?"

"I am great thanks, Ros. You're looking well. I hope you're not working too hard?"

Ros smiled. "You know what it's like Jonty. We moan about being overworked and underpaid, but what about you? You have escaped once, but now you want to come back to the zoo with the lions."

That made Jonty smile.

"Let me get you a drink," continued Ros. "Coffee? White with one, right?"

"You have a good memory, Ros."

At two o'clock precisely, Superintendent John Quinn came out of his office and strode up to Jonty, smiling with his hand held out ready for the inevitable handshake. Jonty accepted the invite and shook Quinn's hand.

"You are looking well, Jonty. Please…" With that, Quinn made a slight bowing action and gestured for Jonty to go into his office.

"Ros, can you arrange refreshments?"

"Already in hand, sir," was the reply from Ros. As Quinn turned away, Jonty turned his head to Ros, who gave him a wink with both her thumbs pointing up and mouthing "Good luck."

They were thirty minutes into the interview and it was all mostly routine stuff – which, with Jonty's experience, was straightforward. Up to now, Jonty felt he was cruising through it.

"Jonty," said Quinn, "I know you are looking into the death of Dave outside the force."

Jonty remained quiet, taken aback by the Superintendent's statement. He nodded to Quinn in acknowledgement.

131

"I would love you back in the team," Quinn continued. "My issue is this, Jonty. If I take you back on and add you to any potential inquiry, dependent upon the pathologist report will you return to retirement after the case is closed, successful, or otherwise?"

Jonty had half expected this question. Quinn continued. "How old are you now, Jonty?"

"Sixty-two," replied Jonty in a low, resigned voice.

"And you're in good health?" Jonty nodded back. "I know you are a man of your word, Jonty." Jonty knew what was coming, but it came anyway. "If I give you your old job back, I would want you here until you're sixty-five."

Quinn was watching Jonty. "I can swing it with the powers above about taking on a sixty-two-year-old, but I want some commitment from you. You can have the job, Jonty. I can always do with good men like you, but I will not offer it unless you commit to sixty-five, health allowing."

Jonty looked at Quinn. "Can I get back to you by lunch tomorrow? Let me sleep on it."

"I would be happy for you to sleep on it. A snap decision now may not convince me."

The next twenty hours saw Jonty swaying from accepting to declining the offer in his mind. He enjoyed retirement but, on the other hand, he missed the daily banter at the station. He missed the camaraderie in the local pub after a day's work. He missed the force.

Ros picked up the phone and spoke in her usual welcoming voice. "Good afternoon, Greater Manchester Police, Superintendent Quinn's Office."

"Hi, Ros, it's Jonty. Is the Super in?"

"Only if you are saying yes," she laughed. "I will put you through now." He could hear her laugh tailing off as the call was transferred to hold. Fifteen seconds later, the line came to life again.

"Jonty, thanks for getting back to me." It was Quinn. "Have you considered our discussion?"

"Yes, I have, Superintendent. I would like to take up the job offer. I will give you the promise that I will stay with the force until sixty-five and, as you added yourself, health allowing."

The reply was genuine and warm. "Fantastic news, Jonty. Great to have you back on board."

"One thing, though, Superintendent," said Jonty.

132

"What is that, Jonty?" replied Quinn.

"I can work on the case regarding Dave, and anything that may fall out of it?"

"Deal," replied Quinn. "You were on it, anyway. Let's say a start date of October?"

"How about next Monday?" replied Jonty.

"Next Monday it is."

Jonty smiled. He knew that he could make things happen quicker and more effectively with a team around him and the strong arm of the law as his bargaining power.

Helen, Jake, and Em all congratulated Jonty when he told them of the news.

"And don't forget, eight tonight you are taking me out for a celebratory meal," said Helen. Em looked at Jake and nodded her head knowingly, their suspicion that Jonty and Helen were becoming an item again was taking another step nearer.

Three days after the phone call with Jimmy 'Shep' Shepherd, Jonty was sitting with Jake and Em discussing what steps to take next. Jonty did comment on Jack Evans. "I know Edward Le Conte was doing his job defending Evans, and he does it every day of the week for some criminal or another. But I think it would be wise to keep an open mind about him."

"I agree," Jake said.

"Dave wasn't always a slob," blurted Jonty. "He was smart and quick in his younger days."

"I am sure he was," acknowledged Jake.

"We went on a station day out at Haydock races once," Jonty continued, with the beginnings of a smile. "By the last race, Dave lost all his money backing losers in every race. Instead of pacing his bets throughout the day, he just went for it," His smile broadened as he continued. "We booked an evening meal and we were going to go on for a drink afterwards," Jake was smiling as Jonty told the story.

"Shep said to him, if you run onto the racecourse and jump the fence in front of the stands, we will all club together and pay for your beer tonight" Jonty paused. "Well, that was a great deal for Dave. He ducked under the railings, ran fifty yards away from the fence, turned and faced the fence, then hurtled towards it. When he got there, he threw himself at the fence and landed on the top of it."

Jonty was giggling like a schoolgirl as he told the story. The infectious giggle was now joined by those of Jake and Em.

"Well, the fence was made of thatch," continued Jonty. "He rolled over it, scraped and cut." He was roaring with laughter now as he remembered the story, and he pictured it in his mind. "He rolled over the fence and fell five feet into the water. It was the water jump. Well, we were in stitches laughing at him," Jonty was struggling to get the words out he was laughing so much. "To make it even funnier, there was a local cop waiting for him. He applauded Dave and said, 'Well done son, now come with me.'"

Jonty was now in hysterics, and the more he laughed the more Jake laughed. They were setting each other off.

"If we weren't in the force, we would never have got away with it," said Jonty. "The Haydock cop just said 'I am glad I don't work with you lot, have a great night.'"

The two men laughed for another two or three minutes without talking. As the laughter began to ebb, Jonty said, "He was a good lad, Dave. They broke the mould after him."

Jonty turned to Jake. "One of the driving forces that has opened all this up is our belief that you are Paul reincarnated." He was looking Jake square in the eye now, the laughter had subsided. "We need one last visit to Jameson."

"I know," said Jake.

"Are you okay with that, Jake?" Jonty continued. "The last time Jameson brought you out of the regression was because you were getting highly agitated, and Jameson said he was worried about the pressure on your heart."

"I knew this conversation was coming, Jonty," said Jake. "But I know I have to go through with it to move this case along." He paused. "Throughout my life, I always knew I was reincarnated. I want to help Paul, and I want to help Helen." His voice lowered. "I know we made the conscious decision for me not to meet Sue and Tommy, but it's for them as well."

CHAPTER TWENTY-SIX

LIVERPOOL 1928

17th October 1928 saw the proudest day of Roberto's life, when his daughter, Francesca Maria, was born. Toni had carried Francesca so strongly, her five foot ten frame and wide hips making childbirth easier than most first births. Francesca Maria was born at 7.15 am weighing in at eight pounds six ounces. Her head was covered with a mop of black curly hair, and she had the natural olive colouring that mirrored Toni's fluorescent skin. Their Edwardian home was large enough to accommodate the guests that arrived on 15th October, in expectation of the happy event that was due anytime. The guests included Don Bennito and his wife, Edita, Toni's parents Azzo and Abrianna Carlucci, and Roberto's friend and mentor, Joey Costa, all expenses having been paid by the excited Roberto.

The days the guests spent together were fantastic; it was a time for Edita and Maria to chat the night away about old Palermo, about the times Roberto senior and Benni looked young and strong, and how they used to go to ice cream parlours called Gelaterias. They laughed at how people would give the two young men preferential treatment because of Benni and Roberto's reputation. Edita and Maria knew that something was wrong with the work their boyfriends were involved in, but they also liked the first-class treatment that they received.

Don Bennito asked Roberto to set up a meeting between them and Joey and Giovanni. Roberto booked a private room at the Royal Hotel in the centre of Liverpool. It was a large room with gold-painted plasterwork around the room, with two golden liver birds at the head of the room. The liver birds are synonymous with Liverpool and they sit on top of the Royal Liver Building overlooking the River Mersey. On the top of each tower they stand, the mythic liver birds, designed by Carl Bernard Bartels. The birds are named Bella and Bertie, looking to the sea and inland, respectively. Popular legend has it that while one giant bird looks out over the city to protect its people, the other bird looks out to sea at the sailors coming into port. Alternatively, local legend states that one liver bird is male, looking inland to see if the pubs are open, whilst the other is female, looking out to sea to check whether any handsome sailors are coming up the river.

The room they sat in was probably too large for a meeting of four. They sat around a table that could dine twenty comfortably; but, as money was no longer an object, comfort won hands down. They ordered a meal, which was typically English, comprising a pea and ham soup starter, fish, caught fresh from the Mersey, with chips and peas. This was an old favourite English meal, but new to Benni and Joey. Both Lancashire and London had staked a claim to being the first to invent this famous meal – chips were a cheap, staple food of the industrial north, whilst fried fish was introduced in London's East End. In 1839, Charles Dickens referred to a "fried fish warehouse" in his novel, *Oliver Twist*. This was followed by a dessert of Bramley apple pie and custard. Benni and Joey both enjoyed the change from Italian food.

"Thank you for the hospitality, Don Roberto."

Roberto smiled. "You are welcome, Don Bennito." All four men smiled. They were comfortable in each other's company that only history and family connections can bring together.

"Let us reflect where we are," opened Don Bennito, "and where we need to be to ensure our family still has the standard of living to which we have become accustomed."

"As you are aware, we still have the export and import business working very well," said Giovanni.

Bennito nodded to Giovanni, who was referring to the first-class whiskey and Scotch production that Giovanni was still mass-producing.

"In the US, it is strongly believed that prohibition has a limited time," replied Bennito. "Maybe two or three years, who knows? The one thing we do know is that the beginning of the end has started," They all took a second to absorb his words.

"And, whilst the tapering off should be considered to start from now," continued the elder Don, "there will be a crossover if we plan this correctly." The others looked at him for inspiration. "If we start a new business now that is different, we need to time it correctly," he continued, "we can allow the bootlegging income to fall and we will not forgo any difference in our income streams, as the new business replaces the lost income."

Roberto was always impressed by the simplistic way in which Don Bennito explained things.

"Don Roberto, what are your views?" asked Benni.

136

"Thanks for your valued foresight, Don Bennito," said Roberto. He nodded towards Benni before continuing. "As I see it, England is a rapidly changing political landscape." He looked at Joey and Giovanni; he knew he had to inspire some wisdom right here and now. "Earlier this year, Emmeline Pankhurst, the leading suffragette from Manchester, died. Shortly after, women were granted equal voting rights with men. This was a major success for Emmeline and the suffragettes." He looked upwards as if choosing his words carefully before continuing.

"Two years ago, in 1926, there was an earthquake that shook the very foundations of British capitalism. In the greatest display of militant power in its history, the British working class was moved into action in the general strike of 1926. For nine days, from 3rd May, not a wheel turned nor a light shone without the permission of the working class. In such a moment, with such power, surely it ought to have been possible to have transformed society?"

Roberto took a sip from his wine glass before continuing. "How can such a position have ended in defeat?" His three colleagues looked at him. "If the strike did not make the desired change meant by the working class, and it didn't, I see this as a weakness, and weakness gives us an opportunity."

Don Bennito looked impressed as he took a long, deep puff on his imported Havana cigar. He had taken the opportunity to have four dozen flown in direct from Cuba before he left for the United Kingdom. After all, some luxuries just have to be bought.

"I like your thinking, Don Roberto," said Joey, giving maximum respect.

Roberto continued. "The UK has experienced industrial stagnation. This was particularly marked in the UK coal industry. The declining industry led to lower wages and increasingly bitter trade disputes. This culminated in a general strike. The miners went on strike for better pay and conditions, and were joined by some other trade unions. However, the general strike was only partial and led to the defeat of the miners. During the general strike, the middle class enthusiastically filled in for jobs helping to break the strike and increase a sense of class and social division. My view is that we throw our weight into the weakness of the coal industry." This was received with three nods of appreciation.

"Besides," continued Roberto, "a very recent 1928 survey showed that fourteen percent of the population of Liverpool was living in poverty. This was, of course, poverty in the loosest sense of the word."

He continued, aware that the three men sitting around the table were hanging on to his every word, mentally counting the cash it may bring. "In these days, poor people are living at barely survival levels. Liverpool is suffering a shortage of houses. Overcrowding is common, as is slum housing."

Benni shook his head, genuinely empathetic with the Liverpool plight. "This sounds like old Sicily," he said under his breath.

Roberto nodded in acknowledgement. "The council built houses, but nowhere near enough to solve the problem. This got me thinking, where does that leave us?" He paused for a moment, letting his words digest. "I paid five guineas to a London firm of economists, a Roberts, Fraser, and Son. They lead the field in predicting all areas of future financial situations."

Roberto produced three identical leather-bound reports, each of about forty pages in length. "I have a copy for each of you." Joey was impressed with his foot soldier of days gone by.

"Their remit was to predict the future for Liverpool's financial stability," said Roberto, "which, in turn, should indicate whether we would like to stay in this area to apply our business."

This is impressive, thought Benni.

"After six months of research, calculations and calculated risks," added Roberto, "Dave Flannigan, an economist at Roberts and Fraser, made an important point." His audience waited with bated breath. "Flannigan makes the point that Liverpool would suffer severely from the predicted depression of the 1930s and that up to a third of men of working age would be made unemployed."

"What is your strategy?" asked Benni.

Roberto looked into the eyes of each of his three friends in turn. "I think we should move away from Liverpool, now, If we stay, we will be doing business in a declining city with a declining industry, increasing poverty and no income generation for us to take a share of. Instead, we should move to Manchester, about twenty miles east. We will be in the heart of the mining community. There are over fifty mines, all within fifteen miles of Manchester."

More nods greeted his words. "We can be in first, before anybody else exploits the weakened workforce after the failure of the general strike," he said. "We can offer protection to the mining companies to ensure the miners will not rise again. They may be weak now, but you can bet your bottom dollar that the companies will be worried in case they rise again. We can keep them down and productive – for a fee, of course."

Benni smiled. "The perfect protection racket?"

Roberto looked his Don in the eye. "The perfect protection racket." he said, returning the smile.

CHAPTER TWENTY-SEVEN

Dave's funeral took place following the post mortem. The sky over Manchester was grey; there was a threat of rain, but it was yet to arrive. Those attending would be leaving from Dave's house. Nobody was aware that Jonty had paid two hundred pounds out of his own money to pay for a professional deep clean of the house; it hadn't turned the proverbial pig's ear into a silk purse, but it did allow Dave to be leaving his home for the last time with some dignity. Jonty stood next to Shep, sharing a tot of Scotch while they waited for the cars to arrive.

Dave's daughter, Tracy, approached Jonty. He only recognised her when she was a few metres away; she had grown from the little stick insect of a kid he knew when the families were close, to a beautiful-looking young lady. She was tall and elegant, with very short-cropped black hair. She wore a knee-length black dress that appeared to float around her body as she walked.

"Hello, Uncle Jonty. Thanks for coming."

"Hello, Tracy. I didn't recognise you. I would not have missed today. Your dad and I go back a long way."

"I know," said Tracy. "It seems like only yesterday when we used to holiday with you."

An awkward silence fell between them. Jonty did not know what to say to the girl who was now a stranger. Her father and Jonty had worked in a profession that split families apart like a wood axe splitting firewood. She eventually moved on to circulate and to thank people for coming. Jonty and Shep remained quiet, Jonty broke the silence.

"I'm going out for a bit of fresh air, Shep. Catch you later," was all he could think to say.

Shep nodded in acknowledgement. The small room filled with family, friends, colleagues, and, whilst there was not a prolific number of people, the small room soon made it feel full and stifling. Jonty made his way through the crowd, who were mainly standing and taking the opportunity to catch up with people they hadn't seen in years.

Why do people only meet at weddings, birthdays, and funerals? Jonty thought.

"Have you seen D.I. Shepherd?" Jonty asked on his return.

The third person he asked said that Shep was talking to someone out at the front of the house. Jonty made his way to the gathering of people who were waiting for the hearse to arrive, Shep being amongst them. While people were focusing on the arrival of the cars, Jonty decided to check the garden again. He made a mental note that some flowers had been chopped, quite haphazardly. The dozen or so pretty-looking trumpets that had been deadheaded kept drawing his attention.

The entourage arrived, a black Mercedes hearse with the coffin resting in the back surrounded by flowers and wreaths. There were three separate wreaths at the side in yellow spelling the word 'DAD'. There were two cars for the close family members and then all the private cars followed. Jonty travelled with Shep.

The funeral went as well as any funeral can. The comforting words from the vicar helped Tracy.

Dave had requested a cremation and as the coffin drew closer to the curtains the dulcet tones of Sinatra's voice came through the piped music system. "When I was seventeen, it was a very good year."

CHAPTER TWENTY-EIGHT

It was the Thursday before Jonty was due to start his new job. They had arranged for Jake to see Dr. Jameson again before Jonty got tied up with his new job. Jonty and the three musketeers, as he had recently started calling Helen, Jake and Em, boarded the train at Piccadilly Manchester and were on their way to Euston London for yet another visit with Jameson. They decided to travel down the night before and were having their evening meal at the hotel they pre-booked. They were all relaxed. Helen wore a navy shift dress with her silver-style accompaniments. Jonty donned a pair of grey trousers, a navy shirt and a blue casual jacket. Jake wore a pair of cream chinos, a red and white dogtooth check shirt, and a pair of his favourite red Adidas shoes. Em also chose the casual look with a pair of her favourite tight-fitting white jeans and a navy and pink sleeveless top with a small V-neck showing the now fading summer tan.

Jake ordered a bottle of Champaign. As the waiter poured a glass for each of them, Jake raised his glass.

"I'm not very good at speeches," he began, "but I would like to raise a glass to Jonty and his new job. We all appreciate that he is doing it for the four of us, to finally get closure for Paul."

They all raised a glass and joined Jake. "To Jonty."

Jonty looked at Helen, Em, and Jake. "I also have a speech to make." His voice was a little shaky. Whilst being comfortable with the company he was in, he was naturally just a little shy and was not at his strongest giving speeches, even intimate ones with friends. "I want to thank you, Jake and Em, for allowing us to have the chance to search for Paul's aggressor. Also, for enabling me to be more open-minded in accepting that what happened to Paul was murder and not an accident."

He looked down at the small flowers placed in the vase in the middle of the table and slowly raised his eyes with a look of mischief in them. He felt the weight lift off his shoulders. He felt warm throughout his body, but cold in his hands.

He took another sip of the Champagne and continued. "It has also allowed me to spend time with Helen again." Helen smiled and placed both her hands over Jonty's large hand. "I would like to add that Helen has agreed to be my wife."

"Helen!" Em shrieked, so loudly that she could be heard several tables away. She was genuinely pleased for these two people whom she'd got to know better as time passed. "Helen, how wonderful. I am so pleased for you."

Helen picked up her handbag and brought out a small box with the word 'Cartier' written in gold lettering on the lid. Inside was a white gold single diamond ring. "I put it in my bag before we came down," she said, "because if I placed it on my finger it would be such a giveaway."

Jake turned to Jonty. "Well, you old fox you," He raised his glass again. "Congratulations to my two favourite Brits. May you have a long and happy life together."

Em, half listened, as she was already turning close into Helen and picking her hand up to look at the ring, which Jonty had placed on the third finger of her left hand.

"New job, new wife, new life," Jonty said. He lifted his glass and pointed it towards Helen. "I let you go years ago, Helen. I have been given a second chance, and I am not going to lose you again." He raised his glass. "To my beautiful future wife, Helen."

"To Helen!" Em and Jake said in unison as they raised their glasses and had another sip.

The evening continued in an atmosphere of excitement and they were all in a party mood.

Jake looked at Em and took her hand. "I haven't thanked you enough for the support you have given me on this journey," he said quietly. "I wanted to say I love you very much."

Em smiled back. "I have felt loved by you every day of my life. You are a lovely man and a lovely human being."

They made their excuses around ten-thirty, congratulating Jonty and Helen for a final time. Em could not wait any longer to take her husband to bed, her feelings of lust for him were strong. He was going to be worked hard later that night.

The next morning saw all four arriving in the dining room for breakfast, Helen and Em giggling like schoolgirls as they huddled together over the self-serve buffet-style food. Em was linking arms with

Helen, feeling so close to the lady who, only four months ago, she did not even know existed. Now, she was a woman with whom Em shared secrets.

Em selected a bowl of mixed fruit salad and yoghurt, while Helen chose porridge. Jake and Jonty chose the full English breakfast of bacon, eggs, sausage, mushrooms, tomato, baked beans, and fried bread. Jonty overdid things a little with three eggs and four sausages.

"I'm a growing man," he said to Jake, noticing the expression of surprise on his face.

"Well, you will be growing with that," Jake joked. "It would feed a small country"

Helen and Em sat down to join them. "Enjoy it," Helen said, nodding towards Jonty's feast. "It won't be on the menu when we are married."

They all laughed, except Jonty. "What have I done?" he asked.

Helen nudged Em. "Start as you mean to go on," they all laughed.

"What have I let myself in for?" said Jonty, blushing slightly as he looked down at his breakfast.

They arrived at Dr. Jameson's office about ten minutes before the one pm meeting. As usual, everything was spotless and looked like it had only been placed in the building yesterday. Nicola smiled at them all and welcomed them with a warm "Good afternoon". She scanned across all four of them, allowing her eyes to rest on Jake for a second or two longer, a detail that did not go unnoticed by Em.

Dr. Jameson invited them into the now-familiar office where the previous regressions had taken place. He asked Jonty what he expected out of the day's session.

"Well, Dr. Jameson, first may I thank you for the free service you have offered for the recent regressions. I do not want to take advantage of your generosity, so I fully expect today to be our final session."

Jameson nodded in acceptance. "And how is the case progressing?"

"We have several scattered leads which we need to pull together," Jonty said, keeping the details close to his chest. "The reincarnation has given us a direction to follow, but we can't use it in a court of law, as they would laugh us out of the courtroom."

"What if you start to get stressed in the regression?" Jameson said, looking at Jake. He stroked his chin as he continued. "It can be very dangerous. A lot of pressure would be put onto the heart, much more than you have seen to date. We don't know why, but it is a fact."

"I want to keep going as long as I can," Jake replied.

144

"In that case, I would want to put a heart monitor on you so I can keep an eye on you all the time," said Dr. Jameson. "Also, I would like you to take a lisinopril heart relaxing tablet before you go under."

"What is lisinopril?" asked Jake.

Jameson addressed the four of them. "Lisinopril belongs to a group of medicines called ACE inhibitors. These cause the blood vessels to relax, making it easier for the blood to pass through them. Lisinopril tablets are used to treat high blood pressure, heart failure, diabetic and kidney disease in patients with high blood pressure, patients who are stable but have had a heart attack within the last 24 hours, so on and so forth," Jameson paused for a moment. "A mainstream doctor would not recommend it in these circumstances and you can decline, but I think it is probably a good option just in case."

Jake agreed, but Em was worried. She felt a cold surge run through her body, starting deep in the stomach. "Can't we just call it off?" she eventually stirred up the courage to say.

Jake looked at his wife. "I need to do this, Em."

"Would you like to proceed, Jake?" asked Jameson.

"Yes, definitely," said Jake, looking at a nervous Em biting on her bottom lip.

Jameson pressed his intercom. "Nicola, could you please bring a lisinopril tablet?" He thought for a moment. "Ten milligrams please."

"Certainly, Mr. Jameson," came Nicola's voice out of the speaker in the white plastic box.

Five minutes later, Nicola knocked on the door with a tablet in a small, round, opaque bottle with a blue cap on it securing the pill. She also handed to Jake a disclaimer form, which he read through. It had the normal narrative, including the disclaimer: 'Should anything happen to me during any interaction between Mr. Christopher Jameson (MRCGP), Master of Science (MSc), either physically or mentally, it is solely the responsibility of myself. I am fully aware of any risks either mentally or physically that may occur and I take full responsibility.'

Jake signed the form.

***

Jake woke up to an intense bright light. He blinked as his eyes became accustomed to the environment he found himself in. He blinked a few times more. He saw the shape of a person holding his hand.

"Oh, Jake, we have all been so worried about you."

He recognised the voice – it was Em. He felt tired. His head felt like it was stuffed with cotton wool. He tried to raise it off the bed, but he couldn't. After about thirty seconds, his eyes began to focus and he could see Em. She looked worried, her eyes were red and tired. He looked around the room, his head moving very slowly. He realised he was in a hospital bed.

"Em, what happened?"

"Oh, Jake, we have been so worried," said Em tearfully. "You've been in the hospital for two days unconscious. You collapsed under hypnosis with Dr. Jameson." Em blew her nose with a handkerchief.

"What happened?" Jake asked again. Just as Em was about to answer, a nurse appeared from behind the blue crepe curtain surrounding the bed. She took Em by the arm.

"Doctor Singh will want to have a chat with Mr. Hughes." The nurse gave a sympathetic smile to Em. "Now, try not to bring any emotions to the fore."

"Can I stay with him a while?" asked Em.

"Yes, of course," the nurse replied.

Nurse Ginny Hammond was in her early forties, was married with twins, a boy, and a girl. She had been working her shift two days ago when Jake was brought into the Chelsea and Westminster Hospital with a suspected heart attack. She was a small, stout lady with unruly red, curly hair that was pulled back into an equally unruly ponytail. She had, however, been fantastic with Em, Jonty, and Helen as they worked shifts to sit with Jake, all praying for the moment of awakening to arrive. Now that Jake had regained consciousness, Em had to be strong. Jonty and Helen had left the previous evening. They'd caught the train home at six o'clock. Jonty had a new job to start the next morning.

146

CHAPTER TWENTY-NINE

MANCHESTER 1954

Roberto had made the most of his days since his meeting with Don Bennito all those years ago. The cold January day of 1954 was not a good day for Roberto; he was feeling upset, but no guilt about the warm tears running down his cheeks as he hugged Toni. They were standing by the large inglenook fireplace that was generating a roaring heat into the large sitting room. Giovanni, his brother, was sitting in the cream armchair. He was sitting with his body leaning forward, his arms resting on his thighs, whilst both hands were clasped around a 15-year malt and lemonade. They had just heard the sad news that Don Bennito had passed away.

Roberto had looked up to Don Bennito like a father. He thought of his two years in New York when he was young and fit and it seemed middle age would never come to Roberto. Bennie had died of a heart attack, the third he had sustained in five years.

"I will take the age of eighty-two to die like Benni," Giovanni told Roberto.

"Yes, it was a good innings," replied Roberto in the low, shaky voice that comes with tears. "The tickets are booked to travel tomorrow. We are on a train to London, stay over at the London Grande, and then fly on Thursday from London to New York."

Beginning in the 1950s, the predominance of ocean liners began to wane when larger, jet-powered airplanes began carrying passengers across the ocean in less time. The speed of crossing the ocean, therefore, became more important than the style of crossing it. The transatlantic crossing of London to New York had been reduced to between six and eight hours, a novelty at the time, but it offered significant advantages over sea travel. A journey by sea across the Atlantic took about five days, while air travel cut that down to about half a day.

Roberto joined Giovanni in a drink and sat on the vacant armchair opposite. "Do you remember when we met Benni in Liverpool and we ordered fish and chips?" he said. They both laughed.

"Yes," replied Giovanni.

147

Roberto reflected. "He gave me licence that day to set up the business of protecting the pit owners from further strikes after the general strike. He took a gamble with me."

"He took no gamble!," said Giovanni. "He knew you were good. Your plan was perfect, Roberto. Pure and simple."

They reflected on the plan. At a time when everybody was in turmoil, the owners of the coal mines could not afford any further conflict with the miners, or else the industry would have collapsed. Roberto and Giovanni arranged meetings with all the pit owners and offered a guarantee that no more strikes would take place. The owners of the first two pits took no notice of their advice and both disagreed, with one owner stating, "I will take my chances." His chances were poor, especially as, within five days, both pits sustained large, unexplained explosions, killing sixty men. The authorities crawled all over them, looking for financial retribution for the dead men's families.

Roberto worked hard, secretly preparing for the TNT to be set and timed to detonate for maximum impact. Of the next twenty-five mines he visited, twenty-four signed up as news of the explosions did the rounds, with rumours of planned tactics rife.

The only man not to sign up was Sir Philip Lewis, who was later found dead after an apparent horse-riding accident. Roberto told Lewis and all the other mine owners that he was a fair man and that, for the sum of two thousand guineas each per month, which equated to an annual income of £26,400 per pit. He promised not to charge each pit a different fee, guaranteeing equal rights. Giovanni and his foot soldiers managed this operation. The twenty-four pits brought in a gross income of £633,000. The outgoings consisted of putting the five most influential union leaders on a £2000 per year retainer, which more than trebled their annual salary from the pits, and payment to Don Bennito of £100,000 per year and another £20,000 to pay Giovanni's foot soldiers on an income or no pay basis to give them an incentive to get paid.

The import and export business brought in another £400,000 per year, which tapered down, as Don Benito had predicted, to £200,000 once the speakeasies turned into legitimate night clubs when prohibition was lifted on 5th December 1933.

Roberto was now living a lifestyle that his lateral thinking had bought over the years. He had moved from Liverpool in 1929. The five guineas paid for the professional advice was absolutely on the mark. The move to the outskirts of Manchester worked well; the access to the pits was masterminded by Roberto and he secured, for the next twenty years, an income that could only be dreamt of by the vast majority of people. He still loved Toni just as much as he did the first time he saw her; she had aged well and the comfortable lifestyle she enjoyed held back the ageing process, as she still only looked in her early forties,

"Giovanni and I were just discussing the old days with Benni," Roberto said to Toni.

She smiled. "And I thought you were in the entertainment business!" Toni still did not understand the business, but, like all family wives, she could bypass the detail for the luxury it brought. "I remember when we first came over, I was carrying Francesca. She is now twenty-seven and will be a mother herself soon."

In 1952, Francesca Sartori had met a tall, dark, handsome man whilst travelling to Italy to enjoy a three-week holiday with grandparents *Nonno* Azzo and *Nonnina* Abrianna Carlucci. *Nonnina* is a term of endearment meaning 'little grandmother'.

She had flown over to Italy to the family home before arranging a week's holiday with her grandparents in Limone, on the western shores of Lake Garda. Sat next to her on the plane was a tall, dark, handsome man who was going to Milan on business. He was taken aback by the beauty of Francesca; she had her mother's smouldering jet black hair and the same shade of chestnut brown eyes, which were large and round. She had a small, pixie-like nose, not seen as an average Italian nose, and the fullest lips he had ever seen, which were exaggerated by bright red lipstick. Her close-fitting pinstripe suit was so tight that she had to take half a normal stride as she walked. She wore a maroon flying saucer hat with a navy band around the rim to match her suit, which was the style of the time. She also held a matching soft leather Gucci clutch bag and high heel shoes that highlighted her shapely calves. There was a perfect straight line running up the back of what were expensive nylons.

The man began the conversation. "I am a nervous flyer," he said. "Please don't worry if I get nervous, and feel free to calm me down if you wish."

Francesca had heard hundreds of opening lines by men. This was different and she giggled because it took her by surprise.

"Of course," she giggled again.

"Then I will pray for bad air turbulence," the man's said.

"Would that not make your fear worse?" asked Francesca.

149

"I will take my chances."

Francesca giggled again. They chatted all the way to Milan and, as a result, the flight seemed to last only minutes and not the three and a half hours it actually took.

The man introduced himself as Ray. "Pleased to meet you."

"Pleased to meet you too," replied Francesca.

"When are you flying back?" asked Ray.

"In three weeks," replied Francesca. "And you?"

"Ten days. I have work for ten days."

They went through passport control together and waited for their luggage. Ray escorted Francesca to the exit doors, where he heard a voice in the distance.

"Francesca!" It was her grandfather waiting to pick her up.

She turned to Ray and shook his hand. "It has been a pleasure meeting you, Ray." She turned away, walked five yards turned, and then turned back again. Walking up to Ray, she kissed him on his cheek and giggled again. Then she was gone, but not without Ray enjoying the Munroe-style wiggle as she headed to meet her grandfather.

The time spent with her grandparents was precious to Francesca. She did not see enough of them due to the distance, so any time together had to be coveted. They spent three weeks based at the Hotel le Palme. It sat on the shore of the lake, with a stop outside where you could get the local steamers to the northern towns on the lake. It was an idyllic three weeks, but, like all holidays, the time passed too quickly. *Nonno* Azzo and *Nonnina* Abrianna were both in their late seventies now, and Francesca could tell that the energy in the elderly couple was disappearing quickly. They could both get about, but Azzo now had arthritis in his hands from years of fishing and untangling nets. Abrianna now needed a stick to get around and was bent over at nearly ninety degrees when she walked. Francesca felt a sadness weigh her down. She knew she would see them only a few more times in her life. Her grandparents dropped her off at the airport using the hire car they'd used through the entirety of the holiday.

Francesca sat in the departure lounge, feeling sad, the sudden bursts of emotion still convulsing through her. Her flight was delayed. The plane was still in London, waiting for the fog to clear before it could take off, which meant there would be a two-hour wait at least. She sat in her own world, thinking about her grandparents and remembering lovely childhood days in the hot Italian sun in Sicily, running around the garden

150

with *Nonno* Azzo, and eating perfectly cooked pasta at the long table in the garden that would regularly be full of friends and neighbours, all sitting under the lemon trees and the vines, amongst the sound of birds and animals.

It's funny, she thought, *at the time it was just a normal day. When you look back, you would do anything just to taste it all one more time.'*

Just then, she heard a voice over her shoulder. "A penny for them?" She turned and saw Ray smiling. "Hello!" he said.

"Hello!" she replied.

"I felt too nervous to fly alone," he said. "I need my support mechanism."

Francesca smiled. "Sit down, I could do with cheering up."

They eventually landed in London and got an internal flight to Manchester Ringway, the local airport that had opened in 1938. Just like the outward flight, the return flight went very quickly, Francesca didn't want the journey to end. She liked the look of this stranger in his double-breasted navy suit and slick black leather shoes, with a trilby hat that framed his face to perfection. She had never felt like this before, and she liked it.

For the next two years, Ray and Francesca were inseparable. They married at Manchester Cathedral, with Ray's working-class family taking full advantage of the free bar and a meal, which they had never experienced before, and all went home happy. Ray continued his job as a clothes designer and often commuted to Milan and back or Paris. Occasionally, Francesca would go with him, but not lately, as the baby in her stomach was growing and the young child would be born soon.

***

Roberto, Toni, and Giovanni all arrived in New York, with Roberto in bewilderment at the time they'd saved by flying. They'd arrived in under a day. He thought of the first time he'd come to see Benni on the liner *Mauretania*, which had taken four and a half days.

This was the second time the family had travelled to New York in the last six months. Edita, Benni's wife, had died from old age. She had been in a wheelchair for the last three years of her life; she'd continued to smoke cigarettes and Benni doted on her. When Edita died, a part of Benni died, too. He'd simply given up. Roberto expected him to die of a broken heart shortly after Edita, as they were inseparable.

151

New York gave Roberto mixed feelings. Some very warm memories were cancelled out by the death of Edita and, eventually, Bennito. Joey had been murdered ten years earlier by the remnants of the Socotto Family war following the 'whack' on their family boss by Roberto. Joey had been hanged from a forty-foot high crane, with his body hanging naked, dying with no dignity whatsoever. Roberto wanted revenge and asked permission from Don Bennito, but the old Don was wise.

"Then what, Roberto?" he had said. "They come and hit you or me? Do we then hit again? It is time to pass on this war." The two men sat in silence. "I need to meet the Socotto Family. They have taken an eye for an eye, as we would have done, we need to call a truce and I would like you to join me at the meeting."

"I don't know if I can do that, Don Bennito. It hurts," insisted Roberto.

"It hurts us all, my son." Roberto had never been addressed in that way by Benni, and he felt proud. "But business is what it is all about, that's all. Just business."

Another lesson learned in humility and acceptance at the correct point in time by Don Bennito. Don Bennito was calm and collected at the meeting with the Socotto Family, his voice never ranged higher than a steady tone and never lower than a whisper. The deal was done, the war was over, all were avenged.

Roberto travelled back on the plane with Toni by his side. "What's it all about Toni? This thing called life. We all battle for the best we can get and, in the end, no matter what you earn, it's all taken away."

Toni looked at Roberto. She had never seen him like this before. *Maybe it will change when the death of Don Bennito passes,* she thought, but remained quiet.

On 2nd April 1953, Francesca gave birth to an eight-pound and two-ounce baby boy. Ray could not have been more thrilled. The baby was born in Salford's Hope Hospital, which was the hospital nearest to Ray and Francesca's home in the well-to-do area of Worsley. Within an hour of the baby being born, Francesca's parents Roberto and Toni were at the hospital with a three-foot Steiff teddy bear. Toni felt wonderful, the strange kick of maternal blood flowing through her veins so strongly, like the Grande River flowing through her beloved Sicily. She felt warm and proud. She looked at the flawless complexion of her daughter and a feeling of pride sent a shiver down her back.

Roberto stood next to her, tall and proud. He was dressed in black trousers with a fawn-coloured polo neck top. Toni looked at Roberto, Francesca and the new baby, William. *This is just perfect, with all the people I love in one room together*, she thought. She asked Francesca if she could hold William.

"Please, Granny, I want you to," said Francesca. Toni smiled and Francesca giggled, the same giggle that Ray had fallen in love when they'd first met on the plane to Milan. She gave the baby a nuzzle with her nose, while Roberto looked over and tickled him under his chin.

"Hello," said Toni, gently picking up the baby and holding him in her arms. "Pleased to meet you. You are going to get spoilt something awful, aren't you, William Green…"

CHAPTER THIRTY

Jonty arrived early on his first day at work. It felt so unnatural to be returning to his old job; he thought he had retired forever and yet, within a year he was back in the old office, with the same desk. Everyone came up to him, welcoming him back, along with several quips.

"Glad you're back," said one colleague. "You bring the average age of the office up, so I am now under average."

"What's up?" said another. "Couldn't you find a better cup of coffee on civvi street?"

"Can't you afford your gas bills? So now you want the taxpayer to pay for them?"

The best came from Johnny Groves. "Glad you're back. Can you bring the leaving presents back, as I'm short this month."

It was lunchtime by the time Jonty felt that he could settle down and start the job. The first thing that he did was to look through the files regarding the death of Paul Jennings, to refresh his memory of what happened on that fateful night in June 1984. The paper files had turned yellow with age and there was a musty smell coming off the paper, which made Jonty instantly aware that he was digging into history and quite a way back.

Time always makes things harder to prove. It can mask the truth so much easier, he thought.

Jonty read the statements of Sue, Paul's wife, and Helen. Reading through the emotion in what they had to say, he knew there was nothing tangible to take forward from them.

He then read a five-page statement from Billy. He read it twice over and then concentrated on a paragraph on the third page of Billy's statement: "Paul was my friend, and if I hadn't let him go so early on the night I know he would have been OK. I feel responsible and if I could turn back the clock I would, but the inevitable happened."

Jonty highlighted this comment using a yellow highlighter pen. He read it again. Something in the terminology was not quite right. He thought about the words 'Let him go' and 'inevitable'. *And why did Billy feel responsible?* he wondered. Jonty knew that, when people make statements,

154

they often fall into their natural thought process, as nobody can stay out of their comfort zone very long. *But what does it mean?*

He then re-read the notes regarding the Jack Evans murder trial that Dave had given him before his heart attack. These raised questions, too.

Who is William Green? He seems to have disappeared off the map. Jonty knew that Green was Jack Evans' cousin. *What did that mean? What did the list with the six names mean? And how does this link to Paul, if at all?*

Jonty searched for a current address for Jack Evans, without any success. His last known address was on the Costa Brava in Spain. That in itself sent shivers down Jonty's spine. He knew that, whilst a lot of Brits retired there, or chased the sun, he also knew it was a haven for criminals to lie low, and he knew that Evans was not a retired pensioner, as evidenced by the bruising he'd sustained during the fracas in London. He also knew from the same meeting in London that Green was alive. *That's another plus from London*, he thought.

Five-thirty soon came around. It had been a typical first day, with nothing achieved, but a few new questions had been raised – tentative but raised nonetheless. Jonty left the office on time, as promised, to take Helen out for an evening meal as an 'end of first-day celebration', as Helen called it.

Helen had made a special effort and looked stunning in her black tight dress, higher at the hem than normal, black shoes and her trademark white silver watch, silver neckless, and a black leather handbag with a silver strap. When Jonty arrived home, he'd showered and put on a new navy suit with a crisp white shirt and navy and pink tie. Together, they looked a very attractive couple.

The evening went by smoothly, with Helen asking how his first day had gone. They met at eight and, by nine, the conversation about work had changed to what life would be like together. They discussed the idea of selling their respective houses and amalgamating the funds, allowing them to move upmarket, maybe to the country.

"Not on Billy's road, though," Jonty joked.

The meal was delicious. For the main course, Jonty chose a medium-rare fillet steak with a peppercorn sauce, whilst Helen picked through the most delicately cooked salmon with a lemon and lime sauce.

Jonty asked Helen if there was any news on Jake.

"I spoke to Em today," she replied. "He has made progress again and the doctor told him he will be fine and he can go home tomorrow morning."

She took another bite of the fantastic fish on her plate. "I told Em I will pick her up from Piccadilly station?"

"Good thinking," said Jonty. "Has Em told Jake what happened yet?"

"She has outlined the basics," said Helen, "but not the details, on doctor's orders."

Jonty nodded as if he was agreeing with the doctor.

"He told Em she can tell him in a few days," added Helen.

As they tucked into their dessert and a second bottle of wine, Helen took Jonty's hand and placed it on her thigh, using the tablecloth as cover. She placed his hand under her dress, where the stocking top met flesh. Jonty smiled.

"I assume you can stay at mine tonight?" she asked.

"I think I can manage that," was the reply.

Jonty started his second day at the job feeling fresh and ready for a day's work. He ordered a forensic report following the death of Paul, which arrived in an orange internal envelope with the name of the last addressee crossed out and his added to the next available square. It read that the cause of death was by a hit and run. The weather conditions were described as wet and slippery, as the rain had made the roads greasy following several days of heat. The car involved in the hit and run was a two-year-old black 5 Series BMW. There was no history of repair work having been done on the car in any garages within Greater Manchester. The registration plate showed that the car was owned by a George Cartwright, who had reported the car stolen seven days earlier. The car was never found. This normally would have been a route to finding the suspect and taking it from there, but every road here had reached a dead end.

Jonty sat and thought deeply. He looked at George Cartwright's address, which read 14 Matthew Street, Birmingham.

Why would people be in Birmingham to steal a car? thought Jonty. He rang the number on the file, an outside shot.

"Hello?" came the voice in Jonty's ear.

"Is that Mr. Cartwright?"

"Yes, who is this?"

"My name is Jonty Ball from the Greater Manchester Police. Am I speaking to Mr. George Cartwright of Matthew Street?"

"Yes, what is this about?"

Jonty was empathetic. "Did you have a black BMW stolen in 1984, Mr. Cartwright?"

"Yes," was the reply. "But what…"

Jonty interrupted. "There is nothing to worry about, Mr. Cartwright. It is more about the car than yourself. You have done nothing wrong."

Jonty could sense Mr. Cartwright's relief. He knew that even innocent people can feel guilty for no reason when the police call.

"Would it be possible to meet you for half an hour and just check your recollection? It would help me immensely."

The line went silent for a good twenty seconds before Cartwright replied. "Erm… Yes, how about tomorrow morning, about eleven? I have a day off work."

"Fantastic," said Jonty, ensuring he sounded enthusiastic. "See you tomorrow at eleven."

Jonty booked a car and a PC to travel down with. He contacted the local Birmingham station and let them know he would be on their patch, but keeping the reason vague. "It's about a car that was stolen twenty years ago. No big deal, one meeting should clear it all up."

This was accepted by what was probably a counter sergeant who had too much paperwork on his desk. He would make a note and file it into the black abyss as it would not be considered important, and certainly not his station's problem.

Jonty rose at six the next morning, leaving Helen asleep to rest. He showered and went down as quietly as possible and made breakfast. At six-thirty, Helen walked through into the kitchen.

"Sorry," said Jonty. "I tried not to wake you."

Helen smiled through half-closed eyes. "The words china shop and bull spring to mind," she said. She walked up to him, give him a peck on the cheek, and asked if the kettle was still hot.

Jonty left for the station as planned just after 7 am. The twenty-minute drive was straightforward before the usual morning traffic build-up started. He arrived at the station to find a fresh-faced constable sitting at the vacant desk next to Jonty's, feet up and coffee in hand. Jonty walked up to him and, with a firm hand, swiped his legs so they fell off the desk and to the floor, the coffee spilling on the desk and between the constable's legs. He shot up, making sure the coffee hadn't spilt on his uniform.

"Don't ever let me see you slouch in a uniform, lad, in or out of sight of the public," said Jonty. "I suppose you are the person travelling with me to Birmingham?"

"Yes, sir. PC Frank Rose."

Jonty shook his hand. "Okay, Frank. I am not sure you look old enough to drive – can you?"

Frank felt under pressure and wanted to impress the detective, whom he had heard so much about.

"Yes, sir," said Rose. "I'm twenty-five and I have a licence."

"Great," said Jonty. "You drive."

Five minutes later and they were outside in the car park. The department had released a grey Volvo V40 estate car for them. *Comfy enough*, thought Jonty.

Frank slowly eased the car out of the Salford compound and onto the M602, about two hundred yards away. The car was used for motorway patrolling as an unmarked car. It had blue flashing lights under the front grill if required and its three-litre engine would keep up with most speeding cars. Just at the junction before the entrance of the motorway, the car stopped suddenly. Jonty and Frank surged forward like torpedoes protected only by their seat belts.

"What are you doing?" asked Jonty in surprise.

"Sorry, sir, I forgot it was an automatic," said Frank.

Frank had naturally tried to depress the clutch pedal to change gear. However, in the absence of the clutch, he had slammed on the oversized brake pedal instead, causing the car to do an emergency-style stop.

"Did you say your name was Frank Spencer?" Jonty asked sarcastically.

"No, sir, it's Frank Rose," said the constable. "I don't know a Frank Spencer. Is he in the force?"

Jonty rolled his eyes. "No, I don't think so. Let's get there in one piece, Frank."

Frank didn't make the mistake of hitting the brake after that. He was conscious of the pedal while driving all the way down the M6. They stopped for a break at the Stafford services, where they had a quick coffee, before continuing and eventually arriving at the Birmingham turnoff, as directed by the onboard sat-nav. The satellite directed them to turn off the M6 at junction 6, **signposted** for Aston, Birmingham, Gravelly Hill.

Matthew Street was about thirty seconds from the junction. The street was lined on each side with Victorian houses, being a mix of semi-detached and terraces.

No 14 was on the left-hand side of the street. Most of the parking was on-street parking with the odd driveway prised in between cars where possible. No 14 was one of the semis without a driveway or garage, so on-street parking was the only choice.

A perfect road to nick a car, thought Jonty. *In and out, back on the M6 in seconds.*

Frank parked in the first available space about thirty yards away from the house. They walked up to No 14, which had an old frontage along with nicely maintained gardens. There was a short path that had black and white tiles matching the outside paintwork, along with a small retaining wall that disappeared from view in some places under the overgrown bushes in an attempt to offer privacy.

The door was opened by a man in his mid-seventies, slightly crouched. He wore a pair of grey trousers and a blue T-shirt that looked like a hand-me-down, with a bobbly Royal blue jumper over the T-shirt.

"Mr. Cartwright?" asked Jonty.

"Yes, Mr. Ball I assume?" replied the elderly man.

"Yes, Detective Inspector Jonty Ball, and this is PC Rose." The two men nodded at each other as Jonty showed his card wrapped in its new leather-bound wallet, bought as a gift by Helen.

"Come in, please," Mr. Cartwright said, as he opened his body up to allow them to pass.

He directed them into the sitting room off a long hallway, which boasted four reception rooms leading off it. They accepted the obligatory offer of a coffee. Mr. Cartwright went to the kitchen while Jonty and Frank sat down and waited. The room was clean and comfortable. An ageing antique green suite surrounded a glass coffee table. Numerous photos of people were placed around the room; the people could be identified in age by the clothes they wore. An old wedding photo sat on the Welsh dresser at one end of the room, which Jonty assumed was Cartwright and his wife on their wedding day. The fire was lit in a small cast iron Victorian fireplace with an angled panel painted black with gold and red roses on it, helping to keep out the cool September air. The room was very quiet except for a loud ticking from a mantle clock that sat above the fireplace.

Mr. Cartwright placed a tray containing three mugs of coffee and a plate of biscuits onto the coffee table. Jonty thanked him, followed by Frank.

"Now, how can I help you, Detective?" Cartwright asked.

"Well," responded Jonty, "I don't think we have found the car."

Cartwright smiled. "Lovely car, that. I bought it with an inheritance I was left. I bought it new. I had it for two years and suddenly it went. The insurance company was good, though. I replaced it with a Mercedes in the end." Jonty got the feeling he could be there all day if he wasn't careful.

"What can you remember about the robbery?" he asked.

"Well, I remember that I reported it missing at about eight in the morning. When I went to the car to go to work, it wasn't there."

Frank was transfixed by the thick Birmingham accent coming through from such a frail voice owned by Cartwright, but he listened intently.

Cartwright continued. "I heard a large lorry go past in the middle of the night, but I didn't think anything of it. We always got lorries dropping off the motorway all the time."

"A lorry?" enquired Jonty.

"Yes, I remember at the time one of the neighbours said it was a very large artic and that it was parked with its back tail open, but she couldn't see what was happening. We think that maybe the car was loaded onto the back of the lorry – probably for the foreign market, the police said." Jonty was scribing notes as quickly as he could.

"I never heard from them again," added Cartwright, "so I assumed that's what happened, that it was sold abroad."

Jonty could not believe what he was hearing. "So, you are saying you never heard from the police again and that you didn't know the car had been in an accident?"

"Accident?" said the elderly man in surprise. "It's the first I have heard of an accident."

Jonty and Frank returned to Manchester, with Jonty knowing there was more work to be done.

How could so much not be transferred between the Birmingham and Manchester forces? he thought.

He got on well with Frank on the return journey. Frank told Jonty he was married with a young son and had qualified as a PC about six months ago.

That's why I have him here today, Jonty realised. *Less can go wrong with him here than being a rookie on the beat. They will ease him into it all.*

On the return journey north, Jonty called his support team and spoke to Jenny Smith.

"Hi, Jenny, can you look into the theft of a black 1982 BMW 5 series registration BVB 381Y. And can you contact the Birmingham police, Aston station, and ask them to send over any details they have of the same car being stolen in early June 1984?"

"Will do, sir," replied Jenny. "I haven't seen you yet, but welcome back."

CHAPTER THIRTY-ONE

Jonty returned home from work at around six-thirty. When he entered the lounge, he found Jake and Em waiting to join them for their evening meal. Jonty smiled broadly at Jake and strode over to him. They shook hands as Jake rose from the armchair. Jake appeared to be back to normal; he was physically very fit and the doctor had said that stood him in good stead.

"Nobody will tell me anything that happened," stated Jake.

"Well, let's get some tea first," Jonty replied.

"Tea?" said Em. "That's a drink, not a meal."

"Not in the north," smiled Jonty.

Helen cooked a meal of potato hash, or 'tater ash' as she called it, which consisted of beef minced meat, potato, carrots, onion, peas, and stock. She made it thick and served it up with thickly cut white bread and pickled red cabbage. Jonty gave the red cabbage a wide berth but smothered his meal in tomato ketchup instead.

"Stodge at its best," said Jonty. They all readily ate every last bit.

"I could get used to this northern food," said Jake, finishing his first proper meal for four days.

"Well, if you're comparing it to hospital food, that's not much of a compliment," smiled Helen.

They sat around the table enjoying meaningless banter until Jake asked the question everyone knew was coming.

"So, can you please tell me what happened and how on earth I ended up in the hospital?"

The other three went quiet, waiting for someone to speak. It was from Jake again. "Em told me I was talking in the regression and I suddenly began convulsing and shaking. At that point, I was rushed to the hospital. But what was it that made that happen?"

Jonty took control of the situation. "Jameson took you into regression by asking things about your earlier life as Jake. You spoke about doing some mountain climbing with your dad back home. You then spoke about having a holiday in California with Em – just general stuff."

"Did he take me back to Paul?" asked Jake.

162

"Yes," answered Em.

Jonty continued. "Yes, Jake, just some basic stuff to start with, like football, drinking, a school trip, etc. Then he began talking about Paul and Billy in the early eighties."

Jake looked on in silence. He could feel his heart beginning to beat quicker and he felt nervous. His throat was going dry as he edged forward in his seat.

Jonty continued. "He asked how many times you carried stuff to Liverpool. You said about eight or ten times."

Jake looked surprised. "So it wasn't just the once, as we thought?"

"No," said Helen. "I was shocked and upset."

"Sorry."

Jonty picked up the story. "Paul and Billy were doing the trips every fortnight..."

A vision entered Jake's mind as Jonty recounted the regression.

May 1977

"Billy, I know we have had this chat before, but I need to get out of whatever we are doing. We have been doing these trips fortnightly now."

"Paul, how many times do I have to tell you, none of us can back out of this thing now." Billy was getting quite aggressive with Paul. "I am fed up of hearing it."

Paul felt anger and annoyance. "You lied, Billy. Not only are you involved in it, but you're organising it all." Billy glared at Paul, but Paul continued. "You are making more money than anyone. You were only working at the ordinance factory so you could get your hands on blueprints that would allow your underground team to build up-to-date weaponry from designs by the Ministry of Defence." Billy was tight-lipped as Paul continued. "I want out. I won't tell anybody, we are best of mates."

"So, what is it, Paul?" asked Billy. "More money? What do you want?"

Paul looked frustrated. "I don't want to do this running anymore,"

Billy went quiet for a while. He then replied in a very soft voice, "Okay, Paul." He held his breath for a second. "Here's what I can offer you."

Paul listened. *What have I got myself into here? How did I allow myself into this?* he thought.

Billy smiled. "How much do you earn, Paul?"

"You mean at the factory?"

"Yes."

"About a hundred and fifty pounds a week."

163

Billy looked at him. "I know you're a top engineer. Why don't you work in my factory as the foreman?" Billy stared at Paul. "And I will pay you one and a half *thousand* a week tax-free."

Paul looked at Billy in amazement. "You will pay me ten times my salary to manage what? Illegal guns so you can supply what?" Paul's eyes narrowed. "Supply Angola today, another terrorist tomorrow, and so on and so on."

"You will have a lifestyle you could only dream of," replied Billy.

"For how long?" Paul retorted. "A year, maybe two, before it's all dug up by the law?" He shook his head. "I don't want to watch the TV news each night seeing people shooting at each other, knowing I had produced some of the weapons to make it happen."

Billy looked at Paul. "What can I do, Paul, mate?"

"You are the boss of all this, Billy," Paul replied in a resigned voice. "You're running the show, and don't think I don't know about your house in Cheshire. I overheard Pat O'Neill talking."

Billy's face was red. "Paul, you are getting to know way too much. I need you to keep your mouth shut, do you understand?"

"Billy, despite all this, you are still a friend. I would never say anything to anybody."

"Look, Paul, let me think about it. I will do what I can, is that okay?"

Paul felt a weight lift off his shoulders. It was a step forward, and he had to hang on to the chance. "Thanks, Billy, I do appreciate it."

"It's okay, Paul," said Billy. "Friendship is the most important thing."

Paul instantly felt better. He knew his friendship with Billy would be strong enough to help him through this.

A week later, Paul arrived home after working overtime to help with the deposit for a house he was buying with Sue. He placed a plate of meat pie and chips on his knee. Sue had called to the chip shop for the evening meal, a meal they enjoyed every Thursday, the day Paul got paid. He settled to eat in front of the fire and TV when an article on the local news programme caught his attention.

"A local man," said the presenter, "has died today from a suspected overdose of ecstasy. Patrick O'Neill from St Helens was in a Liverpool nightclub where he was supplied with the Class A drug. Doctors say he ingested around six times the amount usually taken..."

The segment was over in seconds. Paul looked down at his meal, walked into the kitchen with it, and threw it into the bin.

It was my fault he was killed, he thought.

164

"Wow," said Jake, coming out of his recollection. "But what was it that sent me to the hospital?"

Jonty continued, and again Jake's head was full of images. Long-forgotten memories, or random flashbacks of dreams, he could not tell.

June

Two weeks after the discussion between Paul and Billy, Billy rang Paul asking if he fancied a pint in the Broadwater pub. He had some good news for him. Paul agreed, and they arranged to meet at 8 pm the following evening, which was a Friday.

The weather was hot that day, and Paul was glad to get out of the factory for a pint. He was hoping that Billy was going to reprieve him of the gunrunning and not shoehorn him into the factory work.

Paul put on a pair of jeans and Nike training shoes with a pale green shirt. His mullet hairstyle took longer than expected to groom and position. He arrived at the Broadwater at 7.45 pm and ordered a pint of bitter. He had almost finished it when Billy arrived. He was ten minutes late.

"Sorry I'm late," said Billy. "I got waylaid in the office."

"No problem," replied Paul. "What are you drinking?"

"A pint of bitter sounds good to me," said Billy. Paul ordered two pints of bitter and they sat down.

"It's good to see you, Paul," said Billy. "I'll get straight to the point."

Paul hung on to his words.

"I have decided, I wasn't fair with you," continued Billy.

This sounds promising, thought Paul.

Billy continued. "I have decided to let you out of the running, and I won't ask you to work in the factory again. But the offer is there if you want it."

Billy smiled as Paul replied, "Thanks, Billy, mate. That means so much to me."

Billy smiled even broader. "We are friends. I wouldn't do this for anyone else."

"I know that," replied Paul. "God, you have lifted a weight off my shoulders."

"I was thinking," continued Billy. "Let's celebrate with a night out in June. We haven't been out in Manchester for ages."

Paul felt so relieved and excited about the news he had just been given. He had been released by the top boss in Manchester, the boss that nobody knew about, he was so far under the radar.

"Sounds great to me," said Paul. "I would love to." The night was arranged.

Jake looked at Jonty again. "Was I still okay at that point?"

"Yes, a bit worked up, but when Billy reprieved you from the work, the excitement came through. You were very excited, but then the problems started." Jonty continued with the story.

Jake, like Paul, began to recall the memory as he sat on the couch in Dr. Jameson's office...

June 1977

Paul enjoyed the night out with Billy. He was set up with the girl singing 'Young Hearts Run Free' on the karaoke.

"I felt good," said Jake, on behalf of Paul. "Merry, but not drunk. I remember walking up from Deansgate to Peter Street. I had about fifteen minutes to get to Piccadilly Gardens, where I could get the late bus home. I jogged for a while, but the beer was swilling around inside me so I decided to walk. I was just about to cross the road, which was empty except for a car quite a distance away."

Jake continued to describe the regression. "I know I can easily make it. The car accelerated. I slipped slightly, but I made it back onto the pavement. The car was going faster now, it was aiming straight for me. I tried to jump out of the way. I was about a yard on the pavement, but it kept coming. I couldn't think what to do, so I shouted for help. I felt very aware of the cool rain, the breeze with it. The car came closer. I know the driver has hit me. I am in the air... I see the face of... I see the face of... It's Steve Pitt. I did some gun runs to Liverpool with him."

Jake went quiet and closed his eyes.

"That's when you collapsed," said Jonty. "Jameson was convinced you were having a heart attack."

Helen was sobbing. "I am sorry I put you through this, love."

Jake took her hand. "I had to do it, to find some justice for Paul."

Jonty continued. "Jameson said he had never taken anybody up to the point of death before." The others fell silent. "You were so deep into the regression that your body believed it was dying, the pressure of the death experience affected your heart. It's only because you are so fit that you got through it."

"So, who is Steve Pitt?" asked Jake.

Jonty reached to his wallet, where he kept the folded list of six names safely. Stephen Pitt and Patrick O'Neill, who was killed by the drug overdose, were both on the list.

"What does all this mean?" asked Jake. "Are we any nearer to finding out?"

"Well," Jonty replied, "we have always known we can't use the regression or reincarnation as proof of murder. But, what we do have are the names on this list, which you can add to the board when you get home."

Jonty handed the list to Jake, who read it out.

"Paul had been killed by a collision with a black BMW. A black BMW had been stolen from Birmingham two weeks earlier. I will explain that in a few minutes," said Jonty. "Billy was the leader of an underground world, he used his job as a cover. After signing the official secrets act, is he doing the same with his present bank job?"

Jonty paused for a moment. "Two people have died – Patrick O'Neill and Paul. One of the names on the list, Jack Evans, seems to have got away with murder. Another name, William Green, is Jack Evans' cousin. Who is William Green? Some outstanding information about Dave's death and information from Aston police station will be sent to the office in the next few days." He looked at the others, letting his words sink in.

"Billy is at the bottom of Paul's murder, and more. We just have to prove it, logically," declared Jonty. "Now, let me tell you about my first two days at work."

Jonty swore Helen, Jake, and Em to secrecy. He explained that what he was doing was wrong and that it should be kept to the police investigation only. However, he trusted the people in this room more than anyone he could think of. He then told them of the events of his two days in his new job, including the incredibly green Frank Rose. Helen laughed aloud when Jonty spoke about the Frank Spencer comment. It brought her back from the deep sadness she felt after listening to Jake's regression.

Jake and Em did not understand the Frank Spencer comment and watched, bemused, as Helen roared with laughter behind the palm of her hand.

"Frank Spencer was a television character who demolished everything he touched," explained Helen.

"Oh," said Jake, still none the wiser.

"Ooohh Beteee!" said Jonty, copying the character's famous catchphrase.

Helen cracked up again with uncontrollable laughter, generating yet more tears, only this time tears of laughter.

Jake looked at Em and shrugged his shoulders. "The English are mad." Em nodded in agreement.

CHAPTER THIRTY-TWO

1945 NEW YORK

The business with the pit owners was at its peak from 1940 to 1945. Roberto contacted Don Bennito to meet with him regarding potential changes within the business. Roberto, Toni, and Giovanni flew first class to New York, where they booked two weeks in the New Yorker Hotel.

The New Yorker Hotel, the city's largest hotel, was located at the corner of 8th Ave and 34th Street in Midtown Manhattan. The 43-storey hotel had been built in 1929 and opened its doors on 2nd January 1930 – much like its contemporaries, the Empire State Building (opened in 1931), and the Chrysler Building (opened in 1930).

They booked two suites on the top floor, one for Giovanni and the other for Roberto and Toni. Roberto entered the room, following the bell boy, who brought his large suitcase together with the three suitcases for Toni. The bell boy smiled at Roberto.

"My wife seems to think that half a suitcase per day is just about right for a week's stay," said Roberto.

Roberto gave the bell boy ten dollars, which the boy looked at in surprise. He thanked Roberto and quickly left the room.

Not many days like that, thought the bell boy, first kissing, then cradling the crisp ten-dollar note.

The suite had four large rooms. In the bedroom steps were leading up to the seven-foot-square bed, which had a cream duvet placed on the top, matching the cream, thick-piled carpet. There was a large sitting room with a natural wooden floor and a red and cream Persian rug which sat proudly on it. In between, two sofas was a marble coffee table with gold ornate legs and clawed feet. Two large lamps covered with cream shades, in diagonal corners of the room, sat on matching tables made of marble, with clawed feet to match the coffee table.

The bathroom shower was four feet square with a large shower head. The roll-top bath had gold taps and plug, which were mirrored in the 'his' and 'hers' sinks. The towels were very large, white, fluffy, and thick, with matching dressing robes that hung on the back of the wall, all boasting the hotel crest.

Roberto threw off his smart mid-blue sports jacket and expensive brogue leather shoes, flopped down on the large bed, and quickly fell asleep, tired after the long journey. Toni left him to sleep whilst she filled the bath with hot water and the luxury foam she found in the overlarge bath cabinet on the wall. Her last job before indulging in the flower-infused water was to fill a glass from the complimentary magnum of Champagne.

They were joined for the evening meal by Benni and Edita. They sat in the dining lounge on the 39th floor, with fantastic views of landmarks such as the Chrysler Building to the north, the Empire State Building, and One Penn Plaza, due east. To the south lay the equally stunning vista of lower Manhattan.

Benni and Edita had grown to love this family with true conviction. Indeed, while Roberto, Benni, and Giovanni arranged a meeting for the following day, Edita and Toni agreed to have a shopping spree around the famous stores of New York. Toni was very excited about the prospect of a day's shopping with Edita.

Roberto, Benni, and Giovanni met at 1 pm the following afternoon in the Hotel Astor in Times Square. Benni booked a table in a quiet corner, which inevitably was easily agreed. They sat down and perused the menu, all quiet for a while.

Don Bennito was now in his seventies and age was showing in his face and his actions, which were more considered than in the past. He wore a light grey double-breasted suit along with expensive black Italian leather shoes, with a 22-carat gold Rolex watch on his wrist. Roberto dressed a little more casual with a pair of cream flannel trousers, a cream shirt, and a navy blue sports coat, which was a favourite look of his. Giovanni followed Benni's route by selecting a suit, which was a charcoal grey with a pristine white shirt and charcoal grey tie with a solid silver tie pin gripping it tightly to the shirt.

They sat as one, all extremely comfortable in each other's company. If silence appeared, it was never a strained silence, just three comfortable people totally in harmony.

"What is the current state of play with the business, Roberto?" Benni asked.

"The geographical climate of the coal industry will change in the next year or two, Benni," Roberto answered. "There is a strong opinion that the coal industry will be nationalised and the industry taken out of private hands and managed by the government."

"Can we manage the government, Roberto?"

"No, Don Bennito, we will not be able to manage the government," replied Roberto. By this, he meant that they could not manipulate an income from the UK government.

"What is the main reason for the meeting, Roberto, if we cannot put the UK government on our payroll?" said Bennito.

"The government feels that it needs to keep the miners on their side," replied Roberto. "Wages are too low and families cannot survive, and working conditions are very poor. People feel these areas will improve with a national takeover."

"What are our plans, Roberto?" the old man asked.

"Well, Benni, the changeover from prohibition to our mining business ran very smoothly. The simplicity of tapering down the business allowed us to leave, while the new business was taking shape. It was a perfect strategy."

Roberto paused and looked at his old friend and mentor with affection before continuing.

"I feel we have allowed enough time to build the tapering effect that served us so well when leaving prohibition," he said. "The income will continue for about twelve months."

Benni nodded with a tightening of the lips. He agreed that it worked well. *But why use a new formula when there is one that we know works?* he thought

"The new system will start on what the government will call vesting day, meaning the day the takeover is formulated," Roberto said.

"When will this take place, Roberto?"

Roberto took a sip of his coffee. "I envisage around the end of next year. We are in March 1945 now and the owners will soon have the power to end our agreement. I think twelve months is the maximum time we have."

The old Don nodded. "What do we do, Roberto?"

Roberto looked at Benni, then Giovanni. "The war will end soon. Britain and the allies will conquer Hitler. Churchill is seeing it swing his way."

They both sat and listened as Roberto continued.

"All engineering factories have been utilised for the war effort and they have been used to build planes, ships' engines, and guns, etc." He took

171

on board some more coffee. "I plan to find a small company that has been building arms and munitions, large enough to carry on producing the arms but small enough not to be noticed by outsiders."

Benni looked intrigued. "Where is the market, Roberto?"

"As the war ends," Roberto continued, "I see civil wars and uprisings occurring all over the world." He smiled warmly. "That's where we come in. We work on a supply and demand basis, supplying either side of any conflict."

Giovanni noted a wry smile on Don Bennito's lips.

"Or both?" Benni asked.

Roberto smiled. "Or both! With guns to defend or attack, depending on their position."

Benni smiled. "So no bias, just a neutral manufacturer?"

"Exactly," said Roberto as he proceeded to give an example. "Take Greece right now…"

Roberto went on to explain that the first signs of the civil war occurred from 1942 to 1944, during the German occupation. With the Greek government in exile and unable to influence the situation at home, various resistance groups of differing political affiliations emerged, the dominant ones being the leftist National Liberation Front (EAM), and its military branch, the Greek People's Liberation Army (ELAS), which was effectively controlled by the Communist Party of Greece (KKE). Starting in autumn 1943, friction between the EAM and the other resistance groups resulted in scattered clashes, which continued until spring 1944, when an agreement was reached forming a national unity government that included six EAM-affiliated ministers.

The immediate prelude of the civil war took place in Athens, on 3 December 1944, less than two months after the Germans retreated from the area. A bloody battle erupted after the Greek government, with British forces standing in the background, opened fire on a massive unarmed pro-EAM rally, killing twenty-eight demonstrators and injuring dozens. The rally was organised against the impunity of the collaborators and the general disarmament ultimatum, signed by Ronald Scobie (the British commander in Greece), which excluded the right-wing forces. The battle lasted thirty-three days and resulted in the defeat of the EAM after the heavily reinforced British forces sided with the Greek government. The subsequent signing of the treaty of Varkiza (12 February 1945) spelled the end of the left-wing organisation's ascendancy: the ELAS was partly disarmed, while the EAM soon after lost its multi-party character, to become dominated by KKE. All the while, White terror was unleashed against the supporters of the left, further escalating the tensions between the dominant factions of the nation.

Roberto smiled. "This is where we come in now and in any future conflicts."

"We can supply at the right price," Benni replied. "I like it, Roberto, I like it a lot." They raised their glasses and chinked them.

"Salou!" Giovanni toasted.

"Salou!" was the welcome reply.

"What a fantastic idea, Roberto," replied Don Bennito and he smiled warmly. "Usual fees included?"

Roberto matched the smile. "Don Bennito, I could never leave you out. Normal fees included."

They shook hands before Don Bennito added, "My best ever day's work was bringing you, two men, into the family. You are the sons I never had."

A hug for Roberto and Giovanni and the trio were on their way back to the hotel to freshen up, before heading out for the evening with Edita and Toni to see the Rogers and Hammerstein Broadway show 'Carousel'.

CHAPTER THIRTY-THREE

On their return to England, Roberto and Giovanni took time to find and meet with factory owners who were producing munitions for the government. They found six factories that would suit the bill in the Manchester Trafford Park area. This area was chosen because it was the largest industrial estate in Europe and the brothers could easily disguise a small factory amongst the hundreds surrounding it.

The fourth person they met was Reggie Brown, a short, rotund character with a bald head and thick grey hair at the sides, with equally thick sideburns that rolled into a moustache. His double chin was cleanly shaven, which wobbled when he spoke. He was a single man who had never married but was always interested in the gadgets of the day.

He hated being told by the government that his successful luxury car supply business was to be used for the 'war effort' and that he must produce arms and munitions.

He owned the factory, which employed around one hundred men producing rifles from raw parts to the finished product. He ran a small foundry that could smelt the metal into the shapes required for the barrel, muzzle, trigger guard, and bolt; he also utilised ten lathes turning parts for the guns. A small outbuilding housed fourteen milling machines and eight boring machines, of which four were vertical and four horizontal. He had shaping machines, grinding machines, and three surface grinders. In addition to this, he had a small joinery shop that produced the wooden stocks and forestocks for the guns.

The first meeting ended well and the subsequent meetings progressed even better. The final deal was struck: all staff would be retained utilising their skills, and an immediate pay rise of one percent would be paid to keep them onside. Reggie was taking a good income of £9,000 per year. This would increase to £10,000 and he would become the new employed managing director. In addition, Roberto would pay Reggie £50,000 for the business and they would continue producing arms for the government for as long as the war ran. Then, Roberto would find new markets. It was initially agreed with a handshake, and Roberto told

174

Reggie that his solicitor, Daniel Davey, would draw up the necessary paperwork at no cost to Reggie.

On 8th May 1945, the Second World War came to an end. It was a war that neither Roberto nor Giovanni took part in, as there were no records of them existing, which meant the government could not recruit them.

Roberto was busy setting up markets to keep the employees of Brown's Engineering in work. He initially set up a deal with both sides of the Greek civil war, whilst quickly setting up deals for Poland and Soviet Union versus the Partisans of the 1945-1947 conflict. The Indonesian Independence war of 1945-1946 quickly followed. The business started well, with the tapering formula working exactly as it had before. As the munitions increased, the mining project declined.

1st January 1947 saw the nationalisation of Britain's coal industry. Mining communities believed this marked the winning of an epic struggle for decent wages, security, and public ownership of a vital resource.

On Vesting Day, miners and their families marched in their thousands behind banners and colliery bands to the pitheads. They cheered and some openly wept as the blue and white flag of the National Coal Board was unfurled above them. They crowded around the unveiled plaques which proclaimed: 'This colliery is now managed by the National Coal Board on behalf of the people.'

The dawn of nationalisation brought hope to the miners, who had lived with the evils of privately owned pits all their lives. One could almost hear the cheers of heroes and heroines from the past and present celebrating the reality of public ownership.

For the second time, Roberto made a transition from a failing industry only to develop a new, profitable one.

CHAPTER THIRTY-FOUR

Jonty arrived at his desk by 9.30 am on 17th September to a note informing him that the pathologist report on Dave Rowlands was ready for him to collect from Martin McClean's office, which was on the other side of Manchester. Jonty asked Greg Peters to go and collect it. Peters was a young, freckled-faced junior who had recently finished schooling and was in his first year's training as an accountant with the GMP. The word training was not appropriate in year one, as it was mainly taken up in doing errands for more senior staff who did not have the time, or the inclination. This was such a time. Greg would do the fifteen-minute stroll across the city to pick up the report – only, today it would not be a stroll as the rain had set in and was looking like it would not ease. The sky was painted black, as was Greg's face when Jonty asked him to pick the envelope up.

Greg was a decent lad, even though he seemed a little mothered. He didn't wear trendy clothes and always wore a tank top jumper with a brightly coloured shirt, usually red or yellow, with maybe brown trousers and black plastic, faux leather shoes. The coordination of colours did not seem important to Greg, which gained him the uncomplimentary nickname of Rhubarb and Custard. He grabbed an office umbrella and trudged on with his errand.

Just as Jonty started on a bacon sandwich and a coffee around mid-morning, a sodden Greg arrived back at the office. The rain was dripping off his rimmed glasses and onto his nose. There was a distinct watermark up to his shins, where is long trousers had soaked up the rain-puddled flags and crept up the material. He gave Jonty the envelope – which, thank God, Martin's secretary had shown the foresight to wrap it in a plastic waterproof bag.

Jonty finished the bacon sandwich and went to the washroom to wash the grease and tomato sauce from his mouth and hands, conscious that he didn't want to open the envelope with greasy hands. On his return, he looked at the envelope and wondered what the contents might hold. He carefully opened the envelope and took the report out. His eyes accelerated to the second page of the report, which he knew from experience always held the diagnosis.

Diagnosis

In closing, my final verdict is that death was caused by poison. This was heightened by the deceased having an already weak heart following two previous Coronary Conclusions.

I am of no doubt that the poison was delivered by a plant commonly grown in gardens, Digitalis purpurea.

The seeds, stems, flowers, and leaves of the foxglove plant are poisonous. They contain digitalis glycosides, which are organic compounds that affect the heart. When ingested, the glycosides affect cardiac function, causing an irregular heartbeat. Symptoms can also include digestive issues, headaches, blurred vision, and confusion and can eventually lead to death.

Jonty read the report again. *Foxglove.* He went to the computer and looked up an image of a foxglove. Up came images of lovely looking purple flowers with a trumpet head with trailing bell-shaped flowers on a stem. Jonty recognised the flowers instantly. They had been growing in Dave's garden – or, more accurately, they were the flowers that had been missing from Dave's garden.

Had Dave been murdered? thought Jonty. *And if so, why?*

The second thing to make an entrance that day was the report from Birmingham Police about the theft of George Cartwright's BMW in 1984. Jonty inspected the file with the Manchester police so that he could compare the two reports and see if there were any discrepancies.

When Jonty finished reading the reports, it was obvious to him that the two forces did not communicate. However, that was understandable, as the Manchester police had no car to trace and the Birmingham police only had a stolen car to look for. It had only been since Jake's regression that Jonty knew that a black BMW had been involved.

As he read the Birmingham report, Jonty noted that an eyewitness had seen the car being loaded onto a large articulated lorry with a sheeted side, with the words 'VERDE LTD' printed on the side. The report continued to state that an investigation had been carried out and no such company had been found. In the Companies House Register, where all companies have to be registered to conduct business legally, the report

178

remained open, but the last input on the file had been recorded in 1985 stating that no more man-hours would be placed on the case unless a meaningful lead came to the fore.

Jonty looked at the file a little longer. He then did a double-check to make sure that the company was not registered, just in case Aston station had made a mistake. They had not. Verde Ltd could not be found.

By 2 pm, the weather had cleared from rain to a sunny September day. The temperature in the car read 17 degrees as Jonty moved the CRV into gear, its destination Manchester Royal Hospital to meet up with Martin McClean, the pathologist who had carried out the post-mortem on Dave Rowlands. Jonty had known Martin for many years from the numerous post-mortems he had performed that kick-started hundreds of cases. This one was no different, except that the deceased happened to be a colleague and a friend.

"Jonty, how are you?" said Martin. "I heard you were back in town. Can't keep away from us, I hear?"

Jonty smiled and shook his hand.

"Good to see you, Martin. You are looking well."

Martin McClean was a man in his mid-forties. He was tall, lean, and fit, with a slight stoop in the shoulders, as did a lot of men over six feet, as if they were trying to conceal their full height. Martin was a keep-fit fanatic and would run four marathons or more a year. He was always chasing charitable donations, which Jonty always supported. The hem of his white coat fell about six inches above the knee, making it look more like a long jacket on him.

"Martin, I've come to discuss Dave Rowlands' post-mortem," said Jonty, coming straight to the point.

"Yes," said Martin. "At first, I thought it was a normal heart attack. But then I found a trace of powder around the inside of his mouth. I discovered that this powder was derived from the inner side of the foxglove plant."

"Are foxgloves a common plant?" Jonty enquired.

"Yes," was Martin's reply. "A lot of people do not know how dangerous they are if eaten in volume. Or, in Dave's case, if ingested by anyone with an already weakened heart, they can be fatal. Also, if you put them on a fire, the fumes can also do you harm. A very beautiful, but dangerous plant to the uneducated."

Jonty looked Martin in the eye. "Were there any signs of resistance from Dave? You know, if it was forced on him?"

"No," Martin answered. "No signs of any force or struggle, or resistance at all."

Jonty felt a chill run up his spine. "Thank you, Martin." He turned to walk towards the door.

"One thing, Jonty," said Martin. Jonty stopped and turned back as Martin continued. "The amount of glycosides, from the foxglove, found in Dave's body makes me think that they did not get there by accident."

"So, what are you saying?" said Jonty. "I could have a murder on my hands?"

Martin held both hands out with the palms facing upwards and shrugged. "I wouldn't discount it."

"Thanks, Martin. I won't." Jonty made his way out the door.

Jonty called Jake and Em later that day and asked them to be at Helen's for 8 pm that evening. There, Jonty described his day and gave Jake a copy of the report.

"It's something that has a lot of answers, I am sure," he said. "I just don't know what they are yet."

CHAPTER THIRTY-FIVE

Roberto doted on his grandson, William. He was the son he never had. He loved Francesca with all of his heart, but, for an Italian to pass the business on through the family, it was always to be a son in the first instance. William was the nearest Roberto would ever get.

By the time William was five, Roberto had taught him how to ride a bike, ride a horse, and to swim. By the time he was ten, he could shoot game and fish. Roberto loved taking William out fishing, they would fish all around the large lakes of Greater Manchester. However, the greatest days were when grandad 'Pop' Sartori took young William sea fishing, particularly night fishing off Anglesey in North Wales, or fishing from the rocks at Abeffraw headland.

Today, they were celebrating William's fifteenth birthday. Roberto was now sixty-nine years of age and was slowing down, both physically and mentally. Since the death of Don Bennito, the family tie to America had been severed and the UK operation was very buoyant.

Reggie Brown was a good learning curve that allowed Giovanni to learn the engineering side of the business. Reggie had now retired with Roberto's blessing and Giovanni was quickly placed as the managing director of the company, now named Brown's Engineering. Giovanni, like Roberto, had put every ounce of energy into his work since the days of prohibition. He'd had a few relationships with women, but never strong enough to tie himself to anyone in particular. Giovanni liked his freedom.

It was 1968. With the hippie revolution and Carnaby Street in full swing, the Beatles had just released a revolutionary album twelve months earlier called *Sgt. Pepper's Lonely Hearts Club Band*. Manchester was going through a black music revolution called Northern Soul with some fantastic sounds, which were quickly being followed by the Philadelphia sound, Stax Records, and Tamla Motown headed by greats such as Marvin Gaye, Smokey Robinson or The Supremes. Black America was inching forward in freedom and equality after the great speech of Martin Luther King, reflected in the lyrics of Sam Cooke's 'A Change Is Gonna

Come'. It was a revolution, rapid and modern. The world had never witnessed such a huge generation gap as that of the sixties.

William was also getting caught up in the social revolution, and he and his childhood friends were following the same music scenes. They were also football fanatics, Manchester United or City, with the smaller clubs being left in their wake. William chose City, although most of his friends were United fans. It was in the blood to buck the trend in the Sartori family.

The world was also at war, which meant a profit for the Family. The production of guns could not keep up with the demand as the factory struggled to supply the Colombian conflict, the Mozambican war of independence, the Zanzibar revolution, the communist insurgency in the Thailand Chadian civil war (1965-79), and the South African border war. The brothers were making more money than ever; there was a conflict in every corner of the world, which meant that business for Brown's Engineering was booming.

One morning, Roberto called William into his office to have a discussion. It was normal to leave school at fifteen in a 1960s England, with lots of apprenticeships available for lads with the desire to make something of their lives. Roberto and Giovanni had discussed starting William in the engineering business, which had its plus and minus points. In the end, they agreed that he could be more beneficial to the business elsewhere. They arranged, through a few cash-filled brown envelopes, to have the Royal Ordnance factory offer William an apprenticeship in the drawing office. William was told of this at the meeting in Roberto's office. Roberto told William that, on his fifteenth birthday, he would start the apprenticeship with the ROF. William was delighted; he had seen how hard his friends had tried for jobs, and yet here he was, being handed one on a plate.

"You must work hard at this opportunity," Roberto told William.

"I promise I will Pop," William replied.

Roberto stood up and put his arm around William and held him tight. "I am so proud of you, William, and I love you."

CHAPTER THIRTY-SIX

The following year, on a cold January morning at 6.30 am, Francesca climbed out of bed and staggered into the shower. She turned the dial to hot and stood under the cascade, letting the water wake her body and warm the chilled bones against the minus temperatures outside.

They owned a lovely house on Worsley Green, a mock Tudor 5-bedroom house with all the period features. She climbed out of the shower and dried her body, standing close to the large radiator that was fighting, and just about beating, the ice-cold temperature. She put on a robe and called out to Ray, who answered and made the same pilgrimage from bed to shower. They crossed on the stairs and he tapped her on the bottom.

"I love you," he grinned.

"I love you right back," she replied.

He continued to the shower while she went into her dressing room to dry her hair. It was just a normal day. The process was so robotic on these days when Ray travelled on business, that they were almost on automatic pilot. They enjoyed breakfast together – eggs and bacon for Ray and fruit and yoghurt for Francesca. Ray dressed into a smart black business suit with a red tie, and Francesca in smart designer jeans and a Ben Sherman black and white checked shirt under a thick-knitted jumper. She pulled on a leather coat with a large fur collar around the neck.

They climbed into the six-month-old blue metallic mark 2 Ford Cortina 1600E. Ray had always been adamant that he did not want to be part of the family business. A huge argument broke out during the Christmas holidays between Ray and Roberto, both men a little alcohol-fuelled. However, Roberto interpreted Ray's comments as being his true feelings, and the brandy gave Ray the courage to speak his mind.

"I know you are a gangster," he told Roberto.

Roberto laughed. "Ray, where on earth have you got that idea from?"

Ray fired back. "I don't care what you do, but over my dead body will you get William involved in any of it."

Roberto glanced at William and Francesca. They were sitting on the sofa next to the twelve-foot high Christmas tree. Bing Crosby was singing 'White Christmas' in the background as the film played on the television. Francesca pulled William close to her as the argument between the men gained in ferocity.

Roberto finally looked at Francesca. "Get him home and bring him back when he is sober."

The men hadn't spoken in the three prevailing weeks and all had settled back to normality.

Francesca steered the1600E into a departures bay at Manchester Airport at 8.30 am, allowing Ray an hour and a half waiting time in the departure lounge before the next flight to Milan. Francesca returned home by nine.

William was already up, dressed, and had made the fifteen-minute journey to the Royal Ordnance factory. He had been there for six months and had progressed to drawing basic components for the engineers, allowing them to turn the drawings into metal components for the defence industry.

Ray settled into a window seat on the Boeing 737, in the fourth row from the back. He always preferred to sit near the back where he could look down the cabin. He enjoyed people watching and a jet offered some of the best people-watching opportunities available. The captain introduced himself over the loudspeaker as Captain James Cooke and joked that he was not navigating to Australia but flying to Milan. It was obviously a joke that he had used every flight, referring to his famous namesake and explorer from the eighteenth century.

Ray fastened his seat belt as the cabin crew explained the safety exits, pointing their arms in a well-drilled, choreographic fashion. As the 737 taxied onto the Manchester runway, he heard a female voice, about halfway up the cabin, suddenly shout.

"Oh, my God!"

He shook his head. *A first-time flyer and we are not even on the runway yet!*

The plane slowly advanced before making a right turn before stopping at the beginning of another runway. Within twenty seconds it started to move again, at first a roll forward, then a sudden acceleration as it raced from 0 to 60 mph in six seconds.

The woman was now shouting again. "Oh, my God, let me off." Her partner was trying to calm her down.

Captain Cooke pushed the acceleration to a 150 mph and slowly lifted the jet smoothly into the air. The plane had lifted to around 500 feet when Ray heard the panicking girl again.

"Are we in the air yet?"

"We've been in the air for about a minute," was the reply.

Ray smiled to himself. The jet continued on its climb until eventually the passengers were advised they could unfasten their seat belts. The cabin crew started their exodus from the front and the rear of the cabin, asking passengers if they wanted to buy anything from the trolley. Ray purchased a gin and tonic. The stewardess handed him a plastic tumbler with a Beefeater gin bottle and a white coaster with the airline logo emblazoned on it.

The first hour of the flight passed quite quickly. Ray began to flick through the inflight magazine, which was geared up for holidaymakers and flights to the various countries that the airline serviced. He read with interest the places in the South of France, an area that he and Francesca had discussed and planned to visit soon. *I must make that happen for us*, he thought.

Just then, he heard a deafening crash and he instinctively looked out of the window. As if in slow motion, he watched as the wing fell away from the main body of the plane. At the same time, the plane began to roll on its side. The passengers in the cabin began screaming and panicking. The cabin staff were unable to move down the aisle as the plane had tilted onto its side. It was free falling and spinning in the air, like a coin spinning on its side on a smooth tabletop.

Then there was a second explosion as the second wing fell away, followed by a split-second respite as the drag of the wing caused the plane to spiral, and the spinning stopped. The plane fell, like a dart in the air – vertically! The gravitational force pushed Ray's skin tight against his bones. It felt as though the bone and skin had melded and was turning inside out, his teeth clamping in his mouth so tight that he could feel his jaw beginning to crack. His eyes were popping out of their sockets.

Passengers, as well as cabin crew, were flying into him and over his head, the screaming dying down as people could no longer vocalise through their mouths as the gravity tugged at them. All went quiet. Ray could only discern the noise of the wind; he visualised tumbleweed rolling down a Western street, like in a movie. He had only seconds left before he passed out.

Roberto's phone rang. He picked it up. Giovanni's voice was on the other end

"It's done!" The phone went dead.

***

Francesca fell into the house through her father's front door. She was in uncontrollable floods of tears, tears that left a line where they had run and eroded her make-up, like a dry riverbed in the Serengeti. But these tears were not drying up. Her nose was running, her hands trembling. She felt as if her life had ended, right there!

At the same time, Toni came running through to the lounge upon hearing the commotion. Francesca collapsed in her father's arms, inconsolable.

"What on earth is wrong?" Toni shouted. "Francesca, what is wrong?"

Francesca broke free from her father's grasp. "He's dead."

"Who is?" asked Toni, beginning to panic. "Who is dead?"

"Ray!" cried Francesca. "I saw it on TV. His plane blew up in mid-air. It's all over the TV and radio. It was his flight number and there were no survivors…" She was sobbing hysterically and making no sense to Toni.

"Mum, Dad… my life is over."

Roberto put his arm around the daughter he idolised. "This is a bad time for the family," he said. "We must pull together. You and William must stay here tonight."

"I loved him, Daddy."

"I know, honey," Roberto replied.

Toni turned away and walked to a leather sofa in the large hallway. She collapsed into uncontrollable tears that fell into her lap. She gasped for air as her coordination between sobbing, crying, and breathing left her motionless. The front door was still wide open, allowing the cold blasts of wind to gush through the house.

Toni stared at the TV screen, half-listening as the presenter spoke about a Middle Eastern terrorist group that had claimed responsibility for planting the bombs on the plane.

A well-spent hundred thousand… thought Roberto.

Roberto got up and closed the front door in the hallway. Returning to Francesca, he sat down and put his arms around her. "I know, baby, it hurts at the moment…" There was nothing more to say.

186

Francesca tucked into her father and cried uncontrollably. He felt a pang of guilt, which soon passed. It was worth sacrificing hundreds of lives to eliminate the one possible threat to the Family.

CHAPTER THIRTY-SEVEN

Jonty arranged to pick Jake up and drive him to Dave Rowlands' house. He needed a fresh pair of eyes. He waited patiently as he knocked on the door. Em answered.

"Morning, Jonty. How are you today?"

"I am good thanks, love."

Em smiled. She still couldn't understand some of these Northern sayings.

"Jake!" she shouted upstairs. "Jonty is here."

"I will be right down," was the reply.

"Come in, Jonty," said Em. "Do you want a drink?"

"No thanks," replied Jonty. "We best get on our way as soon as we can."

Within five minutes the CRV was pulling onto the M60 motorway as they made their way to Dave's house.

"I'm not sure how I can help with the scene at Dave's house," Jake told Jonty.

"It doesn't matter," replied Jonty. "Anything can help, no matter how small."

They soon exited the motorway and were at Dave's house within twenty minutes. Jonty made sure nobody was around first before making his way to the back of the house, as he knew officially he should not be at a suspected murder scene with Jake.

Jake instantly noticed the broken foxgloves.

Jonty put his arm across Jake, preventing him from stepping forward. "Don't touch them. Forensics are taking them to look for any fingerprints."

Jake nodded. "Of course," he whispered.

He felt useless. He could not add anything to the professional job already being done, and both he and Jonty knew it.

"Has it helped, being at the scene of the crime?" Jonty asked as they made their way back to the car.

"Yes," replied Jake. "But I'm sorry I can't help."

Jonty laughed. "It's a crime scene. Anything that can be found will be."

They both laughed as Jonty drove the CRV back the way they had come, easing onto the M60 and taking Jake back home. He pulled the car out of the inside lane and into the centre lane to overtake a series of HGV lorries. He accelerated past the first three lorries with ease, then Jake and Jonty looked at each other suddenly and looked again at the HGV they were now passing. The lorry was sheeted at the side and carried the signage, in large green letters, 'VERDE PLC'.

Jonty looked in the mirror and took his foot off the accelerator, dropping the speed from 70 to 40 mph. The vehicle behind him flashed its lights. Jonty waved at the driver but continued. The lorries on the inside lane had now started to overtake him. He waited for an opening and then tucked back into the inside lane, about three lorries behind 'VERDE'. The man in the vehicle behind passed, giving a 'V' sign. Jonty blew him a kiss. Jake laughed.

Jonty turned to Jake. "Let's go for a ride."

Jonty kept the CRV two or three vehicles behind the Verde lorry. He asked Jake to take the registration of the large Scania vehicle with the Verde sign. He would check who it was registered to when back in the office.

The lorry continued along the M60, then picked up the M61 towards Preston. Jonty looked down at the petrol gauge, which was just below halfway. A quick search through the onboard computer told him he had 260 miles remaining before he ran out of fuel.

The Scania turned left at the Preston junction of the M6 and began travelling south, then indicated to turn off at the Charnock Richards Service station. Jonty followed from a distance. The lorry continued to the HGV parking, while Jonty parked in the normal car park. He and Jake climbed out of the CRV and looked across the car park to the HGV. Two men clambered down from the cabin and onto the tarmac. Both were similarly dressed in jeans and T-shirts. Both appeared to be strong, well-built men. One was instantly recognisable from the scar that ran down the side of his face.

"Jack Evans," said Jake. Jonty nodded.

Evans and the other man began to make their way to the car park that Jonty and Jake were in, so they both jumped back into the CRV to try and hide from view. Evans and his partner met two other men who were walking towards them from the car park. The men shook hands and shared a joke about something.

Jonty and Jake watched the men stroll over to the parked Scania and Evans lifted the side canvas slightly. Jonty had, in the meantime, taken his camera from the rear seat of his car. He learned years ago that he should always carry a camera in case of unforeseen opportunities – this could be such an opportunity.

It was difficult to see what the men were looking at behind the canvas, but Jonty noticed the rear wheel of a car – it was an expensive-looking alloy wheel. Three of the men climbed into the back of the lorry while Evans climbed back into the cab. Within a minute he was out again, his head turning, making sure nobody was watching them. He had two number plates in his hand and what looked like a screwdriver. Another ten minutes elapsed, then the men jumped out of the trailer and lowered the tailgate. Two ramps were erected and off the back came a dark blue, two-door Aston Martin Vantage 4.7 V8 S. Jake took a sharp intake of breath, then whistled.

"What a car," he purred.

"That must be worth a hundred thousand plus," Jonty added.

One of the men took the keys and drove the Aston Martin into the car park, making sure he overlapped the markings in the parking bay ensuring nobody could park close enough to knock it with an opening door.

Jonty looked back towards the Scania, where he could see a brown envelope exchange hands between the other man from the car park and Evans. All four men then reunited and strolled to the services – for refreshment, Jonty guessed.

Jonty jogged up to the Aston and took a photo of the registration plate and then the front windscreen. He could just about see the Vehicle Identification Number. He quickly took a photo of it, then returned to the CRV, and waited. After about thirty minutes the four men returned, laughing and joking. They shook hands. One man got into a Mercedes C class, while his partner got into the Aston. They both drove away to rejoin the M6.

Jonty and Jake stayed still and watched as Evans and the man he'd journeyed with climbed back up the steps of the lorry and the engine cranked up. Jonty switched on the ignition of the CRV and remained in place until he saw the Scania hit the slip road and disappear. He knew he could allow a few minutes as he would easily catch it up.

Jonty saw the Scania on the inside lane of the M6 going south and was now indicating to join the M58 towards Liverpool. Again, Jonty

190

followed. The lorry continued to Liverpool, driving through Aintree, past the famous racecourse that held the Grand National, and to the city centre. A couple of turns to the right and Jonty found himself following the lorry into a derelict area of Liverpool docks. Jonty parked short of entering the dockyard parking on the dock road. He and Jake then went by foot to the entrance and hid behind a set of containers packed three high, with about a yard distance between them. The cover was good.

The lorry drove to a remote corner of the yard, where two men came out of the shadows and welcomed Evans and his mate. The VERDE covers were again rolled back, this time revealing the entire content of the lorry. There were approximately a hundred wooden storage boxes, each measuring around four feet long, three feet high, and three feet wide.

A small crane lifted the first box off and lowered it to the floor, whereupon one of the men from the docks lifted a crowbar and prized the lid off the wooden trunk. Lowering his arm, he took out of the box a brand new, modern-looking rifle. He handed it to his partner and picked another rifle out to inspect. They both tried the mechanisms, looking down the sights. Each pulled the trigger and caressed the death machines. The men smiled, nodded to each other, and turned to Evans and his mate. They shook hands and another large brown envelope was passed between the parties. The crane then kicked into motion, unloading all the boxes and dropping them into a rusting container on the dockside with the markings L&S Skip Hire templated on the side.

After a further hour, the container was loaded, awaiting a ship to continue its journey. Evans and his companion then got back into the Scania and left the yard.

Jonty and Jake, however, had seen enough after only fifteen minutes. They had returned to the CRV and waited for the lorry's exit. When the lorry eased out of the yard, Jonty was in a position to follow it. They stayed again within a comfortable distance to Trafford Park in Manchester. The lorry indicated and drove into a factory yard, where it then reversed up to a large, double door frontage marked Brown's Engineering Spares and Parts. It was one of five large bays, all with the same Brown's Engineering logo.

The doors were kept open as Jonty and Jake watched as the Verde side sheet was torn off the side of the articulated lorry to reveal a further canvas marked up with Brown's Engineering. Within five minutes, the Verde lorry had been transformed into a Brown's Engineering vehicle.

191

CHAPTER THIRTY-EIGHT

Francesca never got over the death of Ray. The family supported her and, whilst the feeling of loss never went, she learned to live with the facts. She had a beautiful son who needed her support to get through the loss of his father. So, while William leaned on her, she in turn leaned on her father. Roberto was resilient and fantastic in helping them both get through what was a traumatic period in their lives.

Teams from the country's investigation unit went to the crash site, which was spread over a twenty-mile radius. They collected evidence and confirmed it was a bomb that had caused the plane to explode over Belgium. The report recommendations pointed no blame on the air carrier and that no changes were required with respect to the safety of the aircraft. It was, however, investigating ways to ensure that a potential terrorist could not access a plane so easily. The report continued to add that it classed the explosion as an act of terrorism. It stated that there had been 318 passengers and seven staff members on board, all reported dead.

The next five years passed. The more years that went by, the stronger Francesca felt. She met a new man two years after the passing of Ray. At first, she felt that Ross was a companion and nothing else, and it helped take her mind off the tragic event of the past.

She was attracted to Ross – who, at the age of 51, was older than Francesca. He was a stockbroker in a practice based in Manchester city centre, working in the second most prominent area of finance after London's Square Mile. He didn't have the instant appeal of Ray's outstandingly good looks, or Ray's humour. Instead, he was more of a grey, conservative man. He stood five foot ten inches, and he had thick, closely cut hair that was once blonde, but age had now turned it a salt and pepper colour. He had a love for horses and owned four, which he kept in his paddock at his country home. The house, which dated back to 1764, was located in the area of Mere in Cheshire, with a balcony overlooking the mere set within the local golf course.

What he lacked in humour he made up for in his sensitivity towards Francesca. He was not the type that Francesca was usually attracted to, however, which made Toni question the relationship.

"Are you sure you want to marry Ross?"

Francesca looked at her mother. "Yes, Mum. I think his sensitivity is exactly what I need. And whilst I was not attracted initially, I have grown to love him. I enjoy sharing time with him."

"Are you sure you love him?"

"Yes," replied Francesca. "Ray was my soulmate. But, as Daddy keeps saying, life must go on."

Francesca eventually married Ross Jones five years after the death of Ray.

The bond between Roberto and William grew stronger than ever, with Roberto bringing William more into the business. William changed his surname to Jones when his mother married Ross Jones. Roberto thought this was a good thing, as it removed the surname one step further from the family, therefore offering more protection.

William became a major part of the business for Roberto and Giovanni. He learned his trade as a draughtsman and would spend time memorising the drawings for the factory. As advanced technology was becoming quicker to produce with the onset of computers aiding in design and production, Roberto knew he needed to be at the cutting edge of the industry if he wanted to be a step ahead of all those happy to supply the numerous wars and civil wars across the world.

William was able to produce the drawings and plans for the next project on the Ministry of Defence's agenda. Roberto could then produce an exact replica from the factory; in some cases, he was able to supply the item before the MOD signed it off because he did not have their rigid procedures to conform to. This meant that rebels were obtaining new UK-designed ammunition before the British Army. This made Roberto and Giovanni the world's leading providers to all the black markets in guns and ammunition. The guns they produced were of a high standard thanks to the skills acquired at Brown's Engineering.

William was enjoying the lifestyle. His £10,000 salary from the ordnance factory did not go far, but the £90,000 from the factory input funded the lifestyle he desired.

In 1980, a birthday party was held to celebrate Roberto's 80th birthday. The years had been good to Roberto and Giovanni. Roberto had groomed William to such an extent that he was comfortable that today, on his birthday, he would pass on the mantle of godfather to William. He and Giovanni had discussed this in great detail and felt that now was the time to allow William to take the reins, although Giovanni was not as keen as Roberto on the handover.

Toni and Francesca were busy organising the party that was to be held in the large house at 2 pm. The invites stretched to around eighty people.

Roberto had invited several family members to his office to witness the resignation of Roberto and the induction of William, The attendees were few. There was Roberto, of course, dressed in a grey pinstripe suit with black shoes, a white shirt, and red tie. He had bad arthritis and walked with a constant limp, his face weathered, with wrinkles that were once laughter lines. His voice was weaker than it once was and no longer held the authoritative tone. His hair had changed through the years from jet black to grey, and finally white and thin. It blew in the breeze today as a light wind came through the open window.

Giovanni was not far behind in the aging process. He, too, was of white hair; he had a few age spots dotted around his face and red threads running through his nose, which was red at the tip, following years of indulging in the best red wines and Scotch that money could buy. He'd always had a taste for the Scotch ever since the heady days of prohibition. Days he always thought fondly of. It was his favourite time. He, too, was to stand down today, allowing William to take over the management of the factory.

William was standing in the room, proud, tall, and strong. He was exceptionally good looking and the girls of the area always knew him as hunky Billy Jones.

Also attending the meeting with Roberto, Giovanni and William was the leader of the el Salvador revolutionary government junta, who had successfully deposed President General Carlos Humberto Romero in a coup on 15th October 1979. He was here to tie up a deal with Roberto for arms to supply the cause. Roberto invited him to introduce the smooth transition to William, who would take over from today. Also present was David Wright, who sat on the Manchester City Council, as well as being on Roberto's payroll, and Edward Le Conte, Roberto's defence lawyer. He was also on the payroll but was rarely needed, as the path that Roberto trod in the world meant that he never left a trace.

The age of fifteen was a pivotal point for William. Whilst, before, he had been the beloved grandson for Roberto, with whom he had shared many magic moments, now he was experiencing a slow awakening of the world in which Roberto lived and ruled. He was told of the tradition of the family; he had been told of Don Bennito and Joey; he knew of the first assassination by Roberto all those years ago. Most of all, he learned the tradition and values of a mafia family from Sicily, and that he was born into a unique position of being soon promoted to the only Don in the United Kingdom.

The inauguration took place quickly. Don Roberto made a nick in his and William's arm, and they crossed arms, allowing the blood to mix. Roberto took off the ring he'd worn with so much pride since becoming the Don all those years ago and placed it on William's finger.

"Be wise in your decisions, my son," said Roberto. "Be loving to the family and friends." He opened his arms, gesturing to those in the room, confirming their friendship. "Be ruthless to protect the family and friends."

Roberto then slowly eased out of the leather-bound mahogany chair, pushing it away from the large mahogany desk that had served him so well over the last fifty years, and limped slowly out of the room. The attendees gave Roberto respect by first allowing him to leave the room. Then, one by one, beginning with Giovanni, they approached William. Bent on one knee, they kissed the ring and said the simple words, "Don William."

CHAPTER THIRTY-NINE

Jonty was sitting at his desk when his phone rang. It flashed up in his small screen, indicating that it was an internal call.

"Jonty Ball speaking."

"Jonty, it's Danny." Danny Piper was a desk sergeant whom Jonty had worked with on many occasions over the years. "I have a man in the cells asking if you are available for a brief chat?"

"Who is it, Danny?"

"His name is Jack Evans. He was brought in at three this morning on a drink-drive charge."

"I will be down in a few minutes, Danny."

As he walked down the stairs, Jonty caught a glimpse of the man sitting in the cell. He glanced, took one step forward, and stopped. He turned and took a longer look. It was Jack Evans staring back at him, smiling. Jonty continued down the stairs and entered the cell.

"Well, Jack, what can we do for you today? A glass of the house red, maybe?" Jonty said with a smirk.

The smile was returned unexpectedly. "That would be good, Jonty. Thank you."

"Why are you here, Jack?" Jonty asked, the smile disappearing.

"I'm here because of drunk driving," said Jack coldly. "I planned to get caught so that I could chat with you privately about something else."

"About business?" Jonty asked.

"About off-the-record business," Evans replied.

"Where and when?" Jonty pushed.

"Do you know the Lime Plaza in Chester?"

"Yes," Jonty replied.

"How about there on Thursday, say two in the afternoon?"

Jonty agreed and told him he would have Jake with him. Jonty left, wondering why Evans wanted to talk about his business now, after all the time he had been involved in crime.

On Thursday, at 2 pm, Jack Evans sat down with Jonty and Jake.

"That was some ruck in London." smiled Evans. "You were both good." He clenched his fist and pointed it at Jake and Jonty. "Respect."

196

Jonty smiled. "It's a pity we had to take a bear on."

"I can't remember the last time I was hit so hard," said Evans, nodding towards Jake.

"It wasn't hard enough," Jake replied.

Jonty's face straightened. "Why have you brought us here today, Jack?"

Evans now sat upright. "I heard you were back, Jonty. I got drunk and drove on purpose to get arrested so we could arrange to talk."

Jonty was now looking hard at the foe opposite him. "So, it was a plan to instigate a private chat?"

Evans nodded. "I saw you following us to Liverpool docks."

Jonty looked at Jake. They both held a deadpan face.

"Don't worry," smiled Evans, "I didn't tell anybody. I needed to find a way of talking privately with you. I couldn't think of another way."

Jonty intercepted. "It will be an expensive one when you receive your fine and lose your driving licence."

Evans smiled. "That won't happen, trust me."

Jonty looked puzzled. *What is Evans saying?* he wondered. However, the drink charge was not important to Jonty, so he let the comment pass.

"What are we here for, Jack?" Jonty reiterated.

"I need your help, Jonty," replied Evans. "I want out of this life. I'm getting older. There are only two ways out of this life – die old, or opt-out and get killed."

Jonty listened as Evans continued. "I have moved house every year for as long as I care to remember, just to keep one step ahead of the law. We are moving again today. I have to, as I gave the address at the station."

"Why did you do that?" Jonty asked.

"Because I knew you would come knocking at the door, Jonty."

"So you're not just a bag of muscle, then."

They all went quiet as the waiter brought three coffees and placed them on the table in front of them. Jonty looked Evans up and down. He was expensively dressed in a Hugo Boss lemon shirt over an equally expensive pair of black Armani jeans, with a pair of blue boating shoes and no socks.

"What do you want out of this, Jack?"

"I want a new identity."

Jonty laughed. "This is not America, you know. We don't have a witness protection racket."

Evans looked down at the floor. "Well, it's about time you did."

"What do I get in return?" asked Jonty.

"Information," was the instant response.

"About what?"

"The biggest racket you have ever seen."

"How much do you know really, Jack?"

Evans lifted his head and looked Jonty in the eye. "I don't know it all. Everybody knows only what they are involved in. But I know enough to get you way down the path."

"Okay," said Jonty. "I will need some information now – as a deposit if you like."

Evans sneered. "No way, Jonty. We deal first."

"I need to know you are serious, Jack," said Jonty. "You want me to go to my superiors and try to get something that is not even accepted in this country. So no guarantees."

"Okay, okay," replied Evans. "Just a few snippets, then, to show I am serious."

Jonty didn't need a second opportunity to get out his notebook and pen.

"Okay," he said, "let's say I ask two questions now?" He looked at Evans for a moment. "That will show me how serious you are."

Evans did not respond verbally. Instead, he nodded and put his head down, like a man ready for the gallows.

Jonty looked at Evans. "How did you know we were in London the day we fought? Who sent you? And who were the other men?"

Evans grinned. "That's clever, Jonty. That's three questions in one."

Jonty stared back coldly. "That's the first question."

"I will answer the third part first," said Evans. "One of the other men was James Morgan. He's a Londoner and is the boss in London. He has a team of about twenty men, split into four small teams. He was there because it's his patch, and he would be expected to manage anything that happens in London. I don't know him that well, but judging by the help he didn't give me and Downsy, I wouldn't want to rely on him."

"Downs?" asked Jonty.

"George Downs is like me, he's a foot soldier from Birmingham. I've worked with him in the past. A good guy. Never seen him get beat in a fight until he met you, Jake. Full respect, mate."

"What were you doing attacking us?" asked Jonty.

"The plan was to just rough you up and put the wind up you," replied Evans. "A message had filtered down that you had been asking questions at the police station. It was presumed that, as you had retired, you would be easily persuaded to walk away." Evans smiled. "I guess not, eh?"

"I guess not," Jake intervened.

Evans continued. "I have a boss by the name of Ken Fitzroy. He has a boss by the name of Billy Jones. I guess the order came from him."

Jonty and Jake stared at each other. However, they quickly refocused so as not to give too much away.

"Who is Billy Jones?" Jonty asked.

"Billy Jones is the top boss," said Evans. "He runs everything. What he says goes."

"What type of things does he ask you to do?" Jonty pressed.

"Come on, Jonty," replied Evans. "Enough for today. You're pushing your luck. Not too much at once, eh?"

Jonty was intrigued. "Okay," was his reply. "But, how did you know we were in London?" Jonty had wanted an answer to this question since the day of the brawl.

"Billy Jones saw you both together with your wives in the Midland Hotel," said Evans. Again, Jonty and Jake looked briefly at each other.

"Does he know you both?"

"Yes, he does," said Jonty. "He is good at maths, as he can put two and two together."

Evans continued. "I think he must like you or something because we were told to gently persuade you and not go heavy."

That's what you call gentle? Jonty thought.

"Okay, question number two," he continued tamely. "What is Verde?"

Evans' head shot up, just as he was about to take a sip of his coffee. He stared at Jonty. The sheer speed of the head turn was proof enough that Evans was lying.

"I don't know," he said.

"You will have to do better than that," said Jonty. "You were driving the lorry."

"Maybe that's one for the back burner, too?" said Jonty.

"Maybe," Evans replied.

Evans felt relieved that Jonty was not pushing it further. Jonty was happy that Evans had offered the information he wanted. He also knew that pushing to far now may result in Evans pulling away for good.

"Okay then, one more question?" Jonty proceeded.

Evans nodded.

"Who is Steve Pitt?"

Evans sat bolt upright. "God, Jonty, you *have* done your homework."

"Come on, Jack," Jonty pressed. "You have evaded two questions. Give me this."

"Pitt is a nasty piece of work," replied Evans. "He would always be called in for big deals."

"Like a hit?" asked Jake.

"Yes," was the quiet reply from Evans.

"So, Jack, what do you mean when you say you want out? Out of what?" Jonty pushed again.

"Well, when I first got into all of this in the seventies, it was a good way to earn money. It still is." Evans paused for a moment. "But, as you get older, you want a steadier life. You must know what I mean, Jonty?"

Jonty nodded but stayed quiet.

"I can't get out," continued Evans. "If I was seventy-five and of no use, then maybe." He looked for reassurance, but none came. "I'm in my fifties, Jonty. I want a life I can enjoy, not looking over my shoulder, or not being able to refuse a job." He looked at them both again. "I didn't want to go to London to battle with you two, but my life's choice won't allow me to choose." He looked at Jonty. "You are my only hope to get out of this, Jonty."

"Out of what?" asked Jonty.

"Organised crime… the British mafia!"

As they went their separate ways, at the door Jonty turned to Jake, knowing Evans was out of earshot. "It looks like the head of the British mafia knows we are on to him."

CHAPTER FORTY

William, who was now using the name, Billy, except in the family, was sitting with his grandfather, two years after being made godfather. They held regular meetings, as his thirst for knowledge from the wily old fox never waned.

"Keep it simple, never over complicate," Roberto was saying. "The problem with keeping things simple is that it can be complicated keeping it simple."

Billy did not have Roberto's vision, and this was another meeting to utilise his fluidity of thought. His brain had not aged at the same pace as his body. Today, they were speaking about the need for the community to deal with the international crime of money laundering.

Roberto, as always, was a few years ahead of anybody – and, again, it was impeccable timing. The United Nations was working towards the Vienna Convention to ban illicit trafficking in narcotics drugs and psychotropic substances. This was the first multilateral agreement that particularly dealt with money laundering; it was signed by 171 countries and was implemented in 168 of those countries. However, the Convention dealt mainly with drugs, and, whilst drug trafficking was an area that Roberto never directly touched, he knew it overlapped areas that involved his clientele.

Roberto pointed out to William where the future risks lay. "We cover most of the world with our export business," he said. "The governments of the world will be determined to identify and remove the persons involved in the illicit trafficking of the earnings and of their criminal activities and, thus, abolishing their main inducement for doing so."

This worried Roberto, as he was living proof that the article he was reading to William was the lifeblood that ran through the veins of the family. "We have two, maybe three, years to be in front of the game, William."

Of course, Roberto was familiar with the money laundering concept. In the twenties, money laundering became especially relevant during the prohibition era, as bootleggers of alcohol or operators of illegal casinos had to account for their incomes, and would open cash businesses.

According to some, laundry businesses were a suitable and popular option, leading to the term 'money laundering'.

Roberto enjoyed the business meetings with William. William's thirst for knowledge always warmed him. He felt that he had passed something worthwhile down a branch of the Family tree, whether it was showing his grandson how to fish all those years ago in Anglesey, or how he should be thinking when running a business, today.

Roberto continued chatting with William and discussed the basics of money laundering. "Our business needs three steps to survive. That is, cleansing the money from abroad, hence the phrase money laundering. We need it to look clean as if washed. We can do this in three easy steps…"

The old man paused for a moment to clear his throat. "Placement. The funds are furtively introduced into the financial system. You see, where the family receives income, for instance, Peru or Columbia, we need an outlet where the money can start its life and be moved into a legitimate place, let us assume a bank." Roberto smiled. "Once we have made this step completely, we can move onto the second stage."

Again, Roberto paused before he went on. "Layering. The money is moved around through numerous accounts to create confusion." He looked at his grandson for acknowledgement that he understood. A nod from William allowed him to continue. "You see, William, the more times we can move the money around, the harder it is for authorities to track it." William was still following so far.

"Let us say," continued Roberto, "that we receive an invoice billed to the factory for a new set of machine parts. That could be the first layer. Then we move the money to the bank through the company bank account, that is another layer. The company then might buy something in line with its business, let's say twenty tons of steel. We may use a couple of tons out of the batch and sell the rest on to somewhere else – let's say British Steel. We sell at a fifteen percent loss, which means the buyer has got a great deal, as he's paying eighty-five percent of its market price, therefore building an extra profit margin. At the same time, we have a payment going into our company's business account from British Steel. It could not be cleaner than a government-owned company and well worth the fifteen percent fee." He looked at William.

"I think I understand that," William said. "So, we are happy to make a loss to make the money look clean?"

"Exactly!" said Roberto. "And don't forget, we have already added the fifteen percent on at the front end client transaction." He paused. "Now then, if the first two points are done correctly, the third will look after itself."

He paused to take a sip of water from the glass on his desk.

"Integration," he continued. "It is integrated into the financial system through additional transactions until the dirty money appears clean. It's now ours to spend in any format we want – cash, cheques, banking system… It's clean." Roberto looked at William. "Do you understand what I have just told you?"

"Yes, I think so…" was the feeble response

"I need you to understand it, William," said Roberto. "If you do nothing else, get a true understanding of money laundering."

"I promise," William replied. "What do we need to do to ensure we are protected?"

"Good question," said Roberto. "We have been using the ordnance factory to allow you access to their blueprints."

Roberto thanked William for his efforts in producing the blueprints, before continuing. "The times that are coming mean we have to use you in a different role, William. Also, we will need you to spend more time in the family business."

William looked puzzled. "What are your thoughts, Pop?"

Roberto looked at William proudly. "As you know, Gordon Wallace, an executive of the national bank, is on our payroll, allowing the money to move between the bank and Brown's Engineering. I have had lunch with Gordon several times recently to discuss the money laundering proposals and he has agreed that we can place you in the bank by name only. You can spend as much time in there as you wish, whilst coordinating the accounts from both Brown's and the bank's perspective." Both William and Roberto knew that William was the head of the family, but Roberto always played the strategy correctly.

William looked at his grandfather. *I will never be as good as him as a Family head*, he told himself.

"We will have to place your titles in a career progression process and show on the books a fitting salary," continued Roberto. "So you will start as a trainee branch manager earning thirteen thousand a year. However, you will still be taking two hundred and fifty thousand per year from the family business."

William felt warm inside. *How good must this man have been at the top of his game?* He knew the answer. *Very good.*

"Finally, to end this meeting," Roberto said to William. "Be in the Broadwater Arms next Friday evening. We have arranged for Kenny Webb to be there. Of course, he doesn't know a thing, so just say that you are looking for a job. He will be asked earlier in the day whether he or his colleagues know anybody who may be interested in a new role within the bank."

William smiled. "Then let fate take its course." They both laughed.

"Now, let us go," said Roberto, standing up. "I am keeping you away from your grandmother. I know she is aching to see you." He put his arm around William's shoulders and walked to the lounge with him.

Billy was having a quiet drink as agreed when he 'happened' to bump into an old work colleague, Kenny Webb as planned.

"Kenny, how are you doing?" said Billy. "I haven't seen you for a while. Let me get you a drink."

"Hello, Billy," said Kenny in surprise. "I would love a pint of lager, mate," Billy ordered a pint for Kenny and a Coke for himself.

After twenty minutes of small talk and reminiscing, they fell silent.

"How are things, Billy?" Kenny asked.

"Not so good, Kenny," said Billy. "I have been looking for another job, but with no success. The factory is not what I want."

"My boss told me today that the bank is looking for some new talent, but was struggling to find the right person for the role."

"Wow, that sounds good," Billy said, trying to sound excited and surprised all at once.

I bet you would be perfect," Kenny said. "You are good with figures, which is important. And you've worked in a government factory, which shows honesty."

"How do I get an application form?" Billy asked.

"I will get one for you if you fancy giving it a go?" Kenny told him.

They spent the next half hour talking about old times again before Billy made his excuses and left.

Billy put in his application that he was trustworthy, hardworking, and flexible in working hours, whilst enjoying an autonomous-based role and that he could work with little supervision. His job in the drawing office required numerical ability and he could utilise this in a banking environment, where maths was imperative.

The application turned into an interview. Billy was himself — self-confident and showing his natural presence. The interview turned into a job offer, which he immediately accepted. The last twelve months had been good and this position should help in the longevity of Brown's Engineering, its client base, and Billy's future.

CHAPTER FORTY-ONE

Jonty travelled back from Chester with Jake, happy that a little more knowledge had been gained. The name George Downs was on the list, and Paul Fitzroy, who wasn't on the list.

"It makes sense why Pitt was driving the car when he killed Paul if he was the hitman," Jake said.

"Yes, it does," replied Jonty. "We just need a few more steps to get to the proof."

"What is the next step, Jonty?"

"I need to see if I can conjure a deal for Evans, then get him talking."

They continued on their journey back to Jake's home, where they had arranged to meet Em and Helen. Em had offered to cook an American-style, Iowa meal for them of steak de burgo, which was a mid-west specialty, mainly to the Des Moines area.

"You won't see too much of this dish outside of Iowa," said Em, "but boy is it good. Followed by a batch of puppy chow."

"What?" Helen shrieked when she was first told what they were having.

Em consoled her. "That is a typical comment from someone out-of-state, together with a weird, semi-disgusted look. Mention it to an Iowan and they will instantly ask you to share. Trust me, Helen, you will enjoy it."

The next morning, Jonty was in the office early. He was a little hungover from the wine consumption at Jake and Em's the evening before, where Helen and he had enjoyed a fantastic night. The food Em had put together was glorious, unfortunately with just a little too much red wine.

Trying to focus, Jonty decided to look at the report from Aston police station. Nothing seemed out of the ordinary at first. *William Green, Verde,* he rubbed his index finger between his nose and top lip as he thought. *Verde is Italian for Green. I wonder?*

Later that morning, Jonty found himself knocking on Quinn's door.

"Come in, Jonty," said Quinn. "How are you settling in?"

"Quite well, thank you, sir," was Jonty's reply, but he wasn't there to talk about his comfort in the office.

"Take a seat," said Quinn.

"Sir!" replied Jonty. Quinn was still reading some papers in front of him. "I would like to reopen a case."

"Which case is that, Jonty? We have thousands."

"The death of Paul Jennings?"

Quinn's head slowly rose.

"As I recall," he said, "you were on that case and it was closed as an accidental death. What has changed?"

Jonty chose his next words carefully. "Nothing that I can substantiate at this point, sir. But I would like to reinvestigate if that's okay with you?"

Quinn tossed his pen on the desk in front of him. "Jonty, we do not have the resources or funds available for this."

Jonty was expecting this. "I will work on it alone, sir, until a new case comes up for me to work on. I have spare capacity at the moment until I get up to speed, and it will help me to get back into the swing of things."

Quinn looked over the top of his faux tortoiseshell-framed glasses. "Okay, Jonty. But only until I think that your workload is being affected."

"Thank you, sir," With that, Jonty felt that now was not the time to bring up leniency on behalf of Jack Evans' testimony. Jonty then thought for a moment. *I need to gamble a little here, or I will be caught between Quinn giving leniency and Jack Evans giving information.*

Once he was back in his office, Jonty rang Jack Evans on the mobile number Evans had given him. Evans had decided to take only one phone call off Jonty, then throw the mobile phone away and buy a new one, as that would prevent any chance of leaving a trail. He promised to let Jonty know each new number. The discussion was short.

"Jack, it's Jonty here. I have good news."

"Okay," was the reply.

"I need to speak about the drink driving incident."

"Okay. When?" Evans asked.

"As soon as we can."

"Send me a formal letter requesting that I need to bring ID as requested by the desk sergeant," said Evans. "I will sort from there."

"Deal," said Jonty, ending the call. *God, this man is good at covering his tracks,* he thought.

On the morning of 5th October, an envelope dropped through the letterbox at the home of Jack Evans. It was a letter typed on official Greater Manchester Police headed paper setting out the salient points.

Dear Mr. Evans,
Following your arrest for being in excess of the legal drink-drive limit, we requested that you bring proof of a legal current driving licence and proof of valid motor insurance for the car you were driving at the time of the arrest.

I can confirm I have checked the current Ministry of Department certificate and this is acceptable.

If you do not produce this information then further action may be taken against you for withholding information.

I trust this is to your satisfaction,

Yours sincerely,

Daniel Piper

Jonty had requested Danny, the desk sergeant, to send the letter.

Within minutes of opening the letter, Jack rang his boss, Ken Fitzroy. Fitzroy was a no-nonsense hoodlum from Liverpool. Fitzroy and his close friend, Pat O'Neill, had been up in and around the dock area of Liverpool. They ran a small-time import and export business trafficking drugs to and from Liverpool docks. They then sold the drugs on the streets of the city.

When Billy heard about their tough reputation, he drove to Walton Vale, a hard area of Liverpool, and offered them a job working for him on their turf. They initially refused and told Billy he could work for them if he knew what was good for him.

Billy had smiled and waved his arm in a forwarding motion to the driver of the hired E class Mercedes. The two scallies laughed.

"So, you're looking for a ruck?" said Fitzroy.

"No," Billy replied. "I want to work with you, not against you."

Fitzroy sneered at Billy. He was six foot four and spent a lot of time working out; his arms looked like they were going to burst under the tight short sleeves of the Nike T-shirt.

"I don't like Mancs," he said, using the term used for somebody from Manchester. Fitzroy continued. "Don't come on our turf and tell me how to do business." He was now glaring at Billy. "It's either my way, or I am going to knock you back to Moses."

The two men advanced towards Billy, but by this time the driver had eased out of the car door and was walking to join the 'discussion'. Fitzroy glanced over, then looked again at Steve Pitt, recognising him.

"Steve, how are you?" Pitt remained straight-faced and put his hand in the pocket of his expensive-looking, calf-length black leather coat. Fitzroy knew that Steve Pitt probably had a gun in the pocket. He also knew that he would take anybody on head to head in the city, except Steve Pitt.

"Well, you never said you were a friend of Steve's," said Fitzroy with a noticeable change in demeanor. "That makes things different."

Billy looked at Fitzroy. "In what way is it different?"

Fitzroy laughed. "In a way that we can discuss things."

Twenty years had passed since that meeting and it didn't take a mathematician to work out that there was more money for Fitzroy and O'Neill working for Billy than they would ever earn working alone. Fitzroy had been loyal ever since.

Evans, using his normal mobile phone, told Fitzroy about the letter and asked how he should handle it.

Fitzroy replied in his thick Liverpudlian accent. "I can't believe you were caught drink driving, Jack. You know we need to keep clean about things like that, to stop the law finding out about us." Silence ensued for a few seconds, then Fitzroy continued. "You have compromised us here, Jack. You need to take the evidence and try to follow the procedure. We don't want more heat than we need."

"I don't know what came over me, Fitz," said Jack. "I am sorry."

Fitzroy came back. "You acted like a prat, let's get through it as clean as we can."

Fitzroy always felt nervy about Jack. He felt in control of everybody in his team, except Evans, and the reason was that he was not sure who would win in a toe-to-toe fight. He put the phone down.

The whole exercise had been set up by Jack to allow him to go to the local nick. If anybody saw him, they would know that the reason he was there was to discuss the drink driving offence.

CHAPTER FORTY-TWO

Jack Evans was careful to choose the day when he would turn up at the local police station. He needed to time it for when his boss would be away meeting people about potential new orders with Billy. He agreed to this with Jonty.

At the station desk, he gave Danny Twist the driving licence and insurance documents as requested. As Danny was photocopying and carrying out the formal paperwork for Evans to take away, Jonty appeared from round the back of Evans and quickly passed a piece of paper to him. On it he had written: *Meet me at the Crowne Plaza in two hours, ask for James Roberts.*

Two hours later, Evans arrived at the Crowne Plaza. It was 11.15 am. He walked through the quiet lobby to the reception, where a smartly dressed receptionist looked at him and smiled politely.

"Good morning, sir. How can I help you today?"

"I am looking for Mr. James Roberts."

"Just one moment, sir." The receptionist picked up the phone and Jonty answered.

"A Mr. Ratcliffe is here to see you, Mr. Roberts."

Jonty replied. "Could you send him to room 412, please?"

"Yes, sir, I will do that."

She gave Evans the directions. Evans took the elevator, then walked along the corridor to room 412. The door was ajar. He walked through it to find Jonty sitting by the coffee table. Jonty stood up and the men shook hands.

"Why use Ratcliffe as a name?" Jonty enquired.

"Because I am going to rat up somebody who has paid me a good wage for years, and I feel on the edge of a cliff," said Evans grimly.

Jonty tightened his lips and nodded slightly. "It's all worth it, for the price of freedom."

"We'll see," was Evans' retort.

Jonty began the meeting by lying through his back teeth. He knew it was the only way forward. After all, his priority was to find Paul's killer, not protect Evans. He felt no guilt whatsoever. He felt comfortable and relaxed. He was going to look forward to this one-to-one meeting.

"The first thing I have to say," said Jonty, "is that I have around forty photos taken of you on your journey to Liverpool with the Aston Martin and rifles."

Evans looked surprised. He hadn't noticed Jonty when he had transferred the Aston Martin at the service station.

"Where were the guns being exported to?" asked Jonty.

"What's the deal?" Evans answered the question with a question.

"I have had a few chats about your leniency of the sentence in return for information that may lead to the person responsible for the death of Paul Jennings." Jonty looked at Evans, waiting for a reply. None came, so he continued.

"The GMP are willing to enter such a deal," he lied, "depending on how significant and how detailed the information you give is. They will not commit to an amount of leniency. That is as far as I can go at the moment, Jack."

Evans considered this for a while. "I am not guilty of anything."

Jonty smiled and then spoke. "No, but you're not far away."

He looked at Evans again. "I know about the Aston Martin, I know about the handover of gun-running, and I know that the VERDE sides are changed back to Brown's Engineering every time a dodgy deal is completed."

Evans stared at Jonty, refusing to say anything.

Jonty looked harder at Evans. "Now, Jack, I am not accusing you of anything, and I don't know what will come out of this conversation, but it needs to be meaningful. If we can do it today, we won't have to meet so often officially."

Jonty let the words hang, before continuing. "And that reduces the risk of you being found out by Billy boy, doesn't it?"

Evans nodded. He didn't want any more of these meetings. The fewer the better.

"Okay, Jack, let's start with the information you know," said Jonty. "Where were the guns being run to?"

Jack stared at him. "Why not ease me into this, Jonty?"

Jonty smiled. "Well?"

"The guns were heading for Mexico to arm two of the major cartels in the Mexican drug war."

Jonty looked shocked. "You're supporting a war that has seen over sixty thousand killed?"

Jack put his head down.

"How do you feel about that, Jack?"

Evans' face turned red. "I feel bad, Jonty. I know how much blood is on our hands."

Jonty continued. "Who were the men I saw you with?"

"They were middlemen," replied Evans. "They are the link between our business and those we supply. We call them Agents."

"And the Aston Martin?" said Jonty. "You changed the plates in the Scania. I have pictures."

Evans smiled. "Don't kid a kidder."

Jonty threw down an envelope. Evans picked it up and opened it. He pulled out clear photographs of him taking the plates into the back of the Scania and the Aston being rolled off the lorry. Jonty showed Evans an image of the plates on the car and the Vehicle Identification Number on the windscreen.

"The VIN has probably been changed by now, Jack," said Jonty. "But not when I took the photo."

Evans stared at the photos. "And what about the private number plate put on the car."

Jonty moved nearer and lowered his voice. "They belong to a scrapped Ford Mondeo, not a £100k Aston Martin."

Evans looked like a schoolboy caught stealing apples, only these were big apples.

Jonty continued. "I am guessing your bosses will not be happy when I push this in their direction, Jack – which I will do this afternoon if I don't get the answers I'm after."

Evans was still red-faced. "Okay, Jonty. The Aston was a different deal. We steal cars to order and export them." Evans was feeling pinned against the wall here. He hadn't planned on Jonty knowing so much. "It was an order for Dubai. I don't have details of the client."

Jonty stared at Evans. "You could be in big trouble here, Jack."

Both men knew that Evans needed Jonty more than ever.

Jonty got up and began to make them both a coffee. He switched on the kettle and waited for it to boil.

"Right, Jack," he said, turning to Evans. "I need the story here. Let's start at the beginning."

Evans nodded, then started with the opening line, "I am a soldier for the mafia!"

Jonty laughed. "There is no such thing as the British mafia," he said, shaking his head at the same time. "A lot of crooks look up to the American mafia as some type of…" He looked to the ceiling as if searching for the correct word. "Idolisation."

He turned away and finished making the coffees, placing the cups on the coffee table.

"But come on Jack," he continued as he sat down. "You and I know there is no such thing in Britain."

Evans looked at him with a serious face. "I am a soldier for the mafia."

Jonty thought better of a second skit. "Okay, tell me how that works then, Jack?"

This time, Jonty was a little more serious as Evans explained.

"We are brought up in the organisation on the past and the wealth of the organisation…" Evans paused and took a sip of his coffee. "It all began in Liverpool in 1908."

"Hang on," Jonty interrupted. "Can I record this for my own use and off the record?"

"How can I trust it's off the record?" Evans responded.

"We can't do this without trust, Jack," said Jonty. Evans nodded, not realising that Jonty had already broken the rule by lying minutes earlier.

Evans reiterated. "As I said, we are all told the history of our family and it started in Liverpool in 1908."

For the following hour, Evans told Jonty how Roberto and Maria Sartori had brought their sons, Roberto Junior and Giovanni, to Liverpool. He told of Roberto Senior dying and how Roberto Junior went to New York to meet Bennito Rossi and stayed there to learn the trade of a gang boss. He spoke of the imports and exports of alcohol run by Giovanni to support the prohibition era of a non-alcoholic America. He then spoke of Roberto's first hit in an Italian restaurant called Verde, which became folklore in the family.

Jonty stopped him and lied again, only this time it was a smaller lie.

"I know that the HGV with Verde on the side was also linked to the stolen BMW that killed Paul Jennings, twenty-odd years ago, along with the recent activity I photographed." He nodded to the envelope containing the photographs on the table. "What is Verde?"

Evans looked at him. "Verde is nothing."

Jonty lifted his chin slightly, encouraging Evans to continue.

213

"The lorry is owned by a company called Brown's Engineering," said Evans, "which in turn is owned by Roberto Sartori. If he wanted anything doing that wasn't to be detected, he would have the number plates changed and the canvas sheets on the side of the vehicle with a company logo of Verde. Then he would be able to transport whatever he wanted."

"In this case, for the Paul Jennings hit," said Jonty. "The black BMW?"

"Yes," Evans answered.

Jonty continued. "So, it was nothing to do with Italian being Verde for green?"

Evans shook his head. "No, it referred to a shooting in the twenties at the Italian restaurant in New York, called Verde. It has become folklore."

"Then what?" asked Jonty.

Evans continued to tell the history of the Family, of the meeting between Benni, Roberto, and Giovanni, where Roberto had discussed his plan to phase in the pit owners to continue with an income after prohibition.

Jonty again intervened. "So, at this point, there is extortion going on in British coal mines? Taking advantage of the working class, who were penniless after a national strike that went wrong?"

"Yes," replied Evans.

"And all this is being overseen by a Don in New York?" Jonty asked in disbelief.

Evans nodded at the same time as he replied. "Correct."

"I can't believe it," said Jonty.

Evans looked at him. "I know this is off the record, Jonty. That's why I am telling you."

Evans said this to make sure that it was recorded on the tape. Then he continued to tell Jonty how the extortion racket continued until the National Coal Board took over the pits. That, during the Second World War, Roberto Sartori had bought Brown's Engineering, which was doing its bit for the war effort by making rifles for the forces. However, the overall plan was to mask it until Roberto could build weapons and sell to the black market for wars and civil unrest in foreign countries.

Jonty again intervened. "Why was this Roberto chap not an entrepreneur? He had a brilliant mind."

Evans shrugged his shoulders. "He is brilliant at what he does."

"Is?" quizzed Jonty "Is he still alive?"

"Yes, but he is an old man now."

"Then who is the godfather?"

"Billy Jones."

Jonty knew that this would fit in place somewhere, but where he was not quite sure.

"I thought Billy Jones was a bank manager?" he said. Instantly, he saw an image of Billy's luxurious house in his mind's eye.

"It is a front," Evans confirmed. "Initially, Roberto got Billy a job at the Royal Ordnance Factory as a draughtsman."

Jonty looked lost at this.

"The reason for this," explained Evans, "was to allow Billy to get any new technology weapons to Roberto by copying plans and drawings." He paused and drank some more coffee. "Roberto could then manufacture them and get them to the black market before approval was given at government level."

Jonty guessed. "Too much red tape?"

"Exactly."

"So how did Paul get involved with gun running?" Jonty asked.

"Billy bullied him into it," replied Evans. "Billy always wanted to keep the gun running as far away from the family as possible, so he would bring in non-connected people and use them. He'd then kill them off before any of them could say anything."

Jonty looked down for a moment, deep in thought. Then he looked Evans in the eyes. "Are you saying that, even if Paul hadn't wanted out, his days were numbered?"

"Yes, he would have still been murdered."

"Tell me how the structure works, Jack?"

Evans continued to explain, whilst Jonty jotted everything down on paper.

"The Family no longer has links with America," said Evans. "That ended when Don Bennito died, but the Family is still run to the same format."

"Which is?" asked an intrigued Jonty.

"The top of the structure is the godfather – the Don, or whatever he may be called. Everybody knows this title from so many films, but it is a phrase used mainly by the media. The title is currently held by Billy, passed on from Roberto.

"The next position is the underboss, who is and has always been Giovanni. The underboss is second-in-command in the hierarchy of the mafia crime family. Giovanni is ready to stand in for the boss at any given moment. The underboss is usually groomed for an eventual takeover – although, in this family, it was Billy who was to take over, owing to age."

Jonty was enjoying this. It was so different from normal day-to-day police inquiries.

Evans continued. "The next position is the boss. Again, this would be Billy in our Family. As we are small, we have a flatter structure. The boss, or capo, is the head of the organisation. The boss is a dictator and has the power to order anything from anyone in the organisation. The boss makes all the important decisions, much like the CEO of a company would. Roberto, in particular, is greatly respected and widely feared by his subordinates. All of the men in his outfit would pay him a tribute and shower him with gifts, even though he is an extremely wealthy man."

Evans paused for a few seconds whilst Jonty took in everything he had said. He then continued.

"The next level is the consigliere or chief advisor. He is the boss's right-hand man. The consigliere is not officially part of the hierarchy of the mafia, but he plays one of the most important roles in a crime family. He is the close, trusted friend and confidant of the family boss. The consigliere is meant to offer unbiased information based on what he sees as best for the family, via legal stuff and such like."

Jonty sat, listening in fascination.

"He's not supposed to factor emotional concerns, such as retaliation and blood feuds, into his decisions," continued Evans. "The consigliere is not required to be a direct relative of the boss. Instead, he is chosen solely for his abilities and the amount of knowledge he possesses. Generally, only the boss and underboss have more authority than the consigliere in an organised crime family."

Jonty interrupted. "Who is the Sartori consigliere now?"

The name he then heard came as a shock. "Edward Le Conte."

Jack continued. "The next level is the caporegime. This would be Ken Fitzroy. The capo is the captain or lieutenant of a division within the mafia. He heads a large crew of soldiers, like Steve Pitt and myself. He can order them to do anything, such as murder, assault, bombing... anything. The captain reports directly to a boss or underboss, who hands down the instructions. He ranks much higher in the hierarchy of the mafia. He is also in charge of handling most of the money."

No wonder they were below the radar for so long, thought Jonty, who was feeling a reluctant respect for this Roberto.

"Soldiers such as myself or Steve Pitt," continued Evans, "are the lowest-ranking members of the hierarchy of the mafia, or *la cosa nostra*. We do the majority of the work as I said before… making deliveries, picking up cash, committing murder, assault, battery, bombing, witness intimidation, killing jurors, bribing law enforcement, politicians, government officials, and members of the constabulary."

Jonty interrupted aggressively. "Do you have any police officers on your books now?"

"Yes." was the unexpected reply.

"Who?"

"I don't have names," replied Evans. "It would be the boss or consigliere who would usually make that transaction. That would not be passed down to soldiers."

"Have you murdered?" Jonty asked bluntly.

"No," was the curt reply.

"Okay, continue," urged Jonty.

"Finally, there are the associates," said Evans. "They are not actual members of the mafia, but they work for the mafia. Rather, anyone who teams up with them on a criminal enterprise of some kind. They could be anyone who does business with the mafia."

Jonty interrupted yet again. "Like the gun runners, or Aston Martin agents I saw?"

"Yes," replied Evans. "It could also be someone who does dirty work for the mafia, including murder, assault, arson, assassinations, drive-by shooting, contract killing, witness intimidation, jury intimidation, killing jurors, car bombing, and bombing buildings and houses, along with other criminal and organised crime activities."

"Are there any more activities?" Jonty asked sarcastically.

"There are also the Italian newcomers, who have yet to be made, called cugines," said Evans, ignoring Jonty's comment. "They play a minor role in the operation of the mafia. Associates cannot turn down an order from the mafia. If the mafia gives them an order, they have to follow it, and they are on call for the mafia twenty-four hours, three hundred and sixty-five days a year. They are also fair game on the streets, as they are not protected by the organisation, unless they are a very important and valuable member of the mafia. Anybody can be an associate in the mafia, however, only Italians or Sicilians can be made."

Jonty thanked Jack for being so candid. However, the guilt had now kicked in, as he was not sure if he could return the information with the support he had originally promised.

"One other question, Jack," said Jonty. "Who is William Green? I know he is your cousin, but where does he fit in?"

Jack looked at him before replying. "William Green is Billy Jones. His mother remarried from Green to Jones after her husband died in a plane crash. Billy changed his name with the marriage."

Jonty took a moment to write all this information down.

"One final thing, Jack," he said again. "You may need to give evidence to get the preferential treatment."

Evans looked at him. "I will need protection, too."

"Deal," replied Jonty.

They decided to end the meeting there. Jonty could not believe all this was happening in the UK. He felt exhausted and weary. The amount of information he'd downloaded was deeper than any case he could ever remember.

Jack gave Jonty his new mobile number, yet again, and made himself another coffee to allow Jonty time to get away from Chester so they would not be seen together.

CHAPTER FORTY-THREE

Toni screamed out loud as she saw Roberto crumple to the floor of the luxurious bedroom they had shared all the years together. He lay on the floor, inert. Toni's screams brought Giovanni rushing across the landing into the room.

"Giovanni, help! He has collapsed!" screamed Toni.

Giovanni looked around the room and saw Roberto's mobile phone on the bedside cabinet. He picked it up and rang 999.

"Hello?" was the reply. "Is your emergency fire? police? Or an ambulance?"

"Ambulance," Giovanni coolly replied.

"I am putting you through right now."

Within seconds, Giovanni heard a female voice. "Hello, what is the problem?"

"My brother has collapsed on the bedroom floor and he is motionless," Giovanni stated.

"Is he breathing?" asked the operator. Giovanni reached over to his brother's arm and felt for a pulse. A light one was found.

"There is a pulse and he is breathing lightly," Giovanni confirmed.

"How old is the gentleman?"

"He is ninety-seven."

The operator asked for the address and noted it down. "An ambulance will be with you shortly," she said, then ended the call.

Toni took a three-minute shower, then changed from her gold satin pyjamas into a pair of jeans and a blue and gold fleck angora jumper, ready to assist her husband on the journey to the hospital.

The paramedics arrived within fifteen minutes and looked at the old, grey man lying on the plush Persian rug, covering an equally expensive-looking solid beech floor. Roberto was motionless as Toni watched the paramedics get to work on him.

The leading paramedic asked Toni to get some aspirin for Roberto. Guidelines on aspirin are clear, and it is very beneficial for almost every patient. This was the thought process of David, the lead paramedic, his name clearly in sight on his name badge.

David continued to explain to Toni what he was doing in a bid to keep her comforted and calm. "Our priority is to do a good patient assessment. This will identify any immediate problems, such as low blood pressure, slow/rapid heart rate, or breathing problems. That's what we are doing now."

He then asked his assistant, Greg, who wore a matching green-coloured uniform, to attach the 12-lead ECG machine.

"The sooner we do this, the sooner we can alert the hospital and the sooner Roberto can get treated," David continued.

He knew the 12-lead ECGs were crucial to identify a heart attack in the field. Within the hour, David was happy to transfer Roberto to the ambulance and take him on the thirty-minute drive to Manchester Royal.

During the trip, Greg administered nitro-glycerine, which helps dilate (open up) the coronary arteries, thus providing more oxygen to the heart and reducing the patient's pain and the damage caused. He ensured he managed Roberto's blood pressure, whilst also administering heparin, which helps keep the clot from growing any larger. With Toni's help, he made sure Roberto was changed into a hospital gown ready for when they arrived at A&E.

Giovanni changed equally as quickly. He drove behind the ambulance as it raced to the hospital.

By the time they arrived at the Manchester Royal, the medical staff were waiting, ready to take Roberto into theatre, where he would undergo a coronary angioplasty. Whilst this was happening, a doctor took Toni and Giovanni to one side to explain that angioplasty was an emergency procedure to treat Roberto's heart attack.

"A coronary angioplasty aims to widen your narrowed or blocked coronary artery by inflating a balloon inside it," said the doctor. "The surgeon will usually also insert a wire mesh tube called a stent to hold your coronary artery open."

"Will he be okay?" Toni enquired.

The answer was not what she expected. "The next twenty-four to forty-eight hours will tell us how well Roberto is doing," replied the doctor. "He is, however, a frail man, but sometimes that can be better than a younger man with a stronger heart."

Giovanni took Toni by the arm and thanked the doctor.

When the doctor left, Toni began to pace the room, waiting for any news on the progress of the operation. She wanted to be anywhere but there in that hospital, with Roberto on an operation table, fighting for his life. She thought back to the first time she ever saw Roberto in *Piccolo Italia*. He looked so handsome; his face glowed in such a way she had never seen before. Her right hand went to her left shoulder and imagined she was feeling the cream, fine-knit cardigan she remembered wearing that day. She was transported back to that very moment in her mind when she was twenty years old.

Her thoughts shot forward again to 1979 when she and Roberto had taken a holiday break to the old Sicily. She remembered how they were made so welcome as Sicilians. Giovanni looked at her. She was smiling, in a daydream. She was caught in the holiday, on a day trip that was called 'The Godfather Tour'. It was designed to take holidaymakers to all the places made famous in the 1972 film *The Godfather*. They visited the church where a young Michael Corleone married Apollonia; they visited the bar 'Vitelli' in Savoca, a village near Taormina, where Michael had ordered a hit. Toni unconsciously began to laugh, which, in turn, made Giovanni laugh.

"What are you laughing at?" he asked.

Toni told him that she was thinking back to their trip in Sicily. A guide had asked Roberto whether he had enjoyed the trip. She smiled and looked Giovanni in the eyes.

"He replied that it was okay, but all a bit far-fetched for him. God, I love that man."

They both laughed, just as Francesca came bursting through the door. The sweet thoughts of the past were swept back to the present day. Francesca ran up to her mother and held her tightly. Francesca was in tears; she felt it impossible for such a man of strength to be in a vulnerable position. She felt hot in the head and cold in her hands, her throat trembling as she tried to catch air as she sobbed.

"How is he? Where is he? He is alive, isn't he?"

"Of course he is," said Toni. "He will never die." She put her hands on Francesca's shoulders and stood square on to her. "Your father has had a heart attack and is having an operation now as we speak."

She looked at Giovanni. "Sorry, Giovanni… what was the operation called again?"

Giovanni showed the tender trait he had possessed throughout life as he answered. "A coronary angioplasty."

221

"That's right," Toni thanked Giovanni and looked back at Francesca. "The next two days are critical. It's going to be a long forty-eight hours."

Roberto was wheeled out of the operation room four hours later and into a private ward, which was very comfortable. Dr. Sayed, the surgeon who operated, came over to speak to them.

"It went as well as we could have expected," he said. "I have opened the arteries and we will see how it goes."

"What are the odds?" asked Toni.

Dr. Sayed smiled. "The question everybody asks." He projected a very gentle voice. "I know it seems a long time to wait, but nature will take its course. However, from my point of view, it went as well as it could."

That made Toni and Francesca feel better.

"Can we sit with him?" Francesca asked.

"He is very poorly at the moment and unconscious," replied Dr Sayed. "But twenty minutes will be okay." He smiled. "Then, come back tomorrow for a little longer. You need to get some sleep, too."

CHAPTER FORTY-FOUR

Jake walked down the path of the rented house. Em left him a shopping list and asked him to go to the local supermarket. He had rushed this morning and he was wrongly dressed for the chilly mid-October morning. The mornings were taking longer to catch the daylight and he'd slept a little longer than planned. The tree-lined street saw burnt-orange trees dancing in the autumn breeze, trying to shake off their leaves in readiness for the winter. The leaves were resisting and not yet ready to fall. Jake hadn't put a coat on and he was feeling a little cold in just a thin, cotton, long-sleeved shirt accessorised by his faded Levi 501s and a pair of soft leather brown shoes. Just as the car lights flashed back, confirming he had pressed the remote unlock on the car keys, he heard a voice from over his right shoulder.

"Well! Well! If it isn't our resident Yank."

Jake recognised the voice. He turned around to see Billy Jones standing in front of him. With him was another face from his memory, Steve Pitt.

"Hello, Billy. What are you doing around these parts?" asked Jake, trying to keep calm and collected.

"More to the point, what are *you* doing around these parts?" Billy replied menacingly.

"I live here," said Jake. "We are spending some time enjoying Manchester. Em loves it round here. We will be going home soon."

Billy looked at him. "Well, before you go, we must go out for a meal with the girls. What do you think?"

"Great idea. We would love to," Jake responded.

"I'll be in touch," were Billy's parting words.

On his return from the supermarket, Jake told Jonty of his encounter.

Jonty did not like the idea of Jake and Em going for a meal with Billy and Maggie.

"I think you could be walking into a trap. I would like to be there," said Jonty with unusual urgency in his voice.

"He hasn't got in touch yet," Jake said, trying to make it appear less important.

"He will," replied Jonty, knowing Jake was trying to defuse the situation. "Why don't you come along with me? I am meeting up with Martin McClean, the pathologist working on Dave's post-mortem. He says he has something to tell me regarding the DNA result."

Martin McClean was waiting for Jonty when he and Jake arrived at the Willows pub, where Jonty offered to buy lunch.

"Hello, Martin," he said. "This is Jake Hughes, the man I told you about."

"Hello, Jake, good to meet you."

"And you, sir," Jake replied, with typical American manners.

Jonty turned to Jake. "Martin has something to tell you."

Jake stared apprehensively at Martin, who smiled.

"You look worried, Jake," said Martin. "The only thing you have to worry about is the trick that Jonty has played on you." He looked at Jonty.

Jonty laughed. "Tell him, Martin."

"Well," began Martin, "Jonty has asked me to do some fingerprint testing from the stem of a deadheaded foxglove flower." He stopped when he saw Jake's confused look. "Sorry, I must explain. I know Jonty doesn't mind you knowing this information and I don't mind breaking confidences, just this once."

Jake remained silent, looking confused

"As I was saying," Martin continued, "I have done a fingerprint check on the foxglove that Jonty brought to me. I compared it against the DNA fibres of clothing found under one of Dave Rowlands' fingernails to see if it's the same person. It matches. However, I ran it through the central fingerprint and DNA system and it drew up a blank. We think we have the murderer's DNA, We just don't know who the DNA belongs to"

"Yet!" Jonty finished off the sentence.

"That's great news," followed up Jake. "But what does it have to do with me?"

"Nothing," said Jonty still smiling.

Martin took over. "What *does* have something to do with you is..."

Jonty interrupted again. "Listen to this, Jake."

Martin looked at Jonty and smiled. "Jonty arranged to take a swab from Helen's mouth and..."

"Sorry about the next bit," Jonty said to Jake as he interrupted yet again, trying hard to hide his excitement. Jake, on the other hand, was looking from Jonty to Martin and back, feeling confused.

Martin took over again. "Jonty picked up one of the hairs that he found on a table."

Jake was still confused. *What are they so excited about? What is going on?* he thought. He was soon put out of his misery.

"There is a ninety-nine percent chance you are related," Martin stated.

Jake looked astonished. "Related to who?" he asked.

"Helen, you numpty," Jonty responded.

Jake felt a shiver run down his spine. His throat constricted and a tear came involuntarily to his eye.

"Does Helen know?" he asked Jonty.

"Yes, I know." He turned to see Helen and Em standing directly behind him. They were both crying. Helen walked up to him and gave him a tight hug.

"I love you," she said. "Thank you for making me realise who you are."

Em was next and they all hugged as a threesome. Jake released a hand and pushed it between Helen and Em to shake Jonty and Martin by the hand.

"Thank you," Jake said, aiming it at everybody in the room.

The room suddenly felt warm. The tears were flowing as they turned emotion into a full-blown cry, mixed with laughter and love. Martin shook Jonty's hand and quietly slipped away.

Helen felt the death of Paul was finally erased. She knew she had him back. She may have to share him these days with Nate and Claire, but she had him back with no debate about the crazy American.

Jonty spent some time relaying the story that Jack had told him in the hotel in Chester two days earlier. They all hung on every word and, as the story unfolded, it all started to fall into place, just as it had with Jonty.

Jonty was worried about Jake's safety following his brief conversation with Billy, which made him decide to move quickly. He went to Quinn and asked for the authority to search the premises of Brown's Engineering.

"Who or what is Brown's Engineering," asked Quinn.

Jonty sat down and asked Quinn if he could spare half an hour. Quinn agreed and asked Ros to provide some refreshments. She brought them in with extra biscuits to show how happy she was to have Jonty back on the job. The next forty-five minutes were used as a catch-up session, with Jonty bringing Quinn up to speed with his findings from the meeting with Evans. He told him about the chase of the Scania, from dropping off the Aston Martin and the guns at the closed-down area of the old Liverpool docks, to the dropping off of the Verde side sheets at Brown's Engineering in Trafford Park.

After hearing all this, Quinn scratched his chin and thought for a moment. "It all sounds fantastical, Jonty, but without…"

Jonty interrupted before Quinn had time to finish. "I thought you might say that, sir."

Leaning down to the floor, he picked up his tan, leather briefcase, and placed it squarely on his lap. He unclipped both latches and allowed the case to spring open. He reached in and took out a large A3 padded envelope, which he placed on the table in front of Quinn. Quinn looked at the envelope for a couple of seconds before slowly picking it up. He tipped it upside down and around forty-five photographs fell onto the oak desk, some upside down and some face-up.

"They tell the story of a foreign car sale industry," said Jonty, "along with the arms sales industry that has been active under our very noses since the end of the Second World War.

Quinn laughed. "Nonsense."

Jonty looked at him and said in a strong, no-nonsense voice, "If you don't allow this, I am going to request it from a higher authority."

His eyes never wavered from Quinn, who physically shook. This made Jonty move his head back instinctively. He was not expecting such a reaction. *What's going on here?* he wondered. He thought Quinn always played hardball.

"There is enough evidence here to search, I am sure," Quinn smiled. "You're right, Jonty. Forgive me." He looked more in control now. "I will organise it through the magistrate. Are you sure we have everything for the Criminal Evidence Act 1984?"

"Yes, sir," replied Jonty. "We need to enter the points required."

Jonty smiled as he quoted the requirements which they both knew off by heart.

"Consent to enter the premises or vehicle will not be forthcoming from the occupier," he continued. "The material which is the subject of the search is likely to be of substantial value to the investigation of a criminal offence. The evidence sought is likely to be 'relevant' and admissible at trial. The evidence sought by the police under search

226

warrant does not consist of legally privileged or other material likely to be excluded at trial."

He looked Quinn square in the eye. "I believe all the points are covered, sir. Unless you can convince me I don't have each point covered?"

"I agree, Jonty," replied Quinn. "But it will be tomorrow."

"Too late, sir," said Jonty. "This needs to move today!"

Feeling cornered and in a checkmate position by Jonty's argument, Quinn agreed reluctantly.

"Thank you, sir," said Jonty, standing up. "I will deliver this for you." With that, he left the office.

CHAPTER FORTY-FIVE

Jonty turned up at the office to sign out a car from the carpool. PC Frank Rose had been ordered to accompany Jonty again. Jonty had grown fond of Frank, and they had shared a few meals in the canteen together. Jonty loved the younger man's innocence; he viewed him as a cross between a mummy's boy and a throwback from the past. Jonty often looked out for Frank to share time with, although he was still unsure if he was strong enough to make it as a copper.

They were given a police van as requested, just in case they found the side sheets of the lorry. They also had the support of two patrol cars with two officers in each vehicle. The team of six officers and three cars then set off on the journey to Brown's Engineering, where Jonty had agreed to meet Shep.

When they arrived at the factory gates, Frank pushed the intercom button. A voice came through the speaker.

"Ah, Jonty, what kept you?" Shep asked. Without waiting for a reply, the gates swung open.

Frank smoothly accelerated through the gates, followed by the two squad cars.

Jonty and Frank arrived to find Shep setting up the team to search the premises. He had been to Billy's home earlier to inform him that he had a search warrant. Billy had then rang Gerry Ashworth, his floor manager. He had informed Gerry "to assist Detective Inspector Shepherd in anything he required".

Gerry was a tall, thin man in his mid-forties. He wore Air Force blue trousers with brown Hush Puppies and a grey shirt and navy jumper that had bobbles on it from excessive wear, age, and too many washes. His grey hair and black glasses certainly gave the impression that he was a simple man who lived within simple means.

"Do you think we have anything?" enquired Jonty.

"No, It seems a little weak, but let's look anyway," Shep responded. "Why don't you look over in the far workshops?" he suggested. "I will look over in the spares department."

"Great thinking, Shep," said Jonty. "I'll start over here."

Jonty walked to the perimeter building, while Shep headed straight into the spares department. As soon as he could, Jonty doubled back on himself. *Shep seemed very keen to do the spares with Gerry,* Jonty thought to himself.

Jonty quickly left the building and crept to the spares department via the rear entrance. He entered through a small door at the back of the spares department and hid behind a large, disused vertical boring machine. He could see Gerry and Shep talking. Gerry pointed in the direction of the gable end wall where Jonty was hiding. The two men walked down the white-lined aisle designed to encourage safety in the workplace. They approached near to Jonty, who quietly moved around the machine to keep on the blind side of the two men. Eventually, they stopped and Gerry pulled down a large, dirty, brown cover that had oil spillage on it. Behind it was the Verde sheeting.

Jonty overheard heard Shep say, "We need to destroy these covers right now, Gerry." Gerry nodded in agreement.

Jonty watched the two men struggle to pull the covers down. He began taking photos, confident that the noise of the camera shutter opening would be masked by the noise being made from the cover movements.

The two men dropped the covers onto the back of an internal electric-powered truck with an eight-foot trailer attached to it.

"Let's hide them in the trees for now, before Jonty finds them," Shep said. "Hurry, he won't be in the other building much longer."

Gerry nodded again as he climbed on the footplate of the standing area for the driver and eased the vehicle forward. Jonty left via the same door he'd earlier entered and returned to the building he had agreed to search. A few seconds later, Jonty exited the door into the works yard.

"Any luck, Jonty?" Shep shouted over.

"No luck here, Shep. How about you?"

"Same here. Are we wasting our time?" Shep answered with a question, then continued. "I have a life to get on with." He let out a laugh.

"Yes, I think we are wasting our time," replied Jonty. "Let's go home." He patted Shep on the back, as he had now reached Shep and Gerry in the yard.

He went to the van where Frank was waiting. "Wait a minute," Jonty said.

He texted Jake: *The Verde covers are in the trees. I may need to go but will return in fifteen minutes.*

229

A few seconds later, Jonty's phone pipped. He looked down at the screen and read Jake's reply: *On my way.*

Frank and Jonty got back into the van and drove behind Shep. They drove for about two miles before making it look to Shep that they were turning off the road and heading back to the station. However, as they turned into Westinghouse Road, they parked and waited a minute before making a U-turn and returned to the factory. When they arrived, Jake was already waiting for them, dragging up the Verde signs from the foliage where they had been ceremoniously dumped. Frank looked on, wondering what was going on.

"Come on, Frank," said Jonty. "Open the doors on the van. We need to load these side sheets in it."

The three of them folded the sheets as best they could and just about managed to fit them in the back of the van.

Later, after Frank and Jonty had dropped off the side sheets in the station compound, Jonty rang Martin McClean and asked to meet him in confidence.

"Of course," was Martin's reply.

They agreed to meet at the hospital morgue at 7.15 am the following Monday, before the main staff arrived for the day. As Jonty arrived, there were remnants of the night shift changing staff. From the bleary-eyes, it was easy to distinguish who was finishing the shift from the fresh-eyed who were starting. Martin was already in the morgue office waiting for Jonty's arrival.

"It seemed a good idea at the time," declared Martin, as the two friends made the customary handshake. "What is so important that we had to meet so early?"

Jonty put his hand in his navy suit jacket pocket and pulled out a small plastic box, about an inch square. He carefully opened it and pulled out a hair.

"Could you do a DNA check on this?" he asked. "And measure it against the DNA you found under Dave's fingernail and on the stem of the foxglove?"

"Yes, of course I can," replied Martin. "That's a novel way of thinking, Jonty. It would match up the same person, and worth a try."

"What's the best timescale you can do?"

"Best I can do is about twenty-four hours, Jonty."

230

"Thanks, Martin, see you tomorrow." Jonty was just about to leave through the door when he stopped, Colombo style, and spun towards Martin.

"Oh, and Martin… can we keep this strictly between ourselves please?"

Martin looked up, nodded, and answered at the same time as he peered over the top of his glasses. "Of course, Jonty."

Jonty went to meet Martin the following day and, as promised, he had the results of the fingerprints analysis.

"What is the bottom line, Martin?"

"You have your match, Jonty."

"Thanks, Martin."

CHAPTER FORTY-SIX

"I can't believe what you're asking, Jonty," said Quinn. "Are you serious?"

"I am, sir."

"What proof do you have?"

Jonty replied. "Well, sir, apart from the photos that you have just seen, which I accept could be open to debate, I also have a positive fingerprint match linking him with the murder scene at Dave Rowlands' home."

Quinn looked pensive in his smartly pressed uniform. His jacket was hanging on a Victorian-style coat stand, with his cap sitting snuggly on an adjacent peg that ornately curved first outwards, then back towards the stand. It was all finished in highly polished mahogany. This matched exactly the large desk that Quinn sat behind and facing Jonty.

On the wall were framed certificates of Quinn's achievements and awards from over the years, ranging back from the 1970s to the present. There were also framed photos of Quinn. Jonty looked at what he presumed was the earliest photo of Quinn as a young man; he had daringly long hair – for Quinn, at least, compared to the standards of the day, it would still have been classed as short. In one particular photo, where he was seen receiving a commemoration from the Mayor, they were both smiling with a hand each on the silver platter being awarded to Quinn. It was a sunny day; the setting was obvious, as Manchester town hall sat proudly behind them in Albert Square. Time had faded the picture to an opaque yellowing.

Quinn contemplated for what seemed an age. He looked at the wall, he looked at the ceiling. He looked down at his desk. He then repositioned the papers on his desk from the left-hand side to the right, with a squaring up of them in the middle.

"Okay, Jonty," he said eventually. "But you are not doing this alone."

Jonty looked relieved. "Thank you, sir. I think doing this alone would be wrong, too."

Quinn sprang into action by pressing the intercom button. "Ros, could you ask Detective Inspector Shepherd to join us, please?"

"Yes, sir."

"Oh, and Ros, immediately please."

"Yes, sir."

Shep entered the room within five minutes, smiling.

"James," said Quinn, who always addressed Shepherd by his full first name. "Come and join us. Please sit down."

Shep sat down, shook Quinn's hand, then Jonty's.

"James," continued Quinn, "I have asked you and Jonty to this meeting to give me some feedback on the search at Brown's Engineering the other day."

"Yes, sir," Shep answered calmly. "What would you like to know?"

Quinn looked at Jonty. "Where did you check and what did you find Jonty?"

"I checked the parameter building," replied Jonty. "I looked around and found nothing. When I left the building, I saw Shep in the yard with Gerry, the manager of Brown's."

"Thank you, Jonty," said Quinn. "And James, where did you search?"

Shep looked relaxed in a pair of highly polished shoes, a pair of light blue chino trousers neatly creased, with a salmon pink, soft cotton shirt covered by a mid-blue wool casual jacket.

"Well, sir," he said, "I searched the spares department with Gerry, as Jonty said."

"And?" continued Quinn probing for more.

Shep continued to appear calm, with his hands crossed loosely on his lap. "We were looking for side covers to fit a large HGV lorry."

"What was the logo printed on the covers?" Quinn continued to probe with another closed question.

"Verde, I believe, sir."

"Any success with your search, James?" The question was the million-dollar one.

"No, sir," replied Shep. "Like Jonty, we found nothing, we stayed and looked for around thirty minutes, then I met Jonty in the yard and we left at the same time in separate cars."

Shep looked at Jonty. "Didn't we, Jonty?"

Jonty looked back. "Yes."

"Can you explain these photos, James?" Quinn closed in on Shep.

Shep fidgeted in his chair. He crossed, then uncrossed his feet. "What are these, sir?"

He needed thinking time. Jonty and Quinn looked at him. Shep felt the tension bearing down on him. He felt his chest being squeezed. His eyes scanned over the photos spread over the desk. He saw one of him and Gerry tugging the cover sheet off. He saw another of them both dragging the side sheets over to the company electric truck with the words VERDE LTD in bold green letters clearly in view. He didn't know what to do. However, just when he thought it couldn't get any worse, Jonty spoke.

"James Shepherd, I am arresting you on suspicion of the murder of Mr. David Rowlands..." Shep's eyes shot towards Jonty.

What Shep didn't know was that, when Jonty had patted Shep on the back at Brown's Engineering before they left, Jonty had noticed a few stray hairs on his coat. Jonty had picked up a hair as his hand left the gesture. The hair was the final piece of DNA evidence linking James Shepherd with the hair under the fingernail.

Jonty continued. "You have the right to remain silent, however anything you do say may be used as evidence. If you do not mention anything when questioned, and, you may later want to rely on this in court, it may be discounted."

He paused for a moment and cleared his throat. "Anything you do say may be given in evidence. Do you understand?"

Shep looked at Jonty in amazement. "Jonty, what is this?"

"Do you understand?" Jonty repeated.

"Yes," was Shep's reply, very quietly, his head now bowed.

Jonty continued. "You have the right to inform someone of your arrest, should you wish to do so. You have the right to legal advice, and you have the right to look at the police codes of practice."

Shep smiled at the last point. He knew them as well as Jonty and Quinn, who remained quiet.

"I would like to contact a solicitor," was Shep's reply. They all knew that Jonty could not question Shep until he had spoken to his solicitor.

Quinn hit the intercom. "Ros, could you ask Desk Sergeant Twist to come along to the office immediately, please?"

The usual "Yes, sir," was heard.

Ros, outside, put the switch down and looked bemused. *What on earth is happening here?* she thought.

A few minutes later, Danny Twist entered the room. He instantly picked up on the sombre mood, and he decided to refrain from adding any niceties. He saw a head-stooped Shep in the corner, and Jonty in a similar position, both looking despondent. Quinn was sitting back in his chair, his hands together as if in prayer, with his two index fingers resting on the cleft of his chin.

"You wanted me, sir?" Danny broke the tomb-like silence.

"Yes, Sergeant Twist, and thank you for coming along so promptly."

Danny was still confused. He was aware that it must have shown in his face, but Jonty and Quinn understood why.

"Sergeant Twist," said Quinn, "Detective Inspector Shepherd is being arrested on the suspicion of murder."

Jonty lowered his head further. He felt bile rise in his throat. He swallowed it back down into a stomach that was riding heavy on the end of a friendship – two, in fact, including Dave.

"Please will you do the necessary paperwork and formal procedures required?" asked Quinn.

"Yes, sir," a shocked Danny replied.

He walked over to Shep and clasped a pair of handcuffs on him.

"I don't think they are needed," Jonty whispered, his voice cracking with emotion. "Please take his fingerprints and let me have them as soon as possible."

"Thanks," said Shep to his old comrade, as he rose and left the room with Desk Sergeant Daniel Twist.

CHAPTER FORTY-SEVEN

Billy Jones called Gerry and arranged to meet him at the factory.

"What happened on Saturday, Gerry?" he asked curtly. Gerry told him the story as it unfolded.

"And you say the side sheeting has now disappeared?"

"Yes," said Gerry.

"What do you mean? They can't just disappear!" snorted Billy. He looked like flames would be exploding from his nostrils at any second. "What did Shep say when you contacted him?"

Gerry shuffled his feet nervously. "I have tried numerous times to contact Shep," he replied. "I just keep being told that he is unavailable at the station and his mobile keeps going to the answerphone."

Billy was shunting to and fro, his teeth and fists clenched with rage. He knew something had gone wrong, but he wasn't sure quite what.

"I have to go," he said finally. "I'm visiting my grandfather in hospital later."

Billy left and drove off in complete silence, with no music on and his mobile phone switched off. He arranged to meet Maggie at the house before going to the hospital together to visit Roberto, who was responding slowly to the operation he'd endured five days earlier.

Roberto had shown some signs of recovery following the operation. He was able to talk in a low, sometimes unclear, voice. Giovanni had been advised by the Staff nurse to talk for a few minutes only.

"Billy is too headstrong," Roberto told Giovanni. Giovanni nodded in agreement. "It's all about lifestyle and show with him."

"What is the answer, Roberto?" Giovanni quizzed.

"The time will come for you to talk or make a decision, my brother," said Roberto. "I do not feel I have the strength to continue with it."

Giovanny nodded and clasped both his hands around his older brother's left hand as he looked at the ever-increasing weakening man in front of him. He thought of the days when they had both been strong when they took the world on and won. Now, his brother was a white-haired skeletal figure who, after a two-minute discussion, felt the need to close his eyes and rest.

Billy strolled in, back arched, allowing his head to be behind his neckline, showing arrogance. His feet were pointing outwards at five to eleven, looking like many other Manchester men with a walk that seemed to be growing into a national statement, synonymous with the Manchester music scene of the eighties.

It looks like arrogance has moved in, Giovanni thought as he watched Billy stroll down the ward.

Billy's good looks already drew heads towards him, which was always a bad thing discussed often by Roberto and Giovanni over the years. *The natural good looks we can't control, the unnatural man-made arrogance we can,* thought Giovanni as he watched Billy stroll down the ward, chewing gum. He strutted like a peacock in white expensive training shoes, tight faded blue jeans, and a tight white T-shirt showing off his well-defined physique, smiling with his olive skin and pure white enameled teeth.

Billy was followed by a more subdued-looking Maggie, his wife. Age had added some weight and the gorgeous size ten had given way to a now size fourteen. She wore a pair of white Gucci jeans under a powder blue puffed-out shirt tied with a white belt at the waist, fighting to mask the extra pounds that the years of fine wining and dining had finally delivered.

Billy shook Giovanni's aging hand. Giovanni, always well dressed, wore a traditional charcoal grey two-piece suit with a white shirt, and a grey matching tie. The highly polished black Italian shoes finished off the appearance of a smart, wealthy gent. He half rose to shake William's hand and Maggie leaned over to kiss Giovanni on the cheek.

"How is he?" enquired Maggie.

"He is still very weak, it is still touch and go," was the not so happy reply from Giovanni. "The good news is he has been talking lightly, but not for long."

"That's good," William responded. He looked over to the other side of the bed and saw a cardiac monitor, a pulse oximeter, arterial lines, intravenous lines, and chest tubes. An oxygen mask covered half of Roberto's face.

"How are Toni and Francesca coping?" asked Maggie.

"They are both coping well, considering," Giovanni answered. "Toni is here most of the time, talking to him about old times, trying to trigger a response, but without much success."

Maggie and William looked and listened, straight-faced. However, Maggie seemed more concerned than Billy, a point that Giovanni did not miss.

"I sent Toni home," said Giovanni. "She had been here for forty hours without a break." He shook his head as he spoke. "She needs a good rest."

He stood up and offered his seat to Maggie. "Let me get a coffee for you both," he offered. "William, you come and help me. It will be nice to catch up."

Maggie nodded her head in agreement. Both men walked out of the ward and towards the lift, which took them to the lower ground to purchase the takeaway coffee.

"I hear things are getting a little hot?" Giovanni said, looking at Billy.

"Yes, but nothing we can't handle," replied Billy.

Giovanni looked at Billy in bemusement. "Le Conte tells me that Shepherd has been arrested, and the Verde covers have been taken as evidence against some of our business?"

Billy hadn't known about Shep's arrest.

"You should know all this as the boss, William," said Giovanni.

"How does Edward know?" Billy asked.

"Shepherd has been arrested and he asked for Le Conte to act as his solicitor," said Giovanni. "Another bad move. That is another possible link to connect us."

Giovanni looked around to check that nobody was within earshot before continuing. "I do not like the Family consigliere being officially involved in protecting associates."

Billy's face turned a pink shade, and then claret. He knew this was a spot he would need to manoeuvre out of, but he also knew it was not his greatest strength. And, with his grandfather, and mentor, unable to assist on this one, he felt stuck. A feeling of emptiness devoured his body. A swilling of blood raced through his head, like an unsecured half barrel of wine rolling in a ship's hold during a gale force wind on twenty-foot-high waves. He felt his stomach churn and regurgitate the bacon eaten hastily due to bad time management, which meant it was eaten on the run. This typified the real William: no self-control, no time management, no leadership, and no cool head in times when one was required.

Billy's strength was in managing thugs like Steve Pitt and Ken Fitzroy, an important skill in the grand scheme of things. However, as boss, he needed to be tactical as well. This was a skill he learnt from his astute grandfather.

"You need to make it go away, William," Giovanni said in a low, determined voice. William nodded.

On their return to the ward, Giovanni handed Maggie her drink.

"I am sorry it took a little while, Maggie," he said, smiling, "but here is your coffee. I can guarantee hot, but cannot guarantee it is from an Italian machine."

"Thank you," Maggie smiled back and grasped the coffee with both hands.

CHAPTER FORTY-EIGHT

Edward Le Conte refused to act for Shepherd, citing a conflict of interest as he had worked with him on many cases in the past. It was a very weak reason, but a reason nonetheless, and a solicitor is not obliged to take a case on if they prefer not to.

Jonty sat down with Shep and Neil Wynne, the legal aid solicitor Shep had been appointed. The fact that Shep had changed his legal representative from one of the most expensive defence lawyers in the North West of England to a legal aid lawyer had not gone unnoticed by Jonty. Legal advice at the police station is free of charge to any person who has been arrested or is being interviewed by the police. Wynne started with the usual bread and butter opening.

"You are not obliged to say anything to the police and we advise all clients to maintain their right to silence." Shep nodded in understanding.

Jonty then spoke, with no acknowledgement to Wynne. "Today is Wednesday, October twenty-four at two-twelve pm in interview room five at Manchester police station. Present are the defendant Mr. James Shepherd and his representative, Mr. Neil Wynne from Hampshire and Turner legal practice. Detective Inspector Jane O'Sullivan is making notes. Also present is Detective Inspector Jonathan Ball."

Jonty paused and looked Shep in the eye.

"You are being charged with the murder of your ex-colleague and friend, Detective Inspector David Rowlands. What do you have to say regarding the charge?"

"Not guilty!" was Shep's reply.

"Come on, Mr. Shepherd," said Jonty. "You did it and we both know you did it."

"DI Ball, you cannot just throw out accusations without proof," Wynne said in an alarmed voice.

"Well, how about the fingerprint on the foxgloves and the DNA under Dave's fingernails?" replied Jonty angrily. "They both match your client's fingerprints. They are the same. Also, there is a note in Dave's diary

240

stating that Mr. Shepherd was due for an evening meal with him on the day he died."

Shep never moved from his position. He was looking down at his handcuffed hands. He wore blue jeans and a matching sweatshirt.

"No, it's okay, Neil," Shep said. "Jonty, can we speak off the record? Just me and you? Then we can start again with the on-the-record details if you wish?"

Jonty spoke into the recorder. "As requested, Mr. Shepherd would like to speak off the record. I am happy to accept this as it may help to forward the inquiry. The time is two twenty-nine pm. Mr. Wynne and Detective Inspector O'Sullivan will leave the room and just Mr. Shepherd and myself will remain. Detective Inspector O'Sullivan will remain outside the door in case I require further assistance."

Wynne looked at Shep. "Mr. Shepherd, I strongly recommend you do not proceed with this course of action."

"Thanks for your professional advice, Mr. Wynne," replied Shep. "I think I know what I am doing."

Within two minutes they were alone. "What's going on, Shep?" said Jonty. "How could you kill Dave?"

"I didn't, Jonty," replied Shep.

Jonty looked at him. "Then tell me about the DNA and fingerprint evidence, along with the diary note?"

"I *wasn't* due to see him that day and I didn't kill him," said Shep. "I think I must have been set up."

Jonty looked at him. He thought he knew this man so well, but now he wasn't so sure.

"Okay, Shep, what about the Verde cover? You tried to conceal evidence."

Shep sighed. "There is a world of difference between trying to pervert the course of justice and murder!" He spoke in a voice just above a whisper, leaning forward as if to keep what he was saying from prying ears.

"Well," said Jonty, "from one mate to another, you have one chance and this is it."

"Can I have a cigarette?" requested Shep. Jonty got up and opened the door, requesting DI O'Sullivan to find some cigarettes.

"I was paid for giving them information now and again, nothing important to start with," Shep began.

"Them? Who are you referring to?" Jonty responded.

241

"The Sartori family," Shep answered.

Jonty recognised the name from his Chester meeting with Evans. "Roberto and Giovanni?" Jonty asked in an even voice.

"Yes," Shep answered in surprise, looking up at Jonty. "How did you know about them? You have only been back for five minutes."

"I have my ways," replied Jonty.

The two men looked at each other in silence for a few seconds.

"And?" nudged Jonty.

"Well," continued Shep, "around the mid-seventies, Edward Le Conte approached me and asked if I would like to go to dinner with him, all expenses paid. I said yes."

There was a knock at the door and DI O'Sullivan entered with the cigarettes. Jonty passed them to Shep, whose hands were shaking as he took one from the pack.

"I started getting friendly with Le Conte," continued Shep, after taking a long draw on his cigarette. "And why not? He was a pillar of the community. You know him as well as I do, Jonty."

"I thought I did." was the response.

"We got friendly and, after about six months, he discovered I had a gambling issue – as you know." Jonty nodded in agreement. "He said that, as a friend, he could offer an opportunity allowing me to earn some extra money that would cover the debts." This sounded familiar to Jonty and he recollected the gun-running chat with Billy and Paul.

"What did you have to do to earn the money, Shep?"

"Nothing, really," replied Shep. "Just inform Le Conte of things if he asked anything – cases, people, you know the type of thing."

"Did you give him any information?"

"Not for about two years, but then he took me for lunch in a posh restaurant. He asked if there was any investigation on a case that involved the accidental death of Paul Jennings."

Jonty looked at him in surprise. He felt betrayed by the man sitting in front of him.

"I said that there was," continued Shep, "but that it looked like an accident and we were investigating the car as we believed it was a drunk driver." He took another second to collect himself. "I told him about the report from Aston police station linking the stolen BMW with the Verde lorry."

Shep took another long drag of the cigarette and leisurely blew the smoke upwards with a craned neck. "Le Conte asked me to make it go away. So I destroyed the fax from Aston, thinking if anything went off I could say it never arrived or that it must have got mixed up with other faxes."

Jonty looked at him. *How simple, but so effective*, he thought.

"The contact ended there," continued Shep. "They never sent anything and I never asked." He paused for a moment. "Le Conte forwarded one thousand pounds for that, on top of the five hundred every month they were paying me just for being on the books."

"How were you paid?" Jonty asked.

"They told me I needed to open an account with the National Bank. The money came in every month as if I were an employee of Brown's Engineering."

Jonty was beginning to see the importance of Billy Jones being an area manager. He could direct the money laundering, just like a conductor would to get the right sounds from an orchestra.

"I was never needed again for years," continued Shep. "I took the money and I got used to the level of income. I became dependent on it. I owed two grand on losing bets, but they cleared it for me."

"Until?" Jonty reacted.

"Until last week, when they told me to make sure that the Verde side sheets could not be retrieved. Luckily, I was asked to carry out the search with you." Shep looked at Jonty. "You know the rest. But I tell you, Jonty, I did not murder Dave."

His eyes looked like a dog waiting for acknowledgement from its owner.

"Look, Jonty," he added, "I know I am in trouble, but there is a difference between a ten stretch and life."

CHAPTER FORTY-NINE

The phone rang for the twentieth time in the last hour, although you would not believe it the way Sarah Windsor answered the call.

"Good morning, Sarah Windsor, Sir John Frasier's secretary speaking." The voice at the other end was straight and to the point.

"This is Detective Inspector Jonathon Ball. Please put me through to Sir John."

Sir John was in a board meeting, and Sarah was under strict instructions that only a world-ending problem would give her reason to disturb him.

"I am sorry, but Sir John is in a board meeting," she replied. "Can I ask him to call you back?"

Jonty thought for a minute. *No need to cause any unwanted speculation*, he told himself.

"Yes, that's fine, thank you," he replied. "But please stress the importance."

Two hours later, Jonty's phone rang. "Jonty Ball."

"Mr. Ball, this is Sir John Frasier," said the caller. "I am very busy, so could you please tell me the urgency of the call?" The voice was plummy and very upper class, like velvet soaked in whiskey.

"Sir John, thank you for returning my call," said Jonty. "I am not sure if your secretary told you that I am a police officer."

"Yes," grunted Sir John. "This better be important or you will be hearing from my solicitor."

"Sir, I am in London over the next few days. When are you free? I would prefer to discuss this when we meet."

Sir John could tell from Jonty's manner that this was not a request for a donation to the local Police Ball. "How about tomorrow?"

"Tomorrow is fine, ten okay?" asked Jonty.

"Make it half-past."

"Thank you, Sir John. I look forward to meeting you." Jonty put the phone down.

Billy turned up at Brown's Engineering following a call from Gerry telling him about the letter that he'd opened earlier in the morning. It was written on National Bank letter heading paper:

Dear Mr. Jones,

The National Bank has recently conducted a general review of a series of accounts and has made the difficult decision to suspend that provision of banking services for Brown's Engineering PLC following a review of the bank's appetite to risk.

Yours sincerely,

Sir John Frasier

Chief executive

The National Bank

Jonty had met with Sir John Frasier a couple of days earlier and informed him of the money laundering that was being fed through Brown's. Sir John invited Mike Chapman, the head of internal fraud, to the meeting and they sat and discussed the transactions.

Sir John sat in a large, wing-backed maroon leather chair with deep buttons. A large oak desk separated him from Jonty and Mike, who sat in chairs that were similar to Sir John's in colour and design, but of a smaller build.

Sir John looked very dignified in a navy suit with a grey broad pinstripe running down it. His tailored shirt was pure white and a crisp collar framed a navy tie with the National Bank's crest sitting proudly on it. Jonty estimated Sir John to be in his late sixties. He had a full head of grey hair and veins running down the bridge of his nose. Wrinkles ran across his forehead, but his soft, aging skin showed no wrinkling down the cheek line.

Mike Chapman was an expert on reading the internal systems and had the maximum authority of grade one, which allowed him to look through every part of any account. He opened the account of Brown's Engineering online and talked it through with Sir John and Jonty. Jonty felt that a huge stride was being made. He could feel the adrenalin flow through his veins, invigorating him.

They spent the next forty-five minutes trying to understand the complex setup of the account. The first thing they noticed was an account balance of six million pounds, with a few markers from bank internal auditors to investigate periodically, but nothing was followed up.

The next thing they noticed was a total of fourteen monthly standing orders made payable to another company, Greens Steel Ltd, each for the sum of £200,000. The Green Steel account was also held at the National Bank and showed numerous payments made to companies that included mainly well-known national steel and parts companies. Income was regularly returned at an average of twenty percent lower than the outgoings.

"This is a textbook way of taking dirty money and cleaning it," Mike told Sir John and Jonty.

This account led to another account in the name of a restaurant, 'Verde Italia'. A detailed look at this account highlighted further anomalies. It had a regular monthly income from Brown's, but there were no outgoings normally expected from restaurant items such as food, utensils, cooking oils, alcohol, or wine.

When Mike began to look further into the account, he noticed a BACS system paying a large number of individuals, with William Jones at the top of the list being paid £55,000 per month. Jonty scanned down the list of recipients and noted another fifty names, with restaurant positions next to them, such as chef, waiter, cook, etc. Every payment was made to an individual personal National Bank account in the name of the recipients, which included Edward Le Conte, Jack Evans, Ken Fitzroy, James Pitt, and James Shepherd.

Jonty pointed out that Billy Jones was employed by the bank as an area manager. He outlined that the reason for this was to allow him access and management from the frontline, thus allowing him to run the money laundering from the inside. He felt that there must be other 'employees' involved.

Mike took a sharp intake of breath and whistled.

"This is a classic layering exercise, without doubt," he stated.

"Why have internal audits not picked this up?" demanded Sir John in a very aggressive manner.

Mike's face flushed as he replied. "It has been picked up, Sir John. I will need to investigate why it hasn't been followed up."

"Nothing is more important in your life than getting to the bottom of this. Do you hear me?" Sir John's face was red with rage. He took it personally that somebody could take advantage of him through the bank.

"I hear you, Sir John," Mike answered. He felt a huge weight land on his shoulders, as well as some guilt that this had not been spotted.

He quickly did an internet search for Green's and the restaurant Verde Italia. They looked genuine from the search results. He rang the phone numbers advertised on the websites, but there was no reply from either. Instead, both numbers had the same answerphone message: "I am sorry but we are no longer in business to the public, we are sorry for any inconvenience."

Mike's next search was the Companies House register, which showed no sign of either business.

"They are shell companies," said Mike. "They are used for nothing more than confusing transactions and cleaning up the laundered money by confusing the transaction trail."

Sitting in the three accounts was £19,000,000 being passed around like a game of pass the parcel. Billy was unaware of this at the time, as the forwarding addresses on the accounts were of derelict houses he had bought cheap to be used solely for receiving post regarding the accounts and nothing else. He would be in for a big shock when he drove around later in the afternoon.

CHAPTER FIFTY

Jonty had not seen Jake in over a week. They arranged to meet allowing Jonty to keep Jake up to speed with the things that Shep had told him, as well as the meeting in London with Sir John and Mike Chapman. They were walking through a local park, enjoying the late October sunshine. The chill was setting in as the sun played hide and seek with the pathway behind the trees, which were rustling in the slight breeze. The sky was tinged with pink, which would intensify with the quickly setting sun.

They shuffled through and kicked the fallen leaves of autumn. Jake wore a Berghaus coat that had been bought specially for the coast to coast walk that never was. Jonty wore a grey overcoat with a navy scarf wrapped around his neck. The buttons were open as the day was yet to reach its lowest temperature. The onset of winter, whilst on the horizon, was still a few weeks away.

Jonty had just finished telling his story when a loud crack was heard behind them. A flock of birds flew up from the tree branches above them, squawking in panic. The squirrels scrambled up the tree looking for shelter. A sign of nature's activity told Jonty it was a moment to act; years in the force had made every instinct stand to attention. He pushed Jake past the tree and onto the floor. Looking up for a movement, he saw a body running with a rifle in hand about two hundred yards away. Jake was about to set off in chase, but Jonty held him back.

"It could be a trap," Jonty told Jake. "Or he may try and have a second go."

"It must be Pitt," said Jonty. "He will have been sent by Billy, as the pressure is on them now. And it was probably me he was after."

He paused to look around, checking to make sure they were safe before they made their way back. "To be on the safe side," he said, "I think you and Em best stay with Helen and me for now until this is cleared up. We will also need to stay in a hotel because they know Helen's address."

Jake was happy to hear Jonty's suggestion and he was not about to say no.

He rushed home to tell Em that they were going to move in with Helen and Jonty. He barged through the front door, expecting to see her. He threw open the lounge door, but Em wasn't there. He rushed through to the kitchen, but there was no sign of her.

"Em!" he shouted at the top of his voice. She came strolling through from the back garden, wiping her hands on a towel.

"Jake, what on earth is wrong, darling?" she said. She had never seen Jake so animated.

"Get a few clothes packed," he said. "We are leaving now! Don't ask questions, we haven't the time to discuss it."

Em turned and ran upstairs, having total faith in Jake.

"Hurry, Em, we have to go, NOW!" Jake shouted.

Em grabbed a holdall and scooped into it any clothes that she could lay her hands on. She went to her underwear drawer and tipped the contents into the bag, then ran back downstairs. She and Jake both sprinted out of the house, Jake taking just enough time to lock the front door. As soon as they were in the Seat, Jake turned on the ignition and the car screeched off the drive.

As they turned off the road and did a right-hand turn onto the main road, a black Range Rover came into view from the opposite direction. It turned towards the Seat and accelerated towards them. Em screamed as Jake pulled the steering wheel hard left. The car being small managed to squeeze between a lamppost and a garden wall. The fit was so tight that the driver's side wing mirror caught on the lamppost and clattered against the car door, which magnified the noise inside the car like a drill on a tooth.

The Range Rover took a few seconds to turn around, hampered by its bulk. However, Jake knew that the three-litre engine would catch up with them on the flat roads. He was correct in his reasoning, as the vehicle loomed large in the rearview mirror within seconds. He slammed on the brakes and turned into a small side street. He knew from driving down it in the past that there was a chicane designed to slow the traffic. The driver of the Range Rover anticipated this and followed him, losing no ground at all.

Jake stamped his foot on the accelerator, but the Seat was sluggish. He sped over a sleeping policeman; the suspension was not strong and they heard a loud crunching noise, which told Jake that the Seat had struck something. He looked in the mirror and saw that a black oil trail followed. The car began losing power. Not only had he had cracked the sump, but he had ripped the exhaust off, too. The Range Rover easily took the sleeping policeman. The speed limit on the road was 20 mph, but Jake was doing sixty. He threw the Seat through the chicane, slightly missing the line. A scraping noise on the front wing echoed again through the car. It vibrated for a second but then carried on.

Em screamed. Her hands were shaking and tears rolled down her face. First, her hands were in front of her face, then on the indoor door handle. A churning feeling in her stomach brought a stream of vomit cascading from her mouth; it spread over the windscreen and plastic fascia in front of her. Jake looked at her in concern.

"Are you okay?" he shouted.

"Yes! Just drive!" she screamed back.

The Range Rover slowed and manoeuvred through the chicane. The driver knew that it was now just a matter of time before the Seat stopped altogether. Jake came to the end of the street and did another sharp left. He knew he could not stop and would have to gamble with the traffic. If he chose to turn right, he would have two streams of traffic to deal with, increasing the risk of colliding with another vehicle. The Range Rover followed. Unfortunately for Jake, the road was quiet and this gave a massive advantage to the Range Rover.

Jake suddenly saw an elderly man crossing the road some way in front of him. He beeped the horn three times.

"Get out of the way, old man," he shouted at the top of his voice.

He then watched as the man raised what looked like a high-powered rifle. Em closed her eyes. The old man looked calm and collected as he lifted the rifle. He placed it in the socket of his shoulder, raised the rifle an inch, and dropped it into the perfect position. He looked through the powerful sights. Jake glanced in the mirror; the Range Rover was right behind him. He looked back at the man with the rifle.

This is it, he thought. *We are going to die!*

"Em, I love you!" was all he could say.

Em had just delivered a second portion of vomit all over the car's interior.

The old man took a step to one side and fired. The shell travelled much faster than Jake could react. There was nothing he could do. The shell raced past the Seat and hit the Range Rover. On impact, the car windscreen exploded; the driver lost control and hit a lamppost, causing the vehicle to roll onto its side. Petrol began spewing from the fuel tank like a burst dam.

250

Jake then saw the man quickly take out from his coat pocket a bottle with a rag coming from the neck. The man took a lighter from his pocket and lit the rag. A bright, strong flame raged; the man threw it at the Range Rover's leaking petrol.

Jake heard an explosion behind him and watched as the Range Rover appeared to jump two feet off the ground. He could feel the heat radiating from the fireball that the flamed petrol had generated, even though he was twenty yards away.

Jake dragged Em out of the car and pulled her across the road, thinking of nothing except his and Em's safety. Across the road, the old man was sauntering slowly and calmly away from the scene to a waiting Mercedes.

We do not do business like that in our family, thought Giovanni, as the old-school mobster climbed into the waiting car.

It was difficult to distinguish between the police, ambulance, and fire brigade sirens as they harmonised, like an orchestra playing a well-rehearsed tune, rushing to the attack.

Jonty was driving along the road when he noticed two people aimlessly staggering along the pavement. They appeared to be in shock. They *were* in shock. Jake and Em looked like two young children dropped in a long-lost place of yesteryear, not a Manchester suburb of today. Jonty stopped the CRV alongside them and opened the passenger and rear doors. Jake and Em both crawled in without saying a word; their faces were blackened with soot thrown from the explosion and the oil that had escaped from the sump of the Seat. They could have passed as urchins from a Dickens novel, not the twentieth-century young adults they really were.

Without saying anything to them, Jonty sped to collect Helen from her home. He'd rang her earlier to tell her to pack. She had panicked and the twenty-minute wait felt like hours. Once she was in the car, she sat in silence next to Em as Jonty drove the fifteen miles towards a hotel in Haydock. This would be the perfect location in case a quick getaway was needed. It sat on the crossroads of the M6 and the East Lancashire Road, both easy to sprint along, north, east, south or west if required, and a mid-point between Manchester and Liverpool.

"Are you both okay?" Jonty eventually asked Jake and Em, looking at Em in the rearview mirror.

"Yes," Jake replied. "We are beginning to settle down now. Just the shock of it all."

"Are you okay to talk about it now? Or tomorrow will do if you're not up to it?" asked Jonty.

"We are fine now," said Jake. He looked back at Em, who nodded.

"Did you know the old man with the rifle?"

"No," said Jake. "He disappeared as quickly as he appeared. Without him, though, I think we would be dead right now."

Jonty looked bemused. "The only name that springs to mind is Roberto Sartori. But we don't know much about him."

Jonty continued driving for a few minutes. He was deep in thought. "But he was a brilliant mind in the wrong profession. He could have added so much to society, but instead he chose organised crime." He thought for a second. *It can't be him, though, as he is in hospital recovering from a heart attack.*

CHAPTER FIFTY-ONE

Roberto and Edward Le Conte, the family consigliere, had been
discussing over several months how to best maintain the secrecy of the
Family whilst, at the same time, allowing future generations to blossom.
Edward's daughter, Margaret, and Roberto's grandson, William, had
known each other since being very young children. Edward would often
bring Margaret over to play with William and the two of them would
spend hours running through the acres of Roberto's gardens, swinging
on homemade swings attached to thick tree branches, collecting conkers
in the autumn, picking apples from trees, or boating on any of the three
large ponds in the garden. They were always comfortable in each other's
company.

"You need to disapprove – slightly, of course," Roberto had said, "if
Margaret asks for permission to see William officially."

"The nature of the young is to rebel." Edward smiled back and took a
long draw on the Cuban cigar that was accompanying the expensive
brandy.

The two men had colluded and hatched a plan in 1975. They were to
all go on a family holiday for three weeks to the Amalfi coast and stay at
a top-class hotel. This would enable William and Margaret to spend time
together.

"We then need to hope and pray," Roberto said.

The importance was that the risk was much lower marrying across the
business than outside. And, as Edward, the consigliere, was not part of
the Family, the bloodlines would not clash.

The three-week holiday on the Amalfi coast was glorious, engineered
by Roberto and Edward to pair off Margaret and William. Roberto,
Toni, Francesca, William, Margaret, and her parents, Edward and Susan
Le Conte, had a wonderful time. They saw the young couple spend more
time together and, eventually, spending time together alone. The two
youngsters looked for reasons to be separate from their families. They
would hire a speedboat, or take long, romantic walks. They peeled away
from the families and ate evening meals together, looking out over the

Amalfi with the unrivalled views it surrendered. By the end of the holiday, William and Margaret were a couple.

"A wonderful time was had by all on this lovely holiday," Roberto said on the final evening. "A toast to the Amalfi."

He raised his glass as the family replied, "To the Amalfi."

A wink from Roberto to Edward received a raise of a glass chest high and a knowing smile.

Maggie was looking forward to going to Manchester, where she would be celebrating her friend Jane's twenty-first birthday. Billy had thought it could tie in nicely with a plan he had. It was a job he knew needed doing.

"Let's play out a fantasy I have," Billy asked Maggie.

"Oh, yes? And what would that be?" she answered with a knowing smile.

"When you go to Manchester, let's meet up in a pub and pretend we don't know each other," he replied.

"And?" Maggie giggled.

"I will come over and chat you up, and we can come home together," said Billy. Maggie giggled again.

"Oooh, I like that idea. Let's do it," she teased. Billy knew that Paul had not met Maggie – or, indeed, knew of her. He also knew it was a perfect alibi.

The night of the party drew on. By ten o'clock, the pints turned quickly to Jack Daniels and cokes to ease the pressure on the already bursting stomachs swilled with pints of Boddington's and Holts' Bitter, the local Manchester ales.

As usual, Billy was popular with the girls and he was showing a particular interest in a bubbly blonde doing a bad rendition of Candy Staton's 'Young Hearts Run Free' on the pub karaoke. However, the short skirt and big smile seemed to make up for that in Billy's book.

"I think I am going on to a club with young Candy," joked Billy to his friends.

"No problem," replied Paul. "I should be getting home to make sure Sue is okay."

Paul finished his drink before continuing. "Catch up on Monday. Keep me up to date with Candy, sharing her one and only life," he added, referring to a line in the song. They laughed and shook hands as Paul left to walk out into the city night.

Five minutes after Paul left, Billy turned to Maggie and told her he was nipping to the toilet. She smiled and returned to the girls celebrating the twenty-first – who, like Paul, had no idea Billy and Maggie were a couple.

Billy walked out of the main part of the crowded pub and towards the gents. He made a quick right into a red telephone box that the pub had bought for authenticity. He searched in his back pocket and brought out a neatly folded A4 paper. He unfolded it to reveal a mobile telephone number. Billy dialled the number and Steve Pitt answered.

"He has just left," Billy said down the phone.

"I'm on my way," Pitt replied. "The black BMW is parked around the corner with the new plates on it."

"Perfect," Billy answered. "Good luck."

"Luck doesn't come into it," was the reply, and the line went dead.

Billy walked back into the bar area and headed towards Maggie. "What did you say your name was again?"

"I didn't," she replied with a wink.

CHAPTER FIFTY-TWO

Jonty drove Jake, Em, and Helen along the East Lancashire Road, travelling west in the direction of Liverpool. Their destination was the hotel Jonty had booked them into earlier, where they would stay until everything blew over. Manchester now left behind he was driving past the old Higher Green pithead in Astley, which was easily visible from the road.

He looked at the pithead and thought, '*I wonder if Roberto had that pit under his control in his heyday?*'

Just as Jonty was gazing at the site, in what now looked like open fields, his mobile phone rang. He pushed the button that allowed him to speak hands-free, with the conversation coming out of his radio.

"Hello, Jonty Ball?" he said.

"Jonty, it's Ros," came the reply. "Mr. Quinn would like to chat with you." Jonty looked over at Jake in the passenger seat and pursed his lips together.

I wonder what he wants? thought Jonty.

The phone took a few seconds for Ros to make the transfer. Quinn's voice broke the silence. "Jonty, where are you?"

"I am taking Jake, Helen, and Emily to the hotel that is under police protection, as agreed, sir."

Jake looked at Jonty. He hadn't mentioned that the hotel would have officers protecting them.

"We have just received the names of the two men killed in the rifle shooting yesterday," said Quinn. Jonty looked at Jake again. "Their names were Ken Fitzroy and Steve Pitt."

Jake felt a shiver run down his spine. His hands were sweaty. *They were not messing about by sending in their big guns,* he thought.

"Do you know who they are, Jonty?" quizzed Quinn.

"Yes, sir. They are part of the team that Billy Jones runs."

Quinn now spoke with a sense of urgency. "That would make sense. It would also explain why intelligence tells us there is activity at the Jones' house. I think he is ready to run. Can you drop them off and get to the house as soon as you can? It looks like he is ready to leave."

"Yes, sir." The phone clicked to silence.

"You heard that," Jonty said. "I will drop you off. You will all find shelter, then ring me and I will make sure you are protected."

Jake's head shot round. "No way, Jonty. I am not taking the chance. What if we are being followed right now?"

Jonty shouted back. "You can't come with me! I need to go right now!"

Em felt her stomach tighten and she began to sob. She wished she was back in the quiet of Iowa right now, just anywhere but here. Her hands were sweating. She wrung them together and cowered into the back seat of the CRV. Helen put her arm around her to comfort her.

"Jake is right," said Helen, addressing Jonty. "These are dangerous people. How do you know they are not following us right now?"

"The safest place for us is where the largest police presence is," Jake shouted back. "And that is at Billy's house."

Jonty couldn't argue with that. "Okay," he said, "but you stay put when we get there."

He could not argue for long, as the importance of getting to Billy's house as soon as possible put precedence on everything else at this point.

Jonty drove to the next turning at Leigh and veered left towards the M6. He flicked a switch and the sound of a siren shot out of the CRV. He flicked another switch and the flashing blue lights came through the radiator grill and along the top of the rear window. Instantly, vehicles in front of them pulled over to allow Jonty to pass, and he put his foot down.

"Hold tight!" he shouted.

CHAPTER FIFTY-THREE

Billy pulled back the curtains of his living room. He knew that Steve and Ken had been killed in the attack on the Range Rover. He also knew that the trigger finger belonged to Giovanni. He was now panicking. Two questions were going round in his mind and he tried to think them through.

Would Giovanni come to kill me?

Would Le Conte kill his daughter?

The answer to both these questions was unequivocal, 'Yes'. The Sartori brothers would do anything to protect the family. To protect themselves. Billy was aware that he had made mistakes. He knew he was not as astute as his grandfather; he did not have his intelligence. He was strong and always good with the muscle, but he always knew, deep down, that this was not the role for him.

What did Roberto see in me? he thought.

He was unaware of why Jake was involved. He had seen him with Jonty, Helen, and Em walking towards the Midland Hotel those few months ago.

But how does Jake fit into this? he wondered. *I was only in his company for two hours.* He could not fathom the link.

Was Jake undercover? Surely not. Billy's thoughts were going into overdrive, reflecting how all this could have happened.

The one thing he would never have considered was the reincarnation process from Paul to Jake. And why should he?

Dr. Jameson had explained the odds to Jake and Em. "We calculate that one in a million will have any recollection of reincarnation." He'd let the figure set in their minds. "Let's say there are sixty million people in the UK. That is sixty people who will have any recollection." The figures were being related in easy terms. "And, of those sixty people, only one person per generation will investigate further," Jake and Em were getting the real feel of how rare this was.

"And the other fifty-nine?" Jake asked.

"Of the other fifty-nine," Dr. Jameson replied, "some will think it's silly, some will feel it would make them different and they would be scared. And some will just simply dismiss it."

Jameson looked at Jake. "You are the one, Jake."

Billy could not legislate for this scenario, even if he was aware of it. He was feeling light-headed. Maggie was upstairs. He was assuming she was packing to go on a surprise holiday that Billy had booked for them, something he had done in the past for the lady he adored.

Maggie was feeling excited. She was packing lots of clothes to suit the sunshine she was looking forward to, away from this early dank November drizzle. The weather was already setting in.

She stopped for a second or two to look out of the bedroom window that would normally offer views over the Cheshire countryside for fifteen miles or so. Today, a mile would be the best guess as the mist had fallen, like a wall obstructing the view. The sky was dark and an even grey, which told Maggie the drizzle had set in for the day. She could see a road in the distance with cars snaking along it with their headlights on. Maggie turned and saw all the bright, flowery summer dresses and sleeveless tops she had set out on the bed, waiting to be transferred to the eagerly awaiting open suitcases set neatly as a pair on the end of the cream-coloured duvet caressing the bed. She smiled to herself. The excitement was taking hold of her. She began singing along to the summer song on the radio, which the DJ told his listeners he needed in order to escape this awful weather. Maggie was about to escape it, but not by the fragility of a record. She would be drinking a cocktail on a beach within the day.

Meanwhile, Billy was waiting downstairs. His hands were clammy. He was pacing the living room floor, looking for an answer that never came. He thought he saw a movement in the trees outside the drive.

Calm down, he told himself. He was in the perfect trap.

The police were on one side, closing down on him, no doubt waiting for the answers that would expose the Family. On the other side was the Family itself, chasing him to make sure that that very conversation with the law never took place.

CHAPTER FIFTY-FOUR

Jonty arrived at The Forestry, parking halfway down the road, aware of the importance of not making Billy aware of the police presence.

He brought the CRV to a halt. The large, copper beech was in clear view. Towering above the surrounding walls, it was beginning to drop its leaves on this early November morning.

"Is that where he lives? The bastard who killed my son?" asked Helen. Nobody replied. She already knew the answer.

A man walked up to the car. He was smartly dressed in what appeared to be a black suit, which could only be seen from the knee down. The rest of his body was covered by a waterproof mackintosh, his head protected by a large red and white segmented umbrella. Jonty wound down the window and the man leaned into the car.

"Can I help you, sir?" His next words would have been, "I am going to have to ask you to leave the road, sir." However, this changed when Jonty showed him an ID card.

"My name is Detective Inspector Jonty Ball. I am the lead officer on this case for the Greater Manchester Police."

The man looked around in confusion as he peered in at Jake, Helen, and Em.

"I can explain," Jonty said, knowing what was going through the man's mind.

"We have set up a small unit to manage this," said the man.

He turned and indicated to a large white Mercedes sprinter van further along the road. It had the words 'Johnson Double Glazing' painted on the side. To add to the effect, there was a sheet of bulletproof and shatterproof glass stacked on the side sitting in a wooden frame.

"Health and safety played havoc with the glass," smiled the man, inviting Jonty over to inspect the van.

Jonty climbed out of the CRV and told the other three to remain in the car and not to move.

He observed through the open rear doors of the van two compact shelves fitted down the sides. Two men sat each side and each man had in front of him a computer and a screen, on which flickered different images of the inside of the house.

"We set the cameras up overnight," said the man. "I am Inspector George Lee, by the way. I am heading up a team of Specialist Rifle Officers – or SROs, as we are known."

Specialist Rifle Officers are experienced gunmen who have been trained to use sniper/marksman rifles. They deploy rifle teams in support of SCO19 pre-planned operations, typically setting up to over-watch from vantage points overlooking an incident.

Lee continued. "We have several marksmen concealed in ten trees around Jones' home." He smiled. "He has helped us greatly. The property is a perfect place to hide snipers."

Jonty felt a little lost in all this setup. Lee controlled it all.

"Superintendent Quinn notified my line," said Lee, "and I was instructed to bring it to an end." He turned to one of his men monitoring the screens. "Ged, can you show DI Ball our men's positions?"

The man sitting nearest to the rear doors on the right answered. "Yes, sir."

He moved the joystick set to the right of the screen and the camera panned around the trees. It stopped and focused on a man who stood with statuesque stillness. He was leaning on a tree with a rifle pointing down at forty-five degrees. He had a fixed stare on the house.

"We have a rifle team of six, whose weapons include scoped H&K G3K semi-automatic rifles," Lee bragged.

The other man turned to Lee. "Sir, a black Lexus is coming down the road that is unknown to us."

"Thanks, Harry," Lee replied.

He let the car glide past the white van. It drove past Jonty's CRV, and when it was about fifty yards from the gates a uniformed officer walked out and raised his right arm, requesting the vehicle to stop. However, instead of slowing down, the car accelerated. The officer tried jumping out of the way of the oncoming vehicle, but the car caught him and he was launched ten feet in the air.

The officer fell to the ground with a thud. His knee was bent, but in the opposite direction, it was designed to bend. His arms were twisted and contorted on the floor, his head lolling to the side. Jonty ran up to the officer, just as Lee got there. Jonty looked down. He recognised the face. It was PC Frank Rose, the outrageously innocent bobby he had come to know and love over the previous months. He felt for a pulse – there was one, albeit a very faint one.

"H needs an ambulance!" Jonty shouted. "He is still alive!" He watched his controlled fingers, as if slow motion, dial 999.

Billy didn't need any more hints that there was a generous amount of activity outside his house. The Lexus sped through the gates, virtually forcing them open. As soon as it was inside the gates, the car braked suddenly. Steam, oil, and water poured out of it. A gunshot came from the direction of the trees, causing the two men in the Lexus to reach to the back seat. One picked up two rifles and one picked up a box with six boxes of ammunition inside.

"NOW! To the left!" yelled the driver. He noticed the gunfire had come from the right. They flung open the car doors and sprinted for the trees, zigzagging all the way. Several shots came in their direction, but none landed on the intended targets. As the two men reached the safety of the trees, one fired a few shots back, not intending to hit a target but just to let people know they were armed and it would be more difficult to hunt them down.

Billy looked at his security monitor to see the damage the Lexus had caused. There was considerable damage to the gates. He recognised the car as owned by James Morgan. Morgan was Roberto's biggest hitter; he was a hitman of world-class quality who made Steve Pitt look like an amateur. George Downs was probably his accomplice. Billy never thought he would be glad of a police presence, but had they not been here now he would probably have been within five minutes of death. However, it did not mask the problem that he had police marksmen and a professional hitman on his grounds and both sides had one target: Billy Jones.

The sound of gunfire brought Maggie hurtling down the stairs. "Billy, what on earth is going on?"

"I don't know!" shouted Billy. "Go back upstairs where it's safer!"

Maggie turned and ran upstairs, feeling lonely and petrified. She was crying and the tears ran down her face like a river. She felt her heart pound like a sledgehammer inside her chest. Billy loaded his M24 sniper weapons system. He had never used this before. It had always kept for emergencies, and this was an emergency.

Billy had bought the M24 after hearing it being referred to as a "weapons system". It consisted of not only a rifle but also a detachable telescopic sight and other accessories. The M24 SWS was a long-action bolt version of the Remington 700 receiver, which was chambered for the 7.62x51mm NATO "short-action" cartridge. The "long action" allowed the rifle to be re-configured for a dimensionally larger cartridge.

The sound of ambulance sirens broke the silent standoff out on the road as Billy fired a few shots, just to let people know he was there and armed.

CHAPTER FIFTY-FIVE

George Lee and Jonty kept Quinn up to speed with everything that was happening. It was a volatile situation. All sides were waiting for the other to react, but any false move could give a distinct advantage to this three-sided game of chess. Jonty had been on the loudspeaker to Billy asking him to give himself up. He declined the invitation.

Maggie had tried to change his mind. "It's the only way out, Billy. You're not Butch Cassidy!"

Billy smiled and replied. "No, he died. We are not going to."

The fact that he used the word "we" sent Maggie into a further panic and she ran upstairs. "I thought we were going on holiday." she barked naively, still not understanding that the plan was to keep her quiet for a while.

Another ninety minutes ensued of occasional gunfire, some from the police marksmen, some from Morgan, and some from Billy, in a macho attempt of keeping all attackers at a distance. A radio call came crackling through the microphone in the white van. Quinn's voice came to life.

"Hello, Inspector Lee and Detective Inspector Ball."

"Hello, sir," was the reply made in unison.

"You are doing a grand job there," said Quinn. "But I have been discussing with an emergency action team I have put together how best to handle this situation."

Lee and Jonty both looked at each other, confused. Neither had heard of an emergency action team.

"Keep it quiet down there," continued Quinn. "I will let you know when we have a plan formulated."

Meanwhile, Jake, Helen, and Em were sitting in the CRV, discussing what they thought must be happening. They were all so far out of their comfort zones they had no idea what was happening. An ambulance arrived and they watched as the ambulance crew began to work on Frank's body. After strapping his neck still, they gingerly loaded him onto a stretcher and into the ambulance.

"At least he looks alive," Helen said as they watched the ambulance race down the street with its siren roaring and lights flashing. The sound of the siren slowly descended as it moved further away from the scene until the deafening sound of silence returned.

The speaker in the van came to life again with Quinn's voice.

"Afternoon, both. I assume all is the same, as I have not heard from you?"

"Yes, sir," responded Jonty, feeling like a naughty schoolboy for not having reported anything.

"We have a plan," said Quinn. "I have ordered a helicopter with armed marksmen on board to land in Billy Jones' garden. They will attack the house to minimise fatalities, as the situation currently is like a powder keg."

Lee did not seem happy with this. "Have my line agreed to this, sir?"

"Yes!" was Quinn's reply. "I have just left the meeting. Do you have a problem?"

"No, sir."

"Expect the helicopter in the next fifteen minutes." Quinn signed off.

Lee turned to Jonty. "This does not make sense at all."

Jonty shrugged his shoulders. "Ours is not to question why," was his response.

"Let the team on the ground know what to expect," he told Ged.

"Yes, sir," replied Ged. He wasted no time in telling the armed team spread throughout the grounds to expect a helicopter and that they must make crossfire to protect their colleagues in the chopper.

After about fifteen minutes, as promised by Quinn, the distant unmistakable sound of helicopter rotors came into earshot, slowly increasing in volume as it neared the house. It came into view, first as a speck on the shortened horizon, then slowly becoming larger with the unmistakable dark blue body with a yellow top and yellow lettering reading 'POLICE' under the side windows.

The Euro copter EC-145 helicopter eased its way over the top of the house and spinning in a circular motion, while the pilot looked for a safe landing place. Lee turned to Ged.

"Now, Ged!"

Ged nodded and opened up the airwaves to the listening ears of the waiting snipers in the trees. They immediately started firing their rifles towards where they knew Morgan and Downs were hiding. Morgan and Downs retaliated with more gunfire. They knew that this was not going well for them, but they were tied down and any attempt at making a run to the clearing or driveway would lead to certain capture – or, worse, death! They returned a volley of gunfire, knowing they could not hit anybody. But it also meant that nobody could advance on them as they were not privy to the operation taking place.

The helicopter landed behind the house, unseen by the eye, but a camera in the van picked up the details. Lee and Jonty watched in fascination as the chopper touched down and three armed officers exited the machine, sprinting towards the house. One of the officers was carrying a rope. He tied one end to the door handle on the back door of the house, the other end he tied to the helicopter's left-hand landing skid.

The helicopter rose slightly off the ground and flew a few yards further away from the house. The door flew off its hinges in seconds, the jamb coming with it. As the officers ran into the house, they saw flashing coming through the windows, a sure sign of gunfire.

"Something doesn't seem right here," Lee said to Jonty. "That entrance was too easy and not textbook."

As soon as Lee had said it, one officer came out of the house with Billy and Maggie. Both were handcuffed with their hands behind their backs and a gun pointed at them. They were, shunted into the helicopter. The other officer climbed in after them, slashing the rope that attached to the now fragmented back door. The doors to the helicopter slid shut and it lifted off. As it climbed, the ceasefire order was made.

Lee again spoke up. "Something is not right." He frowned. "The Euro copter EC-145 seats nine people. If they had planned to capture two prisoners, why not have a team of seven for maximum safety? Instead, there are only three, plus a pilot, making four."

Jonty announced on the loudspeaker to Morgan and Downs. "This is DI Ball. I am going to walk down to the house." He spoke slow and clear. "Please do not fire at me. It appears we have both lost the person we were chasing."

Jonty looked at Lee and added through the loudspeaker, "I promise, you will not be shot at."

"Okay. But anything funny and I will shoot." Came the London voice of Morgan.

"I am coming with you," Lee said to Jonty.

Jonty nodded nervously and both men walked towards the house. The copper beech stood there in all its glory. Its leaves lay spread on the autumn lawn, glistening in the relentless November drizzle. The two officers walked through the half-open gates, the Lexus still parked, showing a crushed bonnet reaching as far as the windscreen. They strode down the gravel path, the stones crunching beneath their feet.

They continued to walk around the back of the house to the hole in the wall, which, five minutes previously, had been the back door. They walked through to see holes in the ceiling where bullets had penetrated. On the floor in front of them lay the two officers, riddled with bullets. The tell-tale signs of the bullet entry indicated that the shots had come from the back door area, which instantly told Jonty that it must have been the leaving officer who shot his unsuspecting colleagues.

"We have been stitched up like kippers," Jonty said. "It was a plan to get Billy out. The holes in the ceiling were a decoy to make us think a gun battle was taking place. While one of them was shooting the ceiling to bits, probably Billy, the last one was putting the handcuffs on Maggie and then finally Billy. They left for the helicopter making it look like Billy had been arrested. It was just enough time for them to make their getaway."

CHAPTER FIFTY-SIX

Inspector George Lee ordered an extra five armed men to be brought to Billy's house, under the cover of darkness. They were directed to go behind the house and to the nearest neighbour, whose twelve acres of land joined Billy's.

Crack marksman Inspector Mark Monday knocked on the front door of the house, which was opened by City financier Robin Plumgarth OBE. Monday had quickly read his name on the bronze plaque that sat neatly on the stone gateway leading up the fifty-yard drive. Plumgarth stared at Monday's black SWAT-style suit, starting from his head down to his toes and back to his head again. He took in the six-foot-five figure of the man, built like a prop forward and dressed all in black, with black highly polished boots. Behind Monday stood four identically dressed men all of different builds, ranging from slim and wiry to average build. One was even more imposing than Monday, standing at around six foot seven and nineteen stone of solid mass. Monday would rather have Brad Johnson with him than against him. All the men had H&K G3K semi-automatic rifles slung over their right shoulders.

Plumgarth took in the sight in front of him and casually spoke as if talking to the milkman. "Yes?" A brief second passed. "Can I help you?"

Monday looked at the upper-crust sixty-something gentleman standing in front of him. Wearing a navy wool dressing gown tied in the middle, he looked like a sack of potatoes. Monday showed his ID.

"My name is Inspector Monday of the Specialist Rifle Officers, sir."

Plumgarth said nothing, instead just stared at Monday. He was too stunned for words.

"There has been an incident in an adjoining property," continued Monday. "I will need access through your land to enter the property, if that's okay with you, sir?"

Monday knew he would be going with or without permission, but it was always easier with it.

"Is it that Jones man?" said Plumgarth. "I always thought there was something wrong about him."

268

"I can't go into details, sir," Monday replied. "We will cause as little inconvenience to you and your family as possible, sir."

Plumgarth considered this for a few seconds. "Yes, of course. Anything to assist," he replied. "I will show you the access to my land."

They strolled around the back with all the security lighting setting off as they walked past sensors. Monday could see a wall of aged trees in between the properties, this would conceal them from Morgan and Downs. Monday led his team slowly up to the border between Plumgarth's and Jones' properties. The distance was about one mile in total, with a seven-foot brick wall bordering the land. The team used a rope ladder to climb it. The slim man, Barrett, went first. He hooked the ladder to the top of the wall and slowly climbed. They were still about eight hundred yards away, so would probably not be heard. However, they were all well trained. They manoeuvred the wall, one by one, with the stealth of an owl flying through the night.

The team weaved between the established ash and elm trees, which were quite close together and provided good cover. The land became a little more open as they neared Billy Jones's house, as the oak trees demanded a little more space. It was now one-thirty in the morning and Monday told his team to rest on the edge of the more exposed oak line. As they did not want to silhouette their bodies against the now clear moonlit skyline, they crawled the last one hundred yards to the oak trees on their stomachs, finally reaching the trees in about forty-five minutes. The men reached the point where it was necessary not to speak or make any noise. They had been drilled that, once they arrived at the oak trees, they were to settle under the cover of darkness and be ready to attack at first light.

Sunrise would be at 7.36 am. The plan was that Monday's team would throw five hand grenades to the middle clump of the trees, where Morgan and Downs were dug in. Then, the team on the north side, who were under Lee's control, would start firing to keep Morgan and Downs distracted. This would happen at 7.40 am precisely. The hand grenades would be set and exploded as planned on the edge of the copse, waking and disorientating Morgan and Downs, who by now would not have eaten or drunk anything for nearly sixteen hours.

At the sound of the hand grenades, Lee ordered his men to start firing. Morgan and Downs spun and fired towards the hand grenades, then they heard shots from behind as Lee's men started firing their weapons. They spun around to engage the marksmen. Barrett sprinted across the clearing towards the copse sheltering the two men. Downs saw the move and fired at Barrett, missing him slightly. Morgan kept his gun aimed at Lee's men, whilst Downs had his back to Morgan, trying to engage Monday's team. The dark shadows of the trees gave away Downs' position when the bright flashback from his weapon flashed as he fired. Next to move was Johnson. He moved another twenty yards to the right of Barrett. Downs fired again, but Johnson sprinted, keeping low. Downs was not an expert marksman and all three bullets missed.

Johnson crept between the trees in the copse and met with Barrett. Johnson nodded and they both fired towards Morgan and Downs, the gunfire being returned. This kept Morgan and Downs occupied with the volley of fire coming from two flanks. This allowed Monday to sprint forward. His team followed, one by one until all the men were in the copse. Johnson and Barrett progressed nearer unseen, and within a minute they could see Morgan and Downs no more than twenty feet away.

Monday and his team kept firing above the treetops, allowing the two gangsters the luxury of knowing their position. Downs tapped Morgan on the back and pointed to Monday's position. They turned and made their way towards the gunfire. As they did so, Barrett and Johnson opened with a volley of their own. The first shot by Johnson hit Downs in the leg; he screamed loudly as he fell to the floor. He was desperately clinging onto his leg; it felt warm and aching as the blood steadily poured out of the wound as if a tap had been turned on.

Morgan turned towards the sound of gunfire from Johnson and fired. Johnson positioned himself behind the large girth of an oak tree with his back to it and rifle perpendicular to his body. As Morgan fired and tried to inch his way towards Johnson, he came into view of Barrett, who fired at first sight. As he did so, his foot slipped on some autumn leaves that had fallen on the ground. Morgan was a stronger shot than Downs and he sent a volley towards Barrett. The first bullet caught Barrett's arm, slowing him down; the second bullet caught Barrett flush in the chest, sending him five feet backwards. The third bullet was aimed expertly at his head and it met its target.

Johnson spun from the tree and shouted at Morgan. "Hey, bastard! How about this!"

Morgan half turned, but before he could engage his rifle he felt an explosion in his side. He looked down to see a gaping hole through his designer shirt. He felt another bullet just touch the front of his forehead between the eyes. That was his last recollection of life on this planet.

Johnson then turned to the immobile Downs, whose eyes were so wide open in fear that Johnson could see the whites above, below, and at the sides. He stared up at Johnson, knowing that this man was not going to show any mercy. Johnson aimed at the man on the ground. He cocked his rifle when a voice shouted from behind.

"BRAD, WE TAKE HIM IN!" ordered Monday.

Johnson never wavered. Instead, he kept his sights aimed at Downs' head. Downs was staring back at him; the fear in his eyes was clear to see, as a dribble of urine showed through his trousers to confirm it. He knew Johnson was not going to leave without taking his life. A calming hand came over the barrel and lowered it.

"It's over, Brad. You have done your job." Monday tapped him on his back.

"Yes, sir," Johnson replied.

"Get his rifle and arrest him," ordered Monday.

"With pleasure, sir," said Johnson.

Johnson walked slowly towards Downs' rifle and stamped on the gaping wound left by Barrett's shot. A loud cry of severe pain that grew in the deep crevices of Downs's stomach bellowed from his mouth. Monday did not turn round to see what had happened. He just smiled and continued walking.

CHAPTER FIFTY-SEVEN

Quinn unlocked the handcuffs on Billy and gave him the key to undo Maggie's. He held a gun to the pilot's head.

"Make your way to Barton Airdrome. Now!" The pilot looked terrified. He spun the helicopter and directed it towards Eccles.

Meanwhile, Jonty and Lee were still at the house vacated by Jones.

"They must have a jet waiting at Barton Airfield," said Jonty. "Get a unit there as quickly as you can."

Lee ordered Ged to activate Jonty's request.

"I am driving there, for what it's worth," added Jonty.

As Jonty climbed into the CRV he was bombarded by a million questions fired at him from Jake, Helen, and Em.

"What happened there?"

"Are you okay?"

"Where is Billy?"

"Is he caught?"

"Did anybody get hurt?"

"I will tell you all later," he said urgently. "But right now we need to get to Barton Airport. Billy is getting away!" His foot hit the floor.

They joined the M6 within minutes. Jonty hit 110 mph, sirens screaming and lights flashing. Helen looked ashen-faced. She didn't like travelling at 70 on a motorway, and this was taking her to a new level of fear. Em was screaming like a terrified schoolgirl on a big dipper. Jonty told her to be quiet. Jake, meanwhile, sat quietly. His knuckles were white as he clasped tightly onto the passenger door.

Jonty remained in the outside lane, the traffic giving way to the flashing lights and sirens.

They managed to arrive at Barton airfield within seventeen minutes of leaving Billy's house. The helicopter had landed a few minutes earlier. Jonty could see the orange and white squad cars driving down the runway to cut off the sprint that Quinn, Billy, and Maggie were making towards the Lear jet 45XR. The main reason this plane was hired is that it had the power to go faster for longer.

272

Jonty still had his foot down on the accelerator as he joined and overtook the squad cars. He was only three hundred yards away as the door closed on the jet; the powerful jet engines were already running and the jet taxied towards the runway. Jonty was closing in on the jet when it suddenly accelerated, spun on the grass, but continued to the runway. It accelerated down the runway and lifted off the ground, rising steeply and quickly. Jonty brought the CRV to a halt and got out, watching as the jet slowly turned to a speck in the dark, still sky.

The plane headed west towards the Irish Sea. Quinn opened a glass of champagne and poured a glass for Billy and Maggie.

"I told you we were going on a holiday," Billy smiled at Maggie as he raised a glass. She managed a weak smile back.

***

Toni sat by her husband's bedside throughout the following day, talking to him. She spoke about happy times to him while he was in his comatose state. Music was playing quietly in the background through the hospital stereo. Her mind cast back again. She thought of a time when she and Roberto had gone to their beloved Italy for the first time with Francesca. They were in Limone on Lake Garda, a place Francesca would return to many times throughout her life. She would often say as a child, "It is my favourite place in the whole wide world."

Roberto would take her onto the lake in a brightly coloured yellow and red rowing boat to fish. Francesca would run to the other end of the boat when Roberto caught a trout, frightened by the large creature. She once tipped the boat, but Roberto had taught her to be a strong swimmer. They corrected the boat and both scrambled back in, laughing out loud without a care in the world.

Toni asked Roberto if he remembered it. He didn't reply.

CHAPTER FIFTY-EIGHT

After seeing the Lear jet travel away in the distance, Jonty quickly dropped Jake, Helen, and Em off at the hotel, telling them they would now be safe. He then made his way back to the station where Shepherd was being detained. He marched into the cell, slamming the door behind him.

"We are going to talk and we are going to talk now!" he snarled. "I have you down for murder and you are going to get one chance. Do you hear me? ONE CHANCE!"

Shepherd looked up at Jonty. He looked tired and weary. He hadn't shaved in three days and his eyes were bloodshot. His face had turned into that of a grey old man overnight. Jonty took no notice of his appearance.

"Come on," he demanded, putting his hand under Shepherd's armpit and lifting him off the bench he sat slumped on.

Jonty frogmarched Shepherd out of the cell and into an interview room. The desk sergeant, whom Jonty did not know, shouted out to him.

"That office is booked, sir."

"Then unbook it!" Jonty snarled back as he pushed Shepherd into the room.

He pushed Shepherd into the chair and followed up with a right hook that landed square on Shepherd's jaw. Shepherd and the chair fell backward, planting Shepherd to the floor. Jonty walked over and put the chair back in position. He dragged Shepherd up and told him to sit.

"I am going to book you for murder, Shep, unless you talk, and talk now," Jonty spoke in an aggressive and no-nonsense manner.

Shepherd wiped a dribble of blood from his mouth where his teeth had cut the inside of his cheek on Jonty's impact. "I didn't kill him, Jonty."

Jonty was marching up and down the room, his hands clenching into fists. He was raging inside. He could feel his heart pounding.

"THEN TALK!" he yelled, his face an inch from Shepherd. "Your DNA on the hair under Dave's fingernail and the fingerprints on the foxglove both lead to you. This is all proof."

"Okay," said Shepherd.

"Not yet," Jonty said. "I am going to leave this office for ten minutes, and when I get back we are going to record it. It's going to be an official statement."

"Okay!" Shepherd repeated.

Ten minutes later, Jonty returned. He thanked the constable who had handcuffed and sat with Shepherd while Jonty had been away.

He sat down at the table, opposite Shepherd. "I have asked your solicitor to join us and Detective Inspector O'Sullivan to take notes. Wynne will be about another fifteen minutes." Shep nodded in resignation.

Jonty looked at Shep and continued. "Before we start, Shep, let me update you a little."

Jonty was now calmer. The time out he gave himself allowed him to settle and had put him in a better frame of mind. He spoke, looking Shep straight in the eye.

"You are in a position of no return, Shep. You will be left with egg well and truly splattered all over your face."

Shep looked back quizzically, not knowing what Jonty meant.

"Let me enlighten you, my little turncoat," said Jonty. "Jones and Quinn, as we speak right now, are heading to another country. They have fled the UK because it has got too hot for them."

Shep lowered his head. "God," he whispered. He knew he was one of the few left to cover the dirt while Quinn and Jones were heading for the good life.

"And you have it all," said Jonty. "To either carry the can for them or help clean it up. Quite simple, Shep. You pay or play."

Twenty minutes later, Neil Wynne, the legal aid solicitor, arrived. He was escorted into the room by Jane O'Sullivan. Jonty turned on the recorder.

"Today is October the twenty-fourth at four-fifteen pm. Present are the defendant Mr. James Shepherd and his representative, Mr. Neil Wynne from Hampshire and Turner legal practice, Detective Inspector Jane O'Sullivan making notes, and myself Detective Inspector Jonathan Ball."

Jonty paused for a moment to allow Jane to write down the notes.

"Mr. Shepherd, to update the position from our last meeting, Mr. Jones and Superintendent Quinn have left the country illegally and their whereabouts are unknown."

Wynne looked at Shep. "You are not obliged to say anything."

"I know my rights. Be quiet!" Shep snapped back in an agitated voice.

Jonty nodded to Wynne in agreement.

"It appears that Superintendent Quinn was part of your criminal team," said Jonty. "Can you explain to me his and your positions in this criminal team?"

Shep shuffled uncomfortably. He was at the point of no return, backed into the proverbial corner.

"A few years ago," he began, "Quinn asked me to an evening meal that was being hosted by a Roberto Sartori. I went and had a very good evening and enjoyed the company. He introduced me to Mr. Sartori, who I had a long conversation with." Shep looked at the ceiling, then back at Jonty again before continuing. "I now realise I was being set up."

"Set up in what way?" Jonty asked.

"Set up as an informant for them should I hear anything within the station that may impact on their business."

Jonty looked at Shep coldly. "Like the murder of Paul Jennings?"

"Yes," was the reply.

"What was your part in the Jennings murder?"

"It was my job to make sure any correspondence that linked in with the murder was destroyed, and to make it look like an accident."

"Did you intercept information about a black BMW being stolen from Birmingham that was used as the murder vehicle?" asked Jonty.

"Yes."

"What was your payment for this?" Jonty persisted.

"I received a monthly income from Roberto Sartori."

"Which was paid into a National Bank account in your name?"

"Yes." It was now becoming a predictable response from Shep.

"Did you know that the account it was coming from was money laundered?" asked Jonty. "And that Brown's Engineering made ammunitions to deploy to the underground for civil wars or uprisings?"

Shep lowered his head and nodded.

"I want a verbal response, Mr. Shepherd," said Jonty sharply. "Not a nod of the head."

"Yes."

"What was Quinn to you in all this?"

276

"He was my manager. He took orders off Sartori and would implement them through me if he felt I was the correct person."

"And what if you were not the correct person?"

"Then I guess it was someone else."

Jonty now stared hard. "Are you saying there are other bent officers, Mr. Shepherd?"

"Mr. Ball!" interrupted Wynne.

"Sorry," replied Jonty, not convincing anybody that he was sorry at all.

"Were there any other people within the GMP working for Mr Quinn and Mr. Jones?" he continued.

"There must have been, but we were always kept apart," said Shep. "I don't know who they are."

Wynne intervened again. "Mr. Ball, this is a very nice story, but you told me you were going to charge my client with murder today. Can we continue with that, please?"

Jonty grinned. "Mr. Wynne, I said I *might* be charging your client with murder. I am surprised you feel compelled to think that you are expecting it. Do you think he is guilty?"

Wynne blushed slightly at his small error.

Jonty turned back to Shepherd. "Did you murder Detective Inspector David Rowlands?"

"No!" was the instant response.

"Then who did? You have DNA and fingerprints all over the murder scene."

"DI Ball!" Wynne butted in again.

"It's okay," Shep said, holding up his hands to Wynne. "Quinn found out that you were looking into the Jennings case."

"He would have known. I told him," Jonty said.

Shepherd nodded. "He called in Dave, and…"

Jonty interrupted. "By Dave, you mean DI David Rowlands."

"Yes," Shep continued. "DI Rowlands told Quinn that he had information about Roberto Sartori and people who were working for him."

Jonty frowned "So it could have been several people, you included?"

"It could not have been me," Shep replied.

"Why is that?" Jonty asked.

"Because, a few days later, Quinn asked me to accompany him to Dave's – sorry, DI Rowlands house – as he agreed to talk to Dave at his home about what Dave knew."

Shepherd took a drink of the water that had been placed on the table for him, then continued. "Quinn said he would cause a diversion so that he could be left to speak one to one with DI Rowlands about the information he had." He took another drink as he had developed a very dry throat. "When we got there, Quinn looked out of the window and commented on some purple flowers he saw in the garden and asked if he could take a cutting."

"And?" Jonty pushed.

"Dave said he could," replied Shepherd, "Quinn asked me to take some cuttings. That was my cue to leave them alone."

"Then what happened?" Jonty asked.

"I took the cuttings, wrapped them in some brown paper, and returned after about ten minutes. I gave them both enough time to chat."

"That's how your fingerprints came to be on the flowers?" Jonty asked.

"It must be," Shep said. "If Quinn knew DI Rowlands' working roster, which he did, all he had to do was break into Rowlands' house when he knew he was working and use the poison to stir into his food in the fridge, then wait!"

Jonty's mind was working overtime.

"But how did your hair get under DI Rowlands' nail?" he asked. Then a light flashed in Jonty's memory. *Martin in pathology had said how devastated Quinn was to lose a team member. It's quite possible that Quinn asked to see Rowlands. That would give Quinn enough time to plant one of Shepherd's hairs under the fingernail.*

"That ends today's interview," said Jonty. "It is now seventeen thirty hours. Mr. Shepherd will return to his cell whilst further investigations take place." He then turned off the recorder, much to everybody's surprise.

CHAPTER FIFTY-NINE

Brown's Engineering closed down, with only a handful of employees being aware of the gun-running they were contributing to. Gerry was not quite the unassuming person he seemed on the surface. He was a major part of the business, producing the artillery to a high specification, and would be involved in flights abroad to close deals with many types of leaders, from presidents to guerrilla fighters.

The Lear jet turned left halfway across the Irish Sea and headed south. A big red sun was setting to the right of the plane as Billy, Quinn, and Maggie settled down for to sleep after an exhausting day.

Meanwhile, at the hospital, Toni clung onto her husband's hand and laughed as she described the vision of Roberto and Francesca falling into the lake at Limone. She described to Roberto her memory of the surroundings.

"It was thirty degrees in the shade, with no clouds in sight," she told him. "The Tremalzo mountain was casting a shadow over the town with the lemon groves in the distance, with the multi-coloured yachts and sailboards floating across the lake. It was a palette of colour..."

The tears were streaming down her face as she spoke. She felt unable to help the husband, who always had the world in the palm of his hands.

"Francesca wore a little purple bikini, which she loved and made her feel grown-up," Toni continued. "You wore a pair of blue knee-length swimming shorts. You looked so tanned and handsome."

She was sobbing and a brief thought crossed her mind. *If you are going to take him, Lord, please give me the strength to get past this point?*

Just then, Giovanni arrived and asked how his brother was doing. He saw the tears flowing down Toni's cheek. She shook her head, just as the heart monitor flat-lined. She looked at her husband and shouted for a nurse. Roberto had lived a full life, had loved his family and had put all his trust in his much-loved grandson, William.

***

Jonty went to see PC Frank Rose in hospital. He had suffered a fractured skull, broken pelvis, ribs, and ankle.

"He will be like new, but it will take a while," Dr. Singh said.

Jonty smiled and felt good at hearing this. He planned working closer with Frank in the future.

I will take him under my wing, he thought. *Poor sod.* He smiled to himself as he left the ward and walked out to the car park.

It was early December. Jonty, Helen, Jake, and Em decided to have a meal at the Midland Hotel the day before Jake and Em were due to fly home to the States. As they walked through the entrance doors, Jonty, Helen, and Em all wolf-whistled at the plaque of Rolls and Royce. They looked at Jake and laughed. Em was linking arms with Helen.

"It will be lovely to be home for Christmas," Em said to Helen.

"Aw, I will miss you both so much," Helen replied, smiling at her. "You look after that boy of mine."

"I promise," Em smiled back. "You must come over to see us."

Helen squeezed Em's arm. "I would love to," she answered. "Don't forget, next summer you have a certain wedding to attend."

They both turned to Jonty and giggled.

"Am I missing out on something?" Jonty asked with a smile.

"Just talking wedding plans," Helen replied.

"It's been five weeks since Billy and Quinn left," Jake said to Jonty. "Any news?"

"Nothing," was the reply. "Quinn must have been highly paid for him to give up a good salary and his pension."

Jake nodded. "Round one only," he said. "I am sure we will meet up with Messrs Jones and Quinn again." He looked at Jonty for a moment. "I guarantee it. I have a score to settle with Jones from a previous life."

Jonty looked at Jake. "And I also have a score to settle with Quinn. He murdered my mate, Dave."

THE END

280

Printed in Great Britain
by Amazon

23354562R00158